To Abu Ba

Thank you
hope you enjoy reading it

[signature]
02/07/2013

SPICES OF BRICK LANE

Forid Afzal Uddin

authorHOUSE®

AuthorHouse™ UK Ltd.
500 Avebury Boulevard
Central Milton Keynes, MK9 2BE
www.authorhouse.co.uk
Phone: 08001974150

© *2009 Forid Afzal Uddin. All rights reserved.*

No part of this book may be reproduced, stored in a retrieval system, or transmitted by any means without the written permission of the author.

First published by AuthorHouse 9/22/2009

ISBN: 978-1-4490-0229-9 (sc)
ISBN: 978-1-4490-0978-6 (hc)

This book is printed on acid-free paper.

Chapter One

Sylhet, East Pakistan, 1950

Twenty five year old Karim Ali was desperately looking for work that paid good money. There was no work in the village, apart from family farming with his father. Karim's friend, Rokib, had told him that there were people from Sylhet who had filled vacancies on British ships that went to England and many people had already gone from their surrounding villages. 'It would be a good idea to go to England and work there,' said Rokib. Karim agreed with Rokib's idea of going to a foreign country and they were excited by the prospect of going to England to earn a lot of money. With so much internal happiness Karim spoke to his father, Motlib, about wanting to go to England with his friend and earn money for the family. His father told him that it was an excellent idea and that if he could get there, he would be able to help his brothers and sisters live happily. Motlib spoke to his relatives, who agreed that it was a good idea and said that if he managed to do well then others would follow him. Karim and Rokib said 'Allah Hafiz' to their loved ones and set off for Chittagong.

Chittagong was the main sea port of East Pakistan where all the foreign vessels docked. In Chittagong they managed to get jobs on ships which travelled from Chittagong to Calcutta. Calcutta was another famous sea port of India where ships docked. The ship left Calcutta and docked at many destinations before arriving at Docklands, London.

On the ship Karim and Rokib worked very hard as seamen. They respected their white masters just to get into England. There were other Sylhetis and Indians working on the ship. Due to work pressure there were times they didn't see daylight for long period. They sometimes wondered if they had made a big mistake by getting onto the ship. As the ship arrived in England, Karim and Rokib felt very happy. They did 'a runner' with the other men as well. The British weather was very cold which almost frozen their brain. That was the first taste of the British weather they received and they didn't like it. As they looked around in amazement, they couldn't believe the way London looked. From the village they had the impression that London was a beautiful place. A place of the masters! Everywhere they looked there were broken buildings and roads. They asked others why there was so much damage in London and were informed that it was due to the bombing in World War II by the Germans. They were incredulous to discover that a country like England that had ruled India for nearly 200 years had been bombed by another country.

Karim and Rokib had some addresses of people in England. They found out that some of their village people lived near Brick Lane in East London. They arrived at the villager's home for help and support to settle in the new world. The villagers rented some sleeping space of their room, where ten other Bengali men lived. They all slept on the floor. All of the men were from Sylhet and soon they found out about each others' villages. Karim and Rokib stayed with them and agreed to pay rent as soon as they started work. Within a few days Karim and Rokib managed to find work near Brick Lane in a clothing factory.

Firstly, they had to learn how to use the sewing machine. It didn't take them long to become master tailors as they were very keen to learn. All the owners of the factories were Jews, but they didn't know that. They thought of them as English people because they had white skin. The owners called all the Bengali men by the name of Ali or Ali1, Ali2 and so on as they found it difficult to pronounce their real names.

Although they didn't speak good English, it wasn't a problem as there were so many jobs available. Once Karim and Rokib were paid, they sent money back home to their father so their family could live with ease and feel happy and proud of them. Karim's and Rokib's first aim was to earn enough money to build proper houses in the village so that during the monsoon season the rain wouldn't come through the roof. While they worked hard and earned money, they wrote to their parents to begin to build a strong house with bricks. At the end of every month they sent money back home to complete their dream house for their family. Building a proper house was one of the first things Bengali people did when they earned enough money.

The name Brick Lane meant nothing to Karim or Rokib, but they understood the meaning of the word 'Brick'. Brick Lane gained its name from the local manufacture of bricks. In the early 18th Century it was a long well-paved street frequented by carts fetching bricks into Whitechapel from local kilns.

Karim and Rokib also told their parents to tell their relatives to come to London for work as the earning was good. At the end of the year more of their relatives arrived from the village and they helped them out with jobs and gave them a roof over their heads.

January 1952

The small Bengali community in Brick Lane was very upset hearing the news that the Basic Principles Committee of the Constituent Assembly of Pakistan recommended urdu to be the only state language. It caused a major uproar in East Pakistan where the people spoke Bangla. How racist can a nation get when two parts of the country spoke two different languages and the government abandons one in favour of the other. The people of East Pakistan requested the government to recognise Bangla as the second state language which the government rejected. They were bitterly upset.

February 1952

Karim and Rokib received the news from other Bengalis that in East Pakistan eight Bengali students had died in Dhaka in a language demonstration. They were very upset to hear the sad news and the problem faced by their mother tongue – Bangla language. They became known as the "Bhasha Shahids" (Language-martyrs) and 21st February became an annual celebration of the language martyrs in East Pakistan.

1953 & 1954

Karim and Rokib continued to work hard in the clothing factory. They worked over time whenever possible. Both of them continued to send money back home to their families. Their parents bought land with the foreign money as an investment. Most of the land their parents bought was for rice farming. Rice is the main staple food of Bengali people and without rice the Bengali people can't survive. In Bangladesh people eat rice three times a day, this is how much they love rice. Growing rice and selling it was big business in the villages.

1955

After working for a few years, Karim and Rokib returned to East Pakistan to see their families and friends. As they arrived in the village all the village people treated them as if they were of heroes. They were very happy to be back with their loved ones. Within a short period of time they were married to ladies chosen by their parents. Karim didn't see his wife before his marriage. He had the opportunity to see the bride, but he said that he was very happy with his parents' choice as no parents would find a bad wife for their son. This was a time when young men had trust in their parents' decision. When Karim saw his wife's face he was delighted to see such a beautiful young lady his parents' had chosen.

As it was difficult for Karim to travel to East Pakistan every year for any special occasion, his parents also arranged his brother Rahim's and sister Tozia's marriage, so he could be part of their happiness. Financially, it was difficult for Karim to manage the three weddings. He was the main money provider and he had to borrow money from friends, relatives and managed all the weddings as he had no choice.

Karim stayed with his wife, Sokina, for a few months and enjoyed being back in a culture he was familiar with. He had to leave her and come back to England to earn more money.

1956

Karim and Rokib went back to work and continued to work hard in the clothing factory. They sometimes worked seven days a week. Karim and Rokib missed their wives, families and friends, but they had very little choice. Sokina sent a letter to Karim to inform him that she was pregnant and he was delighted to hear he was going to be a father for the first time. He replied to her and told her that he missed her a lot and she should let him know as soon as she delivered the baby.

Later in that year, Karim received the good news that a son had been born. Sokina gave birth in the new house Karim had built with his Londoni money. The experienced village grandmothers helped her deliver the baby because there was no hospital in the village for pregnant women. Karim was very pleased and instantly sent money to his father for his son's christening. Motlib named his first grandson 'Sabbir Ali.' Karim wished that he had the opportunity to see his newborn child.

1957

Two more of Karim's relatives arrived to London from the village. Karim made them welcome in his rented room which was already cramped with people. He gave the new arrivals a tour of Brick Lane and the surrounding area so if they got lost they could find the house. Karim also found work for them in a clothing factory on Commercial Road. Factories owners didn't have problem with the Asian workers as they were hard working and committed workers.

1958

Rokib met Sarah, a white lady at work and slowly he started to fancy her. Even though he was married back home, he felt he needed a female companion here in London. He went out with Sarah for a few months, took her to the cinema and coffee shops. Sarah was a good looking woman who fell for Rokib's charms. Rokib didn't tell her that he was married back home. Finally, Rokib told Karim that he was going to marry her. Karim told him not to as he had a wife back home but he refused to listen to Karim. Sarah's parents didn't want her to get married to a Pakistani man but she didn't listen to them. Rokib told Karim not to tell anyone back home as he didn't want his family to be upset by the news. He married her and moved into her house. Rokib started to have a better life than his friends as he lived in a house a million times better and less congested than his friends.

1959

Karim decided to go back to East Pakistan to see his young family. He bought clothes for his child, nephews and nieces. Karim went to the Spitalfield market and bought clothes for the whole family to take back home. With Karim, Rokib gave presents to his family. When Karim returned to the village everyone from the village came to see him. The village people had respect for people who went to work in London. The first person Karim picked up was his son, Sabbir. He looked at his son and he was amazed to see how big his son had grown. This gave him a very happy feeling in his heart. He told Sokina how much he missed her and how difficult life was in England. All the friends and relatives visited Karim who explained in detail to his friends and cousins the route to London. He stayed with his wife and family for a few months then he had to return to London to earn more money. Karim had tears in his eyes as did his family; he kissed his son and said "Allah hafiz" to everyone. He would have liked to stay for longer but he was the eldest son of the family and, generally, it's the eldest son's responsibility to look after everybody so he had to get back to work.

1960

Karim felt very lonely in London and working and sleeping became his daily routine. He missed his family a lot. Sokina sent a letter to Karim to inform him that she was pregnant for the second time. Karim was happy to receive the letter and overjoyed happy by the news. He replied back to her with a big smile and told her that he missed everyone and if she needed anything then she should write to him.

In the sixties more and more Sylheti bachelors came to London to work. Most of Karim's and Rokib's relatives came. They helped them settle in and found work for them. Most of the Sylhetis brought their relatives to London to take advantages of the job opportunities that were available in East London. For the Sylheti men working in London, their lives were significantly better than those left behind farming in the village.

Karim received a letter from Sokina that he had become the father of a daughter and mother and baby were both well. Sokina also asked him to suggest a beautiful name for the girl. That put a big smile on his face. Karim replied to her with love and suggested that Sokina should ask his mother for a name.

1961

Sokina missed her husband a lot and she thought about Karim everyday. She was lonely without Karim in the village. Sokina wrote a letter to Karim to stay busy, which somehow made her fell closer to him.

> *Ass-salaamu aaleykum my dear*
>
> *How are you? I hope your health is good and that Allah has kept you well. We are fine with the help of Allah. I have recently been to my parents' home and they are also doing well.*
>
> *Your children are growing up. Sabbir is five now and he goes to school. He always asks me where his father is. Ayna has reached one and she keeps everyone happy with her beautiful smile. If you want to see her beautiful smile then I suggest that you come home quickly. Sabbir misses you and his mother misses you a lot too.*
>
> *I should stop writing now or I will go on and on. You look after yourself and don't forget me. I will be thinking about you. Allah hafiz.*
>
> *From your beautiful wife, Sokina*

Karim was happy to receive the letter from his wife. He replied to her saying that he was okay, missed her and his children very much. He didn't let her know much about the living conditions in London as he thought she would worry about him.

1962

By 1962 the British Government had changed the law concerning foreigners coming into England to work. In order to come to England, foreigners now needed a visa for the first time. Karim and Rokib made sure that they were able to stay in England and return whenever they liked by getting a British Passport each. Before the law changed, Karim and Rokib managed to help more relatives come to London as they didn't want their families to miss out on the golden chance of being in England.

1963

Sokina's loneliness continued and she was upset that her husband wasn't with her. She wanted to keep her mind active so she wrote another letter to Karim, which made her feel more optimistic.

> *Ass-salaamu aaleykum my dear husband*
>
> *How are you? I hope your health is good and Allah has kept you fine. We are fine with the help of Allah.*
>
> *I am very upset with you that you have not come to see me for so long. I miss you. Why are you taking so long to come and visit me? Don't you love me? Your children are growing up and they ask me every day where their father is. They want to see their father. Come home quickly. I miss you. Your children miss you. I pray to Allah that you can come home soon. Don't you want more children? I want more children. Please come home as soon as you can.*
>
> *I should stop writing now or I will go on and on. You look after yourself and don't forget me. I will be thinking about you.*
> *Allah hafiz.*
> *From your beautiful wife Sokina*

Karim received the letter. Read it over and over again. He felt a warm feeling when he read the letter. Then he replied to his wife.

> *Waa-aaleykum ass-salaam my dear wife.*
>
> *Thank you for your sweet letter. I hope you're okay, apart from missing me. How is everyone in the family?*
>
> *I miss you too. I also want to come to Desh every year but I can't afford to come. Of course I miss my children and you, but what can I do? I have to think about the family's rice and curry. Once I have made enough money I will come to Desh forever and spend the rest of my life with you and we can have more and more children. I will try to come next year. Let me know if you want anything from London.*

> *You take care of my children and I love you and miss you. I always think about you and my children.*
> *Allah hafiz*
> *Your silly husband Karim Ali*

1964

After receiving many more letters from Sokina, Karim finally went back home to see his family. Sokina complained to him, asking why he had taken so long to come. He apologised to her and explained that it wasn't easy to come and go as it cost alot of money and he needed to save money for the family.

Karim visited the relatives and he was pleased to see them again after so many years. He also looked at all the land his father had purchased with the money he had sent and felt very satisfied with all the investment his father had made. Karim stayed with his wife for three months then it was time to say 'Allah hafiz' to everyone for another few more years. Sokina told him to return home early. He left her with plenty of love juice.

At the end of the year Karim learned that his wife had given birth to a boy which made him feel very happy and excited. Karim wanted to go back and see his son but that wasn't financially possible.

1966

Karim and Rokib weren't interested in the football world cup that was held in England. They were only interested in one thing, and that was earning money for their families. Karim worked extra hard in the factory. He wanted to be rich and make his parents very proud of him. In his mind he wanted to be the richest man in the village and develop the local mosque and school for the poor village children.

1967

Once again, Karim went back to East Pakistan to see his family and have a break from work. He took nice clothes for his children, nephews and nieces. Karim enjoyed his limited three months holiday with his family. His children didn't want him to return to London but he had no choice.

1968 & 1969

Karim's repetitive work continued in the factory. When Karim felt very low, he took out the letters that were from his wife and read them, which made him feel better. He also visited the local Bengali grocery shop where he found out more about the latest news of East Pakistan. Mainly regarding what was happening about the Bengla language.

1970

In the 1970s, Brick Lane started to change. Most of the Jewish population had moved on, and their place was taken by a new wave of opportunity seeking East Pakistanis whom were looking for work and fleeing the war from East and West Pakistan. East and West Pakistan were one country but they had two languages and that was the main cause of the war. The job opportunities in East London attracted hundreds of Sylhetis to make the long journey. For the Sylhetis coming from their muddy villages to Brick Lane, earning a few pounds a week meant a lot for their family. One week's wages of a person was more than enough to look after the whole family in the village for a few months.

1971

Karim wanted to return to East Pakistan to meet his family but due to the war he decided to delay his visit until it was safe to go back. The Prime Minister who was based in West Pakistan wanted the national language to be urdu, which the East Pakistani people rejected as they spoke Bengali. The West Pakistani army suddenly attacked East Pakistan with bombs and guns.

In the village a group of West Pakistani soldiers came with a Bengali traitor. There were a few Hindus left in the village from the 1947 partition of Hindustan, including a doctor and his family. Karim's father, Motlib, didn't want the doctor to go. The doctor was a kind man and had helped the village people alot since he became a doctor. He was a very rich man and owned a lot of land in the village. The traitor told the soldiers that Motlib was harboring the Hindus, which was true. Motlib explained to the soldiers that the Hindus came to him for help but he'd said that he couldn't hide them in his house. The doctor and his family hid in the big jungle behind Motlib's house. In the jungle

Motlib and his sons helped the doctor build a little tent for his family. Motlib's family provided food for the doctor's family at night when no-one would notice them. Most of the young men in the village hid in jungles to avoid the soldiers and looked for the opportunity to attack them with hand-made weapons. It was very difficult for the young men to get hold of guns, as most villagers worked on farms and they were never involved with arms dealers.

Everyone in London was very worried about their loved ones in East Pakistan. Karim was very concerned about his brothers as they were so young. East Pakistanis were killed by the order of the President of West Pakistan - Agha Muhammad Yahya Khan. The 'bastard' couldn't use his brain so he used his force. Thousands of Hindus fled East Pakistan leaving their wealth behind. Some Hindus managed to sell their land before they left and others came back and sold their land later. Motlib managed to buy many plots of land for very little money as the Hindus were desperate to sell. East Pakistani people couldn't understand why the Muslim leaders were killing other Muslim brothers and the Hindus just because they belonged to another religion or didn't speak urdu. Allah didn't prescribe urdu to anyone! Why were they killing innocent men, women, and children to promote urdu?

The soldiers had found a young man thought to be a Hindu in the village and wanted to kill him. The man said that they shouldn't kill him because he had converted to Islam. They refused to believe him. The man said that he knew all the Kalimas and he was a true Muslim. They still refused to believe him. One army officer asked him to read the Kalimas, which he did. Then he said, 'If you are a true Muslim, have you been circumcised?' 'Yes,' the man replied. The soldier said 'Prove it!' and pointed a gun at him. The man knew if he didn't, he could be killed in front of everyone the man pulled up his lungi and showed them that he had indeed been circumcised. They laughed like a bunch of animals and left the scene. As the soldiers walked towards their vehicle, some village men who were hiding in the roadside forest shot them dead. Everyone went near the dead bodies, kicked, spat and pissed on them. Then they dug holes for the bodies in the forest and hid the vehicle too.

Sheikh Mujibur Rahman fought for East Pakistan's independence. But the racist West Pakistani government jailed him. India joined East

Pakistan to fight for their independence. The West Pakistani army were scared of India and conceded defeat like disabled headless animals after the unjustified killing of three millions Bengalis. The world watched how the West Pakistani army hung their head in shame. East Pakistan became the independent 'People's Republic of Bangladesh.' Sheikh Mujibur Rahman was released from jail and he became the father of the nation. When the army left the villages the traitors were caught and executed by the villagers. The doctor thanked Motlib for saving his life. Motlib said, 'I did what a human being is supposed to do; to try to save life, not kill.'

1972

Karim had waited for the war to finish. As the war ended he went back to a new country called Bangladesh. Within a short period of time Karim had seen four changes in name of his birth place; Hindustan, India, East Pakistan, and now Bangladesh. Karim was very pleased to see everyone in his family alive. He found out that one of his friend had been killed because he was a teacher and the soldiers though he might encourage others to attack them. Karim stayed in the village for a few months to see his parents, wife, children and other relatives.

Karim felt it was important to bring his family to London before his children become too old and missed out on a school education. He planned to apply for his family's UK visa. Karim's brother Rahim heard that he was applying. Rahim couldn't resist the temptation to ask his brother for a big favour. Rahim spoke to Karim asking if he could take his son to London along with his family. Karim told his brother politely that he could take Rahim's son but the problem was that it would be very difficult to bring up so many kids. His brother's son should stay in Bangladesh, be educated and Rahim could see his own child grow up. Karim also told Rahim that once his son became of a workable age Karim would try his best to take him to London. Rahim wasn't very happy with his brother's decision, but he had no choice other than being patience.

Rahim spoke to his father and asked him to speak to Karim about him taking his son to London. Motlib had no option but to speak to Karim and told him that Rahim was very upset. Karim didn't want to say no to his father. He told Motlib it wasn't going to be easy to bring up kids in London and, again, that he had his own children to look after. At the end of the discussion Karim told his father that he would put Rahim's son's name on the application, and that if he got the visa then he would take him. That put a big smile on Rahim's twisted face. It was a time when almost every family had one or two extra children on their application forms. So many families managed to bring extra children with them. The advantages were that when the child grew up, then he could help his parents by sending money home. Who say's Bengalis were not intelligent!

Karim's younger brother Sahim heard the news that Karim was taking Rahim's son. Sahim also couldn't resist temptation, approached Karim and asked him politely to take his baby son with him. Karim asked him if he was crazy! Sahim told him that soon his son wouldn't be a baby, and would learn to walk and wouldn't trouble them. Karim wasn't having any of it. He told his brother straight, 'You are insane, how could you say that? Listen to me, it's not the last opportunity to go to London, there will be more opportunities later on. Make sure you educate your children and I will try my best to take them to London.'

Karim spoke to his wife and the children regarding what kind of questions the immigration may ask. He asked Sokina to learn some basic English and to practice how to sign her name in English. Sokina only knew how to write her name in Bengali as she had only been to school for three or four years before leaving to help her mother with housework. Education wasn't important for the village girls as they were meant to be housewives and give birth to children.

Karim took his family to Dhaka, the capital city of Bangladesh to get visas. He kept it secret from the village people. Karim ensured the children were dressed in clothes of the same colour. With the application forms Karim went to the Bangladesh's immigration headquarters. The immigration officers invited Sokina for an interview to ask her some questions; 'What's your parents' name?' She answered that question.

'How many windows are there in your house?'

'I have to count.' She took time to count then gave an answer.

'Where does your eldest son sleep?'

'He sleeps in the same room as his grandfather.'

'How many rooms are there in your house?'

'I have to count and tell you.' She counted and told them.

The immigration officers asked the same questions to Karim and hardly found any differences. They were given the visas to come to London. Luckily for them, the immigration officers didn't ask any questions about Rahim's son. In the waiting room Karim met another man who went to get visas for his family but he forgot to take the passports, actually he said he didn't know he needed passports to get the visas. Maybe he wanted the visa stamps on his forehead! When Karim returned to the village he only told his close relatives about the visas, in case their enemy might grass them up. Some people in the village were jealous of Karim's wealth.

Karim returned to England with his wife and the children. At first, his family lived in a relative's house. Karim applied for a house with the London Borough of Tower Hamlets. The council gave them a house on Hanbury Street. They were not lonely as there were a few other Bangladeshi families who already lived there. Karim told his children not to go out of the house as they might get attacked by racist people.

Either side of their house white people lived. Karim said 'Hello' and 'How are you?' to them, but Sokina never spoke to them. She didn't speak any English but she wished that she could speak English so she could speak to the female neighbours whenever she was out in the garden. After few days, someone wrote on their door, 'Pakis are not welcome here, go back to Paki land.' Karim cleaned it. Sabbir asked his father what Paki meant. His father told him it was short for Pakistan. Karim told his children to be very careful when they went out of the house as some of the white people didn't like foreigners. The children listened to their father obediently.

On the first Friday in London, Sabbir asked his father where the mosque was. He wanted to go to the mosque for the Friday's prayers. His father told him that there was no mosque. They did the prayer in a house. Sabbir couldn't believe it. He said, 'Abba what kind of country is this, we don't have a mosque to do our prayers!' 'This is a Christian country and we don't have a mosque here yet, but Insha-Allah, soon we will make one,' replied Karim.

Sokina stayed at home as she had nowhere else to go. She cooked rice and curries for the family. Karim told her not to open the door to anyone and to be careful when she opened it. Sokina told Karim that

London was so boring and she couldn't believe why people were so desperate to come here. She wished she could have stayed in Bangladesh but knew it would have been difficult for the family.

Karim's oldest son Sabbir was too late to go to school as he was already sixteen years of age. He joined a local college and took any course that was on offer just to learn basic English. Karim told his son to learn as much English as he could so he could read his own letters and wouldn't have to ask others to read them for him, like his father had to do sometimes.

Ayna, Karim's oldest daughter, started secondary school in Year Seven and quickly made some friends. There were a few Bengali girls, so it wasn't too difficult for her to settle down in her new school. She wanted to learn and try her best but she found it very hard as she didn't understand the language. Ayna followed a Bengali girl to her lessons and slowly picked up the English language.

Karim's second son, Samir was only six years old. He joined a local primary school. Sabbir's cousin was five years old and he joined Samir in the same school. It was impossible for them to understand the teachers as they were alien to this country.

After a while Karim showed Sokina the way to the primary school so she could take the little kids and bring them back. Sokina didn't like going out as she found the weather too cold all the time. Karim went back to factory work knowing that he had to manage his family here and also maintain his parents and brothers' family.

Sabbir's second day in college wasn't very good. In the college he was attacked by some white kids who beat him up badly. He ended up with black eyes and bruises on his head. Sabbir didn't want to go back to college. He cried and said to himself 'What kind of country is this where people hate me so much?' He felt that if he had been beaten up like this in Bangladesh, then he would have got the boys killed. Sabbir wished he had some backup to attack the racist youth. His father told him to go back to college for a few more months, then finish so he could learn some English, which would help him in daily life. Sabbir did as his father said, then he was attacked again. After that Sabbir didn't go back to college again. That was the end of his education in England.

Once he recovered from the injuries, his father found him a job in a clothing factory in Brick Lane. Sabbir learnt tailoring and earned a few pounds a week which he gave to his father. Due to respect Bengali kids always gave their earnings to their father. Karim gave his son two books to read that he had studied when he first came to London. The books had basic sentences in English and Bengali which Sabbir found easy to read and understand. Sabbir read the books with great interest, again and again. Sabbir wanted to read more books and learn more but wasn't sure where to go. He asked his father where he could get more books from. Karim knew there was a library on Whitechapel Road and took Sabbir to the library and made him a member. With self interest Sabbir often went to the library and borrowed books that he could read and understand. Sabbir thought it was important for him to learn English as he was going to work and live in London.

1973

Sokina found it very boring staying at home. Sometimes other Bengali ladies came to their home and she also visited them for company. To keep her busy, she wrote a letter to her sister Priya in Bangladesh;

> *Ass-salaamu aaleykum*
>
> *How are you, sister? We are fine with the help of Allah. I looked forward to coming here but I don't like this county. It is so cold. I stay at home all the time and do all the house work. One good thing is that I don't have to use fire wood for cooking anymore as we have gas in the house.*
>
> *Your nephews and nieces go to school. I take them to school and bring them back when the school finishes. Your brother in law goes to work in the factory. Give my salaam to father and mother. I want to come home but am not sure when Allah will enable us to return again. Pray for us.*
> *Allah hafiz, reply soon.*
> *Your sister Sokina.*

Karim took Sabbir to the Spitalfield market, which was the local market where they could buy almost everything. The Spitalfield market took its name from a hospital and priory known as the St. Mary's Spital founded in 1197. The area was built after the Great Fire of London.

Spitalfield's market was first established in the 1680's and the houses around the area date from around 1685 when the Huguenots fled France, bringing their silk weaving skills. Karim told his son that there were many bargains available in the market and he often went to the market to buy fruits, vegetables and other necessary things.

It was becoming difficult for Karim to maintain the family and help his father and brothers back home. He decided to do two jobs. During the day he worked in a factory and in the evening he worked in a local Indian restaurant. Karim's fourth child, a girl, was born to make it a very busy year for him. The family named her Amina. This was a strange experience for Sokina as it was her first child that was born in London, which was quite different from the village. In the village the elderly village ladies helped while in London the nurses helped her. She was surprised to see so many different types of equipment the hospital had in the delivery room. Sokina asked Karim why there were all sorts of equipment and he explained to her that when babies were born prematurely the equipment was used to help them survive.

1974

Whenever Karim or the other Bengalis wanted to pray, they didn't have any facilities. They had hired a community centre where they carried out the Friday prayers. There was no mosque that they could have used for Friday's prayer, the most important prayer of the week. The Bengali population had grown by this time and so all the Bengali men got together and looked for a suitable place to buy or rent.

At the end of Spring, Karim planted some coriander seeds in his garden, which he had brought from Bangladesh. Coriander leaves are strongly flavoured and Bengali people use them in their everyday cooking to give extra aroma to food. Sokina helped Karim with the gardening, just by standing there and talking to him, while he did all the work.

Karim's eldest sister from Bangladesh wrote a letter to him in Bengali. Letters were the main ways of communication.

Ass-salaamu-aaleykum brother

> *I hope with the mercy of Allah you and your family are fine. I am fine with your prayers. I have recently visited mother and father and they are well.*
>
> *As you know, brother, your nephew has become a grown up boy and there isn't much work for him to do here. We are hoping that you could try and take him to London. It would help our family a lot if Muslah could go to London as we desperately need an earner for our family. It is getting harder for your brother-in-law to do farming as he is getting old.*
>
> *I hope with the help of Allah you will be able to help us. Hope to hear from you soon.*
> *Allah hafiz*
> *From your loving sister Tozia*

After reading the letter Karim replied to his sister.

> *Ass-salaamu-aaleykum aapa. I hope you and your family are fine with the mercy of Allah tala. I am fine with my family. My children are going to school. Your bhabi is finding it very cold here.*
> *I will try my best to bring Muslah to London. I will be looking for a passport and if I can find one then I will send it to you. Meantime, make sure he goes to college as it is important for him to learn English when he gets here.*
> *Give my salaams to brother-in-law and my love to my nieces and nephews. If you need anything, do write to me all the time. Make sure you visit mother and father and if they need anything you write to me. Also pray for me to be rich and stay healthy.*
> *Allah hafiz*
> *Your brother Karim.*

Chapter Two

1975

Karim's wife Sokina gave birth to their fifth child, a boy, in East London hospital. After a few days and many discussions with everyone, they named him Amir Ali. Karim wrote a letter to his parents to inform them of their new grandson. Motlib couldn't read or write so he had hired a friend to read the letter for him. This friend also wrote back to Karim to say that they were happy to hear the news that they had another grandchild and Karim should take everyone back home for them to see. In the letter Motlib also informed Karim that a plot of land had been falsely claimed by Moskond and Motlib had made an appeal against the claim. Moskond had produced dodgy land registry papers and claimed the land was his.

Karim went to the local grocery shop to get some rice and spices. He was shocked to hear that the president of Bangladesh – Sheikh Mujibur Rahman - and most of his family members had been assassinated. He had tears in his eyes. The lovers of Bangladesh became very upset and heartbroken to hear the news. The man had fought for Bangladesh's independence for many years. Since he became the first President, the countries law and order wasn't very good which happens to any new country. There were many theories why he was assassinated. But the main question is how could the assassinators kill a man that was known as, 'The father of the nation?' A man who put his life on the line, a man who fought for the country's independence, a man who was jailed for standing up for this country.

Hearing the sad news Sabbir had tears in his eyes, too. He couldn't understand why people would kill their President and his family. It was difficult for him to digest the news. In his head he tried to analyse what could be the reasons for Sheikh Mujibur Rahman's death, but he couldn't find any justifiable explanation.

1976
A building was bought by the local Bengali community on the corner of Fournier Street and converted into a mosque. The building was built in 1744 as a Huguenot's church. It was sold to the Jewish immigrant society in 1897, after that it became a synagogue. Praying had been a problem for the Muslim Bengalis over the past twenty five years and they didn't have the financial muscle to buy one until 1976. This was a great achievement for the small Sylheti community that lived around Brick Lane and it was time the Sylhetis started to put their stamp on Brick Lane.

Karim received a letter from his sister, Tozia. He liked receiving letters from back home as it enabled him to keep him in touch with his relatives. Tozia had been thinking very hard about sending her son to London.

Ass-salaamu-aaleykum brother
I hope with the mercy of Allah you and your family are fine. We are fine with your prayers. I have prayed to Allah for your family's health and wealth.

We ask you to accept our proposal for your daughter's marriage. We think Muslah and Ayna would suitable for each other. If you accept this proposal then it would be very good for us as our son will be able to go to London and earn money for the family.

I hope with the help of Allah you will be able to help us.

Hope to hear good news from you soon.
Allah hafiz
From your loving sister Tozia

When Ayna finished her school Karim told her that she should stay home and help her mother cook food and there was no need to go to college. Ayna would have liked to go to college and learn more new skills. She had to listen to her father, which she did and never argued. Her understanding was that parents always want the best for their child and there must be many good reasons why she shouldn't go to college. Karim's reason was that there was no point going to college as she would soon be married. It was a time when a lot of Sylheti men didn't allow their daughters to go to college or even finish school. Some parents stopped their daughter going to school at the age of fifteen. They didn't think in advance that if their daughter was educated then she would be in a better position to educate her children and the children would became more successful.

1977
Sokina gave birth to Karim's sixth child, a girl. Karim was pleased to have another daughter. He liked girls more than boys because they made tea for him. They named her Azima Begum, which rhymed with the other sisters' name, Ayna, Amina and Azima. Having six children may sound unusual to a white person but to Bengali people it was common. On average Bengali people have five to six children. It was, and still is, common in Bangladesh for people to have many children. One reason could be that being Muslim they are not allowed to use condoms. Fifty years ago people in the village had as many children as possible, because many were lost to illness and disease.

On a Sunday Samir was playing football in the local Allen Park with his friends. A group of white youth told them to get lost from the park. Samir and his friends knew if they didn't leave the park they would get beaten up. They left the park upset and couldn't play the beautiful game. Samir came home and told his father what had happened and his father told him not to worry and that they did the right thing to leave the park. His father was worried about his safety and he told his son that the next time he went to play football he had to leave the park as soon as he saw the white boys and he should not get into any fights. It was a time when Bengali children couldn't go out and enjoy themselves freely and they didn't feel welcome in society by the white youth.

1978

It was May 1978 when Aftab Ali was stabbed and killed in St Mary's Gardens. He was a young Bengali man aged only twenty six. Aftab Ali was killed just because of the colour of his skin. The small Bengali community was shocked and they demanded justice for Aftab Ali. Every time they went out they had to look over their shoulder for their safety. Whenever the Bengali people went out they went out in groups hoping they would not be attacked by the racist.

Next summer Samir was playing football in Allen Park again with his friends. Some white youths came and told them not to play in the park and asked why they were there. Samir didn't want to argue because he wanted to avoid a beating. They spoke in Bengali and started to run but on the gate there were a few white boys waiting for them. The white youth started to punch and kick Samir and his friends. They ran in different directions for safety, leaving their ball behind. The white youths told them that they didn't want to see any Paki in the park. Samir came running home and told his father what had happened. Karim told his son that they did the right thing to run. He also told his son that they were here in London to make money and once they made enough money they would go back to Bangladesh and Samir could play football there. Temporarily they stopped going to the park and Samir discussed with his friend how they were going to attack the white boys for revenge.

That same summer, Karim and Sokina planted coriander seeds and other herbs in the garden. He managed to get some pumpkin seeds from a friend and sowed them. Tomatoes and potatoes were the other common vegetables they grew. Within a few weeks the pumpkin seeds germinated. Sokina watered the plants and if the next door's white woman was out in the garden then the only word Sokina said to her was 'Hello.' She was unable to answer any other questions in

English. Sokina just shook her head left to right to mean that she didn't understand. The white woman wanted to talk to Sokina and to find out more about her life, but that wasn't possible. Sometimes Karim translated for Sokina.

April 4, 1979

This was a day for the Bangladeshi people to celebrate as Bangladesh's number one enemy, zulfikar ali bhutto, ex- prime minister of Pakistan was killed by hanging. Allah had listened to the pain of the millions of Bangladeshi people he had killed through his power. Allah insulted him in front of the world and then had him killed by his own people. The people of Bangladesh celebrated the news and thanked Allah for justice. It helped to ease the pain of the people who had lost their loved ones in 1971.

Sokina received a letter from an uncle. The uncle wrote to her that he needed help to get his daughter married and asked if Sokina and her husband could help, saying that Allah would reward them in paradise. After reading the letter, Sokina told Karim about it and he gave five thousand taka for the wedding. Most of the people who lived in London always helped their relatives and the poor people in their villages. They felt privileged to be in a position where they could help others.

Samir was bullied alot in school and suffered many physical bruises and mental trauma. Being a minority, he didn't get much help from anyone else to help him survive his school days. He had had enough and told his father that he wanted to quit. Karim understood why he wanted to leave but he wanted his son to learn enough English so he could read his own letters and move around London without relying on anyone. At the end of school Year 10, Samir left school and his father found him a job in a clothing factory in Brick Lane where he learnt tailoring.

There were many tailoring post available in Brick Lane and the surrounding areas. Most of the big retail outlets used to get their garments from England rather then all over the world. The garment market was very popular around Brick Lane. When Samir received his first pay, he gave his wages to his father. Karim gave Samir five pounds for his pocket money and gave the rest of the money to Sokina to save up for the family.

1980

At the beginning of the school summer holidays Karim took his family back to Bangladesh for the first time. He intended to find a suitable 'life partner' for Sabbir and Ayna. When the family arrived at the 'village home' they actually thought that they had come to the wrong place because of some of the relatives' behaviour. Marriage proposal started to come before they landed in the village. All the close relatives came to see them. Karim's sisters stayed in Karim's house for the next few days and they slept on the floor. Both of his sisters were waiting for the opportunity to talk to Karim about something that they had wanted to get off their chest for many years.

At night Karim invited everyone to come to his big room to first receive presents and then to discuss a few things. The rooms in the house were very big, four British double beds would fit in a room. Karim opened the suitcase and gave everyone a present. The first presents went to his father and mother, woolly jumpers to keep them worn.

Everyone sat around the room, some people sat on the bed, others on chairs and stalls. Karim said to them that his intention was to get Sabbir married first, then Ayna. He asked everyone to look for a suitable wife for his son and a suitable husband for his daughter, as he didn't intend to stay for too long. Karim's father, Motlib, gave names of a few people whose daughters may be suitable. Motlib said that one thing he was sure about the girls was that they were from an excellent caste but he didn't know any of the girls personally. Karim's brothers, Rahim and Sahim, also mentioned a few other girls' names. But his sisters didn't mention any name or make any input.

The next day Karim's sisters, Tozia and Shazia, attacked their father one at a time for not mentioning their daughters' names 'for proposal'. Motlib told them that it wasn't too late and at the next opportunity he would mention their names. Both sisters put Motlib in a dilemma and he wasn't sure what the best solution was. If he mentioned one grand-daughter's name then the other one would be upset. He thought the best solution would be to speak to his son and let him know about the situation. Motlib spoke to Karim and informed him of his sisters' intentions. Karim was also confused and looked for a suitable solution which would not upset his sisters. Karim asked his father for his opinion. Motlib said that it was important that Karim helped his sisters but how could he help both of them as he only had one son? Karim said that he didn't mind either of the nieces as both of them were good looking and decent. But the question was, how could they choose one over the other? Father and son agreed that they would leave the choice to Sabbir and that should take care of the sisters.

Meanwhile, so many other people came to see Motlib and Karim regarding the marriage proposals of Sabbir and Ayna. Many distant relatives came whom had hardly visited them over the past ten years. Many brokers came with albums of girls' and boys' pictures and offered money in the region of five to ten laks. One broker offered ten laks for Karim's daughter and a plot of land in a prime location in Sylhet town to the prospective bride. It was getting crazy but the best answer Karim could give was, "First we'll get Sabbir married then we'll think about Ayna's marriage." When a 'Londoni' arrived it was common in Sylhet for hundreds of proposals to come from all sorts of directions. Everyone wanted to send their son or daughter to London. For some people, London was seen as 'heaven on earth! in terms of earning money and having a wealthy life.

Sabbir had someone in mind whom he looked out for but couldn't find. He asked around for the person indirectly. He was informed that the person had gone to another country. Sabbir was very disappointed to hear that as the person had given him something that he wanted to give back. This was a person that he couldn't get out from his mind. He kept it secret as the person had left a lasting impression in his brain and heart.

Sabbir wanted to make the village home look nice before he got married. The paint work was out of date so he went to the local bazaar with his cousin Sodrul to buy some paint for the home. Sodrul became Sabbir's personal adviser. In the local bazaar Sabbir's friend had a tea bar and he spent some times in there relaxing. His friend,

Khutumona, mostly sold teas, biscuits, cigarettes and 'paan' with betel-nut. Khutumona told Sabir that his grandfather had served tea to the British rulers in the 30s and 40s. The bar was open everyday in the evening for the daily 'bazaari'. There were no freezers in the village to freeze fish so people shopped for fresh fish everyday. In the bazaar Sabbir noticed how all types of people mingled together and bargained for fish, vegetables and other products. Fresh fruits, vegetables or fish were never sold for a fixed price. Sodrul spoke to a few people and found two painters in the bazaar. He negotiated the price to paining the house. Sabbir told the painters to paint the outside of the house black and white. From the ground one foot was pained black then the rest white.

Sabbir was given two pictures of Tozia's and Shazia's daughters and provided with basic necessary information such as her education and personality. Sabbir also saw the girls floating around the house but they never came to speak to him. The girls found the experience very embarrassing. They knew what was going on but were too shy to come and speak to him. He was told that if he liked anyone he could choose one of the girls. Both girls had their own beauty that was given by Allah. One looked taller and the other looked chubbier. He liked both and was in a dilemma whom to choose, so a face to face viewing was arranged. Sabbir waited in anticipation looked at them one at a time and asked them a few questions. Both of them were too shy and were hiding their faces. One of the questions Sabbir asked was "What makes a good wife? One of them answered that it was a woman who could look after the house appropriately and the other one's answer was a woman who could bring up the children appropriately. Sabbir found both of the answers to be intelligent. He gave them the opportunity to ask him questions but they never took the offer up.

Sabbir thought and analysed which girl to choose but he found it difficult to make the final choice. He turned to his mother for advice. Sabbir went into his mother's room and told her while no one else was listing "Mother I am finding it difficult to chose which one should become part of our family".

"That shouldn't be difficult, you have seen the girls, chose the one you think is right for you."

"Can you help me chose one?"

"It's your life. You have to make this decision. You are a big boy now."

"I like both of them. Can I have both of them?" He said that jokingly and with a smile.

She laughed and told him "That is not possible. You are only allowed to take one wife to London."

"Anyway mother, give me your opinion about your preference?"

After a bit of hesitation Sokina said what she thought: Shazia's daughter, Sima, would be her choice as she thought that this girl was proactive, always helped out in the kitchen and spoke politely but the only problem was that she had a tooth out of position, towards the front of her mouth.

"That is not a problem as it can be fixed easily in England," said Sabbir. By now he was pretty sure which one to pick and knew that if she turned out to be no good, then he could always say it was his mother's choice, a typical Bengalis back-up plan.

Many more wedding brokers came to see Karim for his daughter's proposal and offered many types of bribe. Karim didn't listen to any of them. He was pissed off with the people's attitude and the way they behaved. For some people it was like a business trying to get married to a 'Londoni' man. The brokers would be well paid if they could arrange a wedding, in the region of ten to twenty thousand taka. They didn't think about whether the pair would get on well with each other or if they were a suitable couple or not.

Sabbir bought a Honda motorbike to compliment his image as a visitor from England. Most people in Bangladesh drove a motorbike rather then a car as it was a hot country. With a motorbike it was easy to commute from the village to the bazaar. Sodrul taught him how to ride the bike. He was taught by Sodrul that where it was wet on the muddy road he had to keep his legs wide apart in case the bike slipped. Whenever the motorbike was free Sabbir's cousins took it for a ride. They loved it because few people had a bike in the village. They had always wanted a decent motorbike and they washed it every morning and kept it nice and clean for Sabbir.

After a few days and nights thinking and analysing, Sabbir chose to marry Sima. Karim's family made it official as soon as possible and the wedding took place within three weeks. Shazia's husband wasn't rich enough to cover the cost of the wedding, so Karim gave his sister fifty thousand taka to help out. As there was no wedding hall in the village, a self-made hall was prepared in the courtyard of Shazia's house. Bamboo bars were used to make the pillars and tins were put on the top in case it rained. Perhaps they could have watched TV and found out if it was going to rain on that day. Then again there were no TVs in the village and if there had been one, nobody would have understood the weather information. During the wedding, pictures were taken but no video filming, as it wasn't in fashion then. The meat from two cows was prepared for the guests and rice and curries were prepared in very large pots. People from both families arrived and sat on long blanket, on the ground - no chair table business! Most of the young men helped out servicing the guests. Poor people from the village turned up, ate and requested more food that they wanted to take home with them in their bags. They came prepared with plastic bags and containers and left with similes on their faces as they were given all the left over rice and curries.

The following week, there was a local football match between two rival villages. Sabbir went to watch the match with his friends to see if it was any different than games he'd seen in England. They went early to find the best grass space available as there were no seats or roof yet constructed in the football stadium. Both teams had hired players from different parts of the country and didn't want to lose the game. They played in bare feet because no boots were allowed. As the match started the abuse at the 'away' team started simultaneously. Home fans were swearing at the 'away' team players as soon as they came near the touch line, there was no mercy. "You son of a bitch! If you score against my team, I will kill you after the match!" a support shouted out. Sabbir's friend commentated for him and told him which players were hired and how much they were hired for. He wanted to laugh at the swearing he was hearing from the supporters. "You son of a dog! Don't pass the ball!" another supporter shouted out. The most expensive player they had hired cost ten thousand taka (£100), which was a lot of money for the village team. The home team players started to play well. That kept the fans happy and they scored half way through the first half which was pleasing for the crowd. But the 'away' team weren't out of the game. They had a fair share of the shots on target and it promised to be a good second half.

During the half-time break a man came around to sell Bombay mix which Sabbir bought. It was spicy and made with lemon, salt and coriander. It was a very tasty snack for Bengali people and sold very well. There were many Bombay mix sellers in the stadium. It was a little business for poor people. They got to earn some money but importantly it was enjoyed by the nation. Some boys as young as eleven were selling it. Next to Sabbir a few other people bought it but refused to pay the man. They told him that they had no change. The seller said, 'Please pay me, don't kick a poor man's belly, I have to feed my children with this money' then they quickly paid and sincerely apologised for the delay. Effective words can have a sharp meaning!

The second half started and the 'away' team started to attack; they were a goal in deficit. Within ten minutes they scored, but the home team complained furiously to the referee that it was an offside. "The referee took bribes!" a group of supporters shouted out continuously for a few minutes. The referee stood his ground and the goal stood. The 'away' team continued to play well and scored again through open play and this time there was nothing that the home team could complain about. The home supporters were getting more and more aggressive and abusive towards the away team. They were throwing plastic bottles at the 'away' team's players and it was getting hard for the 'away' team to play properly. The ball managed to reach the 'away' team's penalty area, and for no obvious reason, the referee gave a penalty for a push. The 'away' team couldn't believe it. Maybe it was best to concede a penalty and go home alive. The match ended in a draw and the 'away' team managed to leave the pitch in safety.

Sabbir couldn't believe what had happened and how racist people could be towards their own people just for a football match. For Sabbir this was an unbelievable experience and he thought people had behaved like animals! For him it should be fare and if you win then you win and if you lose then you have to accept it.

At home many of Karim's relatives were nagging him to get his daughter married to their son. His sister Tozia wanted Ayna for her son Muslah. Karim's father spoke to him and told him to get Ayna married to Muslah as it was important to help his sister. Muslah was a decent boy. He didn't have much education but that didn't matter since Karim wasn't looking for an educated boy. He was merely looking for a decent boy who would look after his daughter well. Karim agreed to the marriage as he also wanted to help his sister out. He gave his sister fifty thousand taka to help her as well. No one asked Ayna if she was happy and if she agreed with the proposal. She was told by Sokina that she would be married to Muslah, and that was it. She didn't complain to anyone about her parents' decision as she respected their agreement.

A month after Sabbir's wedding, he and his wife went to Dhaka to get a visa for Sima to come to London. Sabbir stayed in his aunt's house and his uncle took him around Dhaka as he didn't know how to travel around the unknown city. It was also the first time Sima had been to Dhaka who had wanted to see the capital of Bangladesh for long time. For a lot of village people seeing the capital city of their own country was a 'big thing'. Their uncle and aunt took them around Dhaka and showed them some of the famous and historic attractions and they felt happy became more knowledgeable of Bangladesh.

They went to Bangladesh's high commission's office. Sabbir had most of the important documents with him to show to the immigration officers. He also had pictures of their wedding. Sabbir reminded Sima to remember her new date of birth because her original one would have made her under age to get married. After a short interview with the immigration officers, where the officers asked Sima to confirm her name, date of her marriage, husband's name and her date of birth, Sima was given a visa to come to England.

After staying in Bangladesh for a few months they returned to England with fresh fruit and vegetables. Sima received her first taste of the British weather which blew her mind away and instantly gave her a negative view of the country. At first she found some of the food difficult to eat. She wasn't used to things like bread, butter, jam and cereal. This was a typical reaction of many Bengali village women. Soon Sima, learned to like toast well done with pineapple jam which she had never had in the village.

Syed left school at the age of fifteen due to racism. He told Karim that the white boys were beating him up for no reasons and called him a "Paki" all the time. Karim found him work in a local leather factory.

Slowly he learnt how to make leather jackets. When he was paid, he gave the money to his uncle and Karim gave him ten pounds from his pay for his pocket money and saved the rest for his parents. When Syed's father needed money, Karim sent it to him.

1981

Sima complained to Sabbir that she didn't like the way of life in London and felt claustrophobic in the house. "I am stuck in the house almost twenty-four-seven", said Sima. "What can I do?" "This is London's life", he replied.

"I don't like this life in London".

"You'd better get used to it, as we will be living here in London for a long time".

"I want to go to Bangladesh for one year's holiday".

"I am not listening to you, anyway to avoid getting bored, you should read the Qur'an, English books and watch cartoons and news on television which will help you to improve your English".

Sima said that she wanted to go out and see London but Sabbir never had time for her. He was too busy working seven days a week.

Sima became pregnant for the first time, which was happy news. Sokina was also happy that she was going to be a grandmother and to have a little friend to play with. Every time Sima needed to go to the hospital for checkup, Sabbir had to go with her as she didn't speak English. This was a big problem for the Sylheti men who married women from the village. They had to go with their wives to translate all the time. Almost all the women from villages didn't understand any English because they hardly completed their primary school education.

Sabbir took Sima to Whitechapel Market to give her a break from staying home all the time. He told her to follow him carefully and also gave her the home telephone number and the address in case she got lost. Sabbir met other Sylheti men in the market and exchanged general conversation. At the end Sima told him that she really enjoyed the new shopping experience and would like to go out like that every week. He told her it wasn't possible as he was too busy with the factory work.

Sabbir decided to take Sima to West End to show her some of the tourist attractions. He took her into the big shops and gave a good tour of Oxford Street and bought her an expensive bottle of perfume. She enjoyed the day out very much and told him to take her to more places. He told her he didn't even know London well so how could he show her around?

Later in that year Sabbir's first child, a son, was born in the London Hospital. Sima wanted to give birth at home. Sabbir told her "People don't do that here in London. They go to hospital in case anything goes wrong". Sima prayed to Allah for things to go well. Nothing went wrong and Sabbir and Sima became happy new parents. A nurse in the hospital taught Sima how to change the baby's nappy. She stayed in the hospital for a few days, then she was discharged. All the relatives came and saw the baby and gave clothes as presents. Sabbir, Sima and Sokina spent a week looking for a suitable Islamic name. Karim was asked to give names and he gave the name 'Yasin,' which is a name of a sura in the Holy Qur'an.

Ayna's husband Muslah arrived to London from the village just after six months of getting married. Karim's sister was very happy with Karim for bringing Muslah to London by getting his daughter married to him. Initially he stayed in Karim's house because he had nowhere else to go and had very little idea about London. He quickly applied for a council property. Most Sylheti people lived in council property when they brought their family to London. It was a huge opportunity for people to be given houses by the government. The council first gave them a temporary house in the borough of Tower Hamlets. Sabbir found Muslah work in a local factory and Muslah sent his earning back home as expected by his parents. It was the main reason why he got married to a 'Londoni' girl.

1982

Karim was informed by a friend that there was an Indian restaurant for sale in Brick Lane. An Indian restaurant that wasn't doing too well, but it made enough money to cover the costs. Karim felt that it would be a good idea to buy this restaurant so all of his children could have a secure job. Also, it was close to home, so everyone can help out.

Karim first spoke to his oldest son, Sabbir, who agreed that it was a good opportunity to have a business and if they bought it then they would try to see if they could improve it. The family agreed to buy this restaurant. The restaurant was of a medium size with over fifty seats and had three rooms upstairs. They had to borrow money from a bank and relatives to acquire this business.

Everyone became involved in the business. They employed one of their cousins who was a chef and retained one of the experienced waiters so they could learn the trade before letting him go. Sabbir and Samir worked in the restaurant full time and Karim helped out during the weekend in the kitchen as he had some previous experience. In the evening Muslah worked in the kitchen to extend his bank balance. Karim rented out the above rooms to other single Bengali man who worked in the factories. From time to time Karim visited the restaurant just to see how his sons were doing and if they were running the business appropriately. Karim told Sabbir to try to learn the art of cooking. He felt it would be good to be multi-skilled. Sabbir watched the chef cooking very carefully. With his eyes he measured the amount of spice the chef used for different curries.

When Sima had the chance and Sabbir was in a good mood she complained about not liking it in London. She found it boring staying at home all the time. She wanted to go back to Bangladesh for a long holiday. She said to Sabbir, 'Why don't you make a lot of money so we can go to Bangladesh and stay there for ever?'

'I wish there was a tree that I could go to and collect lots of money,' he replied.

'I hope you make a lot of money from your restaurant so we can go back home sooner.'

'You keep on praying, I am sure Allah will make us rich.'

'I have been praying a lot since I arrived here.'

'Good, you need to pray more.'

According to Sabbir she didn't understand what she was talking about, money didn't come easy and when people came to London they hardly ever returned to Bangladesh forever due to their love of the currency.

'You won't be bored anymore, I will buy you something that will keep you busy, it will help you go back to Bangladesh sooner rather than later,' said Sabbir. That put a smile on Sima's face. She wanted to know what it was that he was going to buy for her. He told her it was a surprise and that if he told her then it wouldn't be a surprise anymore. 'Whatever it is, I want it as soon as possible, as I want to go to Bangladesh,' she replied.

Sabbir fished around and bought a sewing machine for her but it was so big that he wasn't able to bring it home. It was a 'Brother' sewing machine that people used in factories. He asked his friends and brothers to help him to get the machine into the house. His house was crowded enough and it became even more crowded. Sabbir felt that this purchase would pay dividend if it was used appropriately. He gave her a few lessons on how to sew clothes. He told her to look and learn and that she should press the peddle slowly. Sima practised in her spare time.

Sima told her husband that everyone in the family wanted to celebrate Yasin's first birthday. She asked Sabbir whether he would buy a birthday cake for his son. He told her that there was no problem celebrating something that was useful and beneficial. He didn't think birthday celebrations were a good thing to do as it was something English people did and it was un-Islamic. 'Money is not a problem; if you want I can give you twenty pounds to put in his account,' he said. Sima didn't want to argue. She knew that if she did then he would get pissed off. Sabbir's sister bought birthday presents for Yasin. He told his sisters that they would spoil Yasin and that when he grew up he would expect everything to be given to him. He thought it was important to control kids when they were young. This was a problem to the Sylheti people who had their own religion to follow at the same time as living in a foreign society where children wanted things that clashed with their religion. Children were not allowed to celebrate things like birthdays.

1983

Sima became very good at using the sewing machine. Sabbir contacted some of his friends and managed to find work for her to do at home. In the beginning Sabbir showed her how to do the real work and the way to do it quickly. She made ladies skirts. Sabbir told her that with the money she earned, she would be able to buy whatever she liked but mainly she could help her parents back home with it.

When Sima saved up some money she gave it to Sabbir to send it to her parents. The money helped her parents with their daily needs and made them proud that their daughter was able to help them financially. That was one of the reasons why they got her married to a Londoni man.

Sima continued to complain to Sabbir that she didn't like it here in England. She said that if she had known her life would be like this, she would have tried her best to avoid marrying him. Then again, she knew she didn't have much say in terms of whom she had to get married to. She told Sabbir that she wanted to go back to Bangladesh for a long holiday. He told her to be patient and that the time would come soon because he had been working hard in the restaurant to earn extra money.

Sabbir's restaurant wasn't doing as well as he intended. He wanted to make money more quickly. He wanted to be rich for many reasons and he never discussed his reasons with anyone. Sabbir worked very hard to improve the business. He worked in the kitchen when it was busy and helped out at the front, too. Sabbir worked like a 'runner' as it was his business and wanted to improve it as fast as possible. Whenever he had the chance he distributed menus door to door with special offers. From his advertisement he received good returns. He wanted to make the business a success as he had a very important hidden ambition to fulfil. When he worked, it helped him to let go off the other things he had in his mind. Sabbir felt that if he wasn't busy doing something then he had flashback of the past memories, which had traumatized him greatly. He decided to keep the memories to himself until it was appropriate to tell anyone.

1984

Four customers came into the restaurant, ate their meal and then one by one started to leave the restaurant. The last customer said that he would only pay for his part of the bill and not the others. Sabbir told him that if he didn't pay then he wouldn't be allowed to leave. The customer said that if they didn't let him out then they would be killed by his mates. Immediately, Sabbir locked the front door and called the police. Two police officers arrived and made him pay the bill.

The next day the four customers came back into the restaurant, and started to smash the glasses and pull over the tables. Sabbir and the other waiters backed off, went to the kitchen and called the police. They shouted, 'We don't want any Pakis here, go back to your country!' Quickly all the restaurant staff got together. 'We are not here to go back, we are here to take back what you lot have stolen from us!' Sabbir shouted. With kitchen knives and wine bottles Sabbir and staff attacked the hooligans. There were injuries on both sides. The hooligan ended up with stab wounds. The police officers came and arrested the men. Sabbir had to close the restaurant for a few days. Some of the furniture and glasses were broken and damaged. Sabbir tried to fix what he could and had to replace some of the tables and chairs. The racist may have thought that they could get rid of the Bengalis from Brick Lane but their antics made the Bengalis stronger as a unit. Sabbir never thought about giving up his restaurant. He had ambition, determination and he wanted to make the restaurant a success.

Sokina's father wrote a letter to her regarding that he needed some money to get one of her sister married. A proposal had come from a 'Londoni' groom and they didn't want to miss the opportunity to send her there. Sokina asked her husband and sons to help. Her sons were happy to help their grandfather. Karim sent fifty thousand taka to help with the wedding.

Sima persistently complained to Sabbir that she needed to go back to Bangladesh to see her parents and friends. She was missing them a lot. She had enough of London and wanted to go back as soon as possible. Sabbir understood her situation and told her that he would try his best to send her at a convenient time. She continued to work at home and earn extra money, which also allowed her to take her mind off the village.

While Sima worked on the sewing machine Sokina looked after Yasin and helped with the cooking. Sokina tried to use the sewing machine but she found it uncomfortable, so she gave up. During the Eid time, she bought everyone clothes and sent money back home to her parents.

Sima became pregnant and gave up work for few months before the child's birth. At the end of the year Sima gave birth to a daughter. Sokina named the child - Khadijah. Khadijah was the Prophet Muhammed's first wife's name. Sabbir became exceptionally happy to have a girl. The more he looked at the child the more confused he became. He couldn't work out how amazing a child's birth was. The process was unbelievable. From a drop of water to a human! How could that be possible, he asked himself. He also reflected that he was also born from a drop of water and now he was able to talk, think, make decisions, and have his own children. Then he gave up trying to understand the process. But Sabbir thought "If every human thought about the process their mother had gone through to give birth then they would never disrespect their mother".

Chapter Three

1985

Sabbir's restaurant business had picked up and it started to do well. He wanted his restaurant to stand out from others. On the menu he created two extra dishes, Shatkora and Komla curry. These are two top Bengali home curries that are regularly eaten by Sylheti people. Sabbir wanted to give the Sylhet to his customers. He enjoyed creating new items to give customers something new to taste and also increased the price a little bit too. When customers asked him why he had changed the menu, he told them that he had added new items, but he never mentioned the price increase. Anything that kept Sabbir busy was good news for him as it stopped him constantly thinking about something that had happened to him at earlier age. For Sabbir an active mind was better than a non-active mind. His past haunted him like a ghost and continued to give him psychological flashbacks. Whenever he had the flashbacks it made him think about what had happened and how he was going to solve the problems. He had planned many solutions but it was very difficult for him to implement any as the target was in another continent.

Sokina's sister arrived in London from the village with her British husband – Badol Miah. Badol Miah lived in Shadwell, not too far from Karim's house. Sokina visited her sister with Karim and the children. She was very happy that she had a close relative in London that she could visit, talk to and spend some time with when possible. She could also have a holiday at her sister's house.

Sabbir's restaurant's chef, Gozafor Miah, who was thirty years old, was a friendly and hard-working man who loved cricket. He kept up to date with cricket news through the Bengali newspapers. Gozafor Miah's love for cricket made him create his own team with the restaurant's staff. He bought a cricket bat, a tennis ball and invited the restaurant staff to join him in the local Allen Garden to play. During summer time they played in between their long lunch break from work. They invited a few other workers from the other restaurants to form a team. Sometimes Sabbir joined in the fun. It allowed them to mix together and have a social time as well as enjoy their break. They also caught up with village news.

Karim and Sokina sat in the living room watching TV. Azima came and sat next to her father to talk to him. She told him that she didn't want her father to get her married at an early age. Her father and mother couldn't believe that their child had the audacity to say that. They found it embarrassing for a child to discuss marriage with them. They realised that the western culture had influenced their daughter to think and speak to her parents like that. Karim promised his daughter that he would not get her married at an early age. Azima then said to her father that she wanted to go to college, then university, as she wanted to become a teacher. Karim didn't like her ideas and ambition and told her that a girl in their society did not study. Girls were meant to stay home and look after their husbands and children. She replied that white women work and therefore she should work and earn lots of money. Her ideas provoked him and he was really annoyed with her ambitions. Karim was very surprised to hear what she had to say. He suddenly thought that he had made a mistake by bringing his family to London. Sokina told Azima to go to her room as she had said enough for one day. Karim and Sokina found it difficult to understand why their daughter was thinking like that and did not know what they would do if she really was determined to go to college and university. They thought that if she went to college or university she would definitely end up with a boyfriend and their family name would be destroyed.

They decided without informing her that when she turned sixteen they would take her back home and get her married there so she wouldn't be able to go to college and university. A typical Sylheti man's plan!

Sabbir told Sima that she would be going back home. She became over excited with the prospect that she was going back to Bangladesh for the first time since she came to London. Sima raided Whitechapel market to do her shopping for Bangladesh. Sabbir didn't want to go with her as for him, ladies took too long to shop! They could not make up their mind when selecting something. He told Sima to take his sister with her. Sabbir gave her a few hundred pounds to do the shopping. Sima bought clothes for everyone. She knew that when she arrived in the village the relatives would come and expect to get something.

Karim had a discussion with his wife and children about retiring in Bangladesh. Sabbir understood his father's situation and the hard work he had done over the past forty years. Karim also no longer wanted to suffer the cold British weather. Sabbir didn't want to go to Bangladesh as he loved the restaurant and didn't want to leave the restaurant to Samir. Sima asked Sabbir to go with her so he could have a break. He also wanted to complete unfinished business in the village so he decided to go after all. Karim intended to stay in Bangladesh forever but Sabbir had other ideas that only he knew about, concerning what he was going to do during the holiday.

They went to Heathrow airport and put the luggage on the scale for weighing. They had two pieces of luggage over their weight allowance limit, but Sabbir knew a guy who worked for the Bangladesh airline so he did not have to pay anything. After a very long journey they arrived at the Sylhet Osmani airport. Rahim and Sahim came to the airport to pick them up. In advance Rahim had paid the custom officer five thousand taka. The custom officer let them out without checking their luggage. From the airport they went to the village by a mini bus. Everyone was happy to see them after such a long period of time.

In the village, Karim employed a female worker, Nazma, who helped the family with cooking and washing up. It was very cheap to employ a female worker, because there were lots of unemployed females. Nazma was paid two hundred taka (five pounds) a month and also received free food and accommodation. She had to do alot of hard work and all the washing by hand, as there was no washing machine. People in the village never had heard of washing machines or ever seen one. Sokina looked after her well and gave Nazma her old saris and presents to give to her parents. At the end of most months, Nazma's father visited her to collect her wages which helped her family to survive.

Sima mostly stayed in her parents' house as she had missed them alot over the past few years. She gave presents to her parents, brothers and sisters. Her parents were very pleased to see her but most importantly they were eager to see her children. Her parents liked their beautiful grandchildren so much they didn't know what to do with them!

Karim asked Sabbir to buy a plot of land in Sylhet town. He believed that it would be worth a lot of money in the future and it would be a good investment for the family. Sabbir paid ten laks for an empty plot and left it as it was, hoping to do something with it in the future. Alot of Sylhetis bought land in Sylhet town with the money they earned in England. It was one of the most common ways they invested their money back home.

In the village mosque the Imam made an announcement that a man had died. Most of the men from Karim's house went to see the dead body and discover the cause of death. He was a very young man, aged thirty. People were saying that there had been a fight in the local bazaar and that someone had stubbed him with a pair of scissors. Within a few hours of the man's death, all his relatives were informed and he was buried in the afternoon. In the local bazaar, in the evening, everyone was talking about the man and most people came to understand that there had been an argument between two people about the national political parties. A fight had started, the victim went to break up the fight, then someone stubbed him. There were others who were wondering about what would happen to his wife and the children. Who was going to look after them and would anyone marry a woman who had two children? It was most unlikely that anyone would marry her. Politics in Bangladesh can be very dangerous and small disagreements can lead to huge fights. Some people are so hot-headed, perhaps because they eat the hottest chilies called 'naga'. Naga is so hot it interacts with the brains cell from the moment one consumes it. People get a buzz of some kind of drug. There are people who are addicted to 'naga' and they have to have it when they eat rice and curry.

Sabbir met all his friends, the people from his caste and village. He particularly looked for someone in particular, the person he couldn't get out of his mind. He remembered the person almost like a lover. This person always stayed active in his mind, but he wanted to erase that memory.

The village people felt Sabbir was different and very unlike Londoni, who got on well with everyone, including the low cast people. Sabbir gave his friends presents, like shirts, t-shirts and cigarette from London, or perhaps the duty free cigarettes he bought in the airport. For the village people, smoking a cigarette from London was a big thing. It was the closest taste of London they could get. Sabbir searched for friends and people from his caste who might know the special person he had in his mind. Within a few weeks he managed to find a few young men whom he could trust and rely on. He told them that whenever he requested them to come to his help, that they must do so. He had a plan to catch 'a big fish.' Sabbir also told them he would pay them well if they could help him with his mission. One young man asked him, 'Are you planning to get Moskond?' 'No, he's not a fish! I will tell you when the time is right!' he replied.

In the evenings, Sabbir went to the local village bazaar. He sat in his friend's tea bar to catch up with the day's news. Almost every man went to the local bazaar each day to socialize and buy fresh fish and vegetables grown by the local people. Sabbir bought all of his friends and village men teas, biscuits and cigarettes. He mingled with them like a 'deshi' man. Sabbir observed from the tea bar how people mixed together and chatted in Bengali which was a beautiful sound to his ears. All the village friends and others liked him as he bought them free drinks each time he was in the bazaar. Sometime it cost him fifty taka, which was about a pound, so it wasn't a problem to him. He needed supporters for his hidden agenda. Sabbir didn't have to do any shopping as it was done by his uncles, but he went around the market to see what people were selling. Most people were selling fresh fruits and vegetables that they had grown in their garden. The fish were fresh, probably caught earlier in the day. If the fishmonger failed to sell his fish within the time limit, then he would try to sell it for a large discount and if that doesn't work then he would make it a dry fish with help from the heat of the sun. All the shop keepers and the shoppers were male. Females never went to shop in the bazaar because they were not allowed to mix with men. Sabbir found out that the person he was looking for had been in the village a few months ago, but had returned to some place in the Middle East. He had to postpone his mission for the moment. He was really disappointed that he was unable to meet this person and ask some of the questions that he had thought of over the years. One of the questions he had planned to ask was, 'Why did you choose me?' but he had to be patience.

A few days later, the guys asked Sabbir when they were going to catch this 'big fish' that he had mentioned, as their hands were itching. Sabbir said, 'Be patient. It's going to be as soon as we get a sunny day.' After a few days there was a sunny day and some of the guys came eagerly to Sabbir. He couldn't believe it how crazy some of those guys were! Then again, they had nothing else to do in the village as they were unemployed. They were young and hot-blooded and just what he was looking for. Sabbir told them to bring some fishing nets because he wanted to catch some fish from their big pond before he went to back London. They asked him if he was joking. They thought he had meant he wanted to catch a man. The guys had some big fishing nets and they placed the nets from one end of the pond to the other. They gave the nets a few hours in the water for the fish to get caught. They watched and noticed the net move. After five hours they took the nets out from the water and found lots of fish stuck in the nets. Sabbir gave the guys a fish each for their help and kept the other fish.

In the evening he went to the local bazaar and sat in his friend's tea bar. The guys told him that they never thought he wanted to catch real fish. Sabbir told them he wanted to see how they reacted and hinted that there might be a real human fish to catch in the future!

A few weeks before they returned to London, Sima shopped in Sylhet town and bought few saris for herself and clothes for the children. She also bought gifts for Azima and her children. Sabbir bought some fresh limes and lemons, as they tasted really fresh, to give to other relatives in

London. The close relatives came a few days in advance to see them off. Some came hoping they would receive any unwanted clothes, which they did. Sokina and Sima gave their old saris to the relatives and the poor village people. She also gave a sari to Nazma. Sabbir gave some of his shirts and trousers to his cousins and friends. Receiving old clothes put smiles on so many people's faces.

After staying in Bangladesh for a few months everyone booked their ticket to return to England except Karim who stayed to have a beautiful rest in what he called his real home.

They arrived at the London Heathrow Airport and received their luggage. They couldn't believe the modification the luggage took from Bangladesh to London. Two of the bags had been tampered with. They assumed it must have happened in Sylhet or Dhaka airport. Some bastard had cut through the luggage and taken stuff out! Sabbir said to himself, 'Do you think by complaining to the Bangladeshi airlines anything will happen?' 'No!' These sons of animals cut people's luggage and steal things. They put people through unnecessary problems. Why don't they sell their mothers if they are so desperate to steal other people's goods? Perhaps they should put a note in the luggage department, 'Please do not steal other people's goods, if you are so desperate then sell your mother.' That might teach them a lesson. Maybe not!

Sabbir had been unable to find the special person he had searched for in the village, but he wasn't going to concede defeat. He decided to be patient, and remembered that good things came to those who were patient. The children returned to London with many illnesses, such as mosquito bites and 'rotten feet.'

Next day Sabbir went to work as he couldn't keep away from his restaurant. To him the restaurant was like another wife whom he enjoyed spending time with. By default, Sabbir became the most responsible person in the family in London as his father had stayed in Bangladesh.

Karim's sisters and Nazma looked after him in the village. One sister after another sister visited him and they all stayed for a few weeks. Tozia and Shazia got to see their brother for a long period of time and Karim visited the relatives that lived far away and asked them to visit him. He wanted to know what had happened over the past thirty five years in great detail from them.

After six months in Bangladesh it became difficult for Karim's sisters to stay and look after him. They decided that it would be better for Karim to get married again. His new wife could help with the housework and she would be able to look after him better. He would also get better company from her.

Karim had to go to the main town to make a telephone call to speak to his wife in London. He asked Sokina what she thought about the proposal. Sokina was very upset with the idea and she wanted a divorce. After putting the phone down Karim thought about the situation. He felt that Sokina was correctly upset and that he had spent thirty years with her and he shouldn't upset her. On the other hand, he was in Bangladesh and she was in England. He was planning to living in Bangladesh as long as for the rest of his life and he needed company.

In London Sokina cried inwardly as she realized she was going to lose her husband. She spoke to her sisters in London who told her not to let him go and to persuade him not to marry again. After a few days thinking, she felt that he was on his own and that his sisters and Nazma weren't the best people to look after him. She understood that it would be better for him to have a wife as they were in two different parts of the world.

A week later Karim called again to speak to Sokina. After a long time listening to the positive and the negative sides of their argument, Sokina decided to put Karim out of his misery by giving him permission to get married. There were two conditions; one was that when Karim returned to England he couldn't bring his new wife with him and the other was that when Sokina returned back home he had to live with her. Sokina didn't know that the law didn't allow him to bring a second wife to London and Karim readily agreed to the conditions.

Karim's sisters found a young lady thirty years younger than him by the name of Rukshana. She was a divorcee but had no child from her previous marriage. The reason her husband divorced her was that she didn't produce any children and her husband's family thought something was wrong with her reproduction system. Karim didn't mind if she had problems and could not have children. He already had children! Rukshana had been married at the age of fourteen and had been divorced for fifteen years. She only stayed with her previous husband for six months, which was the time they gave her to get pregnant. Her family found it very difficult to get her married again because most people in Sylhet wouldn't marry a divorcee. Rukshana's parents had wanted her to marry for many years. Her parents weren't concerned about Karim's age as their main aim was that their daughter needed to have a husband, somewhere to live and to find some happiness. It was a very low key-wedding because both parties didn't want to make a fuss. Rukshana's parents also had very little money.

Karim gave his new father-in-law ten thousand taka to arrange the basic food. The wedding took place at night as they didn't want too many people to know about it. Only Karim's close family went to the wedding. An Imam read the relevant rites. They said, 'Kobul' and were married. Rukshana was just pleased to have a husband. It didn't matter to her what he looked like or how old he was. Rukshana arrived to her new home feeling excited. For so many years she waited for a new home. Everyone was happy in Karim's family as she looked very beautiful.

1986

Samir told Muslah that he wanted to marry a white girl called Jamie and asked Muslah to tell his mother. In Bengali culture it is disrespectful if a child talks about their marriage to their parents. Jamie was a good looking English girl but Sokina didn't want her son to marry a white girl as Jamie wasn't Muslim. Also, how was she supposed to communicate in Bengali and any children would not grow up as Muslim. Sokina knew she couldn't do anything if he married a white girl. The only thing she could do would be to kick him out of the house. She told Sabbir who felt upset to hear that his brother was going to marry a non-Bangali girl.

Sokina told Muslah to tell Samir that they could take him to Bangladesh and find him a beautiful girl there if he decided to go. Samir rejected the offer and insisted he wanted to marry Jamie. Sokina and Sabbir decided to let Samir marry his girl-friend. Sabbir knew the girl because she had come to the restaurant many times with her parents and friends. He had known there was something going on as sometimes the bill hadn't been paid. Samir and Jamie were married in a local church and brought her to their family house straight afterwards. There wasn't enough space in the house for them to live and Jamie didn't speak Bengali make it difficult for Sokina to communicate with her. They moved out to a rented house and Samir continued to work in the family restaurant. Sabbir felt he couldn't disown his brother because blood was stronger then a mistake. He felt that when there were many types of beautiful women available, people would try to taste them. Maybe he would learn later when he wouldn't be able to get the Bengali fish curries. Then he would come back to get married to a Bengali girl!

One of Sabbir's uncles, Kolim, arrived in London through some kind of 'visit' visa. Sabbir and Sokina paid him a visit where he was staying with his brother near Brick Lane. Kolim told them that before he left Bangladesh he had visited Sabbir's father and that he was okay. Sabbir remembered how when he was young he had been to Kolim's house in the village and Kolim had given him a shirt, so Sabbir took his wallet out and gave Kolim fifty pounds as a gift. Kolim asked Sabbir to find him a job. The only work Kolim could have done was in a factory or a restaurant. Sabbir spoke to a few people and within few days he managed to find Kolim a tailoring job on Commercial Road.

During the summer, Sokina took over the gardening as Karim wasn't in London any more. She planted the usual herbs which helped her keep her mind occupied. When Sokina spoke to her sister on the phone, she told her what she had planted and from time to time they exchanged seeds of different plants. Ayna came to her mother's house with Muslah almost every week. She didn't have many other relatives to go to. On her way out she took fresh coriander from her mother's garden to season her own cooking.

Sima nurtured the children, cooked food and worked at home sewing skirts and she was able to help her parents with the extra money. Sima thought about her next holiday to Bangladesh. When would she be going back again? The village was on her mind all the time. To Sima her body was in London but her mind was always in the village.

One day in the restaurant a customer ate his food and at the end, instead of paying the bill, he told the waiter to call the police. He had no money to pay the bill! Rightly so, Sabbir called the police and two officers came and spoke to the man. They found out that the customer came from a local mental hospital. A police officer told Sabbir that they would contact the mental hospital and try to get them to pay for the bill. Sabbir told the police officers not to worry about the bill as the customer was an ill man. He also told the officers to come to his restaurant and try his curries. He always looked for new customers; it didn't matter what job they did.

1987

Surprisingly, Karim's new wife Rukshana soon gave birth to a son. Everyone was surprised as everyone knew that she had had problems getting pregnant before. Karim telephoned Sokina to tell her the news. Sokina asked him if the mother and the child were well and he replied that they were well and the child was gorgeous. She told him not to overdo it or people would laugh that he was having children at his age!

Nazma and Rukshana's sister helped Rukshana in the house with the cooking and washing up. All the baby's clothes had to be hand washed. There was still no electricity in the village, but cabling work had begun to bring electricity to other towns nearby.

A few of Karim's relatives visited him and asked him whether he would agree to his daughter's proposal for marriage. The relative knew he had a daughter in London about marriageable age. Karim told them that his daughter was too young, as she was only fourteen, but when that time came he would see what happened. The relative wanted him to give his 'word of promise.' He didn't! In Sylhet, people thought it was okay to get married at the age of thirteen or fourteen. There were times when girls were married at a very early age, such as twelve. Some people think getting their daughter married at an early age takes the financial burden from off their shoulders.

1988

Yasin told his parents about the letter his school sent home about Parents' Evening. Sima asked Sabbir to go as she didn't understand English. He told her that he had too many things to do. Sabbir was too busy in the restaurant most of the evenings, so hardly visited his children's primary school for Parents' Evening. From time to time Sima went to Parents' Evening, but she didn't understand much English - the children translated what the teacher said. Sabbir assumed that the children would learn and be educated without much parental support. In the eighties and early nineties this attitude was a major problem in the Bengali community as a lot of parents didn't support their children's learning due to mis-understandings. For some parents it was acceptable for their son to leave school fifteen or sixteen so he could work in a factory or restaurant. They thought that the wage a son could earn from a restaurant job was enough and never understood the benefit of further education.

These were the Sylhetis who didn't receive any parental advice in their new local communities. But slowly they were learning about the benefits of education and were taking over the Spitalfield and Brick Lane area.

1989

Sima continued to pester Sabbir about wanting to go back to Bangladesh. He understood her situation but couldn't send her back home every few years due to the children's schooling. Sabbir told her that he had made a mistake by marring a Bangladeshi girl. Sima told him that she made a mistake by marrying a Londoni man! Sabbir jokingly proposed to her to let her go to Bangladesh forever if she would allow him to have another wife here in London. She refused. Sima told him that she didn't want to share her man and he wasn't giving her enough attention as he was always busy at work. How was he going to satisfy two women?

Rukshana decided to write a letter to Sokina to see what sort of response she would get and if she could have a friendly relationship with her so called partner. Sokina received a letter from Rukshana.

Ass-salaamu aaleykum appa.

I hope you are fine. How are Yasin and his mother? We are fine here with the help of Allah. I hope you are not upset that I have come to this family. My parents are very happy that they have managed to get me married and now I have somewhere to live and a new family.

When you have time, try to come to Bangladesh. I would like to see you all and the kids. Give my love to Ayna, Amina, Azima, Sabbir, Samir and Amir. Also give my love to Sima, Yasin and Khadijah.
Allah hafiz
Your sister, Rukshana.

Sokina didn't want to know Rukshana as she had a grudge against her for marrying her husband. Then she thought about it, and felt it wasn't her fault so she replied.

Wa-aaleykum ass-salaam.

I have become happy by receiving your letter. It was nice of you to write to me. With the help of Allah we are fine here. I am happy that Allah has made you happy by giving you a new family.

Life is very different in London. We have to stay in the house all the time. If you need anything from London then do write to me. Ayna and Muslah are fine and they do come around when Muslah has a day off.
Allah hafiz
Sokina

Karim telephoned Sokina and told her that when Amina finished school she shouldn't go to college, but should stay home and learn how to cook rice and curry. Sokina told him that she wanted to go to college and how she was very good at her studies. He told Sokina there was no point, and that whether she was good at studies or not, her next step was to be a house wife, get married and look after children. The next time Sokina saw Amina, she told her what her father said and Amina became very upset. Sokina also told Sabbir and his reply was 'If that's what father wants, then that's it. No-one can argue with father.' It was common in the seventies and eighties for most children to obey their parents' ideology, due to respect and possibly the threat of getting kicked out of their house. But slowly the children's ideologies were beginning to change with the British weather and culture.

Rukshana gave birth to her second child, a son. At the age of sixty four Karim became a father again. Karim loved fatherhood like he never had before. He was now able to spend more time with his young children, which he could never do before due to his work commitments.

A new surgery was opened by a Bengali doctor - Dr. Zakaria, near Brick Lane. Dr. Zakaria qualified in Bangladesh and also did further studies in London. The doctor went around Bengali people's houses to 'fish' for customers. He visited Sabbir's restaurant, introduced himself and requested that Sabbir joined his practice. It wasn't long before Dr. Zakaria realized he knew Sabbir's father who was from the neighbouring village. The doctor needed certain number of clients in order to run his practice, and alot of the Bengali people changed their doctor. They thought that they could speak and explain in Bengali the symptoms they had and some Bengali people needed dodgy documents. They felt that Dr. Zakaria would give them what they needed without a fuss.

During the Christmas period, Sabbir gave free bottle of white or red wine to his regular customers and decorated the restaurant with cheap Christmas decorations just to make others feel comfortable even though he didn't celebrate Christmas. For him it was another opportunity to make some extra dosh. He wanted to make his regular customers feel at home and welcome in his restaurant. Peter and Lee were allowed to have anything free. They were allowed to choose from the wine list and the food menu. Peter and Lee were Sabbir's best customers as they were coming to his restaurant since he had taken over.

Chapter Four

1990

Gozafor Miah's love for cricket still hadn't died out. He always enjoyed talking about cricket and kept up-to-date with Bangladesh's cricket results from Bengali newspapers. In the summer time he continued to go to the local Allen Garden during his long lunch break to play cricket with the other staff. If anyone refused to go then he made them work hard in the kitchen. Gozafor Miah knew the names of all the Bangladeshi cricket players and when he took a shot, he told others which player's shot it was. On his day off he took his son to the Allen Garden and taught him how to play cricket with a tennis ball. When he slept, he dreamed of playing in Bangladesh's team in the national stadium in Dhaka.

Sima was very happy as Sabbir told her that he would take her to Bangladesh during the summer holidays. She raided Whitechapel market with Ayna and bought presents for the relatives. Sokina bought clothes for Rukshana, her sisters and brothers and their children. She also bought dry nappies for Rukshana's children because they didn't have any kind of nappies in the village.

Sokina called Karim and informed him that they were coming back home. Karim told Sokina to bring Amina with them because it was her time to get her married. Sokina asked him to make the house clean and buy all the necessary items such as pillows, blankets, lungis and sandals for the grandchildren.

Sabbir went to his uncle Badol Miah's travel agent to book the holiday. The travel agent was based near Brick Lane where Badol Miah did all sorts of businesses. The tickets were very expensive because it was the busiest time of the year to fly. There were no direct flights from London to Sylhet, even though most of the passengers were going there. The Bangladeshi government didn't allow direct flights because if the passengers didn't stop at Dhaka Zia International airport then no-one could steal from the passengers' luggage. The aim of the government was to make life as difficult as possible for people. Sabbir had to stop at Dhaka, and then take a domestic flight from there. He decided to visit the aunty and uncle who lived in Dhaka and they agreed to pick him up from the airport.

When they got out of the airport they were attacked by new waves of fans as if they were superstars. All of the new fans were saying, 'Please give us some money, we have nowhere to go, nowhere to live, please give us a fat coin.' Sabbir took his wallet out and gave all the small Bangladeshi taka to the children, most of whom were half naked. The beggars refused to move out of the way and they wanted more money. His uncle shouted at them and told them to get lost. They got into an eight seater car but the beggars followed them for as long as they could and continued to beg. Sabbir's uncle told him how most of the children were not beggars, but were controlled by a gang. These children collected money and at the end of the day, the gang leader collected it from them. Sabbir found the news very disturbing to his brain.

Soon the road was blocked with a bamboo trap. A man came to the car with a pad on his hand and said, 'You have to pay fifty taka Road Tax.' They didn't want to waste time so Sabbir's uncle paid the money. Sabbir wasn't sure who the money was for, whether it was for the local gangster or the government. His uncle clarified that it was most likely a gang who were collecting the cash. Even if it had been for the government, most likely the government wouldn't get it. If it was a road tax, why didn't they manage it like they do it in England? Maybe no-one would pay. Maybe if people paid, then the people who were in charge would steal it all.

They stayed and relaxed in the aunt's house for the night. Next day they took a domestic flight to Osmani airport, Sylhet, which took forty minutes from Zia international airport, Dhaka.

When they arrived in the village, many proposals came for Amina and many bribes were offered. Karim's one intention was to get his daughter married to the closest relative who had a decent boy. His criteria was a boy who looked nice, who was polite and who would look after his daughter and respect her. They showed Amina a few pictures of grooms to choose from, to show the relatives that the choice was hers. Sokina told her daughter to choose her brother's son - Sufian. Amina was left with no choice and she didn't want to upset her mother because her mother had done so much for her. She went with her mother's choice and didn't complain about the person she would be getting married to. Sufian looked average, nothing special, just a typical uneducated Sylheti boy. Everything was arranged and Amina got married a few weeks later to Sufian. Then the process of bringing him to London started.

Sima spent most of her time in her parents' house. The children didn't complain much as they found English toilets to use and liked the vast space available around the house. Yasin liked the village very much and he was surprised to see so much free space. With Sabbir's cousins, Yasin fished in the pond and they made fishing rods with bamboo sticks.

A few years earlier Karim had tried to sell some trees from one of the plots of land that he had bought a long time ago. A powerful village man, Moskond, came and told him that the plot belonged to him and that if Karim cut down a tree then he would cut Karim's hand off. Karim didn't want to start a fight so he reported it to the police and proceedings started regarding whose land it was. Moskond said that he had land registry documents to prove that the land belonged to him, where as Karim's father also had land registry documents proving the same thing. Over the past thirty years, Karim's family had been selling trees and bamboo from the plot and suddenly now they had a problem. The other families in the village didn't want to get involved, although they knew the land belonged to Motlib's family. People didn't want to get involved with Moskond or his family because they had too many strong men in their family.

Karim didn't let his son Sabbir know anything about this because of his temper, but during Sabbir's holiday he found out what had happened from Munna Bhai. Moskond was a well-known foul-mouthed village gangster who had committed a few murders. He killed a witness in front of many people, but no one dared go to the police and give evidence. Once he had killed a man who refused to give up a plot of land that Moskond claimed was his, even though the man had land registry documents which he had for more then a quarter of a century.

Everyone in the village was scared of him but Moskond didn't fear anyone. Moskond claimed that when he died, Allah would not find him. He had built a concrete coffin in which he told his brothers and children to bury him in when he died. He also claimed that Allah had forgiven him for every murder he had committed because he had visited the holily place Mecca for hajj and asked Allah for forgiveness. He thought he was a clean man like a new born baby. Sabbir wasn't very happy about what Moskond did or his ideologies, which conflicted with his. Sabbir was interested in finding out how he could teach Moskond a lesson for telling his father that he would 'cut off his hand.' He found it difficult to live with the thought that there was a person in the village who thought he was bigger or stronger then him. This kind of bigotry unsettled him and Moskond became an extra item on Sabbir's menu! Sabbir was still looking for someone else in the village that he couldn't let go from his long-term brain cells. A person who was attached to his daily life and front of his brain, a person whom had a lot to answer for. Is it a lover? Is it an enemy? He refused to discuss it with anyone except himself but it was the first item on his agenda, but no-one else knew.

Sabbir used his financial resources to plan how he was going to get Moskond. One of the major problems was that Moskond hardly went out of his house, he mostly stayed home so no one could attack him. If he went out, he always had a bodyguard with him which made it harder to get him. Munna Bhai told Sabbir if he wanted him killed, it was possible, but it would take time. Sabbir told him that he didn't want him killed yet. He worked hard with his criminal advisor, Munna Bhai and concluded that the best way to get Moskond was to attack him when he came out for shopping and beat him up at night as there were no street lights. That wasn't possible as he hardly came out of his house. They had to wait patiently for a good opportunity.

Even though Sabbir was on holiday, he was thinking about the restaurant and wondering whether his brother was managing it smoothly. He called his brother to find out about the restaurant and also spoke to Gozafor Miah to check everything was going to plan.

Sabbir and Munna Bhai hired a gunman and planned that the gunman would wear a mask, go to Moskond's front gate, claimb a tree and shoot him in the legs, then drive off. They drove close to Moskond's house but it was busy with people coming and going. They didn't get a decent opportunity to execute their plan. Then they realized, technically, it wasn't feasible and gave up on that idea.

But Munna Bhai came up with another idea. He would send an old man into Moskond's house and when he opened the gate the old man would go in and shoot him. This was a risky plan too, for the hit man, if he got caught then there would be a huge fight between both families, which Sabbir didn't want. Sabbir wanted to do a clean job with no traces of evidence or DNA left behind. Perhaps he had the idea from CSI movies. Then again, in the village the police probably never heard of DNA. Sabbir didn't want his village friends and backup to do anything to Moskond. He felt they might 'grass him up' later or may blackmail him. Through Munna Bhai, he hired a gang from outside to keep an eye on Moskond's movements.

Once they noticed him with another man, and they kept track of him. Moskond went into a restaurant to eat. Munna Bhai told the gang to 'beat the shit out of Moskond' but to leave him alive. The gang went into the restaurant, leaving two motorbikes at the front and two at the back to escape. They were armed with knives but were not allowed to use them in case they killed the man. With a wooden bar, first they hit Moskond on the head, then on his body for a good few minutes and then they left.

Moskond ended up in the local hospital. Sabbir sent an anonymous person in the restaurant to pay for the damages. He also paid twenty thousand taka for the gang's fees. People in the village were surprised to hear Moskond had received a beating and many people were happy to hear such good news. At last someone had stood up to Moskond! In the local bazaar Moskond's relatives were saying that the person who had done it was a coward because he didn't show his face and didn't have the guts to say who he was, knowing he could be killed. Sabbir felt that Moskond needed a chance to learn and decided that if Moskond didn't attack Sabbir's father again, then Sabbir would leave him alone. Sabbir told his father to sell some trees from the plot of land where Moskond had given him problems. Karim told him that he didn't want any trouble and that once he had won the case, he would sell whatever he liked. Sabbir told Munna Bhai that if Moskond was a problem again in the future then he should inform him by telephone.

Sabbir decided to see the plot of land he had bought in Sylhet town the last time he was in Bangladesh. The price of the plot had tripled since he had bought it. When he arrived at the spot he couldn't recognise it. It was very different from before and it looked smaller. No-one looked after the land and some people had grown fruit and vegetables on it. That wasn't a problem. The problem was that the land looked smaller than he remembered and he needed to measure it to confirm its size. Sabbir came back to the village and informed his father. They went back to the plot and measured it and found out it had diminished in size by one-fifth in five years. Sabbir calculated that if he didn't do anything with it soon then in a few years time there would be nothing left! They went to investigate who had taken the land, to see if it was the adjacent owner on the side or not. They found out one adjacent owner had moved his boundary into their land. They went to visit the man and spoke to him politely. He denied any wrong-doing. Even though Sabbir had land registry documents for the land, the other man said that the land was his. They had no choice but to sue him, which cost them unnecessary money. At the same time Sabbir built a brick a boundary around the other side of the plot to prevent others from putting their nose into his land. It cost Sabbir one lak to pay a lawyer to get the part of the plot they actually owned from the other man. Police officers came to help Sabbir's employees removed the boundary to where it should have been. Then they built a brick boundary so the evil man couldn't push in again. At one stage Sabbir wanted to hire a hit man to get the man killed but his father stopped him and told him that wasn't the right thing to do "Be patient and Allah will give justice." This is Bangladesh where people try to mug people in the daylight. There were many cases where people stole others' land. In doing so many people died as people hired hit-men to do their dirty jobs.

Soon the family's holiday time was up. Sabbir returned to England with his family but Sima didn't want to return. Sabbir felt disappointed to return as he was unable to fulfil one of his top missions. He had failed to find the person he was so desperate for. He promised to look for the person until he died and not give up. Sabbir felt that until he found that person he wouldn't be able to stop thinking or put a full stop to that incident, which he decided not to talk to anyone about it.

Sabbir went back to his restaurant work the next day because he was a workaholic. He found out from his regular customers that Samir and Gozafor Miah had controlled the restaurant well and served quality food as usual. Sabbir gave a Bangladeshi 'lungi' to Gozafor Miah as a present and a fat end of year bonus.

1991

While everyone was eating dinner together as a family. Sabbir's son asked him, 'Abba why don't we use a knife and fork like English people?' 'Firstly, our prophet used to eat with his fingers, secondly we are not English and thirdly the food tastes much better when you eat with your fingers,' replied Sabbir. Yasin was satisfied with the answer but he still had a dig at his father, 'We have to wash our hands, but they don't.' 'They have to wash their knife and fork and it goes into everyone's mouth.' Yasin twisted his face with disappointment. A few minutes later Yasin said, "Abba, why do white people do everything different from us?" "Because they are a different colour from us and we follow the rules of our Prophet." Everyone had to eat with their fingers. The children had to learn to use their fingers at a young age.

Sima went back to work sewing skirts as usual. She went out with her neighbour and bought raw materials from Whitechapel market and made a salwar kamiz for Khadijah. Sima also made Asian dresses for Khadijah and Ayna's children. When ever Ayna wanted to make something she used Sima's machine. Having the machine, allowed everyone to save a lot of money. The raw materials were cheap to buy, but ready made clothes cost much more.

Sabbir visited Dr. Zakaria to see him regarding his heart burn. He was surprised to see so many Bengali men waiting to see the doctor. He spoke to Dr. Zakaria who told him to cut down on 'naga chili' and gave him some medicine. Sabbir couldn't help but ask the doctor why there were so many Bengali men waiting to see him. The doctor told him that they were not ill, but that most of them wanted sick notes so they could claim sick benefit and work at the same time. Dr. Zakaria gave the men the sick notes even though some of them were not sick at all.

During the summer holidays Sabbir invited Dr. Zakaria to come to his home and circumcise his son. It is part of being Muslim, which allows one to stay clean when one urinates. The sooner it was done the better it was. The doctor gave Yasin pain killers to do the job and was paid fifty pounds in cash for the extra work. Relatives came to see Yasin and gave him gifts to cheer him up. It took Yasin three weeks to recover fully from the pain.

Gozafor Miah continued to play cricket passionately. On his day off from work Gozafor Miah trained his son how to play cricket in his local park. He refused to allow a British passport for his son because he wanted to see his son play for Bangladesh one day. His son preferred football more than cricket but he told his son that cricket was better than football as when a player bats, he needs to stand up like a tiger and strike the ball that comes at a speed of over 100 mile per hour. He encouraged his son and told him that he wanted to see him on TV playing for Bangladesh.

Karim called from Sylhet and spoke to Sokina and told her that he had won the case against Moskond. It had cost him two laks which he had to pay the judges to give the verdict. When Sabbir heard that it cost him two laks for no reason, he was pissed off, which in return gave him unwanted anxiety in his brain. Sabbir called his father and told him that they needed the two laks back from Moskond. Sabbir felt like going to Bangladesh, holding a gun on Moskond's head and getting him to pay the money. His father told him that it didn't work like that in the village; there was no such thing as 'compensation,' and he should learn to control his temper as he was getting older.

In Amir's school a gang beat him up badly. They kicked him on the face and gave him ugly bruises. When he went home, Sabbir saw the marks. Sabbir felt like he wanted to chase the boys and do the same thing to them. Amir had a fight with one white boy but a gang beat him up. Sabbir took him to the hospital and the X-ray showed that there were no broken bones.

The next day Sabbir went to school, informed the head teacher and gave the names of the boys. Amir stayed at home for three weeks before returning to school. Sabbir wanted to come after school with his mates and beat up the suspects. Then his brain worked logically and he felt that his brother should learn to stand up for himself. Sabbir told Amir to make his own gang and beat up the white boys who gave him the beating. Amir spoke to his friends and told them about his plan. The white boys teased him about how they kicked him, and how he screamed for help.

Amir had had enough of the teasing and he decided to take some action. He planed to attack the white boys after school with his friend. As school finished, Amir and his mates attacked the gang members. Amir stabbed two white boys with a Stanley knife. He was the only one with a weapon as he intended to cause bodily harm to his opponents. Soon the coppers came and everyone did a runner. Two white boys ended up in the local hospital. Amir came home and told his brother what had happened. Sabbir told him to go to one of his uncles' house with his passport. In the evening two police officers came to Sabbir house and wanted to see Amir. They told the police that he had gone out with his mates. Sabbir spoke to Badol Miah and managed to get an emergency ticket to Bangladesh for Amir. Sabbir's family thought it would be best if Amir went to Bangladesh so the police wouldn't find him. Amir took a flight to Bangladesh within a few days and joined his father, step brothers and sisters in the village. Relatives wanted to know why he had suddenly gone to Bangladesh.

The next day, two police officers came to Sabbir's house again and wanted to know where Amir was. They told the police officers that he had moved out with a friend and had not returned home.

1992

Sabbir's aunty Priya, Kolim's wife, arrived in London with a dodgy Bangladeshi passport that her husband had bought from another man. Kolim paid £100 pounds for the Bangladeshi passport and had changed the picture to his wife's photo but immigration didn't stop her at Heathrow airport. Sokina visited her sister, gave her a sari as a present and told her to visit her home. Priya stayed with her husband in Kolim's brother's house and both of them lived illegally. There were no worries for her as she was staying at home but his status was at risk. He had to go to work and there were times when restaurants were raided by immigration officers.

Sabbir's step-mother gave birth to another child, a girl. No one could believe this lady's luck. She couldn't stop giving birth! Karim wanted a daughter as he missed playing with his other daughters when they were young. He was enjoying life like he never had before - a few young children around and free time to spend with them. Some relatives were laughing at him. Why was he having kids at his age? What could he do when he had a lot of venoms left within!

Amir roamed around the village on Sabbir's old motorbike as if he was having a holiday. Amir visited the relatives' house and received VIP treatment. Karim told his relatives that Amir was in Bangladesh because he missed his father and wanted to spend some time with him. Most Bengalis didn't like to tell any relatives any negatives things about because it brought bad name to the family. They tried their best to hide any negativity as they wanted to show their family in a good light.

Gozafor Miah bought a Bengali newspaper on his way to work and found out that 250,000 Rohingyas, which is a third of their population had fled over Burma's border into Bangladesh to escape the inhumane persecution. They were called one of the world's most persecuted people and some argued that they were also one of the most forgotten. The Rohingya people of western Burma's Arakan State are forbidden from marrying or traveling without permission and have no legal right to own land or property. Not only that, but even though groups of them had been living in Burma for hundreds of years, they were denied citizenship by the country's military government. For decades this Muslim group of ethnic-Indo origins had been considered the lowest of the low in this mainly Buddhist country. These people had been regularly beaten by Burma's police, forced to do slave labour and jailed for little or no reason. The kitchen staff discussed what would happen in Bangladesh as it is a poor country. 'As humans it is important to help others,' said Gozafor Miah. 'How can you help others when you're poor yourself,' replied Goni. 'We are already over-crowded in Bangladesh, do we have any space?' 'Exactly who's going to provide shelters for these people? 'I think our government must help these people because they need help, we are refugees here and the British government has helped us with houses and jobs,' replied Gozafor Miah. 'Yeah, but the reason the British government helped us is because they stole our wealth,' Goni counter-attacked.

In the restaurant two customers ate most of their dinner and then they called Sabbir to have a look at the food. When he looked at their plate there was a hair. Sabbir apologised and offered to provide the same dish again but the customers refused the offer. They said that they wouldn't pay the bill as the hair made them feel like puking. He was pretty sure that they had planted the hair in order to not to pay for the food. Sabbir argued that they had eaten most of the food and he was willing to take the price of the dish that had the hair in it but they wouldn't have it. There were other customers in the restaurant and Sabbir didn't want to argue with them. He let them have the food for free but he kept their picture in his photographic memory. A few weeks later the same customers returned but he told them that his restaurant was fully booked.

Sabbir went to pick up Yasin from a local mosque where he went to learn Arabic. Learning Arabic was must for Yasin and it was Sabbir's duty to make sure his son learnt the language of Allah. Sabbir noticed red marks on his son's face and asked Yasin what happened. Yasin said that the Imam had slapped him. Sabbir took his shoes off, went inside the mosque, told the Imam politely not to beat up children like that, leaving finger marks on their face. The Imam said that if they didn't beat up the kids, the kids didn't learn. Sabbir told the Imam politely that next time he shouldn't hit his son on the face.

But the next day Sabbir noticed more marks on his son's face. Yasin told his father that the Imam had slapped him again. Sabbir was really pissed off. He took his shoes off and went inside the mosque to beat the Imam. On the way he had a second thought, he knew that if he did what was in his mind then he would be locked up. Instead he called the police and had the Imam arrested. Sabbir showed the marks to the police officers and the police officers told Sabbir to get a report from the doctors so they could keep the bastard locked up for child abusing. Some of these Imams had problems adjusting to the British law. They thought they could do what they did to the young children in Bangladesh; beat them up all the time. Who's going to educate these Imams?

Imam being arrested became big news in the local community. There were some people against Sabbir for grassing up the Imam. A few old men from the community came to Sabbir's restaurant to see him. The first man said that Sabbir's father was a very nice man to soften him up. Then they asked him to drop the case because it would bring a bad name to the mosque and the Bangladeshi people. He refused to listen to them. He told them, 'What the man did was wrong and he needs to pay, not only did I give him a polite warning not to hit my son on the face but the next day he did the opposite. He didn't hit my son, he actually hit me! Now I will show him who I am.' The old men told him that if he didn't drop the case then the community would stop him from going to the mosque.

'You can't stop me from going to the house of Allah; it's for everyone to pray.'

'We can stop you.'

'I don't want to be disrespectful to you all, but let me tell you, if I am stopped from going to the mosque then don't blame me if anyone gets killed. Don't forget all the money I gave for the building work. I will tell the government the amount of money you people scam. For example, I know you people claim benefit and work in the mosque and get paid. I know the Imam claims benefit and gets paid from the mosque! What's going to happen? A big headline in the local newspaper – Scammers in our Society.'

The old men left Sabbir's sight quietly and they said to each other that they couldn't believe that there was so much fire inside Karim's son.

Gozafor Miah won Sabbir's heart and mind with his hard work in the restaurant. Sabbir sensed that he might lose Gozafor Miah, as others might offer him a partnership in their restaurant as he was a very good chef. He didn't want to lose Gozafor Miah. So he offered Gozafor Miah ten percent profit to work until he retires. Gozafor Miah accepted the offer but Some of Sabbir's relatives criticized him for giving someone profit like that. He told them that it was important to have an excellent chef that one could trust and rely on. When Sabbir went to Bangladesh the restaurant's income didn't go down and customers were satisfied. According to Sabbir's understanding, Gozafor Miah worked as if the restaurant was his own and he deserved the extra rewards.

Chapter Five

1993

Amir returned to London after two years of hiding in the village. Sabbir thought the police probably forgot about the case and would leave Amir alone. Amir didn't live at the family home in case if the police came after him. He started to work in Sabbir's restaurant as a waiter and lived in the restaurant's room upstairs. Sabbir told Amir not to meet his old friend, they might 'grass him up.'

Sabbir walked through the Whitechapel Road to go to a relative house. On the way, in the Whitechapel Road a young boy asked him if he had any spare change. Sabbir was surprised to see an Asian beggar; most importantly, anthropologically, with the facial structure and colour he looked like a Bengali. The boy looked scruffy and looked like hadn't had a shower for long time. While Sabbir checked his pockets for change an idea came to his opportunist brain cells as usual. He took a coin from his pocket and gave it to him. Sabbir was a man who didn't give money easily so there must have been a string attached to that coin. The boy asked him with a soft voice, 'Do you have a spare cigarette bro?'

'I don't smoke but I might be able to buy you a cigarette depends of what answer you give to my questions.'

'What's your question bro?'

'Do you have a British passport and if you do, would you like to sell it?'

The semi-drunk boy said, 'What you gonna do with me passport man?'

'Don't worry about it, if you want to sell it, I will buy it.'

'How much you gonna give bro?'

'I will give you hundred pounds.'

'Na man, it must be worth much more then that bro.'

'Alright, I will give you one fifty that's it.'

'Give me five hundred bro.'

'No way.'

'Wha man, it's a British passport, it must be worth a lot.'

'I don't have time, my last offer two hundred, take it or leave it.'

'Okay bro, two fifty.'

'Fine, bring it here tomorrow this time.'

'Okay bro, see you tomorrow.'

'If I don't come, I will send someone else.'

In the evening Sabbir called Jamal, one of his cousin. Sabbir told Jamal the discussion he had with the drunk boy, asked Jamal to come and collect the passport as he didn't want to take the risk incase the police came. Jamal usually dealt with dodgy passports, which includes Bangladeshi and British passports. He sold many dodgy passports to people in Sylhet. Jamal looked for vulnerable people and targeted them and persuaded them to sell their British passport. The success rate of people entering into London with dodgy British passport was good. So people had confidence in Jamal. The next day Jamal collected the passport and paid for it. Later on in the evening he came to the restaurant. Sabbir paid him back the money for the passport. Following day Sabbir gave his uncle, Sahim a call back home and asked him to look for customers. The price he put on the passport was ten laks if the person could get into London. If the person couldn't get into London then they just paid for the flight and expenses of changing the picture. Sabbir sent the passport back home to his uncle who found hundred of customers who were willing to pay the price. It was crazy in Sylhet that people were ready with 'dosh' to go to foreign country like England and the USA. Sabbir told his uncle to select someone who was educated, had confidence and looked like a foreigner.

The passport picture was changed in Bangladesh and the young man was trained by his uncle. Sabbir and Jamal wrote down some of the possible questions the immigration officers were likely to ask. The client was also told if he got caught then he had to say that he bought the passport in Bangladesh. They gave the following instructions, questions and answers in English and Bengali to the client to learn also told him to practice English. In addition they gave a few videos that showed London.

What is your name? My name is Abdul Kuddus.
How old are you? I am 18 (eighteen years old).
Where do you live? I live in Whitechapel man.
What is your home address? Cannon Street, London, E1.
What colours are the buses in London? The buses are red.
How big are the buses? They are very big, double decked and single.
What is your nearest underground? Whitechapel.
What line is Whitechapel? District line.
Where is the London hospital? In Whitechapel.
Which school did you go to? I went to Stepney Green School, in Benjonson Road, Stepney, London, E1.
What college did you go to? I didn't go to college man.
What did you do after you left school? Started work in a restaurant.
Where do you work? Brick Lane man.
What restaurant do you work in? Sizzling Spices.
What's your boss's name? Jamal Ali.
What do you work as? I work as a kitchen porter.
What do you do for living? I work in a restaurant man.
What does your job involve doing? I wash plates, dishes and make simple things like salad. Some times cook rice and make chapattis.
How do you get to work? I walk to work.
What does the Fire Bridge do? They kill fire / put off fire.
"Make sure you get blade one on the side of your head, look around the airport and put your hands in your pockets and flick your hair time

to time." This was a typical interrogation process of the immigration officers.

Bangladesh's immigration wasn't a problem as they paid the person who was in charge. When the client arrived in London Heathrow airport the immigration officers asked him some questions which he was able to answer and they let him get through. Jamal and Sabbir collected ten grand. They gave a grand to Sahim for his dealing and shared the profits between them.

Azima had previously complained to her brothers that a Bengali boy had been messing around with her on her way home from school. This boy kept on telling her that he loved her. She told him that she wasn't interested and to leave her alone. But he refused to listen. She had enough of him and felt that he needed to be taught a lesson before he went too far. Sabbir knew his responsibilities as an elder brother and that he needed to protect his sisters from any problems. Sabbir and Jamal decided to give the boy a visit. After school they waited outside her school, waited for him to approach her. When he approached her, Sabbir got out of his car and spoke to him politely. Sabbir told him, 'This is the only and the final warning I am going to give you. You better leave my sister alone, and if you don't then there will be consequences.' 'What you going do about it, it is a free country,' the boy said. 'If my sister complains about you once more, Insha-Allah I will show you what we will do.' Then he returned to the car.

The next day the boy arrived again after school and he attacked Azima. He was sarcastic towards her, 'Are you going to get your brothers? I am not scared of them!' he said. Wisely she ignored him and came home. Azima told Sabbir what had happened. He was annoyed as he didn't want to punish a Bengali boy. The following day Sabbir called Jamal and waited near Azima's school. Sabbir noticed the boy, opened his boot and told Jamal to get the cricket bat out. Jamal went out and hit the boy with the cricket bat and left him on the street. They disappeared. A few hours later the police came to Sabbir's home then to his restaurant but he denied any charges. The police had no evidence against him but continued to investigate and look for witnesses.

Sokina telephoned her husband to let him know that Azima had excellent GCSEs results. Karim didn't get excited about his daughter's results. He told Sokina what was the point of girl getting excellent results, tomorrow she will go to another man's house. Sokina told him that Azima wanted to go to college. He said that she can't go to college and she should learn how to cook. Sokina also told him that Azima won't like it staying at home. He replied that was not her choice. When Sokina told Azima that her father didn't want her to go to college, she was very upset. She said that she wanted to go to college because she didn't want to stay home like her sisters. She wanted to work and earn money. Sokina told Sabbir about it. He tried to understand the both parties and where they were coming from. He didn't want to upset anyone; to him both had their own rights. Sabbir understood why his father didn't want her to go to college and understood why she had the ambitions.

Slowly many elderly Sylheti men's attitude towards education had started to change, Bengali boys and girls started to go to college and university. It was something Azima wanted to do too. Sabbir told Azima that he will speak to father and try to convince him to let her go to college. Ayna and Amina also telephoned their father and tried to convince him that he should let her to go to college. She was so good at learning. After everyone's persuasion Karim agreed to let her go to college but with one condition that she had to wear the hijab all the time and was not to talk to any boys. A new era had started for the Sylheti children as they went to further education to improve their lives.

1994

Amir was roaming and puffing in Brick Lane during his lunch break with his mates, a man approached them and said, 'Brothers you are enjoying life like if it's a heaven but our brothers and sisters are dying all over the world, if you have a few minutes then come to this meeting.' The man gave a leaflet which contain pictures of dead Muslim children and had information such as, a Muslim must help other Muslims in the world; Come to the meeting if you can help your Muslim brothers and sisters. Amir and his mates decided to go the meeting which was held in a house near Brick Lane to find out how they could help other Muslims. In the meeting they met other local Bengali guys they knew. There were twenty chairs for the new guests to sit on. Three men sat at the front of the guests and had a table front of them with some leaflets, videos and information on the desk. Behind them they had a big poster, hand written, 'young muslim fighters.' The guests were offered soft drinks.

The first man, an Egyptian, that's what he said, spoke about how the West had killed thousands of Muslim people including thousands of children in Chechnya and Palestine. He distributed pictures of dead people to make an impression and arouse the minds of the guests and create hatred for the killer of the Muslim.

The next man said, 'Unless we do something the West won't stop killing our brothers and sisters; the west gives money to Israel so the Israelian can kill our brothers and sisters in Palestine everyday; you don't hear when the Israeli kill our brothers and sisters but when one of our brothers gives his life in the path of Allah to kill the Israeli terrorist you get massive headline on the television as Muslim suicide killed; the West is against us Muslim; if you give your life in the path of Allah, you are guaranteed to go to paradise and you will be given seventy virgins in heaven; so why do we need to live for sixty or seventy years. Pray and hope to go to heaven when we can try to help our Muslim brothers and sisters, if we die, we are guaranteed to go to heaven; it is a short cut way of going to paradise.'

A third man showed a video, which showed how the Israeli were killing Muslims. The video made the young guests click. There were anger in their eyes. The man said, 'If you can help then give us your details and we will contact you Muslim brothers.' The guests gave their details on a pad. Most of them were up for it to be the soldier of Allah.

―

Ten year old Khadijah asked her mother why she had to wear the hijab as white people don't wear it. First Sima told her, 'Because we are Muslim, we need to wear a hijab and it looks nice when you wear it.' Khadijah said that she didn't want to wear it as it messed up her hair.

Sima raised her voice and told her, 'I don't want to hear anything like that again, you wear the hijab like I do and if you don't wear it then Allah will give you sin and when you die you will go to hell.' Khadijah stopped as she was scared to go to hell and wore the hijab. When Allah is mentioned children are mostly scared to do anything against their parents. It's a psychological technique that some mothers used to scare young children.

Karim tried to sell some trees from one of his plot of land where he had problems. Once again Moskond told Karim that the land wasn't Karim's. Karim told him that he had won the case and the land was his. Moskond told him that he didn't care about the case. The land was his and Karim shouldn't sell anything and if he did then he would beat up Karim. Karim didn't want to fight as it was embarrassing if people heard about it. Moskond used his physical strength, he had a few strong brothers. When Munna Bhai heard that Moskond had threatened his uncle. He asked his uncle if he wanted Moskond dead. Karim told him that there was no point of fighting, he will report to the police. Munna Bhai called Sabbir and told him the news. Sabbir's anger reached its limit. He felt like going to the village and shooting Moskond. Munna Bhai asked Sabbir if he wanted Moskond dead. Sabbir told him he wanted him close to death. Munna Bhai said that he would arrange that smoothly. Sabbir sent some money to Munna Bhai to arrange Moskond's pain.

One evening in the restaurant's kitchen the cook and the porter had a punch up, which Gozafor Miah had to break up. They were fighting over who was from a better village. Gozafor Miah heard them argue before but he never stopped them, he enjoyed their cussing and time to time he helped them continue. One and another were insulting each other then they punched each other. Sabbir told them if they fight again, he would call the immigration officers and send them back home. There had been some problems when people from the same town worked in the same place. There isn't much to talk about, apart from the latest news, how to get a visa and bring people from Sylhet, they 'cussed' each other's village. It's like a football team - whose village is better!

Yasin stole twenty pounds from his father's pocket. This Sabbir noticed when he checked his wallet. He asked around in the house to see if anyone had stolen it. But no one owned up. Sabbir noticed that his son wasn't behaving as usual and asked him what was wrong with him. After a few times of asking Yasin admitted that he had stolen the money from his father's wallet because a boy in school told him if he didn't give him twenty-pounds then the boy would kill him. Sabbir was shocked to hear that another Bengali boy had threatened his son. He felt like finding the child and beating him to death. Sabbir didn't tell his brother Amir, otherwise Amir would have gone to the school, found the boy and beat the shit out of him. Sabbir went to the school and spoke to the head teacher. The boy was called to the head teacher's office and admitted bullying. The police were called. They came and arrested the boy.

Sabbir told his son if anyone ever bullied him then he should tell him or beat up the person who bullied him, other wise he wouldn't have any chance of surviving in this area. Sabbir told Yasin if he found it difficult to beat up a boy then he should take something from home such as a kitchen knife and make sure the boys who bully him are finished. Then he said, 'Don't take knife just tell me and I will go and kill them.' He also told Yasin not to worry about school as he can find another school for him. Sima told Yasin not to listen to his father and never to take any weapon to school. She also asked Sabbir, what was he teaching his son, did he want his son in jail. Sabbir told his wife if his son doesn't stand up then other will eat him. The reasons behind Sabbir's anger were that he was bullied at college, his brothers were bullied at school. He didn't want his son to suffer the same fate.

Munna Bhai called Sabbir and informed him that his gang had stubbed Moskond a few times. Sokina asked Sabbir why Munna Bhai recently been calling a lot. Sabbir told her that Munna Bhai needed some money to fix the motorbike. Moskond was taken to the local hospital. Sabbir asked him if anyone saw them doing it. He told Sabbir

Spices of Brick Lane

that they carried it out at night when Moskond was returning home from the local bazaar. There were no clues as they drove off from the scene.

Karim didn't know who had assaulted Moskond. But he thought that there was another enemy after Moskond. He could have sold some of the trees while Moskond was in the hospital. When Karim spoke to Sabir, he told him that someone had stubbed Moskond. Sabbir told his father that when people do wrong Allah punished them through others. Karim thought that if he did sell some tires then when Moskond recovered he would think Karim had him 'done.' The psychology in the village was like a chess game; everyone thought about the opponents' movement. These people didn't have to study a degree to learn it, it was natural.

Amir and his friends were contacted by the young muslim fighters. They asked Amir to attend another meeting, which he did with his mates. They told them that they will train them how to fight for their Muslim brothers and sisters. For the training they had to go to Afghanistan. They were also told not to inform their parents that they were going to Afghanistan. They should tell their parents that they were going to Pakistan to learn more about Islam. That's exactly what Amir told his family. Sabbir didn't have a problem as he thought learning more about Islam was important. Amir and his mates went to Afghanistan through Pakistan. During his training he met big boss Osama bin Muhammad bin Awad bin Laden, known in Europe as Osama Bin Laden. The one and only man known to provoked the USA and George Bush's brain. Bin Laden must have encouraged the new recruits that they had chosen the right path and they will be successful in their objectives. Since Bin Laden came to light and on people's visual display unit he suddenly created a new fans base in certain parts of the world. In some parts of the world people were wearing t-shirt that had his name and picture on it. In one village in India there were some men that had named their sons as Osama Bin Laden. They look at Bin Laden as a warrior rather then a terrorist. Can someone explain that to the American's why would someone do that?

1995

Munna Bhai called Sabbir and informed him that Moskond had recovered and had returned home from hospital. He asked Sabbir if he wanted Munna Bhai to damage Moskond again. Sabbir told him, 'Maybe Allah doesn't want him to die yet, let him live now and we will see if he gives us anymore problems.' Moskond told people in the local bazaar that if he found out who had done it, he would kill them. He had so many enemies so he wasn't sure who had done it. He had a feeling it may have been Karim as he had the financial capacity but Karim never threatened him so that confused him.

Out of nowhere Sokina's cousin Panna called from Bangladesh for the first time. Sokina picked up the phone, first he asked her how she and her family were. Then he wanted her home address. She didn't know the address. Most of the village ladies didn't know their own address. It's simple because they couldn't read or write English. She passed the phone to Sabbir. Sabbir asked Panna why he wanted their address. Panna politely said that he was trying to get into London with a number two passport referring to unauthentic passport. Sabbir couldn't say no, but due to cultural politeness he gave the address. Once he put the phone down, he told his mother that her cousin wasn't coming to stay in their house. He already had too many people living in the house.

Sokina told Sabbir that she had no choice and if Panna came then he didn't have anywhere else to go. She also told Sabbir that his father used to say that 'If anyone comes from Sylhet then we should help because when your father first came to London others helped him too. If you help people they will pray for you and you will get rich quicker.' 'Mother, we don't run a charity here,' he replied.

A few days later someone knocked on the door. Sabbir answered the door and a man appeared, 'How are you nephew?' Sabbir had a feeling who he was, but pretended not to know. 'I am fine.' Sabbir felt that it would be rude if he didn't let him in, so he told him to come in and sit in the living room. Panna introduced himself, ''I am your uncle, you must be my big nephew Sabbir? 'Yes I am Sabbir.' The man only had a small bag with him, un-usual for a Bengali to come to London with such a small bag. Usually Sylheti people come to London with all sort of vegetables and dried fish as its cheap in Bangladesh. Quickly, Sabbir informed his mother that her cousin had arrived. She knew her son would be annoyed if her cousin says he wanted to stay in their house. Sokina met him; he gave salaam to her and said, 'Thanks to Allah, I have managed to come to London.' She asked him how everyone was in the village. They discussed how he managed to get here and how were all the relatives in Bangladesh. Sabbir became interested when he heard how he came to England. He had the sharp mind. He was already thinking about using the same process to bring more illegal people into London. Sabbir became nice to Panna. He wanted to know more about Panna's routes.

Panna spoke a little English. He used to own a shop in the village but went around Bangladesh buying goods for his shop. He had enough confidence to use a fake British passport to get into London.

Sima worked at home tirelessly sewing skirts. Sabbir helped her when ever he was free during the day. Usually he worked on the machine a few hours before going to the restaurant at lunch time. She had saved up a few thousand pounds and wanted to send her parents to Hajj. She asked Sabbir if that was alright. He told her that it was fine. Sima telephoned her parents and told them that she would be sending them the money they need for Hajj and they should get their passport ready. Sabbir didn't have any problem with that as he wanted to see his wife happy and he knew his wife would get rewards for the good charity.

Rukshana gives birth to her fourth child, a daughter. Once again she couldn't believe her luck with children. She was enjoying her life more then ever as she managed to become mother again. It was getting embarrassing for Karim that he became a father at this late age. Maybe he was having too much free time to play with his wife. Or it could be she was so pretty that he couldn't keep away from her.

Sokina telephoned Karim to talk to him and let him know that his daughter did really well in her A-level results. Again he wasn't happy and wasn't interested in her education. He felt that it was waist of time for a girl to study. Karim told Sokina to bring Azima to Bangladesh so he can find a suitable boy for her. She told him that Azima wanted to go to university. She knew what he was going to say. 'Is she out of her mind, girls don't go to university, she can't go to university, she had already done enough, a degree isn't going to help her with cooking and nurturing children, it's time for her to get married and start a family,' he said. A lot of the men those days didn't know the value of their daughter's education and no one can blame them as they came from totally different culture and ideology which had its own structure, advantages and disadvantages.

Sokina told Azima that her father didn't want her to go to university. He wanted Sokina to take her to Bangladesh and get her married. Once again, Azima didn't like it and she told her mother that she wanted to go to university and get a degree. Sokina said "Why do you insist on going to university when soon you will be married and a house wife. It is waste of time."

'It's not waste of time; I will learn new things and get paid to learn,' said Azima.

Sokina then said that she would speak to her son and see what he said. She spoke to Sabbir and he didn't like the idea of his sister going to university as the family will be out of touch for three years and she could get up to anything. Azima tried her best to persuade her brother and had her other two sisters to persuade him. Once she had her brother on her side, then all of them telephoned their father and persuaded him to let her go to university. After hours of negotiation with Karim, he failed and had to listen to his son and daughters, and let Azima go to university. Azima promised that she wouldn't do anything wrong to bring shame to the family's name. She enrolled at Queens Mary's University to study Business Finance.

Sabbir's restaurant's business had started to pick up. More and more customers were coming into the restaurant, which helped him to make more profit. Sabbir was seeing more cash coming into his pocket after excluding all the overheads. He never showed the actual income of the business as he didn't want to pay VAT and other taxes to government. As usual he worked very hard planning and running the restaurant.

He visited the restaurant at every lunch time to make sure all the work was done up to excellent standard and all the tables and cutleries were clean. If he had to buy anything that was missing, he bought it during the lunch break.

One day at lunchtime a dodgy dealer came to Sabbir's restaurant with a few bottles of red and white wines. The price was very good but Sabbir didn't know if the wines' quality was good. He bought two bottles of the wines for testing and took the man's number. Sabbir gave the wines free to a regular customer to check the validity. He asked the customer what they thought about it. They told him that it was the real stuff. He bought more wines from the dodgy dealer. Sabbir never missed a good opportunity to save money.

Sabbir felt it would be a good idea to teach his son how the restaurant business was run so his son can take over when he retires. He asked to Yasin to join him in the restaurant, which he didn't refuse. During the weekend Yasin went to the restaurant and helped his father at the front of the restaurant. Sabbir asked the other waiters to explain the basics to Yasin. Yasin didn't have problems communicating with the customers as he spoke good English. In the kitchen Gozafor Miah shook Yasin's hand and told him that when ever he wants to eat anything he should let Gozafor Miah know, everything was free for Yasin. Gozafor Miah ordered Goni to make a Tandoori chicken for Yasin, which he did. Gozafor Miah decorated it with salad, slice of lemon, touch of coriander and gave it to Yasin. While Yasin ate the starter Gozafor Miah asked him if he liked football. Then he asked him if he liked cricket. Yasin said that he was good at spin bowling and he played in the school team. Gozafor Miah had found a new friend who liked cricket. Very quickly Yasin learnt the basic 'waitering' skills. He enjoyed entertaining the customers. Time to time he enjoyed looking at the half naked young lady customers, whom unveiled their assets to impress on lookers or partners.

Yasin asked his father for advice regarding what GCSEs to take. Sabbir told him to take the subjects that he was good at, but he ought to take business studies as it would help him learn about business. He was already thinking about the next manager of his restaurant. Yasin didn't mind studying business studies to keep his father happy.

One of Sabbir's 'illegal' cousins, Mahiz, needed to see a doctor but due to his status he couldn't register with a doctor. He telephoned Sabbir to find out if there was a way he can join a doctor. Sabbir told him that there was nothing to worry about. He could get Mahiz medicine without any problem. He told Mahiz to visit Dr. Zakaria who he telephoned in advance and informed that his cousin would be visiting him. Dr. Zakaria was happy to see him as he received twenty pounds in cash for the prescription. Sabbir's illegal cousin told the other illegal friends and they queued up for Dr. Zakaria.

One evening a few young white girls came to have dinner in the restaurant. Minto - one of the waiters in the restaurant tried his best to woo them with free drinks and told them they would get more free drinks when they come back next time. He lived up-stairs at the restaurant to save rent money. Minto thought about having an affair with a British woman. The main purpose of his affair was to get a visa on his Bangladeshi passport. He arrived with a student visa and had been studying computing at local university during the day. In the evenings he worked in the restaurant to supplement his living expenses. He realised that one of the quickest way to get a visa was to get married to a white woman who was a British subject. Otherwise he had to return to Bangladesh or try to stay here for fourteen years, and then apply for a residential visa. Going back to Bangladesh or waiting for fourteen years didn't sound promising to him. He discerned out that he could make so much more money by staying in London.

Minto usually looked smart with his restaurant uniform and was clean shaven. He didn't speak fluent English but he knew what he was chatting about. The same group of girls came to the restaurant again. At the end of their meal Minto gave them a free shot of Sambucas. One girl asked him how much tip he wanted. He told her that her phone number would be enough as a tip. He managed to get her mobile number probably because of the free drinks. It didn't take long before he gave his first text message just to check the girl was still interested in him. He managed to find out her name – Claire! Then he arranged a date with her to get to know her. Minto asked Yasin what he should wear. Yasin told him to dress smartly with dash of perfume. Minto newly suited, and booted ended up going to the local Genesis cinema with Claire. Then they had a dinner in a pizza restaurant. Minto paid for the food to impress her.

Sabbir's family had enough of Brick Lane and its hustle and bustle. They wanted to go somewhere quieter with less Bengalis. As money was floating into Sabbir's pocket from his restaurants businesses he didn't have a financial problem. Sabbir asked his mother to visit some of the potential houses. She didn't bother because she never liked travelling. Sokina told him to find a house with big kitchen and two toilets. After many months' search and investigation, they bought a four bed room house in Upton Park. Sabbir put a twenty percent deposit to buy the house. He rented out the house on Hanbury Street. Upton Park was an area where some Bengali people lived, probably moved from Brick Lane area. Sabbir thought it would be a good idea to move there as it provided better atmosphere then Brick Lane. It was only about six miles away and fifteen minutes drive from Brick Lane. It wasn't a problem for Sabbir to travel to work. Their new house was on the Queens Road, only five minutes from Green Street, where most of the Bengali people visited when ever they bought gold and wedding saris. Sabbir's family weren't going to miss the Spitalfield and Whitechapel markets anymore. They found a new market in the name of Queens Market adjacent to Upton Park station.

Sima heard about the Queens market and kept nagging Sabbir to take her to the market and show her around. As usual his excuse was that he was too busy to take her when ever he went to the market. One of the main reason he didn't like shopping with Sima was that she took too long looking at things before making her mind up. He decided to show her around the market. He planned in his head that whenever he was busy she could come to the market with the kids and do the basic shopping. Sabbir took her to different shops and told her which shop was good value for money. She bought some material to make salwar kamizes for the children. Sima was surprised to see such a long queue outside some of the meat shops. Maybe the people never had meat before. She liked the market as it offered fresh fruits and vegetables. At the end of shopping Sima told him that he should have shown her the market before. The goods were cheap in the market. She told him that she could come to the market by herself because it was close to the house. Sabbir told her, 'Very good that will be good exercise for you.'

Sabbir's children needed to buy clothes and school goods. He decided to give some time to them and took them to Stratford shopping center. This shopping center is located on Romford Road in Stratford, only five minutes drive from their house. He felt that he needed to show them around as they were new in the area. The children could visit next time whenever they needed something. The children browsed through the shopping centre and bought what they needed but couldn't find some of the school items they wanted. Sabbir told them that next time he would take them to another shopping centre where they might find them.

The following week Sabbir took them to East Ham shopping centre which is different from the Stratford shopping centre as it was in the street rather then in a blocked area. The children went to the relevant shops and bought what they needed. In a shop Sabbir noticed half priced marked on the parker pens. He bought one pen per child and told them to improve their hand writing.

Moskond sold a tree from the disputed plot to another person. Karim asked the man why he was cutting down the tree. The man told Karim that he had bought it from Moskond. Karim asked him how he could buy it from Moskond when the land was his. The man refused to stop cutting the tree. Munna Bhai wanted to kill the man; Karim stopped him and told him to get the police. Karim had to pay the police five thousand taka to come to the village. The police took a report and stopped the man from cutting the tree. Karim never informed his son as he didn't want Sabbir to get involved in it. Later on Munna Bhai called Sabbir, told him what had happened. He also told Sabbir that he felt like killing Moskond. Sabbir told him to be patient and soon they would take their revenge. He also told Munna Bhai to keep an eye on Moskond's where about and that he was likely to go to Bangladesh next year. When he returned something sizzling awaited Moskond.

Minto had Claire in his direction and convinced her to be his wife. They got married in a local registration office. Minto moved into her apartment. He treated her very well in order to achieve his main objective.

Chapter Six

1996

Sabbir had lived in London for nearly quarter of a century and had experienced many changes in life and society. He needed to find a secondary school for his daughter. Sabir thought about sending Khadijah to a girls' school. He and his wife decided to send Khadijah to a Madrasa for female. They felt that if she went to a public school then she might become a naughty girl and may end up having a boy friend which would give the family a bad name. By attending a madrasa she would learn the values of Islam and develop a good understanding of the Muslim religion. A Madrasa for female had been established by the local Bangladeshi people near Whitechapel because they realised that there was a need for one. It cost Sabbir two thousand pounds a year which wasn't a problem to his bank account. Khadijah didn't mind going to the madrasa as she was a little girl and didn't have the ability to make her own choice. There were hundreds of other Bengali girls at the madrasa.

Yasin wanted a computer to help him type up his course work so he asked his father for one. Sabbir didn't hesitate. He went to the Becton's supermarket and bought Yasin a Pentium-100 PC, it was one of the top ranges of PC available in the market, which made Yasin a very happy young man. Sabbir's children became proactive in the line of education and technology. They wanted to be successful as they had the influence from their aunty Azima. Azima became a role model for the children.

Due to curryholic customers' demands a few more restaurants opened up in Brick Lane. The competition to get customers became harder. Everyone was fighting for the same customers. Sabbir employed a tout who stood near the restaurant's front door and offered special offers to passersby before they went to the other restaurants. He gave offers like; first round drinks free and a ten percent discount on food. Most of the other restaurants also had touts working for them. This was something Sabbir didn't want to do but because of competitions he had to compete for customers. Some customers didn't like the touting and complained to the local authority.

It was early May. Sabbir gave his son two months off from work as he had exams. He wanted his son to do well. Azima helped Yasin with some of the course work. Yasin did well in his GCSEs exams. He decided to go to college to study business as encouraged and advised by his father and aunt. Sabbir wanted Yasin to study business so later on his son could manage the restaurant.

Sima went to Green Street to do her shopping for Bangladesh. She was going within a few weeks. She didn't miss shopping in Whitechapel markets, she felt the products were cheap in Green Street too. Sabbir never liked going shopping with his wife. She never liked taking him to shopping too. He made her hurry up. He told her not to buy presents for the relatives but give them money instead so they could buy what ever they liked. Sima told him that the relatives would feel good if they receive something from London. He agreed. She took Azima as usual and shopped in Green Street, bought presents for the close relatives. The saris were expensive compared to the prices in Bangladesh. If they bought it in Bangladesh then the relatives wouldn't like them much as if it were from London. The relatives' wanted gifts from London. It didn't matter where they were made. They wanted a taste of London. But why? Perhaps the British's empire's nearly two hundred years of ruling wasn't enough taste for them. Most likely they didn't even know that the British ruled them as most of them were illiterate.

Sabbir returned to Bangladesh with his wife and children for his wife demanded holiday and to see his father and the relatives. On the way to Bangladesh they had to go via Dhaka and were supposed to fly within a short period of time. For a diabolical excuse they were kept in the airport for another six hours. They were told that the flight to Sylhet was full. Biman Airline knew how many people they had booked for the Sylhet flight but they were not bothered about the passengers. They knew passengers from London would have to wait. If they complained then they wouldn't listen. There was no other quick means of transport to get to Sylhet. They could have gone by coach but that would have taken a long time and that wasn't advisable as coaches were robbed very often.

Sabbir thought, if people couldn't manage something uncomplicated as that how the hell were they suppose to go forward. "This is what kind of bastard management we have in our country, no fucking organisation, no fucking wonder why we are not going forward, always going backward." Sabbir thought. He and his family were really disappointed but were without choice - they had to wait!

When Sabbir's family arrived in the Sylhet Osmani airport, the custom officer told them that they had to open their bags because they had illegal items in them. 'How can I have illegal stuff, I am from London and everything has been checked there, so how can you say that,' Sabbir asked. The officer refused to listen to him. 'Use your computer system to check if I have anything illegal then that will be displayed,' said Sabbir. They told him that they didn't have any computer system and they had to check manually by opening the bags. He refused to let them open the bags. They refused to let him go until he opened his bags and checked his luggage. He offered them a fifty pound bribe but they requested two hundred pounds. Sima told Sabbir to pay up so they could go, but he refused to bow down to the bastards. Both parties couldn't come to an agreeable solution. Sabbir didn't want to give the bastards any money even though he had lots of it. They had to open his luggage. Sabbir told them that he would show them his luggage without messing up the clothes. They weren't having it. When they opened his luggage they went through them like some kind of animal. They threw things out from his luggage. They tried their best to steal much clothes as possible. They found nothing illegal but refused to say sorry. Sabbir looked at their faces and in his memory he said: 'If I had a gun now I would have shot you son of a bitch.' This is what kind of bastards we had in our country; they harassed people for no good reason but just for greediness. All they wanted was money whether it's right or wrong it didn't matter to them; they were some kind of people that would sell their mother to a pimp for money; they didn't have any humanity in them.

After so much bother and anxiety Sabbir arrived in the village home with his family. Everyone was pleased to be home at least. The children weren't very happy with the facilities. Most of the things were very different from the West. Firstly, they were put off by the journey, the bumpy roads to the village. When they saw the house they didn't like the way it looked and the surrounding area. According to the children, they thought they arrived at a jungle. The house was in the middle of no where. It was the monsoon season. There was mud everywhere. The children had to stay in the house. There was no back garden. At the back of the house there were so many big trees which made the house look horrible. Karim's house was the biggest in the village, in-terms of the size of the plot and the number of rooms. Every time the children wanted to do something there was some kind of problem. There were small holes at the top of the house's side walls in the bed rooms. The children thought that insects may get inside the rooms through the holes. Actually they were permanent twenty-four-seven ventilation. They were provided with insect net top of their bed to prevent insect bites. The Children were given the best beds that were available, which were made from their own trees that would last for over hundred of years. They weren't used to sleeping in strong beds; they didn't have back problems that they needed such strong beds. Yasin felt the difference in living in East and West was gigantic like the physical distance. They complained to their father about every thing. The children told Sabbir that they didn't want to come back to this village again.

Sabbir realised that as soon as possible he needed to give the children some positive image of his village home other wise they wouldn't come back again. He needed to win their hearts and minds. Quickly, he bought some soft blanket for the beds. Arranged for an English toilet to be fitted within the shower room. Labourers were available in the village. He hired them and got them to work as many hours as possible. They quickly made a beautiful shower room with an English toilet. That put the smiles back on the children's faces. Sabbir employed a few more people to cut down the branches of the trees around the home to give it more space and make it look nice. The children watched the men jump up the trees like monkeys without any aid and cut the branches of the trees. Cutting down the branches of the trees also benefitted Sabbir's uncles, who were able to get fire wood for their cooking.

Sabbir kept the most important information in his non-volatile memory. He informed Munna Bhai to keep an eye on Moskond's movement, especially the days he went out and what places he visited. Maybe he was using the skills he had learnt from the movies he watched in England. Munna Bhai hired a few local rickshaw drivers to keep careful eyes on Moskond. Rickshaws were mostly used by people to travel from one local place to another as they had no doors which helped the air to float freely from all the directions.

The weather condition improved in the village with the sight of sun. The children were able to go out, visit the local people in the village. They had Sabbir's cousin, Bandil, with them who took them around the village and introduced them to others as grand children of Hajji Karim Ali. People offered them tea but they refused as they didn't want anyone to waist their money. It was Bandil's duty to look after the children and entertain them. He had nothing else to do when he finished school that's if he bothered going to school. It was a good excuse for him to bunk school. Bandil spent most of the time with the kids listening to their needs and complained. He made a few fishing rods with bamboo sticks from their jungle, took the children for a fishing treat. Bandil showed them how to catch fishes with dead insects. They fished in their big pond for a few hours and managed to catch a few fishes which were cooked and offered at their dinner.

The next day Bandil took the children to the pond, told them to watch. Bandil swam and planted a fishing net from one end of the pond to the other end. He told the children to watch and in few hours time they will see some fish stuck in the net. The children kept on telling him to show the fish. 'Be patient,' he said. After two hours Bandil took the net out from the water and there were some big fish stuck on the net. It took Bandil good few minutes to get the fishes out from the net. The children enjoyed watching the fishing technique. They learnt something new in their holiday.

Sabbir's uncles had fifteen cattle. They were kept on the far side of the house's court yard. The children were shown the cattle. They were surprised to see so many animals. In the morning an employee - Tazul milked the female cattle, and later they were offered the fresh milk to drink. During the day chickens run around the court yard freely and ate what ever they could grab from the ground. The children were also shown the sheeps their grandfather had. Motlib liked sheeps. He had six of them. They looked beautiful with the soft wool. The children like the sheeps too and it didn't take them long before they were touching the sheeps' body protection. Yasin asked his grandfather if he could take a sheep back to London. 'Yes, but how you going look after a sheep in London,' said Motlib. 'That is a good point dhada; I think I won't take one.'

Sabbir wanted to take the children to some of the nicest places in Bangladesh so they could enjoy their stay and would want to come back again and again. He arranged to take them to Jaflong, a very famous tourist attraction. He hired two eight-seater cars and took the family out. Sabbir took his cousins so they could keep their eyes on the family. There was a risk of child abduction in Bangladesh as they knew that children had been abducted and never found again. There were reports that abductors took children and sold expensive internal organs to other countries. Jaflong is a beautiful place where thousands of foreign people visited every year. The Water fall was the most beautiful scenario of the place. Sabbir' children didn't think that there were beautiful places like that in Bangladesh. He took pictures of everyone near the water fall. The children had thought of Bangladesh as a poor country with no identity and beautiful places. Maybe Sabbir should take some of the blame for that.

A few days later Sabbir took his family to the some of the tea gardens' of Sylhet. He showed their own tea garden that they had bought a few years ago. The children watched and admired the beautiful tea gardens and the landscape of Sylhet. Sabbir told the children that teas from the gardens were exported to all over the world, including England. Sylhet has three of the world's largest tea gardens.

Munna Bhai tracked down Moskond's movements and found patterns on the days he went out. Sabbir instructed Munna Bhai to make sure his gang damages Moskond so much that he was never able to sell another tree again. One day Moskond was in a rickshaw going towards the local bazaar with his body guard. Munna Bhai's masked gang, blocked the rickshaw and beat him up with metal bars while his back-up did a runner when he saw the gang. They broke both of Moskond's legs but they were instructed by Sabbir not to hit him on the head in case he died. They shortly left the scene in their motorbikes. Sabbir paid the five thousand taka each for their effort. Moskond ended up in the local hospital. The doctors bandaged him and told him that he would never be able to walk again without third parties help.

Moskond thought very hard about who could have carried it out but he found the list was too long as he had too many enemies. Moskond had a feeling it could have been Karim's doing as he had the most money. He wasn't hundred percent sure. Sabbir and Munna Bhai were satisfied with the outcome and they didn't show any remorse towards Moskond as they felt he deserved it. To Sabbir, Moskond was never in his agenda but became an excess item and he had to get rid of him.

Karim told Sabbir that everyone was building big storey building and apartment in Sylhet town. Having a shopping centre would bring good rental income. He asked Sabbir if he could build a shopping centre on the plot of land they had bought ten years ago. Sabbir told his father that he would look into it and how he could develop a contemporary shopping centre.

Sabbir looked for the most important person since he became mature and was able to think for himself. He heard the most eagerly waited news of his life. The person he had been waiting for so long had arrived from a Middle Eastern country. He thought about this issue for many years and the best way to solve it but couldn't find a conclusive solution. Sabbir thought about hiring an outsider to deal with this matter rather then Munna Bhai. But the problem was that an outsider would find it difficult to track the insider down. He didn't want anyone to know about it. He categorically decided that he had nothing to hide and he was going to teach this man a big lesson. Sabbir couldn't forget what had happened between him and Abdul Hannan. He told Munna Bhai to keep an eye on Abdul Hanna but didn't tell him why. As usual Munna Bhai had his boys hooked on the target. Munna Bhai tracked down Abdul Hannan easily. Abdul Hannan was in a restaurant in the local bazaar. Munna Bhai informed Sabbir. Sabbir told Munna Bhai to get his gang together to smash up Abdul Hannan. By the time they went to the restaurant Abdul Hannan had gone. Sabbir felt like sending the boys to Abdul Hanna's house and finishing him off there but he didn't want Abdul Hannan's family to suffer as they didn't do anything wrong. Abdul Hannan survived and went back to the Middle East within short period of time. Sabbir had to wait for the next opportunity. He didn't like the waiting game. This was a game he wanted to complete as soon as possible. It was giving him psychological problems and many anxieties in his jobs undone part of his brain.

A few of the village's poor man approached Sabbir and asked him to help them with some charity which he did. He also gave money to the local mosque and school for improvement.

Sabbir stayed in Bangladesh for six weeks, visited most of the relatives and the relatives visited them too. Before they returned to London they bought presents for the relatives in London. Some of the relatives gave presents to their love one in London. Sabbir had to bring it as they would have been upset if he didn't. The day before they left, they gave their left over clothes to the poor relatives and the village's poor people as usual.

September 1996

Foriz started college at the age of eighteen. A five feet six inch, smart and good looking young man. Foriz's main aim was to get some qualification so he didn't had to work in a restaurant like his other friends. He enrolled at East Ham College of further education in the London borough of Newham, a neighbouring borough to Tower Hamlets. His intention was to do well and go to university, if possible. It was difficult for him to concentrate on his studies as there were so many good looking girls in the college. When beautiful mangoes hangs out from a tree's branches everyone likes to look, admire and have.

Foriz was mainly interested in Bengali girls. He thought that if he could find a decent girl and get to know her then he would marry her. Once he noticed a group of Asian girls in the college's canteen but he didn't have the confidence to talk to them.

The college had mixture of all types of students, Asians, Blacks and White. He met other boys in his class and made new friends. All the friends were looking for girl friends to fulfil their natural desire. Foriz discussed with his new and old friends how they were going to talk to them girls. He particularly liked a girl from the group, who looked fair, medium height, a bit chubby with curly hair. He mainly liked the way she smiled and her facial structure. When she smiled, it made him feel like that he was in another beautiful planet. All the friends planned that first Foriz would go to the girl and ask her if she had a change for ten pounds just to get her to notice him. Foriz found the idea a bit too embarrassing, he gave the idea a miss. Then they came out with the idea that Foriz's friend Joynul would go to the girl and tell her that Foriz would like to get to know her. They also thought that was too direct, and what about if she said no. Joynul had over heard a conversation where one of the girls called the girl that Foriz liked by her name - Shuba. Since Foriz had seen Shuba, he started to think about her day and knight. How was he going to get to know her? It became an obsession with him that he couldn't forget her from his live memory.

Foriz continued to attend his lessons even though he couldn't concentrate. All the friends decided that they had to do something to get her attention. As they sat in the college canteen, Foriz wrote a note with his friends' confidence; 'hi there, I would like you to be my friend, if you don't mind, I like making new friends. If you would like to be my friend then please call me.' Shuba was in the other end of the canteen with her girls. Joynul took the note and gave it to Shuba and told her it was from Foriz.

Foriz waited impatiently for a few days. Shuba's friends told her to call him but she decided to take her time to make her mind up. A few days later she 'texted' him and told him she didn't mind being a friend. That put a smile on his face. Through texting they got to know more about each other. The following day they met in college and developed their friendship further.

Foriz, his friends, Shuba and her friends decided to go out for a day out. They went to ice-skating in Romford. Shuba was close to Foriz all the time. They ice-skated for a few hours where they stumbled on the ice, laughed and joked. Foriz loved every moment of being with her and treated her well with respect. He went to a local chemist and bought her an expensive perfume just to let her know that she meant a lot to him. He really liked her and thought that after investigation if she turns out to be a decent girl then he would marry her. In the afternoon they went to cinema. Foriz and Shuba sat together away from their friends. In the cinema Foriz told into Shuba's ears that he liked her a lot. Hearing the beautiful words she smiled back at him. During the movie they ended up kissing each other passionately.

The next few months Foriz enjoyed Shuba's company and lips. Joynul went out with one of her friend. During beautiful weather most of the lunch time they spent in the Central Park, near the college, enjoyed each other and the natural atmosphere of the park. A lot of the times Foriz laid down on Shuba's laps and she stoked his hair to comfort him which he liked very much.

At the end of the year, Shuba's family went to Bangladesh. She didn't want to go as she had the feeling that they might get her hitched. She was forced by her family to go to Bangladesh. Her parents promised her that she won't get married and when she returned, she will be allowed to continue with her studies. Foriz didn't want her to go, he had the same feeling what might happen. He had little power to do anything.

Shuba arrived in the village with her family. There were already queues of proposal for her and her sister. Her parents told people that they were only in Bangladesh to get Shuba's older sister married. They had no intention of getting Shuba married, that's what they told people when they spoke front of her. One of Shuba's cousins told her that people were consistently telling her parents to get her married. They can save money by not coming back again in few years time. Shuba felt like she was a bird locked in a cage, no where to run, no where to hide, no where to get help from. There was no chance of dialing 999 as no telephone existed in the village house. Her parents turned against their words like two faced snake. Maybe that was their plan, but they never told her, she thought. Shuba did a lot of thinking how she can get out of the mess. There was no way she could contact Foriz and get any help from him. Even if she was able to contact him, how could he have helped her, she thought. She couldn't eat and had many sleepless nights.

Shuba's sister's marriage was arranged with a relative. Her father was paid five laks for agreeing with the deal. Shuba asked her sister for help. Shuba's sister replied "How can I help, I am in the same boat as you?"

More proposals came for Shuba through the back and front doors. A week later Shuba's father told her that it would be good for her and him if she got married now. He wanted to carry out both of the girls' marriage at the same time to save money. There wasn't anyway that she could say no. She didn't have a choice. She had to obey his command due to fear not love. If she didn't, he would have beaten her up. She had seen him beat up her mother. Her life became empty.

Shuba had to get married to a man she had never met before. The groom was fifteen years older then her. During her first night as wife, she had no choice but tried to get to know her new husband. According to her the man looked like he had just arrived from plouging a paddy field, he smelled of mud. He told her, 'Aame tuma ke balo bashi,' that he loved her and then he thanked her for marrying him. They chatted and tried to find out more about each other. Shuba asked him what his ambition was. 'I always wanted to go to America or London,' he replied. Next she asked him what he wanted to achieve by going to London. 'First I need to earn the fifteen laks (fifteen thousand pounds) and send it to my father as this is what my father paid your father to get married to you,' he said. The reply shocked her. This is when she really learned that her father wasn't her father but a bastard.

Later on Shuba's husband told her that he wanted to taste her but she told him, 'Not tonight,' which he didn't like. He had waited very long time for a female to arrive in his bed. While she slept, he abused her slowly but physically, which she didn't like but could do anything about it. She tried her best to go back to sleep again. As she slept again, he did it again. It was getting bad to worse for her. Shuba thought what kind of animal was this. He didn't take no for an answer. She felt like she wanted to scream to realise her frustrations but knew nothing would happen. It was like if she was in a jungle and if she had screamed then the animals wouldn't be able to help her. She felt that she had to suffer because it was written in her Takdir and tried to go back to sleep. She had the worst night of her life. She wished there was some one that could have helped her.

After two months' physical abuse from her husband Shuba returned to England. She felt that her body's behaviour was different, it gave her unusual attitude. She negotiated with her friends and took pregnancy test and found out that she was pregnant. Her first intention was to get an abortion.

Foriz was worried why she didn't come back to college on time. He asked her friends about her. They told him that she had arrived but she had been very busy with things. He asked them what things she was busy with and did they know why she wasn't meeting him. They told him that they were not sure. He told them to tell her to contact him as soon as she could and he still loved her a lot. She returned to college, tried her best to avoid Foriz. She felt that she couldn't face him.

Shuba thought about it and decided that it would be best to tell him about the situation rather then avoid him. She met him and told him what happened in Bangladesh. She also told him that she planned to have an abortion as she didn't want the unborn child. Foriz knew that he couldn't love her anymore as she had lost her purity. She lost one of the most important criteria to be his wife. He didn't want to love and marry a married girl. 'Not to worry, it's part of life that we come across many difficulties and we have to deal with it best as we can,' he told her. They decided to continue to be friends. Foriz told her that if she needed any help then she could always ask him and he would try to help her.

Shuba spoke to her friends and told them that she wanted to leave home as she no longer wanted to see the ugly face of her bastard father. Her friend Lipa advised her that she could get a council house if she became homeless.

Shuba left home, became homeless, and went to the local authority. She didn't tell her parents that she was going to leave them but left them so some of her pain could be eased. She told her young sister that she wouldn't come home, she was living by herself and they shouldn't contact the police. If they did then she would tell the police what they did to her in Bangladesh. The local borough gave her a one bed room house in East Ham. In her new house she found it very scary to live by herself. She never lived in a house by herself before. Shuba invited her friends to stay with her. Lipa stayed with her when she could. It became difficult for Lipa to live with her all the time, she had her own family. Shuba needed some one to live with her as she was pregnant and felt very lonely – too many things were running through her brain.

Shuba asked Foriz politely to live with her, after bit of thinking he agreed. He felt that she genuinely needed support and he once loved her a lot. He didn't want to see her upset anymore. He told his parents that he needed to stay with a friend whose parents had gone to Bangladesh for a long holiday. Foriz moved in with her just for the nights. He brought his lungi with him. Shuba told him that he could sleep in her bed room where as she would sleep in the living room's floor. He told her, 'There is no need, I will sleep in the living room and you needed to sleep well as you are pregnant.' She agreed. Most of the evenings they watched Indian films together without any chemistry. Time to time other friends joined in with them as well.

Shuba happily met her doctor, arranged a hospital appointment to have an abortion. The day she was supposed to have the abortion she was ill through heavy headache and couldn't attend. Then she learnt from a friend that it was illegal to have an abortion if you were Muslim. She wasn't allowed to kill an unborn child. Now she was stuck. She had an unborn child that she didn't want and she wasn't allowed to get rid of it. She thought about it for a few days, argued her views within, came to conclusion that it was meant to happen, and it must have been written in her Takdir that she should mother the foetus, whether it's one day or one week old. Shuba then thought that if she gave birth, there probably would be a new beginning for her. One thing was clear in her mind that she wasn't going to bring the cattle farmer to England. She put her education on hold as it was difficult for her to carry the extra baggage.

Shuba visited the local hospital by herself when required. She felt that she needed someone to help her go through the new experience but there wasn't anyone to help. Shuba gave birth to a baby boy. All her friends supported her including Foriz, everyone bought clothes and many presents for the baby. Shuba didn't tell her parents about anything since she left home.

The baby looked gorgeous. She felt very happy that she had decided to give birth to the child, and she didn't have an abortion. By now she concluded the pain she went through in Bangladesh was nothing compared to the joy she received from looking at the innocent child. For her this was where her life started. Often she thanked Foriz for his help and support. She only had income from the social security benefit; it was financially difficult for her to have a good life. Foriz realised her situation, he sometimes bought her shopping and gave her presents just to see her happy. He never tried to take advantage of her situation or entered her bed room without permission.

One day Shuba was out shopping in East Ham shopping centre. There she bumped into her evil mother. Her mother was very upset with her that she had left home and didn't tell her. She also complained that Shuba had given her father a bad name. In the Middle of the shopping centre Shuba didn't want to have an argument. Shuba told her mother that she didn't give a dam about her father. He wasn't her father anymore. If he was her father, he wouldn't have got her married like that. Shuba's mother said, the decision was best for the family as it would have saved money for them to go back to Bangladesh again. 'You never thought about me and my feeling and what I wanted,' she told her. Her mother asked, 'Whose child is this?' She had a feeling it was Shuba's. Angrily she replied, 'It is the child of the cattle farmer in Bangladesh.' Shuba's mother took a closer look at the child and admitted the child was gorgeous. Her mother understood that she won't get very far by complaining, she decided to listen to her daughter. She asked Shuba how she was doing, how she was nurturing the baby without a father's support. Shuba replied that she wasn't doing very well as she was on her own and didn't have anyone to help her out. Her mother's eyes were full of tears; she hugged Shuba, and told her to come home. 'No,' she replied. Then she said that she would never go home until her father was dead. Shuba's mother asked her to phone her and keep her up dated with the child's progress. Her mother gave her fifty pounds presents for the baby. Shuba first hesitated to take the money then she took it as she needed it.

Foriz became part of Shuba's family. After college he was with her most of the time. He looked after the baby when she cooked rice and curries. She found his help very comfortable and she often asked him to do shopping for her. He happily helped her and enjoyed her beautiful company whenever around her. They went to the local park together, on looker thought they were husband and wife. In her house they watched Indian films, laughed and joked together. Shuba cooked his favourite curries and washed his lungis.

Shuba had started to have more then a 'friendship' affection for him. She wanted to see if he felt the same way. Foriz didn't mind playing but he didn't want to be the first one to make the move. Shuba made his bed ready in the living room, stayed awake to watch a movie with him. They never sat too close to each other. The baby slept in his pram. She pretended to slept on the sofa to see what Foriz did. He didn't do anything to her. He put the volume of the television down so she could sleep soundly. He noticed that she was sleeping awkwardly, her neck was bent. She might end up having neck pain. Foriz thought about what to do then he straightened her body onto the sofa. Shuba was able to feel that he was helping her. She felt that Foriz wasn't going to do anything to her. It wasn't in his character to take advantages of anyone. Slowly she got up and said that she couldn't believe it that she had fallen asleep on the sofa. He told her that she was sleeping awkwardly and he pulled her up on the sofa. She thanked him for that.

Shuba took the baby to the bed room and put him into the cot. Her feeling towards Foriz had totally changed. She couldn't resist his character no more. She came back to the living room and said to him that she felt scared to sleep in her room. 'How can you be scared, you have been living in your room for long time now,' he said. She said that she knew that but she had a bad dream and now she felt scared to sleep by her self. This is why she probably slept on the sofa. He asked what should he do, should he come and sleep on the floor of her bed room. 'That would be really nice,' she replied. Foriz wasn't bothered where he slept as no one saw him that would take piss-out of him. He had a feeling that she might be up to something. They took the blanket and the pillow from the living room to the bed room to make his bed there. He started to make his bed on the floor. 'That's enough Foriz,' she said. She put the light's power down and asked him 'If you don't mind, you should sleep in the same bed with me.' He wasn't sure what to say, took a few seconds and he said, 'Are you sure?' 'Yes I am.' 'There is no problem from me as long as you don't complain if I kick you while I am sleeping.' She told him there was no problem. Shuba told him to hurry up and get into the bed, she put the light off and went into the bed too. She was ready to make love to him. She felt at last she had the man she loved even though it may be sociologically inappropriate.

By now he knew what she was up to and he was also ready for action. 'If the ghost comes now, I don't feel scared anymore,' she said.

'You are making me scared now.'

'If you feel scared you can hold me tight.'

'Thanks for the offer.'

Shuba moved in with the first attack, asked him to pull her fingers as they were stiff. He did that. She slowly went close to him, touched him with her leg. There was no reaction from him. Then she touched him with her hands. Foriz felt that she was ready for the touching game so he touched her with his leg, then his hand. The game continued for a minute or so. Then she jumped on top of him and kissed him, told him to make love to her. He said that he couldn't as he didn't have any protection with him. She told him that she had pills to protect herself. Quickly he took control by getting into the driving seat, visited places with his rubber part of his pencil that he shouldn't have, had the best night of his life and made her happy. She told him that it was the present for all the help and support he gave her. He told her that she didn't have to give him this excellent present but thanked her anyway. They continued to enjoy life together like husband and wife, unofficially.

Shuba's child was growing up. She started to think about his future. She wasn't sure what she would tell the child when the child would ask her who his father was, and she didn't have a future with Foriz. She knew that Foriz won't marry her because she was already married once. It would be very difficult for her to find a legal Bengali man to marry her as she had a child. Her future looked empty and bleak. After many days and months of thinking Shuba came to conclusion that she was in a no win situation. She worked out that she needed a husband that would live with her for ever and the child needed a father who could support him while he grew up.

Shuba spoke to her friends for advice; no one had a solution to her problems. She decided to bring her husband from the paddy field. Shuba calculated this would be the best solution as he was the father of the child, it was written in her Takdir to be his wife so be it. She telephoned her mother, met her and told her that she would bring her husband. There were a few conditions. She told her father that he had to return the fifteen laks he took and give back the land to her husband that was registered under her name as dowry. Shuba's mother was pleased with her that she decided to bring her husband but most importantly pleased to see happiness in Shuba's life. Shuba made it clear to her mother that if her father came up with any crafty plan then she wouldn't bring her husband to the UK.

Shuba kept the council house as she needed it to bring her husband. She went back to college while her mother looked after the child. She arranged through her family some dodgy pay slips and put money into her bank account and applied for her husband's visa. Within three months of her application, he was given a visa to come to London.

Shuba explained the situation to Foriz which he understood very well and they agreed to continue to be good friends. A month before her husband's arrival she stopped seeing Foriz. His final night with her, he enjoyed her company and beauty from different angles. He made the most of the night as he hardly slept and didn't let her sleep either.

Shuba's husband arrived in the UK. There was only one job her husband could do as he had no qualification. He had to work in a restaurant. He managed to find a job as a kitchen porter. She continued to study. He didn't want his wife to study but she explained to him that if she studied then she would earn lots of money and they would be able to buy a house. He would be able to send more money to his parents as this was why he was in London. Then he agreed to let her study.

Sabbir's Restaurant business had picked up a lot and more restaurants were opening in Brick Lane. Sabbir spoke to his brother and relatives about opening another restaurant in Brick Lane. They found a shop and agreed to go ahead with a planning permission for a restaurant. A planning permission was given for an A3 usage. Sabbir needed partners to help out financially, also to work in the restaurant. He asked Ayna's and Amina's husband if they wanted to be partners. Both of them said they would have like to be partners. Sabbir agreed to take them on, gave them 20% partnership each, 10% to Minto and he kept 50%. He gave ten percent to Minto and made him manager of the new restaurant. According to Sabbir Minto worked hard over the years and was a reliable waiter. Muslah agreed to be a sleeping partner. They managed to get a bank loan with their business plan, which Sabbir drew up. The new restaurant cost them eighty thousand pounds to get ready in a contemporary design. Sabbir gave the building work to Peter and Lee as they were the most reliable builders he had and his best customers too. They discussed the restaurant design in great details. Peter gave his point of view and genuine advice as if he were a partner. Peter and Lee did the building work within three months they created a highly reputable restaurant. Sabbir and his partners were pleased with the outcome.

CHAPTER SEVEN

1997

Foriz met Mariam a beautiful girl at college. He liked her because she was very beautiful. They went out with each other for a few months then she dropped a bombshell. She told him that her parents were planning to take her back to Pakistan and get her married there. Mariam wanted Foriz to help her runaway from home and then get married to her. Foriz told her that he wasn't ready for marriage. He wanted to study and go to further education. They broke up. She found another boy who took her offer. He didn't feel upset as he only went out with her to get rid of Shuba from his mind and she only had the looks not a great personality. Only thing he missed was her beautiful red lips.

A table of four customers ate in the restaurant. The bill came to sixty pounds. The customer paid with a cheque and a guarantee card. A week later the cheque bounced. Sabbir remembered the customers that gave him the cheque. A few months later the customers returned and ordered their food. They had changed their appearance a bit. Sabbir recognised two of them but wasn't hundred percent sure. He waited to see if they paid by cash or card. Sabbir had copy of the old cheque, it was returned by his bank. The customers again paid by a cheque. He looked at the cheque, checked it with the old one and it was an identical cheque. Sabbir called the police. The customers wanted to leave but Sabbir locked the door, and invited the kitchen staff to come with their usual weapons to scare them. Sabbir told them that the police were on the way and they had to pay the current and the old bill. They agreed to pay. Sabbir told them that it was good if they paid but the police would be there soon to take them away. The police officers arrived, made them pay and then took them away.

Sabbir received a letter from an uncle from his village. The uncle had been paralyzed on the legs, and he needed money for medication. The man was a decent person and from the same caste as Sabbir. Sabbir thought that it was important to help a needy person as his prayer might help Sabbir in the near future. Sabbir asked his mother to telephone the relatives and asked them to donate too. People gave ten and twenty pounds each. They managed to collect two hundred pounds and sent it to him. The uncle sent another letter where he thanked everyone for the help, and he wrote, that he would pray for everyone to get rich. Sabbir didn't mind helping poor people. He felt the people's prayers may have helped him to be rich and successful.

Spitalfield and Brick Lane were renamed as Bangla Town to mark the establishment of the large Bangladeshi settlers and also to promote the area as a tourist place. The local authority put up a big sign 'Bangla Town' at the entrance of Brick Lane. It looked very attractive and gave the area a new vibe and also changed the face of the area once again. The restaurant owners and the local Bengali people celebrated the achievement. Sabbir hoped this new name would bring more customers from different part of the country. This was a beginning of another era for the Bangladeshi community and the area.

In the evening Peter came to the restaurant and said to Sabbir, 'Now you lot have changed the name of the Road, next you lot will change name of the borough.'
'Why not, when you lot went to India, you changed the name of most of the places, like Kolkata to Calcutta.'

'So what would you lot rename Tower Hamlets?'

'I think we will rename it London Borough of Curry Hamlets.'

'I won't be surprised at the rate things are changing here it looks like everything is going to change to some kind of Asian name.'

'I wouldn't disagree. We are here to take over.'

'This is why I have already moved from this area, I knew you Pakis were going to take over like the Jews.'

'This is the way you British people took over India a few hundred years ago. You Europeans went there to buy spices – pepper, then tactically you lot spiced us.'

'I don't think you Pakis can take over England you fool, then again if you Pakis don't get what you want you probably become a suicide bombers.'

They laughed to together. Peter asked for another beer.

Sokina's cousin Panna returned from work after two years. He told her that he needed a break from work, he wanted to see his wife and children back home. Panna stayed in Sokina's home for a day then took a flight back to Bangladesh. He told Sabbir that after three months he would try to get back to London again with the fake British passport he had. It had five years visa on it. And if things went well he shouldn't have any problem getting in again.

September 2007

Foriz had started university to read Business and Computing at London Guildhall University. In the first few days he learnt that he can email others on the internal email communication system which had command driven interface. Foriz logged into a computer and sent emails to other girls that were online, very soon he received replies. He managed to meet a few Asian girls as he mostly emailed them. He loved the email system and enjoyed meeting the new girls in the university. It was an easy way of meeting girls. Through the email he met Linara, Peara, Nina, Shahanara, Shanaz, Samsia, Zakia, Zara and many more. To Foriz none of them looked outstanding or provoked his chemical hormones. He felt that he wouldn't have mind playing with Peara, she looked a bit spicy and meaty with her fair skin. Foriz tried to play with Peara but she showed too much demand. He left her to Joynul to play with. Foriz told Joynul to keep on trying her and see if he could pull her, he had to look for girls that were easy to pull.

First few lessons Foriz went into his lectures not to learn the subject but to study the good looking girls that were available. He wore latest fashionable gear with all the labels that can be read and seen, labels like Armani, Versace, Prada, Moschino and Burberry were common to him. Foriz thought that top brand would enable him to attract good looking young girls towards him. He asked the teachers obvious questions or questions that didn't carry much value to get attention from the girls. All the time he had an eye on the girls and the other on his lesson.

Within a few weeks he realised he was getting a lot of attention from the girls. He made many female and male friends, mostly female as he was a heterosexual. He wanted a beautiful girl friend to compliment his style and show off to his mates.

For the first few weeks he continued to use the email during spare time or in computing lessons, met girls in the university's canteen.

Foriz sent an email to a new girl called Shilpa. By now he had good confidence that girl would reply to his emails.

>*Hi babes*
>*What's up?*
>*Wanna make new friend, den reply soon.*
>*from Mr. lover man.*

>*What's up dude*
>*I m cool man*
>*I only make friends with good looking guys, r u 1 of them?*
>*What ya study?*
>*from de sexy bitch.*

>*Yew sexy bitch*
>*I m de good looking man u been looking for*
>*I study sexsology!*
>*catch me if u can*
>*from Mr. Sexy man*

>If your dat sexy den I must meet u, wen r u free?
>Yes baby, I bet u r looking for some1 to experiment
>I m in Tower Hill now, where r u?
>I am in Aldgate East branch now, why don't u come ovr here now and I will check your ass out.
>de sexy bitch.

>hi sexy
>no problem bitch, I will come at 3.30 and meet u in the canteen as I hav a lesson soon, is that ok?
>I m hoping I can experiment with u
>The sexy man

>no problem, I see u at 3.30 and den I will decided if I want to experiment with u or not
>bye darling.

Through the email Foriz arranged a meeting with Shilpa. Foriz's first meeting with Shilpa was in the canteen of Calcutta House, which was very interesting. The name Calcutta gave Foriz the connation of something to do with Calcutta the town in Indian. He told his brain to remember next time when he is on the internet that he needs to do a search to find out more about it. Shilpa and Foriz sat on the comfortable section of the canteen which had couches. He particularly noticed that she was vibrating with fire and had extra spice in her looks, clothes and words she used. She looked very pretty, dressed like a westerner with tight trousers and open chest shirt, had short hair like English women. One wouldn't say she looked like a Bengali girl.

Foriz asked her, 'What would you like to drink?'

'I don't really want anything.'

'I insist you drink something with me.'

'As you're insisting, I will have a coffee with one sugar.'

They sat opposite each other; a small around table in the middle stopped them from kicking each others' legs. Shilpa sat with one leg top of other, opened her hand bag, and pulled out a packet of cigarette and a lighter, offered Foriz one. He wasn't interested. He didn't smoke.

'You are a very different kind of Bengali girl.'

'Yes I know, I like to be different, I have my own reasons.' 'So what are your reasons then?'

'If I tell you the reasons then we will be here for the whole night and I am sure you don't want to be here for the night.'

'Actually I don't mind spending the night with a beautiful woman like you.'

They continued to chat and get to know each other. End up asking questions they had already asked through their email communication, just to kill time and extend their stay. It was getting close to six pm, Foriz asked her, 'Ain't you gonna be late for home?'

'No, I am not gonna be late, I don't live with my parents, I live by myself. I have my own apartment.'

'That's nice, you have your freedom, perhaps I could come and watch football in your apartment.'

'Yes, of course you can come and watch football and movies and if you're a good cook then make dinner for me.'

Foriz had started to get the feeling she was interested in him. Foriz took his mobile out from his pocket to make a call, told Shilpa, 'Just wait a second,' he opened his computerized phone book, searched and dialled a number and spoke; 'Mother I am gonna be a bit late today as I am with my friends. Don't worry, I will be home soon, ok, bye.' Shilpa bust out laughing, 'I can't believe it that you have to call your mum and let her know that you gonna be late. Are you a mummy's boy?'

'You don't understand my mum gets worried, I have to let her know where I am and if I am running late.'

'You lied to her, why didn't you say you're with a girlfriend?'

'If I had said that she would have been very upset with me.'

'I know she would have.'

'Shilpa, is it ok if I have your number so I can text you later.' 'Yes, of course you can have my number, I like texts as I get bored at home, you know I am by myself.'

He felt he was getting somewhere. Their conversations came to a mutual end. They decided to call it a day. They chatted and walked out of the university. Shilpa asked Foriz, 'Are you going to walk me to my home or leave me here?'

'If you want, I can take you to your bed room.'

'I don't want you to take me that far, if you take me up to my house that will be enough, but going as far as my bed room, I have to think about that.'

From her reply he thought he was getting very close to her. Foriz accompanied her and walked her to her door. Her one bed room flat was adjacent to Brick Lane.

'I better say good bye now Shilpa and talk to you on the text later.'

'You have come this far, I think it would be rude if I don't offer you a coffee.'

'No, its okay, I don't think it's safe for me to come in, incase anyone comes and sees me with you, you may get bad reputation.'

'Don't worry about people, as long as they have eyes and lips they will be talking, no one can stop them!'

'Ok, Shilpa, I will come in but I won't stay long.'

'No problem.'

Foriz wanted to show her that he wasn't desperate to get into her house. He slowly walked into her living room following her footstep like a novice. Her living room was attached with an open plan kitchen presented well with leather sofas; it looked like a very neat person lived in the house. She told him, 'You sit down and make your self comfortable as I get changed and if you know how to make coffee the kettle is there. I see you just a second.'

'Hey, I thought you were supposed to make me a coffee.'

'Well, the rule has changed now you're in my apartment.'

She disappeared from his visibility. Shilpa went into her bed room, took her trousers and shirt off, and put on an adidas tracksuit bottom and a tight fcuk t-shirt. She reappeared within a few minutes, which helped Foriz to have better picture of her chest and he had started to wonder what she was up to but he paused this thoughts and went with her flow. Foriz had switched on the TV, kettle and displayed two mugs on the kitchen table, both mugs had text, read, 'I love you.' She commented, 'You have selected very interesting mugs. Then she completed producing the coffee, asked him, 'How many sugars would you liked?' 'Half a spoon.'

They drank the coffees, watched TV, laughed and chatted more. It was nearly nine o'clock. Foriz made his way out, she gave him a kiss on the chin. Shilpa needed rest after an exhausting afternoon and evening full of questions and answers.

Later on Foriz came home and had some rice and curry which was prepared by his mother. Then he went into his bed room, laid down and texted Shilpa as she was running around in his mind. 'Hello beautiful woman, thanks for meeting me today, I rally enjoyed ur company.'

'Hiya sexy man, I enjoyed your company 2, thanks for dropping me home.'

'You gorgeous woman, how do u keep yourself so fit?'

'Hi babe, only way to find out if u spend time with me.'

'Beautiful, what are your ambitions?'

'Sweetheart, I like to enjoy life as it comes.'

After texting each other for long period of time and running out of what to text they agreed to meet-up again.

Next day Foriz was ready for her in the canteen with a hot coffee on the table, waited for her to arrive. He had a clean shave and wore Armani shirt and trousers. When she arrived, she arrived very different from previous day, she looked even better. Shilpa had a bit of make-up on, changed her hair style and clothes. They chatted, caught up with the days news, moved out from the canteen, went to a local coffee shop. In the coffee shop they spent more time together looking at each other from close range. They ended up going to her flat again. This time he knew where to go and sit. She went into the shower. He felt that she could have done that after he had left. Five minutes into her shower she shouted, 'Foriz, can you please bring my towel? I forgot to bring it in, it's on my bed.'

He couldn't believe it that he needed to go into the bathroom, she could be naked. He took the towel into the bathroom and found her hiding behind the plastic division of the shower section. Foriz noticed that she was kind of naked on the other side. He quickly left the bathroom.

She returned shortly and said 'Sorry for the inconvenience.'

'No problem, I actually enjoyed doing that for you.'

'What did you enjoy?'

'I enjoyed looking at a beautiful lady in the shower.'

'You didn't get anything to enjoy, you sound like you never had the real enjoyment, its look like I have to teach you a lot.'

'Please do.'

'What do you want to watch darling? Do you want to watch Indian or English film?'

'I don't mind, I watch both. Actually if you got a nice Indian film, I don't mind, perhaps a romantic one. I see you're in a romantic mood.'

'Of course darling, I will put a romantic movie for you. Who do you want to watch? Ashwarya Rai or shall I say who's your favorite actress?'

'I don't mind Ashwariya Rai, she's beautiful like you.'

'So you want to see Ashwarya dancing and shaking her ass?'

'I'll watch Aishwarya; you can watch Salman Khan showing his naked chest.'

'What would you do if you have a girl friend beautiful as Aishwarya?'

'I would just look at her twenty four seven.'

'I am sure she would prefer more then the look.'

While they chatted, she looked through her sets of films, found a movie that had Aishwarya in it, and she played it.

The film included many romantic scenes which aroused their physiological desire. They were sitting apart from each other on the sofa. Both of them were thinking simultaneously about how to get close to each other, but no one was making the move. She felt that if she doesn't make the move he won't. He wasn't sure how she would react if he had made the first move. Shilpa said,

'I feel lonely here on this sofa.'

'You know what to do.'

'What shall I do? I am not sure.'

'Obviously, you can come and sit next to me.'

'You could have said that earlier.'

'Sorry mate, I am a bit slow.'

'I can see that, you are very slow.'

'I am sure I can learn from you.'

'Looks like I have to teach you a lot.'

'Please do.'

She moved over to his side. While they watched the movie they made comments on silly aspect of the movie, laughed and joked. Time to time they looked at each other's eyes. Both of them were thinking about the next move. Shilpa thought he was too slow to react and not going to make the next move. Foriz felt that he was getting close to kissing her and soon his going to be top of her, but wasn't sure how.

Shilpa said, 'It's itching on my back, I can't reach it to scratch so if you could you kindly scratch it for me.'

He loved the idea and waited for something like that to get close to her body. Foriz scratched her back; then he slowly moved his hands all over her body. He ended up playing with her oranges, which she enjoyed as she made satisfactional noise. Foriz knew that he had her under his control. He manoeuvered his face close to hers and kissed her. They kissed each other continuously for long period of time. In between they stopped and took more breath and continued to kiss again. He told her, 'Your lips are so tasty.'

Panna managed to get into England once again with the same fake British passport. He arrived to Sokina's house, and stayed for a few days. Panna slept in the living room as there was no space in the house. He gave Sokina a sari, some betel nuts which he brought from the village. Sabbir spoke to him with interest as he wanted to bring illegal people from the village. 'Uncle, what kind of questions did they ask you in the Heathrow Airport?' 'They asked me where I worked? What I worked as?'

'Did they look at your passport for long time?'

'No, a few seconds.'

Panna went back to his old restaurant job where he became a chef within two years. He worked and lived in the restaurant, never paid a penny tax. The word tax wasn't in his dictionary.

Minto had applied for permanent residency, used his British wife as a decoy. He used real and dodgy documents for the application. A few months later he received visa for three years. He went to Bangladesh, as he hadn't seen his parents for long time, married another woman but he never told Clair about it.

CHAPTER EIGHT

1998

Sabbir bought another house. Money was busting into Sabbir's account from all the restaurants' businesses. Sabbir and his children looked at a few houses and decided to buy a three bedroom house in Upton Park, close to their house, and rented it out. They worked out that later on if they needed another house to live then they can move to the new house. Sabbir decided that it was important to invest in London rather then in Bangladesh as their children will be growing up here.

Sokina received a letter from her friend Maskura regarding her daughter's marriage. Maskura found a suitable boy for her daughter but didn't have enough money to get her married, and needed financial help. Being an open hearted woman, Sokina wrote back to Maskura that she will do her best to send much as she could. Sokina spoke to Sabbir, her sisters and daughters. She collected fifteen thousand taka for Maskura. Sokina asked Sabbir to send the money to Maskura. It became a formality that poor relatives from the village kept requesting for support, and people from London always supported them.

Azima completed her honours degree with a 2:1. She was very happy as she managed to complete it after so many complications. Everyone in the family was happy for her. In her family she was the first one to get a degree. Sokina telephoned Karim to give the good news, he wasn't very excited as usual. He told Sokina that Azima was getting too old, and Sokina was to take her back home to get her married. Karim told her that he had many proposals for Azima and if they don't get her married people will think there was something wrong with her, that's why she was that old. According to Karim and many other Bengalis, girls must be married well before they reach twenty.

Foriz was in a deep relationship with Shilpa. She realised that she needed to tell him the truth about her as she no longer wanted to keep her top secret, and wanted to know if she had a future with him. They sat in her living room watching an Indian movie cuddling each other. 'I needed to tell you something,' she said.

'I hope you are not going to say that you want to dump me.'

'No, I am not gonna dump you, only you can dump me.'

'So are you ready to listen to me?'

'Yes, I am listening, just let me kiss you again.'

'Ok, you know that picture there which shows three kids with me, they are not my sister's children.'

'Don't tell me they are yours.'

'Yes, they are my children.'

He pretended and raised his voice. 'You must be kidding me, how the hell can you have three children, did you buy them from someone and if they are your children where is the father? Did you get the children without a father? Perhaps you liked children a lot that you bought sperm from someone else.'

He was run out of things to say, he stopped and waited for her to respond.

She calmly replied, 'I was married at the age of seventeen and had a kid each year, I divorced my husband last year. I am sorry, I didn't tell you the truth, If you want to leave me you can. But one thing I like to say, I really enjoyed being with you and thanks for everything you have given me and for being a good friend.'

Foriz wasn't sure what to say. He stayed silence for a few minutes, continued to be attached to her, collected his thoughts together. He comfortably said, 'Well, not to worry, it is part of life, hey what's there to be upset about, I have been having an excellent time with you and enjoyed every moment of your time, surely the physicality you provided, I am sure we can continue to be good friends.'

'Foriz don't you love me?'

'I do love you.'

'If you love me, then you should marry me, so you can enjoy me all the time.'

He wasn't expecting that shot from her. He bought time from her.

'Let me think darling.'

'You never loved me.'

'Of course I loved you, you're an extra beautiful, I always wanted a beautiful lady like you but I can't get married to a woman with three kids, my mother will kill me, I would have married you if you were a single woman.'

'I understand how Bengali family works.'

'I am sorry if I have upsetted you but I can't marry a married woman, I have an ambition to marry an unmarried woman.'

'No problem.'

'Are we going to be friends?'

'If you want.'

She was very upset and it showed on her face. He tried his best to make her smile and continued to kiss her around her face and neck.

'How did you keep such a fit body Shilpa?'

'I didn't want to stay home and get fat like other girls so I joined a gym and worked out.'

'From your body figure and shape I couldn't tell if you were ever married.'

'I did hide my belly from you, look, you can see some birth marks, and the skin had stretched.'

One thing Foriz knew was that he wasn't going to marry her from day one. She was too westernized for his liking. He had to find a soft way of saying no to her. She provided the excuse for him, but for as long as possible he wanted to continue to enjoy her physical gift while he looked for a 'suitable girl.'

In Brick Lane everyone was fighting for customers. Some restaurants owner sent their waiters out on the street to speak to customers and offer discounts, which pissed off other restaurants owners. Sabbir felt that some of these owners went too far to get customers, and were making a mockery of their business. He also felt that he lost business because his competitors were getting to the customers first and offered all sorts of offers. Sabbir decided to produce some special offer vouchers for customers in order to not lose his customers. He distributed the vouchers to the local businesses which boosted his revenue.

Everyone went to work early in the restaurant to prepare for the fist Baishakhi Mela which took place in Brick Lane, Weavers field and Alrlen Garden. The Baishaki Mela established as the premier Bengali celebration outside of Bangladesh. The Baishaki Mela brought together the very best of Bengali arts, music and culture to Brick Lane – Bangla Town. It was a unique festival, created by the collective aspirations of the Benali people who wanted to celebrate the Bangali New Year (Shubho Nobo Borsho). The festival had developed into a sensational extravaganza promoting all that Brick Lane and Bangla Town had to offer to people across UK.

September 1998

It was September the start of Foriz's second university year. He eagerly waited for the beginning of year to commence. Foriz knew more fresh girls will be joining the university. In the university Foriz went into a computer room to check his email, and send email to anyone that was new. His search for a suitable girl continued. A few new names appeared on the list of current internal users, a name stood out from the other names - Shabana. He liked the name for some reason that he didn't know. He took a deep breath, composed himself and an email that he believed Shabana will respond to. The email he sent her read;

>Ass-salaamu-aaleykum Shabana
>How are you? I hope your fine!
>Well, I am a student at this university and found your name on the current users list.
>I hope I am not bothering you. I just like to say that if you like to make a new friend then do email me back.
>Once again I am sorry if I have bothered you.
>Hope to hear from you soon.
>From Foriz

Foriz had no idea how this girl looked like whether she was beautiful, decent or not. He sent the email assuming she was just another girl maybe something different. He had already met a number of Bengali girls whom didn't meet his criteria to be the suitable one. He had an impulse that this girl may have the spices that others didn't. It didn't take long for Shabana to reply;

>Wa-aaleykum aas-salaam
>I am fine, how r u?
>I don't mind u emailed me.
>I like making new email friends 2.
>So what do u study?
>from Shabana (the one and only beauty queen)

Within a few seconds of Shabana pressing the send function Foriz received her email. 'Yes,' Foriz said to himself. For some weird reason he was attracted to Shabana's name. He felt like that he wanted to get to know her and see her. His psychic feeling was telling him that she might turn out to be a nice girl that would interest his hearts' desire. He soon replied;

>thanks for your reply SHABANA
>so you call yourself the beauty queen. I haven't seen a beauty queen yet in this university.
>I study loveeeeeeeee and beautiful girls
>what do u study?
>I take it u r Bengali - begum is usually a Bengali name

>I am Bengali or more precisely a Sylheti
>from ur new friend Foriz

Shabana received the email, she read it again then she composed the reply;
>you r very fast at emailing mister.
>once you see me, u will only study me.
>you seem to study a very interesting subject, I wish I had time for that.
>I study Law. I am Bengali and to be exact a Sylheti toooooo.
>what year r u in and were r u at the moment
>from Shabana (the one and only beauty queen)

Foriz received the email and thought this girl was very sweet whether she is beauty or not he needed to investigate her.

>If you're the beauty queen then I must see u now and ask u out, only joking.
>sorry friend, I have to go now as I have a lesson to go to, I will talk to u later
>take care now and look after yourself
>from Foriz, the handsome man

Foriz wanted to show to her that he wasn't desperate to talk to her and made her wait for the next email. He logged off so that she couldn't see whether his online or not. Foriz noted the computer number she was using. He investigated and found out that she was in the Moorgate branch; he left Tower Hill and took the London underground and went to Moorgate to check her out, just for the fun of it.

Within fifteen minutes he arrived at Moorgate branch. He then went into the computer room she was in and found her using the email. He looked at her from behind. She was wearing a black hijab and was of medium height and build. He didn't want to speak to her and didn't want her to know who he was. He wanted to see her face. He logged onto another computer and waited for her to turn around, move or get up. He thought about going to her and asking her for the time but then he thought that would be bit too obvious. After half an hour later, she got up and went out of the room. He managed to see one side of her face, instantly he began to admire it. Now he wanted to see her full face. Foriz followed her, but she went into the ladies' toilet. He waited outside away from the toilet pretended to be talking on his mobile. She freshened herself and arrived out of the toilet. He took a full look at her face. Within few seconds she disappeared from his visibility. But her image stayed in his photographic memory as if he took a picture of her. 'Wow,' he said to himself. Foriz looked through the window and saw Shabana went out of the university but covered her face with a niqab where only her eyes could be seen. He wasn't sure if she was a Bengali as she looked so modest and uniquely beautiful. He wondered if she was a half-caste, half Bengali and half Arabian. Foriz returned to the computer room and sent her an email;

>*Hiya PRINCESS SHABANA BEGUM, the most beautiful Bengali lady.*
>*sorry I had to go b4.*
>*I m not sure if you're on-line now.*
>*I m in 2nd year.*
>*When u get this message do reply, I have something nice to t ell u.*
>*what branch r u normally at?*
>*Foriz, the unknown Romeo*

Shabana didn't reply as she wasn't on-line. Foriz continued to think about the way she looked. When he went home he visualized her picture from his memory which put a simile on his face. Foriz couldn't stop thinking about her and the beauty she had. The next day she read his email and replied.

>*Hello Foriz (Mr. Romeo)*
>*I couldn't reply yesterday, I had gone home by the time u sent the message.*
>*what is it nice that u need to tell me Mr. Romeo? don't tell me that I am beautiful, I already know that!*
>*is this all u do, study girls!*
>*I am mostly at Moorgate, where r u?*

>reply soon
>Shabana, the one and only.

Foriz received the email as he was desperately waiting to get into conversation with her. Then he composed and sent a reply. At same time he also sent messages to the other girls that were online.

>Hi dear BEAUTIFUL SHABANA, the self confirmed beauty
>I m not going to say ur beautiful, because u haven't shown me your beauty yet.
>I heard something nice about u
>yes I only study beautiful girls like u as I can sense beauty
>I m mostly in tower hill, I have a lesson in Moorgate, next time I m in Moorgate I will see u, if that's ok with u.
>reply quickly
>Foriz, the romantic player

Foriz was worried about her as she looked so pretty that other boys might take her. He wanted to act fast. He also knew she was chatting with others and if the others saw her, she could be gone in days, if she decides to.

>Hiya Foriz the fake player
>I am fine, thanks
>tell me what u heard about me?
>if u only study beautiful girls, once u see me, u will only study me but I m not available for studying.
>thanks for the offer, but I don't like meeting boys
>reply soon Mr. Player, what do u play? football or volleyball?
>from shabs, de one

One thing Foriz knew now was that if they didn't meet up then there was no way he could tell her how much he liked the way she looks and that he wanted to get to know her personality.

>hi beautiful SHABANA
>I'll tell u what I heard about u if u meet me.

>if that's the case I would definitely like to study u top 2 bottom.
>why don't u meet boys?
>I m in Moorgate on Mondays it would be nice if u meet me.
>I play love games where I fix people's heart problems.
>reply quickly
>Foriz, de man

>Hello Mr. player
>r u trying to black mail me into meeting u. I don't like black mailers.
>just tell me what u heard about me and from whom?
>if u don't tell me I won't email u.
>I don't meet boys cause I don't want to be friend with boys
>from shabs de one n only unique girl

>hiya beauty queen
>sorry, don't stop emailing me, I kind of like emailing u as u r a different kind of person.
>I wasn't black mailing u; I was just making our conversation longer.
>r u trying to black mail me now?
>I heard that u r a beautiful lady from a friend, please don't ask me what friend that is.
>I thought u r my friend, so how come u don't like to hav boys friends but u talk to me on the email
>Foriz de handsome player

>Hi Foriz,
>for some reason I don't believe u, I told u I was beautiful and u tell me someone else told u that.
>does this friend know me?
>when did u become de handsome man? I haven't seen any handsome boys in this uni.
>anyway, do u have a girl friend?
>Shabana, the princess

Spices of Brick Lane

They emailed each other fast and furiously. Foriz was on fifth gear, nothing was going to stop him. He typed fifty words per minutes. Their spelling and grammar didn't conform to any standard.

>dear SHABANA bhondu
>I know wat u told me but this friend I hav in Morgate told me that seen u and thinks u r a gorgeous woman, n this is why I wanted to meet ya.
>yes I do hav a girl friend as I am sure u would agree that u r a female n u r a girl friend of mine.
>so if u kindly meet me, I would appreciate it.
>I became handsome since u became beautiful
>the reason u haven't seen a handsome boy is because u haven't seen me.
>Foriz de real man

>Foriz you silly billy boy
>yes I am your only email friend but not ur girl friend.
>I meant if u had a girl friend like some one u go out with.
>sorry mate I can't meet u. Tell u the truth I'm not allowed to meet any boys, this is why I m only talking on the email.
>I can be ur email friend for long as I am at de university.
> Shabana the ugly girl

>hi SHABANA bhondu
>please don't say u r an ugly girl, everyone is beautiful as Allah created everyone.
>I'm looking for a decent female friend that's why I'm on the email hoping to meet some1 gorgeous like u.
>what u mean, u r not allowed to meet. r u married?
>I think u should meet me because a beautiful girl like u needs a handsome man like me
>reply soon
>Foriz, de real player

>Foriz u joker,
>how come u reply so quickly.

>so u think u will meet someone decent on the email, good luck mate.
>I'm sure if u were handsome then girls would hav taken u by now. So don't try it.
>no I'm not married, I am just not allowed to meet anyone as that can make things complicated.
>I have few problems with meeting boys.
>Shabs rules

>hiya Shabana the unique lady
>why do u take so long to reply?
>well it is fine if u don't like meeting boys. I understand ur points of view, so no problems; sorry I asked u to meet me.
>girls tried to take me but I saved myself 4 de beautiful lady that I hope to meet one day.
>u r a different girl, unique like ur name
>I'm off now as my fingers need some rest
>take care now and good knight, look after yourself & don't dream about me.
>Foriz unlucky man

>Foriz I hope u're not upset with me.
>it takes me time as I hav to reply to so many other boys.
>good bye
>u take care; I am going to be off now too & I won't be dreaming about u.
>make sure u don't dream about me.
>talk to u next time & don't think of me 24/7
>Shabs de one n only

Foriz decided to call it a day, he wasn't getting very far with her and didn't want to show her that he was desperate to meet her.

On the e-mail Foriz was also talking to other girls but he particularly wanted to meet Lana. Foriz noticed on the email that her computer number was next to Shabana's. He assumed she was likely to be her mate. He emailed Lana and decided to meet her. She was willing to participate in. He strongly felt that she might know Shabana and maybe able to help him. They described what each other was wearing and met in the university's Moorgate canteen. Lana looked beautiful, average height and dressed likea Euro – Asian woman. She didn't wear a hijab but had a scarf around her neck. Foriz liked the way she looked. He had planned what kind of questions he wanted to ask her to extract the information he needed.

'So I am sure you have met many guys on the email?'
'I have met a few boys - some of them were crazy.'
'What you mean?'
'One boy met me for the first time and told me he loved me.'
'That's a bit stupid.'
'That's crazy.'
'Have you met Joy?'
'Yes I have, he was the first person I met. He is another crazy one, sends me millions of emails.'
'He is my mate; he always beats me to the girls.'
'Who else have you met?
'I have met some girls but I like to meet one or two here in Moorgate, the girls in Moorgate are bit reserved, they don't seem to like meeting boys. But they are the best looking.'
'Give me some names of girls you met.'
'I met one good looking girl called Lana.'
'I know that.'
'I met Peara, Shahanara, Bably, Jahanara and many more.'
'Are you a Casanova?'
'Not yet, do you know a girl called Sabba?'
'No, I don't, why?
'I was talking to her on the email and she told me she is in Moorgate all the time, I just wondered if you know her.'
'Is that all you do, email girls?'
'Well, when I have so many admirers I have to satisfy them all.'
'I suppose so.'
'I forgot this Bengali girl's name. She is usually here, her name starts with S.'
'Sima, Sira, Shakira.'
'No.'

Lana had a feeling that it could be Shabana. But she didn't want to say it.

'Describe her to me.'

'I haven't met her, how can I describe her, but she sounded like if she was religious person.'

'Is it Sabina?'

'Yes I got it, it is Shabana, do you know her?'

'I might know her. Why?'

'She chatted on the email but doesn't like meeting boys.'

'You're right, she doesn't like meeting boys because if she does then the boy would say they love her even though they don't even know her, anyway she would never go out with anyone.'

'That's ok, I understand, she sounds unique.'

'She looks unique.'

'When any boy sees her he falls in love with her.'

'She is extremely beautiful. I fancy her too.'

'I didn't know you're lesbian. I must meet her then.'

'I am not.'

'You won't be able to, she won't meet you.'

'I will be able to meet her if you help me.'

'May be in the future I might get you to see her.'

'So she must be your best friend.'

'Well, she is one of my best friends.'

They spoke for an hour, drank coffees together and got to know more about each other. Then they said bye to each other with the exchange of telephone numbers. Foriz's mission was a success as he managed to find Shabana's friend who could be very helpful to him. He intended to manipulate her to get close to Shabana.

In the evening Lana called Shabana and told her that she had met Foriz and he was a good looking guy. Shabana asked her whether she wanted to go out with Foriz. She replied that she wouldn't mind if he asked her out. Shabana asked Lana if she wanted her to email Foriz and tell him that she liked him but she said no. She wanted to see how things progressed in the next few days. Shabana told Lana that Foriz wanted to meet her. She said, 'No.' He sounded like a decent boy on

Spices of Brick Lane

the email. Lana mentioned to Shabana that Foriz had spoken about her and that she had refused to meet him.

After six o'clock Foriz contacted Joynul. 'You clever bastard why didn't you tell me that you met Lana?'

'Shut up man, if I had told you she was good looking then you would have asked her out before I did.'

'Anyway, I met her today. She looks nice and I told her that I love her.'

'No, you didn't, you cunt, I met her but I wanted to get to know her before I confessed that I loved her.'

'Well, your too late, you should have told me you met her.' 'What did she say bro?'

'She said she will let me know soon.'

'I don't believe you man, why do you want to go out with her when you already have a sexy girl friend.'

'You know I am a player, I like playing with the good looking babes.'

'Don't be silly man, let me have her.'

'She is not a fruit that I can let you have, you have to earn her.'

'Look bro I will give you ten pounds if you let me have her.'

'No, twenty.'

'Deal.'

'Promise.'

'Ok.'

'Tell you the truth I didn't ask her out, I was kidding.'

'You bastard, when did you meet her?'

'I met her today in Moorgate.'

'What did she say?'

'She told me that you met her and you sounded like a stupid boy, you kept giving her millions of emails.'

'Do you think I have a chance to go out with her?'

'Only way to find out if you ask her out.'

'Do me a favour, you ask her for me.'

'If I do that that will be another ten pounds.'

'Get lost.'

'Alright, I'll give her an email and tell her.'

'Thanks, did you meet anyone else?'

'I was trying to but she doesn't meet anyone.'
'Are you talking about Shabana?'
'Yes, are there any girls on the email that you haven't emailed?'
'No, I don't think so, I have emailed them all.'
'If you meet Shabana then leave her alone, I want her.'
'Ok, I will leave her alone. That will be twenty pounds.'
'Piss off; did you try to meet her?'
'I did.'
'What did she say?'
'She told me she doesn't meet boys.'
'She told me the same stuff.'
'What we can do is that next time when she logs in, we can give her a visit in Moorgate and see her when she's emailing.'
'No, don't do that bro, she sounds like a decent girl, I think we should leave her alone, if she doesn't want to meet us we should respect that, she is a Bengali girl.'
'Your right man, we should respect her.'
'Anyway if you do manage to meet her before me don't tell her you love her because I am in love with her and I want her, she is my woman.'
'How can you say you want her when you haven't seen her?'
'I got this psychic feeling she is a good looking and decent girl.'
'You must have seen her; you are not telling me the truth.'
'I haven't seen her.'
'How can you love her?'
'Well, Lana told me she is good looking. She wears hijab and niqab. So I am warning you not to go near her as I cannot trust you, you pervert!'
'Deal.'
'Anyway speak to you some other time, take care.'
'Bye.'

That is how Foriz's communication with Joynul ended. Foriz thought 'Well at least he knows not to interfere with his interest. He told him so, didn't he?'

Chapter Nine

1998 Continued

The next day Foriz went to the university and emailed Lana. His main intention was to become her good friend then he can get close to Shabana. Joynul also emailed Lana with the intention to woo her to love him.

>*Hiya beautiful lady, how r u?*
>*thanks for meeting me yesterday; it was nice talking to u.*
>*reply soon, I have good news for u*
>*Foriz 007*

>*Hi sexy man, how are u?*
>*I m cool, when did u become James Bond?*
>*Yes it was nice meeting u, I also enjoyed chatting to u babe.*
>*So what did u enjoy about yesterday?*
>*Reply soon, I will be waiting*
>*Lana 0069*

>*Hi babe*
>*a correction, I m not a sexy man; if I was then I would have been able 2 have any girl.*
>*I enjoy meeting new people, I enjoyed meeting u as u r a good looking babe.*

>u hav a secret admirer
>Foriz the player

>Hi again darling
>I am sure most girls would fancy u, I know someone likes u.
>And who is the secret admirer of me?
>r u single Foriz?
>reply soon
>Lana the sexy bitch

>hiya babe
>I can't tell u who's ur secret admirer is but I am sure soon u'll be able to find out
>ur admirer loves u a lot
>I may be single, it's all depends on who's asking.
>Foriz, de bazigaar

>Hi darling
>u change ur name again?
>I also know an admirer of yours
>what r u doing in the afternoon
>do u know my admirer?
>I know I hav so many admirers.
>Lana 0069

>hiya babe
>I m happy that I hav an admirer
>yes u do know him, u got an interesting positional extension name.
>I am free in the afternoon; shall I come to Moorgate and company u?
>Foriz, de casanova

>hi darling Casanova
>I like interesting positions, how about u?
>yes come to the canteen at 3.30, I will meet u there
>u hav to tell me who the admirer is

>Lana, everyone wants me

>hiya babe
>see ya; make sure u bring ur friend Shabana with u.
>soon u will find out ur admirer
>Foriz, the real player

>hi
>I will try, I don't think she will come
>she isn't that kind of girl
>Lana, octopus

>hi
>ok, Joynul will come with me is dat ok?
>octopus, where did you get that from?
>Foriz

>hi
>no problem but if he comes tell him not to play with his mobile
>I like octopus, I got it from james bond's film
>byeeeeeeeeeeeeee for now
>Lana, octo-pussy

Lana had a feeling that her secret admirer could have been Joynul, he had emailed her non-stop. Foriz simultaneously emailed Shabana. He hope to convince her to meet him.

>Good morning PRINCESS SHABANA, the one and only unique lady
>how r u 2day, I hope u r feeling cool like me
>reply when u get a chance, I will be waiting for ur beautiful emails
>Foriz ur new friend

>Good morning to u Mr. Player.
>I am fine, thank u. How r u?
>I hear u have been meeting girls in Moorgate. So u r living up

to ur nick name.
>Shabana, the one and only

>Hi Pretty woman
>I m cool as cucumber
>I see, u must be a psychic that u know I met some1 in Morgate or hav u been keeping ur eye on me?
>I told u not to dream about me
>I told u I like playing with good looking girls
>reply soon.
>Foriz, de real player

>Hello Mr. Player
>for ur information I wasn't dreaming about u and keeping my eye on u, I was told by someone that u were in Moorgate
>let me know if you like her. I can fix u up
>Shabana, the unknown heroine

>hiya the unknown pretty heroine
>I take it Lana told u that I met her, so u must be her friend.
>so u been finding out about me. u must be interested in me. I m not surprised!
>look like next ur turn to meet me, wouldn't u say so.
>Foriz, reply soon

>Mr. Foriz
>Yes, your correct Lana is my friend and she told me.
>It isn't my turn to meet u mister. There is no turn, I don't drive.
>I don't meet boys, that's a full stop.
>I'm not interested in u mister. Stop dreaming. Ok
>Shabana, the one and only

>hiya Shabana the one and only beautiful girl
>U don't hav 2 meet me but it would hav been nice to put a face2 that such a beautiful name that u hav.
>I know ur not interested but it's ur loss cause I m a man that meets ur criteria.

>I m meeting ur friend 2day after university at 3.30 if u can come dat would be really nice.
>Foriz de lover man

>Mr. Foriz
>Thanks for trying and the offer, sorry I'll not be able to make it, enjoy ur time with Lana.
>U may meet my criteria but I won't be looking 4 my husband.
>My dad has a criteria and my mum's criteria is dangerous
>If u like Lana, let me know, I'll let her know just like that.
>Princess Shabana – catch me if you can

>Hi friend SHABANA
>I'm sure I can meet everyone's criteria
>well, if I like her, I can let her know myself.
>I can tell u now; Lana is too good for me
>I got to go now, bye Shabana-ji
>Foriz de bazigaar

>bye Mr. Foriz
>u sound like a bazigaar
>Talk 2 u later and enjoy ur time with Lana, give my love to her when u see her.
>who says she is 2 good 4 u?
>if she is too good then i m too too good 4 u mister.
>Unique Shabana

>hiya, u silly girl
>Lana is now sitting next to u on the computer no 12; u can give ur love to her now, ha ha ha
>I said she is 2 good for me.
>I play like a bazigaar
>I hav 2 meet u to judge whether ur too good or not. Will I get de opportunity?
>Bye once again, Foriz.

>Oi, Foriz

>Stop it now, r u in this room now?
>U r scaring us!
>How do u know she is on computer no 12?
>If u r, don't come near us, if u do we will scream.
>Shabana.

>Hi Shabs
>stop emailing me, I need to go to my lesson; I m going to be late.
>I may be in the same room, I also know u r on computer no 11, m I correct?
>bye now, I must dash
>I will talk to u again when I finish my lesson.
>Foriz de sharp player

Foriz didn't have a lesson to go to but wanted to stop emailing Shabana to show that he wasn't desperate to meet her. He felt that he needed to do something different to meet her. Joynul also emailed her.

>Hellooooooooooooooo Shabana
>what's up man?
>I know you have a secret admirer
>from JOY the best looking man.

>Hi Joy boy
>how r u?
>for your info, I m not a man
>I m sure if u r good looking den u would have been with ur girl friend right now not on the email mailing all de girls
>and who is this secret admirer of me?
>Shabana the one and only beauty queen

>Ha ha ha haaaaaaaaaaaa!
>I m fine man?
>I can say the same thing if you're sexy then u would have been with your boy friend not on the email.
>I m not going to tell u who the secret admirer is, but tell u this

that he likes you a lot man.
>from Joy of love

>Joy what r u talking about man, no one seen me so how can he like me.
>who is it anyway? I bet he must be a crazy friend of yours.
>tell me his name?
>don't u have any lesson 2 go 2 or is that what u do all day, email girls.
>Shabana the one.

>Miss Bangladesh
>I do go to my lessons but studying girls is another part of my subject which I need in order to keep me going.
>and for your kind information don't you have lessons it seems like your on the email a lot
>looks like u haven't had much luck with boys.
>I can't tell you his name, but if you meet me then I might tell you his name
>Joy of life

>little boy joy toy
>R u trying to blackmail me to meet u. I don't care if I have a secret admirer, I know many un-secret admirer so I won't meet u mister.
>for ur info I m not looking 4 a boy friend. I talk on the email just for fun. Okay!!!! Did u get that?
>but if u tell me who the person is then it would be nice.
>I m off now to my next lesson chat to u later little boy
>Princess Shabana

In the afternoon Foriz and Joynul met Lana in the canteen as planned. Foriz told Joynul that he would take the back seat and allow him to woo her. Joynul bought coffees for the gang. Lana came very smartly dressed with a touch of make up to arouse Foriz. He wasn't interested in her as he already had a sexy girl friend. He wanted to get close to her so he could learn more about Shabana.

'So your friend didn't come with you?' Foriz asked Lana.

'She doesn't like meeting boys, I asked her to come but she refused.'

'How come she talks to us but doesn't meet up,' said Joynul.

'I know, she likes having fun on the email but doesn't like meeting up with any boys.'

'Did she have an 'ex-boy' that hurt her so much that she doesn't like meeting boys?' Foriz asked.

'I don't know that. You have to ask her.'

'Do you have a boy friend Lana?' Joynul asked.

'It depends on who wants to know.'

'We like to know,' both replied simultaneously.

'I don't like threesomes.' They laughed.

'Don't get me involved, I am not interested, you're too hot for me to handle,' Foriz replied.

'No, I don't have a boy friend at the moment just looking around for the right man to come and take me away.'

'I am sure many boys will be interested in a girl like you,' said Joy.

'I know some one in this canteen is interested in you,' Foriz replied.

'Who is it then?'

'I can't tell you now.'

'Why not?'

'First you have to introduce me to Shabana then I will tell you.'

'Why are you so desperate to meet her?'

'I like that name. I am just curious to meet her.'

'You crazy man, first time I hard someone in love with someone's name,' she said.

'Would you like to go to the student union bar?' Joynul asked.

'Why not,' she replied.

They walked from Moorgate through a decorative public park, took the short cuts root and went to the student union bar near Aldgate. They ordered some soft drinks. Foriz said that he would pay for the drinks but Joynul insisted paying as he wanted to impress Lana. Foriz didn't want anyone to see him with her especially Shilpa. He looked for a way out to exit and let Joynul entertain her. He noticed some of his class mates were in the bar and went to say hello to them. They were Bengali, Pakistani and Indian. One Bengali boy offered bear to Foriz. Foriz told him that he hadn't promoted him self to bear yet. They were drinking all sort of alcohol which Foriz didn't like. He thought maybe they were doing it to impress the girls. Foriz didn't like the beer smell. He said good bye to them. Foriz left the bar, out of their sight for a few minutes and called Shilpa. She was at home relaxing. He told Joynul and Lana that he had to go. He left the party to allow Joynul to play with Lana.

He hurriedly shot off to visit Shilpa intending to enjoy some valuable time with her. Shilpa told him when he got to her door he should call her. As told, he called her. She told him to listen to her instructions, which he did. She told him, 'The key is under the carpet; open the door; close the door; make sure the door is shut; take your shoes off; take your socks off; take your bags and jacket off; take your top off; good boy; take your trousers off; now turn your mobile off and come to the bed room.' She was ready for him in the bed, he jumped in, started to enjoy her from the top instantly. Shilpa allowed Foriz to drive through her narrow lane into her 'satisfactional garage.' He enjoyed driving through her lane and reversed gear where necessary to satisfy and complete his driving needs.

Joynul talked and tried with Lana. He felt that he was getting somewhere with her. Lana realised that Foriz wasn't interested in her, and she could have Joynul if she wanted. She felt Joynul was alright but wasn't stylish and smart as Foriz.

Joynul was enjoying his time with Lana, he found her very attractive, someone he would like to be with. He was just impressed by her beautiful figure and wasn't interesting in anything else. At seven o'clock the union bar became full of students. The DJ had the music rolling. Joynul asked Lana if she wanted to dance. She didn't refuse. They went onto the dance floor. Both didn't have much experience of dancing but tried to copy others. He was only thinking about getting close to her body. 'Can I hold your hands Lana?'

'If you want to.'

'Thanks.'

He held her hands and danced. From time to time he let go off one hand and swung her around to mix it up. He knew he was getting close to her and she was allowing him to do so. While dancing he moved his hands on her hips to see her reaction. She didn't react. Joynul went closed to her and gave her a hug which enabled him to feel her soft chest. Then he grabbed hold of her and kissed her. She also kissed him back. He felt happy. They smiled at each other to confirm their affectional agreement. They continued to dance and Joynul continued to do more to experiment with her body. With his hands, he managed to feel her soft bums. She had to go home at nine pm. She had told her mother she was with Shabana doing some extra study at university. Joynul took her to the local bus stop. She went home by twenty-five bus through Whitechapel Road.

At the end of the day Joynul was a very happy young man as it was a very successful day for him. He was able to taste a very beautiful girl. Lana was happy to an extent as she wanted to meet someone who would love and adore her and didn't want her parents to find someone for her.

As she went home she called Shabana and told her what happened and all the things she had done with Joynul. Shabana wasn't very happy with her performance. 'How could you kiss him and let him touch you when you were not married to him, you know you will get so much sin for that. I can't believe you did that - you disappointed me and I am ashamed to be your friend,' said Shabana. Lana told her she was sorry. She was out of control. The event had taken control of her, and what she did was unintentional, but she enjoyed it.

Joynul called Foriz and told him what had happened. Foriz told him that she was under control now and all he needed to do was to play it safe and enjoy her slowly. He also told Joynul to send her text messages telling her that he loved her a lot.

In the evening Joynul texted her because he couldn't stop thinking about her.

'Lana my beautiful friend, thanks for meeting me today, I enjoyed it very much.'

'Halo Joy, thanks to u, I enjoyed it 2, so what did u enjoy about 2day?'

'I enjoyed everything from the moment I met u. What did u enjoy?'

'I enjoyed drinking in the bar and the dance we had.'

'Good to know u enjoyed it. I enjoyed the stuff u gave me on the dance floor.'

'You naughty boy, I didn't give u any stuff, was I drank?'

'I m sure you were not drunk. I like to tell u something Lana.'

'You told me so many things 2day, haven't u finished yet?'

'No, I have not finished yet. I want to tell u the most important thing.'

'I thought u did tell me the most important thing on the dance floor.'

'Ok, no problem I will tell u again, r u ready baby.'

'Yes darling I am ready for u, get on with it quickly.'

'I LOVE YOU VERY MUCH AND IF YOU LOVE ME, I LOVE TO MARRY YOU WHEN WE FINISH UNIVERSITY.'

'Nice to know that I have a lover, I have to think about it darling, Ok, chat to u some other time, bye.'

'No problem, take your time, bye 4 now, love you very much.'

At the end of the texting she knew how much Joynul liked her that she wasn't sure before. Lana called Shabana again and told her that Joynul loved her and wanted to marry her. She asked Shabana what she should do. Shabana told her, 'Do what ever you like; I am not interested in your love affair, I can smell trouble.'

'You cow, I didn't know you have six senses, just tell me what to do or I will kiss him again tomorrow.'

'Shut up you kut-thi and don't kiss him again or he will think you are cheap.'

'Ok, how do I become expensive then?'

'Don't talk to him for a few days and don't email him, see what he says.'

'Ok.'

'Go to bed now and stop thinking about him you silly cow, 'bye.'

A few days went past. Lana didn't reply to any of Joynul's emails or text messages. She played it as Shabana told her. Joynul sent messages included that he was so sorry if he did anything wrong. There was no electronic reply. Foriz also sent her emails on behalf of Joynul, she didn't reply to them too. They sent emails to Shabana and asked her if she knew why Lana wasn't replying. It was another opportunity for Foriz to send more and more emails to Shabana.

>Hi dear friend Shabana
>do u know why Lana isn't talking to Joynul?
>tell her to talk to him, he loves her a lot.
>please find out why she isn't talking to him?
>Foriz your friend.

>Hiya Mister Foriz
>I don't know why she isn't talking 2 him.
>that is her problem. That is her life
>maybe he went too far with her
>Shabana, leave me alone u 2

>Hiya Shabaaaaanaaa Begum,
>I won't leave u alone, I thought we were friends
>Come on yaar, de man is dieing, don't u think u should help
>he is crazy about ur awesome friend
>Foriz, don't leave me alone

>Hello Mr. Middle man.
>why r u so worried about someone else's luv life.
>Shouldn't u be thinking about ur own luv life?
>she isn't answering my calls too. Do u think I am her PA that I should pass messages?
>Shabs the bad girl

>dear Shabana-ji
>I m worried because he is one of my best mate and I don't like to see lovers un-happy
>I don't have to think about my love life
>I found a gorgeous woman to love, she is mind blowing.
>I never said u r her PA.
>Foriz Mr. Problem solver.

Slowly their email conversation had started to divert from the original objectives. And that's what Foriz wanted.

>Mr. Foriz de Crazy man
>So u hav become the problem solver, I don't think so.
>I think u r still a child.
>U should keep away from that lady whose mind blowing.
>I don't won't to see a friend getting blown up.
>Shabana de rude girl

>Hiya Miss. Crazy woman
>what make u say I am a child
>I m sure if I get married to u 2day, I will be a father within 9 months
>I know she is so beautiful, I fink she is a danger to the society as men keep on looking at her when ever she passes by.
>Foriz the player

Shabana had become interested in his love story but not knowing that it was a psychological game Foriz had planned and he took full advantages of the situation.

>hello armature player.
>U r a dirty man, how dare u think like that of me. U hav no chance of getting close to me.
>Stop dreaming and don't talk dirty.
>what game do u play?
>stop copying me, I called u a crazy man, ok!
>U should tell her to veil up or men will end up having accident.
>Have u told her dat u like her?
>Shabana de rude girl

>Dear Shabana de sweet-rude girl
>I didn't copy u
>if she had veiled up, I wouldn't hav seen her and loved her.
>once I get married to her, I will tell her to veil up.
>no I havn't told her dat I like her incase she says no.

>tell me what shall I do or how shall I tell her?
>Foriz, de young player

Foriz wanted to hook Shabana into his email and it stared to work.

>Ok mister
>I see ur not very smart after all, just big talks
>will u force ur wife to veil up?
>Tell me more about her and I will see if I can help u.
>how long have u known her for?
>Princess Shabana

>hi dear friend Shabana
>if my wife is really beautiful like u den I will force her 2 veil up
>she is Bengali, she's about nineteen or twenty
>I hav known her for 2 mnths
>Do u like anyone?
>Foriz

>Ok Foriz
>Shut up. Don't compare me, u havn't seen me, u silly boy.
>if my husband tells me 2 veil up, I will divorce him.
>I see, how do u know her n when do u talk to her
>is she friendly with u?
>No, I don't like any boys.
>Shabs

>Shabana darling
>Shabana how long r u going to be on the email?
>I need 2 go 2 a lesson now but I am free after 2.30.
>will u come to the email if u're free after 2.30 then we can talk.
>Is there any boy that fancies you?
>4i2

>Mr. Foriz crazy
>I m not ur darling. Don't call me ur darling.

>I m free after lunch; yes I will use the email as I'm doing some work on the computer.
>good boy, go to your classes now.
>I don't think any boy fancies me,
>u see the problem is that I m not good looking. I wish I was beautiful
>Shabs

Foriz had a lesson to go to but he didn't bother turning up. He found out what computer room she was in and transported himself to Moorgate. Quietly he went into the computer room as he wanted to see glimpses of her beauty again. She was there with Lana. They were talking to each other and giggling, maybe giggling about the email they received. Foriz wasn't sure why Lana wasn't emailing him or Joynul even though she was in. He didn't want Shabana or Lana to notice him and sat on a computer on the other side of the room. Foriz wore a baseball cap and tried to hide himself in case they notice him. He was ready to play his game.

>hi Shabana bhondu,
>I m back. What's wrong with calling u my darling?
>what do u see? I talk 2 her on de email mostly and met her through email.
>she is very friendly, polite n quite funny.
>Ur not telling me the truth, I m sure there r so many boys that would fancy a beautiful girl like u.
>4iz

>You silly boy
>Didn't u go 2 your class, that was a quick lesson.
>I don't want u to call me ur darling. Full stop.
>So wat is it dat u like about her n what makes u lov her?
>Do u meet her when u r at uni?
>I told u the truth, no boys fancies me that I know of.
>for the last time tell me who told u that I m beautiful or did u make that up?
>Shabs, no one loves me.

>hi Shabana sweetheart
>ok, I won't call u my darling
>have u seen Lana 2day? Joynul desperately looking 4 her
>I did go and I m in the lesson, in a computer room but not listening 2 the teacher
>I met her a few times but I haven't had the chance to speak to her a lot face to face
>mostly I talk 2 her on de email n she talks 2 me all de time.
>I just love the way she looks, she wears beautiful hijabs n niqab, she is Bengali/Arabian colour, and about 5ft 2inch tall.
>She looks so beautiful with the hijab
>I m not sure how long her hair is as I haven't seen it.
>If u feel upset that no boys fancies u then I can fancy you, if u let me.
>well, Lana told me that u r beautiful
>4i2

Foriz was able to hear them giggling like unnoticed roses in their corner. They were deciding what to write. Telling each other, write this, write that. And the emailing was getting fast and furious. They must have been talking to other boys too and enjoying the attention they were getting.

>Mr. Crazy boy
>Stop it now. Don't call me sweetheart.
>who's Lana? Let not talk about her, just talk about ur lov life
>I was right 2 call u crazy, u don't even know much about her and u tell me dat u lov her.
>I don't understand u. If u like her hijabs so much, go to a shop and buy them hijabs.
>Try 2 get 2 know her first, see if u can meet her and find out what she likes and whether she has a nice heart or not.
>Remember looks can be deceiving.
>for ur information, I don't feel hurt dat I don't hav a lover, I don't want one, how can u fancy me, I am ugly.
>so just because lana told u, u believed her
>5h435

>hi beautiful thing!
>why can't I call u sweetheart?
>Joynul asking me 2 go 2 Moorgate and look 4 Lana, is she in 2day?
>that's why I spend a lot of time on the email try 2 get 2 know her and at the same time I email others.
>what's that 5h435? Is dat ur encrypted mobile number?
>I know I sound crazy but I think she looks so gorgeous with the hijab,
>when I look at her, my mouth becomes watery, I feel like I want 2 eat her.
>if u see her u will fancy her too
>I m sure u want a boy friend, most girls like attention.
>I still don't mind if ur ugly, I believe Lana, she is my friend.
>4i2

>Hi Crazy man
>u can't call me sweetheart cause I m not ur sweetheart.
>don't com to Moorgate, she isn't in 2day, u lot will be wasting ur time
>find out if she is really religious or she is wearing it just to keep her parents happy.
>5h435 is not my mobile no, u silly boy, it stands 4 Shabs,
>find out about her family, what would happen if her family finds out.
>U know some parents could kill their daughter if they find out they r involved with boys, so watch what you're doing mate.
>I m not looking 4 attention, I get enough as it is
>why did u write u still don't mind fancying me, u don't even know anything about me. Stop winding me up!
>5h435

>hi my beautiful yaar
>why r u stopping me from calling u all the nice names
>Joynul tells me he will go 2 Morgate by himself, he thinks Lana is in 2day
>yes I hav been working extremely hard 2 find out more and

more about her.
>I hav been using psychological and phychological techniques 2 learn more about her.
>I think she isn't free to make decision.
>tell me Shabana is it difficult 2 lov a girl that wears hijab n niqab?
>I find girls wearing a hijab very attractive.
>if u get lots of attention den u must be beautiful, u sound so nice that's why I want to fancy u.
>4i2

>U Crazy crazy lover boy
>Tell Joynul not 2 come and waist his time, if I see her, I will tell her 2 contact him, why is he so desperate 4 her.
>Has he never had a girl friend b4?
>I think u should leave the girls alone.
>If they wear hijab, we also think they are dangerous because u don't know anthing about them.
>I hate girls with hijabs as I don't know what's in their head.
>I think girls with hijabs have something to hide.
>Have u had a girl friend before?
>why do u find girl in hijab attractive?
>I get attention because I m so ugly n why r u after me when u r after another girl? >U naughty boy!, stop harassing me.
>Shabs

>Hi Shabana and Lana darling
>We know Lana is there with u because u wrote we also think.....so what game r u silly girls playing?
>I m not that dumb
>U scare me man,
>how can u hate girls with hijab, u wear hijab though.
>I like girls with hijab because they look awesome with it. Full stop.
>how can I hav a girl friend, I m not good looking like Joynul
>do u have a boy friend?
>For some reason I think u r so beautiful, I m after u because if

the other one says no to me.
>*Forizo 007*

>*Mr. Stupid Lover man 007*
>*Lana just arrived from her lesson, I will tell her 2 email Joynul, tell him not 2 come.*
>*Lana tells me u look buff and she doesn't mind going out with u 2 at the same time.*
>*no I don't have a boy friend n I told u that before, can't u remember in your fik head*
>*I better tell all de girls with hijabs to keep away from u!*
>*how do u know that I wear hijab, is that a guess?*
>*I will not have one, I don't like boys.*
>*U r such a pervert, it doesn't matter if I m beautiful or not.*
>*Shabana*

Lana had logged on and was online. She emailed Joynul and Foriz. She wrote sorry that she couldn't email because she was busy with things.

>*hello 2 u 2 silly girls*
>*so why wasn't she talking 2 him?*
>*I m not interested in Lana; she is 2 good and 2 smart for me*
>*My mother will kill me if I take home a girl smart like Lana.*
>*I m interested in girl like u, who r dangerous, hijabi and very hard to get.*
>*I know u wear hijab and it's not a guess!*
>*If u don't mind me asking, r u lesbian?*
>*I m not a pervert, I m honest, I kind of fancy ur personality too.*
>*forizo real 007*

>*You stupid little crazy boy*
>*how dare u call me lesbian, I m not lesbian. I just don't want a boy friend; they r not worth the hassle.*
>*Lana is a beautiful girl, I m sure your mother would like someone like her.*
>*how can u be interested in me when u haven't seen me, r u a*

fagla?
>Who says that I wear hijab?
>I do u know? Who told u?
>how many times do I have to repeat myself
>R u talking 2 that girl at the moment?
>how can u fancy my personality? Why?
>Shabs

Shabana was enjoying the unusual attention she was getting from Foriz and the crazy stuff he was telling her even though he was irritating. On the other hand he was enjoying winding her up.

>Sorry mate
>Good 2 know ur not a lesbian, I don't want to see a beautiful girl spend rest of her life without a man.
>I know Lana is beautiful but she is 2 smart 4 me and why r u talking about her, she already has a boy friend that loves her very much
>I hav used my brain to find out dat u wear a hijab, m I correct?
>yes I m also talking 2 the girl that I lov so much.
>the more I talk to her the more I seem to like her
>Joynul is going 2 Morgate 2 meet Lana would u mind if I come and meet u?
>de reason I like u is because incase if the other girl doesn't fancy me; I would like to have a wife like u.
>I like ur personality because u sound so awesome n I m starting to like u more n more.
>Forizo de lover man

>Hello fagla boy
>Stop dreaming, I would never go out with u. Did u get that through ur stupid head?
>u r just a crazy fagla boy. How can u think about going out with me when u haven't seen me.
>stop winding me up, I m not going 2 tell u if I wear a hijab or not.
>And I wasn't thinking about spending my life without a man.

>*Does Joynul want to marry Lana?*
>*What is that girls' name and what branch is she in?*
>*U better stop loving her or you'll fail everything.*
>*Yes I do mind if u come and meet me. I won't meet u.*
>*how can I sound awesome I haven't spoken to u, I better stop emailing u because I don't want u 2 like me.*
>*Shabana, no nonsense*

>*hello de beautiful woman*
>*stop calling me a little boy, I m a grown up man*
>*Lana told me u r beautiful n that u wear hijab*
>*I fink he wants 2 marry her that's what he told me*
>*I can't tell u her name incase u know her because she also studies in Morgate and u might tell her that I m crazy*
>*what kind of man do u want to spend ur life with?*
>*I wasn't winding u up. I told u my opinion. U sound very decent to me.*
>*I know I havn't spoken 2 ya but I find the things u write so nice and sweet and attractive.*
>*the player dat wants to play with ya babe*

Chapter Ten

1998 Continued

Foriz noticed Shabana got up and went out of the room. He assumed she went out to the toilet. He was desperate to catch the full view of Shabana's face again. Foriz went out side the room and waited for her to come back. He pretended to be talking to someone on the mobile. She came out of the toilet and he took an eyeful view of her, which made him very happy. "Excuse me, have you got the time?" he asked her just to look at her a bit longer. She told him the time and he thanked her. To him she looked so complete and intoxicatingly awesome. She went back to her computer. Foriz felt like that this was the woman made for him.

>*Hello mr. liar*
>*Lana tells me she never told u anything about me. so why were u lying 2 me?*
>*tell me who told u dat I wear hijab?*
>*If u tell me her name, I might be able to talk to her n tell her dat u like her.*
>*I would like 2 have a husband who would love me, respect me and also religious.*
>*Not someone crazy like u who don't have respect for woman.*
>*Keep ur option 2 ur self. I m not interested*
>*U r so crazy, how can u find my reply attractive?*
>*I m not that stupid*

>Shabs, girls' power

>My dear beautiful friend Shabana Begum.
>some1 must hav told me that you're beautiful and u wear hijab. I can't tell u dat person's name now
>anyway tell me r u really beautiful or not?
>I have been looking for a wife for long time and I have found her and I need ur help 2 get her.
>when I look at her, she sends me 2 another planet with her beauty, smile, body.
>I m allowed four wives and I meet your criteria why don't u become my wife too.
>Lana gone to meet her man, u r on your own, I think I should come and give u some company
>I m sure if I meet u, I will become normal.
>Foriz da man

>You dirty little kut-ta
>I knew u r a pervert.
>I look the way Allah has crated me. I m sure everyone is beautiful.
>U like one girl n same time u r trying it with me.
>U won't have a chance with me because I m not like others girls; I keep away from pervert like u.
>If I meet that girl u like, I will tell her not 2 go out with u because as soon as u will find another 1 u will dump her.
>I don't need your company, I m fine by myself.
>I won't help u get her. I don't think u love her; I think u just like the way she looks.
>U need to meet a psychopath to become normal.
>Shabs, girls' rules

>Dear Shabana Bhondu
>why do u get annoyed so quickly, I just told u, I met ur criteria and if u wanted I can become ur husband that's all mate.
>fine if u don't want me, it's ur loss cause I m good looking like Lana told u.

>that girl I like is in 2day in Morgate, if I tell u the computer number she is in u can go and meet her and tell me if she is gorgeous or not.
>of course I lov her, I lov her because she is beautiful, looks decent n talks politely.
>I have affection for her
>I don't need 2 see a psychopath, believe me I will be fine if I see u.
>Foriz de lover boy

>Mr. Pervert
>I wasn't getting annoyed, I was telling u the facts. So how religious r u?
>Looks r not everything. Looks dies but personality never dies.
>What computer is she on and what room?
>I m not gonna meet u, u r de last person I will meet
>U r so dirty, trying it with 2 girls,
>what will she fink if she finds out u r trying it with me too.
>Shabs, leave me alone

>Hello there mate
>If I m a pervert then u shouldn't talk 2 me. I think I should say good bye now because I don't want to talk to people who think so low of me.
>I was having bit of laugh and u took it seriously.
>good bye, nice talking 2 u, I hope I didn't hurt u, if I did, I m really sorry.
>Please forgive me 4 de troubles I gave u.
>Foriz de un-known friend.

Foriz decided to test her further and see how she reacts. He wanted to see whether she was enjoying talking to him or not.

>Hi Foriz de cry baby
>Sorry friend, I didn't want to upset u. I was only joking too.
>I don't mean to call u a pervert; I said it as a joke. Come on chill out man.

>Forgive me please and do talk to me as I think u r a nice and funny person. But sometimes u go over the top.
>If you don't talk 2 me then I'll be upset because I'll think it's my fault.
>but one thing, don't say that u like me.
>Tell me what's she wearing n I'll go and check her out 4 u.
>Shabs, just your email friend

Foriz had the reaction he was hoping for. He felt that he was getting somewhere and soon she would melt like butter. He knew that he could wind her up and get away with it.

>Dear Shabana Bhondu
>Good, I didn't want to lose an email friend like u because u sound so mature and decent
>I will tell u all about her but first u have 2 promise me that I can trust u like a best friend and then u have to promise me that u will never stop talking 2 me if I upset u ever again.
>Foriz ur new friend.

>Hi Foriz
>Good to be friends again.
>I can promise u but there is a condition, which is if u say anything that is rude or really rude or hurting then I will stop talking 2 u or I will continue to be your email friend.
>Is that ok?
>Shabana

Foriz stretched his legs, hands and fingers and decided to tell the truth slowly. Out it came...

>dear Shabana-ji
>that's ok friend
>will u be my best email friend?
>I will try not to hurt u or upset u.
>I saw the girl I love twice altogether for about 30 seconds.
>I know she won't be happy if she finds out I was trying it with u.
>Foriz the normal man.

>Hi Foriz
>U bloody fool, u only saw her for 30 sec and u love her. Is ur brain working?
>Where is she at the moment?
>Where did u see her?
>What is she wearing?
>Shabana

>my dear friend Shabana Begum
>I know I could be crazy but I call dat love in first sight
>She is in Morgate. In one of the computer room.
>I saw her once today and once before.
>she told me she is wearing a light blue skirt 2day
>Foriz
>ps I want to tell u something I hope u don't mind. I hav been talking to u for a few weeks and I kind of like u as a person.

Basically Foriz started to describe what Shabana was wearing with a bit of ambiguity.

>Hi Foriz
>Are you in Morgate at the moment?
>What's her name?
>Why do u like her so much and how many times have you met her?
>Describe her to me please?
>Shabs
>ps. good to know u like me. I m sure we can be good friends on the email. I like u as an email friend. R u happy now?

>hi Shabanaaaaaaaaaaaaaaaaaaa
>Yes I m in Tower Hill
>I think she is wearing a blackish jacket
>I can't tell u her name.
>I tell you how beautiful she is, 'if a man sees her and doesn't admit that she's beautiful then he is a fool'
>I told u before why I like her; I find her very pretty and I think

she is decent; I met her twice.
>She is medium built, she is wearing a hijab, I only saw her face and hands a few times as all the other parts of her body are concealed
>Foriz
>ps. I was telling u Shabana that I like the way u talk and I find u a very decent, is there any chance that I could get to know u more then a friend?

She started to suspect that he was referring to her.

>Foriz u monkey, you goru.
>why don't u answer my question fully
>What colour is her hijab?
>Has she given u any hints whether she likes u or not?
>Reply quickly u foga
>U r scaring me
>Shabs
>Ps. what r u talking about now. U r a crazy boy. U tell me u r in love with a girl, n now u tell me u want to get to know me more then a friend. U need to see a doctor urgently. How many times do I hav 2 tell u.

>my dear friend Shabana
>She told me she is wearing a black hijab
>She hasn't given me any hints but I love the way she is
>Do you want me 2 go and see her?
>I know what computer room you're in and also what computer you're using. All the information comes up on my computer.
>Don't be scared, I don't bite
>Of course u can go and talk to her; what will u say to her?
>Reply slowly, I m enjoying this situation
>One more thing, looking at her is like looking at a sight of heaven
>Foriz.
>Ps. I was telling u the truth dat I like u a lot now as I got to know u as a person. By talking to u I can say I like u much as I like the other girl. Why don't u give me a chance to meet u?

>*Fagla Foriz*
>*U r scaring de hell out of me n u enjoying it, u silly goru.*
>*OK what computer room am I on?*
>*Tell me her computer number?*
>*U don't know anything about heaven so don't compare*
>*Reply quickly*
>*Shabs*
>*Ps. I really think u r crazy. How could u say dat. I am laughing now. U r a good joker. Sorry, I won't give u the chance to see me.*

>*my beautiful friend Shabana*
>*I m really enjoying it, do u want to call a friend for help -Lana; she might help u out.*
>*You're in second floor, room B5*
>*She is in room B3 computer no 25 go and check her out.*
>*Tell her I love her so much that I want to marry her and spend rest of my life with her*
>*Reply slowing and slowing*
>*Foriz de lover boy*
>*Ps. I m telling u the truth that I love u much as I love her and if u say yes, I love to marry you instead of her because I like ur personality more then hers.*

Shabana went to room B3 to see if that girl existed. She left her computer on, turned the VDU off. Foriz took the chance and went to her computer, in big letters he wrote 'I LOVE YOU SHABANA AND I WANT TO MARRY YOU,' and minimized the document.

>*U stupid psychopath*
>*U r scaring de hell out of me, I m logging off now.*
>*There wasn't any1 on dat computer, why did u lie to me?*
>*There was no one by the description u gave me.*
>*U r worse then what I thought.*
>*U r making me sick now.*
>*U r the biggest and the stupidest person I have come across.*
>*U r a fool. I hate u. I am gonna log off now.*
>*Lana Help me, there is a stalker in the room.*

>Shabs
>Ps. U gonna make me crazy. Why r u winding me up for. What hav I done 2 u. how could u say u love me n u want to marry me when u don't know anything about me and most importantly u hav not met me. Hav u been let out from a mental hospital? people like u should be locked up.

>my dear best friend Shabana
>Don't log off friend
>She must hav logged off and left.
>some1 told me what she was wearing.
>is there a problem with what she is wearing?
>would u like to play a game with me just for a minutes?
>Foriz, wants 2 be ur man
>Ps. This is what I call love is blind. I am willing to love u even though I haven't met u officially. Not only dat but I m willing to marry u if u say 'yes' to me. I don't have to see u.

>hi Foriz u r a sick man
>I m going to scream.
>I m calling Lana and tell her what u doing to me.
>who told u what she was wearing. Was it Lana?
>What kind of game r u talking about?
>r u in the same room as me?
>Get lost u monkey
>Just admit it who r u really talking about because I think I know who she is?
>Shabs
>Ps. So now u want to marry me. I don't know what to say. How can the uni. Allow some1 stupid like u come n enroll. U r just a mantel child. Well, I will not marry u mate because u r not my type.

>Dear Shabana
>Sorry friend, Lana told me what she was wearing.
>I was only joking, come down, take a deep breath.
>lets play that game to calm you down

>*Foriz*

>*hi Foriz*
>*U scared me man*
>*When I get hold of Lana I will kill her.*
>*I thought u were in Morgate*
>*I m going home now*
>*What game?*
>*Shabs*

Foriz's patience run out and he had to tell her who he was really talking about.

>*My dear friend Shabana*
>*I think u should say hello to the girl I love so much before u go home*
>*she is on computer number eleven near the printer in B5*
>*have u seen her? What do u think of her?*
>*by the way in her computer there is a document minimized, tell her 2 open it and read it.*
>*the game is; in 1 minutes we will see how many emails u can send 2 me and how many I can send to u. And the email must have at least 4 words in it.*
>*Foriz de man*
>*Ps. Well, like I said, I m willing to take that risk and marry u, all u have to say is, yes I do.*

>*U BLOODY FOOL*
>*U ARE JUST A PERVERT N I MEAN IT*
>*I HATE U SO MUCH*
>*I m not ur friend any more*
>*I have seen her, u have zero percent chance of getting close to her.*
>*How dare u talk to me like that? I knew u were talking about me from the moment u told me what she was wearing.*
>*U r scaring me.*
>*So this is your idea, u r the biggest joker I have come across so far.*

>*Did u type that document when I went to check next door?*
>*how could u say that, u don't even know me.*
>*Why did u write that stupid message for?*
>*tell me exactly where r u?*
>*I know u r here but don't come near me.*
>*I m scared to look around.*
>*Ok, let's play your stupid game; I will beat u to it. When do I start?*
>*U r a stupid n crazy boy, I will tell my brother, he will come n kill u.*
>*Shabs*
>*Ps. So u have seen me then. This is why u want to marry me. am I correct?*

>*I m sorry friend*
>*I was just having fun in your expense*
>*lets hav a break n play the game den I'll reply 2 ur message*
>*we start de game in a minute, exactly at 4 pm ok.*
>*I will let u go first, soon as I receive ur next email I will start, ok.*

The game started.

>*YOU STUPID LITTLE IDIOT*
>*you cleaver girl, I love you*
>*you crazy boy with no brain*
>*You are a mental, go to mental hospital*
>*I love everything about you Shabana*
>*I hate everything about you*
>*I want 2 marry u*
>*I want to kill you*
>*Learn how to spell first*
>*Blackpool, Liverpool, u r most beautiful*
>*When did you become a poet, you stupid boy.*
>*I luv u from top to bottom, especially the middle*
>*roast, toast I love u the most*
>*Use your brain before you type*

>I love u from my heart
>I luv u from my brain
>You monkey I hate you
>u beauty I need u
>You mental go to hell
>Go back to primary school
>I want u to be my wife
>I am going to make u so happy when u become my wife
>I will never be your wife
>u dog n goru
>what happened, u r too slow
>I like your beautiful eyes
>u have 2 beautiful............
>I hate everything you have
>you need a new brain
>go and see a doctor
>u need a husband like me who will love u 24/7
>You cow, you dog
>You idiot, you planed this game to tell me all this rubbish
>you are a psychopath
>Last message wasn't four words
>I m going 2 get my brother and beat you up
>don't get your brother u just come and beat me up
>I m going to tell ur mum about u
>tell her u love me too and u gonna be my wife
>only 5 seconds left, I won
>shut up, I won, u cheated, u monkey, u planned it all in advance to get me.

That was Foriz's plan to tell her how much he liked her.

> Thanks for the compliments, I appreciate it friend.
>See I told u, she is heavenly beautiful, my dream woman.
>I always wanted a wife like her. If she becomes my wife I will be the happiest man in this world. I will not look at another girl again.
>Yes, I did type it when u went next door, that's why I sent u there.

>I know I am crazy but just for u. Say 'yes' and become my life and wife
>Foriz ur husband 2 to

>Listen u stupid idiot foga
>stop saying stupid things before u write anything think about what you're writing.
>U haven't met me and u r saying all sort of stupid things.
>U don't even know me and how can u say u love me.
>There is no chance of me being your wife and life, get it!
>Foriz tell me the truth, have you seen me?
>Reply quickly I need to go home soon.
>Shabs

>My future wife Shabana
>Yes I hav seen u before and I came 2day to see u.
>do you remember u went out once when Lana was here and I was outside the door talking on the mobile.
>do u remember some1 asked u for the time?
>yes darling that was me. Don't u wish I m ur man!
>Don't u think I am handsome!
>Foriz

>You are so sly
>I m not going 2 be ur future wife. Do u get it!
>I can't handle u. u r too much 4 me.
>I remember u, I was thinking why was that pervert looking at me like that hasn't he seen a girl before in his life.
>why did he ask me for time, when he had a mobile.
>I m going to kill u.
>It has been a long day, I m going home now and tell Lana everything about u and 2 keep away from u.
>Bye, good night.
>Shabana
>ps. u do look alright but not good enough to be my husband. Happy now! I want my husband to be much better looking then u.

>dear Shabana
>So what do u think of me?
>Do u fancy me?
>Would u like to be my wife?
>If u want to kill, first u hav 2 meet me then I would like u to kill me with ur beautiful hands, at least I will get to touch u.
>Shabana, just meet me in the canteen for few minutes before u go home
>I m sitting right behind u in the same room. Computer number 25
>I can see ur back from here.
>Foriz de clever Goru

>SHUT UP, SHUT UP YOU STUPID ANIMAL
>u talk too much non-sense.
>No, I don't fancy u and I will never fancy u.
>No, I don't want to be your wife?
>I rather die then become your wife.
>No, I don't meet boys.
>I m going home now, don't stop me or talk to me when I leave.
>Shabs
>ps. I want my husband to be much better looking then u. do you get that. Happy now!

>My dear email friend
>Please don't be upset
>Come on Shabana just few minutes, come n talk 2 me friend.
>Please don't say things like die. If u don't like me that fine.
>I m sorry about the stuff I told u, I was just winding u up, I know how can I love u, I don't even know u.
>If I wanted, I could hav come and said hello to u, as u know I can see u from where I m now but I hav respect 4 u
>Just come for 4 or 5 minutes, I know u told me u don't meet boys, but I m ur friend.
>Please please please please please please come
>Foriz

Spices of Brick Lane

Shabana felt that if she didn't talk to him, he might come and talk to her so it was best to meet him where no one else would notice.

>*Ok Foriz*
>>*This is de only time I m going 2 meet u, I will go 2 de canteen n 2 de corner where no one can see me.*
>>*Just five minutes only. Please don't look at me.*
>>*Ok*

>*Ok friend*
>*Thank u for meeting me*
>*U go and I will come after u.*
>*I won't look at u, I will look at ur feet.*
>*Bye for now*

Foriz's persistent nature worked and managed to arrange a meeting with Shabana. He was very excited to see her face to face. On the way to the canteen Shabana put her niqab on.

She sat on a chair, as he approached, she pulled her eyes and looked at him smiling and then hid her face with her hands. Foriz sat front of her and said, 'Hello Shabana, firstly I am very sorry what I wrote, please forgive me, I was just joking.'

'Ok, no problem.' She kept her hands on her face to cover her eyes and looked through her fingers.

'What would you like to drink?'

'I don't want anything. Can I go now please?'

'Please don't say that. I waited nearly a month to meet you, just seat for a few minutes then you can go, I promise I will not bite.'

Foriz left her for a few seconds and bought two soft drinks.

'Shabana please drink yaar.'

'I don't want a drink.'

'Please move your hands from your face, I won't do anything.'

'Ok, please don't look at my face.'

'I won't look at your face; I have seen it two hours ago.'

'You are so unbelievable.'

'Sorry, what am I supposed to do.'

'Can you look somewhere else please?'

'Come on Shabana do you have to wear your niqab now?'
'I always wear my niqab when I go out.'
'I understand but now you're inside so do you mind removing it please?'
'Yes I do mind.'
'Ok, well, as you know I have seen your face before.'
'That was cheating.'
'Please friend, remove your niqab.'
'No, I won't. You're going too far.'
'Sorry, anyway you have such a nice beauty sport on your face.'
'I didn't know you can see though the niqab.'
'Well I can, I have seen your beauty before.'
'How do you observe things so quickly?'
'Allah has given me the special eyes.'

Slowly she removed her hands from her face and opened the drink. Foriz was only able to see her eyes.

'It's already been five minutes, can I go now.'
'Please friend just a few minutes and then you can go.'
'Are you happy now that you have seen me?'
'I am not happy that you're not showing your face. Do you know that I have seen you the first day I emailed you, but I am happy that you met me now.'
'Why did you come and see me without my permission?'
'You told me you won't meet any boys so I thought I do a sly one and find out who you are.'
'Now I know why you were sending me all those messages and I thought you haven't seen me.'
'After all I am not that stupid.'
'Definitely not that stupid but still stupid enough to write so many stupid messages.'
'Did you like my idea of the girl I was in love with?'
'I believed you, I thought there was someone.'
'Are we friends now?'
'No, I can't be your friend.'
'Why not?'

'How can I be your friend, you are a boy.'

'I am sure we can be friend sand talk to each others and help each other out when ever in problems.'

'I don't what to be rude but I don't like mixing with boys. Can you stop looking at my face please?'

'I am not looking at your face, I am looking at a face that Allah has created and gave to you as a gift.'

'Very smart, where do you get these ideas from?'

'My stupid brain, so is this the last time we are meeting?'

'Yes, I would like it to be the last time and please don't talk to me if you see me in the computer room, I have relatives in the university. If they see me talking to a boy then they will tell my parents.'

'Fine, I will talk to you on the phone. Can I have your mobile number please?'

'What, Sorry Foriz, I can't give you that.'

'I don't want to be your friend like that.'

'I thought we were friends.'

'Yes, we are just email friends.'

'So what do I have to do to become more then an email friend?'

'You have to become a girl.' She laughed.

'No problem, it's your life and it's your decision.'

'I hope you understand my situation, I do like talking to you on the email. I was just having a bit of fun on the email, never thought it would get this far.'

'At least I have Lana to talk to; you two friends are so different.'

'I know, she changed a lot, she fancied you but you didn't fancy her. Why is that?'

'I know she did but I liked the other girl I told you about. Now I lost both of them.'

'Sorry to hear that, I am going home now and talk to you on the email.'

'Ok, thanks for meeting me Shabana, I hope to meet you again and again, everyday, you are such a nice and decent girl. You are one in a million.'

'Thanks for the compliments but you have to cut down on the excess stuff you say.'

Shabana was ready to leave. Foriz asked her if she wanted him to take her to the underground. She answered in the negative as she didn't want anyone to see her with him. Shabana went, left him with more desire, lust and affection.

In the evening Shabana called Lana and told her what had happened. Lana asked her if he seriously liked her or if he was having a laugh. She told her that she thought he was serious. Lana congratulated her and told her that she had the better man. Shabana told her, 'You stupid bitch I don't want a boy friend.'

'If you don't want him then give him to me.'

'You know what will happen if I get involved with boys.'

'It's part of life, get in or get out, I got in.'

'Help me man, how do I keep away from him?'

'Like you told me, don't talk to him for a few years.'

'I don't mind being his friend; he is kind of cute and smart.'

'You fucking bitch, you like him. I don't believe it, you're in love. Tell me what did he say to you?'

'I didn't say that, I just said he is kind person. He told me on the email he wanted me to be his wife.'

'Ow baby you're in love, I can see it in your eyes. Well, looks like he's serious, wife means your in business kut-ti.'

'Stop winding me up, I will tell him to get lost on the email.'

'Don't do that Shabana, you might regret, he chose you over me.'

'I think the only reason he chose me is because I wear a hijab.'

'Just ignore him for a few weeks and then we will see what happens, I know he will be on the phone to me soon.'

Foriz called Lana and told her how much he liked Shabana and needed her help. Lana asked him why he liked her; 'I think my mother will like her. She looks religious, very down to earth and family type of girl.'

'You are crazy man, leave her alone. She was on the phone to me crying and told me what you did to her.'

'Why did she cry? I didn't do anything to her.'

'You forced her to see you and have a drink with her; she is upset that you saw her face.'

'I am sure she told you I saw her in the first week but she didn't know that. And I didn't see her face as she refused to take her niqab off.'

'If you look at her once more I will take your eyes out, what ever happened that's past just leave her alone, she isn't interested in boy friend business.'

'I thought you were my friend but now I realised that you're not so, bye and when I get married to Shabana I will not invite you.'

'Yes I am your friend but I am her best friend.'

'Are you gonna help me.'

'I will try my best but she is a very different type of girl. She is a hijabi.'

'I know she is a hijabi. That's why I like her. So what do I have to do?'

'Why are you so interested in hijabi girls?'

'I guess I am born to like hijabi girls.'

'Give me a few days and I will talk to her.'

'I can't wait few days.'

'Shut up, you have to, you have no choice.'

'Tell her that I love her and I want to marry her please.'

'Shut up Foriz, I will do my best.'

'Ok, thanks.'

'Talk to you later.'

'Bye.'

In the next few weeks Foriz sent many emails to Shabana and apologised but she didn't reply. He also sent emails to Lana to help him out but she wasn't very helpful too. Foriz visited Moorgate to track her down but she hardly used the computers. Lana stopped answering his call too. Shabana became his mission; he decided not to give up.

Two weeks later Foriz received a call from Lana. She told him that Shabana was in the Moorgate library. Foriz went to the library and saw her by herself doing some work. He made a rose with a paper and asked a student to give it to her. He hid behind a shelf. On the rose he wrote how sorry he was. She read it and smiled which he captured. A few minutes later Foriz went to her desk and sat front of her. 'Hello Shabana.'

'Hello.'

Shabana looked at his face once then looked down at her work. She quickly looked at her bag and took out her niqab and wore it.

'How are you?'

'I am alright, how are you?'

'Not very good as you decided not to talk to me.'

'Foriz, I know you're here to talk to me, I don't want anyone to see me with you. Can we go to that quiet corner and talk? I have been very busy doing my assignments, I am sure you don't want me to fail.'

They moved to the quiet corner where most students didn't visit.

'Of course not, I want you to get first class degree.'

'Are you up to date with your course work?'

'Yea kind of, I have people working for me.'

'What, do you get others to do it for you?'

'I know a few people who gave me their assignment, all I have to do is change bits and bobs and it will be mine.'

'I am sorry I didn't email you because I wanted to keep away from you.'

'Please don't keep away from me, I promise I will never hurt you.'

'That's not the point; I don't want to hurt you.'

'You will not hurt me.'

'I was using the email just for fun and didn't know it would get this far and you know I never intended to meet you.'

'I know, but Shabana can we be friends at least?'

'It's not possible.'

'I told you before; I have relatives in this university if they see me with any boys they will tell my parents. And my father will kill me if he finds out.'

'Ok fine, be my friend on the email and meet me with Lana in Tower Hill.'

'On the email, don't write any silly messages. I will see what happens but I can't promise you anything.'

'Shabana please remove your niqab.'

'No. I can't.'

'Shabana will you meet me today after university for a coffee?'

'No, please don't ask me to meet you, I told you that was the last one.'

'Please friend, I haven't spoken to you for nearly two weeks, please meet me?'

'This is the problem; you say it so nicely and I find it difficult to say no.'

'Will you meet me then?'

'If I don't meet you, you won't go from here.'

'That's kind of right.'

'Ok, at 3.30pm in that canteen's corner and this is the last meeting.'

Foriz's persistency paid off and Shabana forgot some of the rules that were prescribed by her parents. She was in a dilemma, with one part of her brain she wanted to meet him and with the other part of the brain she wanted to ignore him.

Shabana went to the canteen at the scheduled time. Foriz was already there waiting for her. She sat on the inside chair where it was difficult for anyone to see her. She had her niqab on. He offered her drink to warm her up.

'Why are you smiling Shabana?'

'Am I not allowed to smile? And how do you know if I am smiling?'

'Of course you're allowed to smile; I can tell when you smile, when you smile you look more beautiful, I was asking for the reason behind your smile.'

'The reason is that you are a crazy person.'

'Thanks, every crazy person needs a mature friend like you.'

'Why don't you get a girl friend so you can spend time with her and leave me alone?'

'I have a girl friend sitting front of me.'

'Shut up, don't start again, I am not your girl friend, please get the facts correct.'

'Of course you are, you are a girl and you are my friend.'

'That's ok. I meant, why don't you get a girl friend that will go out with you and, you can spend time with her.'

'I am not interested. I am interested in a decent friend like you.'

'Stop bringing me into it, I don't want to be in your puzzle.'
'I have to bring you into it because you're my friend.'
'Whatever.'

Foriz just couldn't control himself from Shabana's appearance. He just wanted to talk to her about anything that came to his lips.

'Shabana, please remove your niqab?'
'Sorry I can't do that.
'Please friend.'
'I said no.'
'Shabana it has been two weeks and I haven't seen your face.'
'So what.'
'Come on friend, I thought we were friends.'
'Looking at my face is not good for your eyes.'
'Please Shabana remove the niqab.'
'Promise me you won't look at y face.'
'Ok, I will only look at your beauty sport.'

Shabana removed her niqab which allowed Foriz to take a full look at her face.

'Did you have any lessons today?'
'Yes, I missed one this morning thanks to you, but I asked Joynul to collect the notes.'
'You shouldn't have missed your lesson, I wasn't going anywhere. I will be here for three years.'
'I just wanted to meet you; my heart was thirsty for you.'
'You have to stop it; I don't want anyone to like me.'
'You should be please someone really likes you.'
'No, I don't want anyone to like me.'
'What's your ambition Shabana?
'I like to have a nice house, nice car and a good looking husband.'
'I can give you all that.'
'Shut up, you're not going to be my husband, full stop.'
'Why not?'
'There is no chance of that.'
'Why not.'
'I don't fancy you.'
'Why not.'

'I don't want to like you.'
'Why not.'
'Stop saying; why not, why not.'
'Please give me a chance, I know I am the man for you.'
'I don't think my mother and father will like you.'
'I will convince them.'
'I don't think people from your village get on well with people from our village.'
'So what if they don't get on well, long as we get on with each other what's the matter.'
'Stop it Foriz, I don't want anything to do with you. You keep away from me.'
'Don't be silly, don't you want a good looking husband like me.'
She laughed.
'No, I don't, I will take whoever my parents pick for me.'
'What would you do if they pick me?'
'I will tell them you're a nut case and mental and to reject you.'
'Look at me Shabana, and say you hate me.'
'I don't want to look at your horrible face and I don't hate you but I don't like you enough to be your girlfriend.'
'If you don't hate me then it means you like me.'
'Stop twisting what I say.'
'Tell me about your family Shabana?'
'I am not telling you anything.'
'Please Shabana.'
'My mother is a dangerous woman, if she sees me with a boy she will kill me. My father is a religious man and spends most of the time in the mosque, and I have brothers and sisters. How about you?'
'My mother is alright, she is quiet and does all the cooking. My father comes and goes to Bangladesh. He has another wife there and I have brothers and sisters doing their own bits.'
'How did you find out I was in the library?'
'I didn't, Lana told me.'
'She is a cow, she was with me, I told her not to tell you but she did. When I see her, I will kill her.'
'Good she told me, I am getting to see your beautiful face.'
'Have you not seen a beautiful girl before?'

'I have but no one unique like you.'

'There are so many beautiful girls in this university. Why don't you see them, harass them and leave me alone?'

'They don't have the magnetism that you possess.'

'What is it that I have and they don't have?'

'The looks, the hijab, the niqab, the personality, the smile, the skin colour, the lips, the beautiful beauty spot, the shape, the eyes and the body.'

'SHUT UP man, why do you say dirty things? You talk too much. If you say things like that then I will not talk to you again.'

'Sorry friend I can't help it.'

'You better get rid of the things you have in your dirty brain about me.'

'I can't do that. I like the things and images I have about you in my head.'

'I am going home now.'

'Please stay for a few more minutes.'

'No, I can't, I am going to be late.'

'Can I drop you off please?'

'No.'

'Please Shabana.'

'No, keep away from me.'

'Please Shabana.'

'Ok, once I have gone past the university's building on the right then you come and talk to me. I will go by bus.'

Shabana wasn't sure what to say. On the one hand she wanted to tell him to get lost. On the other hand she found someone who loved her so much and gave her so many compliments. In the bus he was reticent and didn't say anything silly to her as others were there. She offered him a chewing gum; probably it was for the company he gave her. Foriz ended up giving her a lift with the 25 bus up to Romford Road, Manor Park, close to her home.

Chapter Eleven

1999

Yasin had started university to learn business studies as expected by his father. He made his father very proud by attending an university. He asked his father if he could have a new PC as his old one was out of date. Sabbir wasn't going to say no to his son who had done well so far, and money wasn't a criteria. Yasin went to a superstore and bought the latest PC, and gave his old one to his nephew.

Sokina prepared Azima to go to Bangladesh as requested by her husband. Azima told her sisters in London that she didn't want to get married to any peasant or uneducated person, her husband must be educated. Her sisters and brothers told her that they would speak to their father and tell him to find an educated husband for her. If he didn't then she should say no to the marriage. 'How can I say no to father, he will get upset,' she said. Sabbir told her that if the groom wasn't educated or good looking then she should phone him, he would speak to father. Everyone in London wanted her to get married to an educated person. Sokina took presents for Rukshana and the step children as they were part of the family also she had to live with them in the same home.

Karim hired a large car and went to the Sylhet airport to pick them up. After haggling with the custom officers, Sokina and Azima managed to get out. Sokina arrived in the village with Azima; as usual expected proposals arrived from the day one. Azima took her honours qualification with her, and showed it to her father. He gave her a pretended smile to make her feel happy. But to him the qualification had no meaning. Azima told him that she had managed to get a job in a bank and she earned twenty thousand pounds a year. He couldn't believe that and asked her if she was joking. He still didn't believe that a girl can earn that much money. Karim asked his wife for confirmation and she told him that it was true. Karim was surprised that his daughter could earn so much money. One thing seemed different about Karim was that this time he told the relatives that he was looking for an educated boy for his daughter and no one else? Some of his relatives told him that though his daughter was educated, she would finally be a house wife. Karim had started to defend his daughter, 'Yes that is true but it will not look nice if I get my daughter married to an uneducated person. She worked hard and she is my only child that managed to get a degree, and I want the best for her.' Karim also mentioned that Sabbir told him that an educated groom will be able to get a good job in London. He won't have to work in a restaurant.

After a few days they managed to track down a distant relative's son who was doing a master degree in Maths and Computing in Dhaka. Through relative he was encouraged to propose to Azima's family and he did. The groom, Kawsar Ali, came to see Azima. He looked smart, he wore a shirt, tie and trousers, European hair style - no lungi. He looked better then Azima expected and was from a good family. Azima was happy with the way he looked. They met and saw each other for half an hour and spoke a few words. But some of Karim's close families tried to create problems. They were saying that he should get his daughter married to a nephew. Karim told everyone on their faces that no more close relatives; he had helped most of the close relatives.

Within two weeks they were married. Azima had all the appropriate documents with her. She went to Dhaka, Bangladesh's home office for her husband's visa. After looking at the documents the immigration officers gave Kawsar two years permit visa. He still had to complete his final MSc exam. He stayed in Bangladesh, Azima returned to London as she had to return to work.

Sabbir telephoned his father and asked him to make passports for his step brothers and sisters. Karim wasn't sure what Sabbir meant and how his Bangladeshi born children could come to London. Sabbir explained to his father that there was no problems. All of the children would be able to come to London because Karim was a British subject. Even though the children were from his second marriage. Karim hired a relative to do the running around to produce the passports. His relatives heard the news – the foreign word. One of Karim's poor cousin approached him and asked him to do a big favour by including his son with Karim's children. Due to Karim's nature he couldn't say no, he included an extra child in his application, like he did nearly thirty years ago.

Karim went to Dhaka to get entry visas for the children and his wife. The immigration rejected his wife because he already had a wife in London. Karim told the officers that he wanted to take his second wife to London. They told him that it was against the British law; he could not have more then one wife in London. He told them that he was allowed to have four wives. The officers told him that he maybe allowed four wives in Bangladesh but not in England. Karim also told the officers that he known many Bengali men had already taken their second wife to London. How had they been allowed? The immigration officers told him the law had changed. They also rejected the child that wasn't his. The child did not resemble his other children. The immigration officers told Karim that the child didn't look like his, but he denied the accusation.

A few weeks later two immigration officers came to the village to investigate Karim's family. All the village people told the officers that Karim only had four children and the extra child wasn't his, the child was his cousin's. Karim told his cousin that the law had changed; the white people had learnt now that Bengali people took too many others' children, it wasn't the same as thirty years ago, when it was easy no checking, just going.

Gozafor Miah became crazy with excitement. His beloved cricket team was coming to England. The Bangladesh cricket team had qualified for the cricket world cup for the first time. He bought sweets for everyone in the restaurant to celebrate Bangladesh's qualification. Through out the evening and night he spoke about cricket like a crazy fan. In Bangladesh four people were killed celebrating the qualification on the street. Can you imagine how many would die if they won the world cup!

Gozafor Miah wanted to go and watch his team play. He didn't know how to get a ticket or how to go to the matches as he didn't speak good English. He spoke to Sabbir to help him out. Sabbir managed to get two tickets and took Gozafor Miah to a match. Gozafor Miah bought Bangladesh's cricket kit and wore it on the match day. Bangladesh didn't do too well in the world cup but they defeated Pakistan in a group match, which made Gozafor Miah ecstatic. For Gozafor Miah beating Pakistan was like winning the world cup. He was singing continuously, we beat Pakistan for a few days, but didn't realise it could have been fixed, which was under investigation later on. Good thing Bangladesh didn't' win the world cup. If they had, thousands of people could have been killed in celebration in Bangladesh.

―

Foriz and Joynul waited for the first Valentine's Day to approach. Firstly they planned what present they should give to impress the girls they love. Then they went to Green Street, the gold market and bought a gold bracelet each. They also bought big Valentine's cards and wrote all sorts of love messages which they had stolen from friends and the Internet. Foriz and Joynul went to Moorgate to give the presents to their prospective Love. Lana promised Foriz that she would bring Shabana with her. They sat in the basement where the canteen was and chatted for a long time. Joynul gave his presents to Lana. She loved it with great smile and excitement. They left to go to watch a movie to celebrate the day. Foriz and Shabana stayed in the canteen as she refused to go to a cinema. 'How was your day Shabana?'

'Not too bad, I managed to do a lot of research for one of my assignments, how about you?'

'Ok, I didn't get much done as I was distracted by a friend.'

'You should keep your friends away when learning because that could make a big difference if you fail.'

'I know, but with some friends it is so difficult to keep them away because if your not with them then one's brain stops functioning.'

'Then it must be a friend that you like a lot.'

'Maybe.'

'I suppose you probably have to work hard as you have to complete many assignments.'

'Yes I have to as the course work and the exams are very important, I bet you don't have to do any hard work as it's your first year.'

'I have to, I don't want to fail and I want to get a good result.'

'I am sure you will do well, you look focused.'

'No point of looking focused if one doesn't put the effort into the work.'

'Correct, you talk like a teacher, I should come to you for motivation.'

'You are with me now, what kind of motivation do you need mister? You look mature and sharp enough to motivate yourself.'

'No, I am finding it very difficult at the moment.'

'So what's the problem?'

'It a friend that keeps on brothering my thinking.'

'Is it a boy or a girl?' She had a feeling it was her.

'Of course it's a girl.'

'Is she poking your brain with a pin?'

'Something like that, she keeps on coming in my way almost all the time since I met her.'

'She must be a dangerous girl. You need to keep away from her or you could be a big loser.'

'I don't want to keep away from her; I like to have her so she won't distract me.'

'Well, if she is something that you can buy then why not but I am sure it's not that simple.'

'That's the problem; one can't buy certain things in life.'

'You're correct, bear that in mind, money can't buy everything.'

'I am sure there is nothing wrong with trying to achieve it.'

'Nothing wrong but there are things you know are very very difficult to achieve, like if I wanted to marry a white man.'

'What's wrong with that?'
'I am sure you know my father will first kill me.'
'How about if it is a Bengali man that you like?'
'I am sure he will kill the Bengali man and maybe not kill me but disown me.'
'You have a very strict family.'
'I do, I suppose.'
'I like to know more about your family, I think I can write a book.'
'I am sure you can, if you do then you must give me fifty percent for the story line.'
He laughed and said, 'You must become a business woman.'
'I have to go now, I don't want to be late home other wise I have to give my father an interview why I am late.'
'Before you go, can you please close your eyes for ten seconds?'
'No, I can't do that.'
'Why not?'
'Incase you touch me.'
'I won't do that, trust me.'
'Ok, I close my eyes, you hurry up.'
Foriz took out the present from his bag and displayed it on the table.
'Open your eyes Shabana.'
She opened her eyes and looked at the beautiful gold bracelet. She knew it was for her. She paused for a few seconds.
'Very beautiful gold chain, who is it for?'

Shabana wanted to say if the present was for his girl friend but decided not to put him on the spot.

'It's for a close friend.'
'I am sure she will like it.'
'If she likes it then I suggest you should take it.'

Shabana found the situation very embarrassing and wasn't sure what to say.

'I can't take someone else's presents.'
'Look at me Shabana?'
She looked at him.
'The present is for you!'
'I hope you are not serious!'
She said with a serious face.
'I am serious. It is for you.'
'Why would you want to buy something like that for me, are you over loaded with money?'
'I only buy something nice for a beautiful good friend.'
'I can't take this Foriz.'
'Why not?'
'I can't accept a present like that from a friend, it's too much. I don't want to send the wrong message.'
'Don't be silly, you have to take it or I will be very upset. You won't be sending out any message as you don't have my mobile number, unless you want my number now.'

Shabana didn't want to take the present. She felt that if she took it then he would think that she liked him. She didn't want to give him that impression. At the same time she wanted to be his friend and she wanted to listen to the compliment he gave her. Girls just like compliments, don't they?

'Ok, I take it as a friend that's all and from now on I don't want you to buy me anything else.'
She gave him a smile and thanked him with a soft tone.
'Can I put it on for you?'
'No, no chance, you are going too far, you better stop this nonsense or I won't meet you ever again.'
'Sorry. Can you put it on please?'
Shabana paused and looked at his eyes.
'Close your eyes so I can put it on.'
'Let me watch please.'
'Don't look at me, look that way.'
Shabana put the gold chain on as he watched her do so.

'You look so beautiful Shabana, I hope you stay beautiful like that.'
'Did I not look beautiful without it?'
'Of course you did but now you look amazingly awesome.'
'Thank you.'
'You are welcome in my house.'
'I am off now.'
'Few more minutes please then you can go.'
'Why?'
'Just want to look at your beautiful face for a few more minutes.'
'No, you are making me do so many sins.'
'Please bondhu.'
'Only two minutes.'
'Five minutes please.'
'Ok, look at my feet not my face.'

They laughed simultaneously. Foriz scanned at her slowly and observed her deeply in his long term memory. She tried her best to look away and ignore him. But inside her she was enjoying the affection he was showing her.

'Ok, let's go, I will take you home.'
'I don't want you to come with me.'
'Why not.'
'I don't trust you.'
'You are getting too many funny ideas.'
'Don't be silly, lets go.'
'Ok.'

From Moorgate they walked to the Aldgate bus stop, caught a 25 bus which took them near her house. He dropped her off to Romford Road, end of Third Avenue. They waved good bye to each others then he went home.

In the evening Shabana called her best friend Lana to tell her what had happened. Shabana said, 'Lana guess what happened today.'
'Did he give you a kiss?'
'No chance of that you know.'

'You tell me what happened?'
'He gave me a present.'
'So what, Joynul gave me a present too?'
'There is a difference, guess what he gave me?'
'Perfume, red roses.'
'No, he gave me a gold chain.'
'No way, he must be crazy about you.'
'That's the main problem; I never wanted that to happen.'
'Shut up you bitch, that's good, you've got a lover.'
'I don't want a lover; you know that, it's your fault.'
'He is good looking and sounds decent, I wouldn't let him go, if you don't want him then let me have him.'
'How can I have him, you know my problems.'
'Just don't respond to him, he will get it that you're not interested.'
'What am I going to do with the gold chain, it's quite big, I told him I didn't want it but he forced me to keep it, now I got it, he will think that I like him.'
'That's true though you do like him.'
'How do I tell him I can't love him?'
'You have to find a way to love him.'
'How do I do that?'
'Just relax now and we will see what happens next.'
'Thanks, he wanted to put the chain on me.'
'Did you let him?'
'No way, I told him there was no chance of that.'
'His so sweet, sweeter then Joynul.'
'I know, he is changing me.'
'Don't let him go.'
'When I put the chain on, he told me I looked so beautiful.'
'Oo you bitch he loves you from his heart.'
Shabana wanted to talk about him non-stop. Lana realised Shabana was in love with Foriz too.

Foriz wanted to meet Shabana when ever it was possible. But she decided to meet him less as she felt things were getting out of hand. There were times he waited for her on the bus top near Aldgate station. She arrived from Moorgate and he surprised her. In the bus they chatted on the way home. He took her up to the nearest bus stop to her home, then he went home. Shabana was confused. She wasn't sure what to do or how to solve the love problem. He was in love with her and she knew it. To Foriz, Shabana was the nearest to the complete girl he found that he was looking for, he couldn't let her go. He had waited for a girl like Shabana to arrive in his life for many years. Foriz felt Shabana was made for him, she was written in his Takdir.

A nail bomb went off in the heart of the Brick Lane, which injured many Bengali people. Luckily no one died. The Bangladeshi people were shocked to see the new methods of racist attacks against them in this age. It was thought that the BNP was behind the bombing. This racist people didn't realise that they couldn't drive the Bangladeshi from there just by bombing. This area belonged to immigrants for many centuries and the Bangladeshis were here to establish themselves, make money like the Jews before they made a move. If there's one lesson the racist people hadn't learned from history, was that centuries of attacks against the Irish, Huguenots, Jews and now Bangladeshis had not driven people away. It just made people stronger and together.

Samir had divorced his wife because he didn't like the life style with his wife. He wanted to eat home cooked curries which she couldn't prepare. Sokina quickly took him back to Bangladesh to get him married. The family wanted to get him married as soon as possible to a Bengali girl before he found another English wife. Even though he was married and over thirty years old, it wasn't a problem to find him a young wife. Karim found a seventeen year old bride for Samir. The bride's parents knew he was married and of his age but they were just pleased to get their daughter married to a Londoni man.

Kolim and Priya's first child was born. They were so happy to have their first child. They had waited over two decades to have a child. Their life became complete as they had a child that they were desperate for. They felt their life was incomplete without a child. Kolim and Priya felt Allah had listened to their prayers and had given them a child after all. One of the reason for her not getting pregnant previously could be that her husband was old and she probably never enjoyed it when he planted the seeds. They used the hospital facilities like a legal citizen of this country. No questions were asked by the health authority. One could find it diabolical that 'illegal' people used hospital facilities and the government didn't charge them for it.

Foriz found out from Lana that it was Shabana's nineteenth birthday. He didn't understand how to stop loving Shabana even thought he knew there were so many obstacles. Foriz decided to buy something special to show to her that he loved her. Once again he went to Green Street to buy her a present and he invited Lana to come and help him choose a present that Shabana would like. They visited many gold shops to choose the present. Foriz wanted something uniquely beautiful. This time he bought a pair of gold bangles.

Foriz tried to arrange a meeting with Shabana. She told him that she was too busy to meet him as she wanted to avoid him much as she could. She knew that he was crazy about her. He didn't give up and persuaded her to meet him. Foriz hired Lana to put in a word to Shabana to meet him. After many emails and Lana's persuasion she decided to meet him as usual in Moorgate's canteen. This time she invited Lana with her, she didn't want him to say anything embarrassing to her. After half an hour Lana left with Joynul. Shabana had no choice but to talk to him and spend some time with him.

'Shabana, why do you avoid me so much?'

'I have been busy and I have to avoid you as you're bit crazy.'

'Is it my fault that I am crazy?'

'Some of it is your fault, have you seen a doctor yet?'

'I have a doctor seating front of me and this doctor knows all the prognoses and the medicine I need, but doesn't give me anything.'

'For your information some doctors are not allowed to sell medicine, they don't have the authority.'
'I am sure if this doctor wants then she can help me but this doctor's heart is like a stone that doesn't have any feeling.'
'Some doctor's 'affection part' of the heart is taken away by others.'
'I am sure if they work at it they can get it back, but they must try.'
'What ever. Have you found a girl friend yet?'
'No, not interested in girl friend business. Have you found a boy friend yet?'
'I am sure you know that I don't want a boy friend.'
'Have you found a husband yet then?'
'No, I am not looking for a husband that will be my parents' job.'
'Have you got the time?'
'Yes, it's four o'clock.'
'I forgot, what's today's date?'
'Check it on your watch? I am sure you know today's date.'
'Ow yea I just remembered.'
'Good.'
'Shabana, will you close your eyes for ten seconds?'
'No. Why?'

She knew why he wanted her to close her eyes. She had experienced it before.

'Please Shabana.'
'I don't want to incase you touch me.'
'You should know better, I would never do that without your permission.'
'I don't feel comfortable closing my eyes.'
'Please bhondu, don't be silly.'
'Do I have to?'
'Yes please.'
'Ok, I give you five seconds.'

Shabana closed her eyes. Foriz took out the presents and left it in front of her on the table. He asked her to open her eyes. She looked at the present, looked at his face, gave him a dirty look. 'This is your birthday present,' said Foriz.

'Why do you spend your money like that? I will not take these present.'

'It's not for you, it's for my friend Shabana.'

'Why are you doing this?'

'I don't have anything else to do, I am unemployed.'

'Get a job then.'

'I already have a part time job.'

'You don't understand what you're doing. You still have a child's brain. You've been watching too may Indian films.'

'Can I put them on for you?'

'No, no, I am not going to put them on.'

'Can you put it on please?'

'If I say no, then you will say please then I have to put it on.'

He watched her as she put the gold bangles on. Then she displayed her hands on the table for him to observe. Shabana was in two minds again. To love or not to love that was the question running through in her head. She was differently enjoying the attention Foriz gave her.

'You look so beautiful with them Shabana. I hope my wife looks beautiful like you.'

'Does that mean I didn't look beautiful without them? You should keep them for your wife.'

'Don't worry there are plenty more in the shop.'

'I can't except presents like these. I will be sending wrong message to you.'

'Please do, I am giving you because you're worth it.'

'How am I going to take it home? They are too big and where will I keep them?'

'Keep them where you kept the other presents'

'I have got the other one with me, would you like to see?'

'I don't believe you.'

'Close your eyes for thirty seconds and I will get it out.'

'I won't close my eyes.'
'Why not?'
'Incase you kiss me.'
'Dream on, you are the last man I would kiss.'
'Am I that ugly?'
'I didn't say that.'

Foriz closed his eyes, she pulled it out from her bag and put it on. Foriz had the feeling he was getting close to her day by day. Shabana had started to melt slowly like butter. Then she told Foriz to open his eyes.

'How do I look?'
'You look so amazing. I should thank Allah for creating someone like you.'
'Thank you.'
'You look like a bride ready to go to your husband's house.'
'I don't think so, it's all in your dirty head, you don't think about the practical side of it.'
'I am willing to go through anything to achieve you.'
'Stop it now. Foriz you are changing me and my way of life.'
'I don't want to change you please stay the way you are.'
'I meant you are getting too close to me and I think that's dangerous.'
'I know I am getting close to you and that's what I want to do.'
'I think your ideas will get you and me in big trouble.'
'Will you let me take a picture of you wearing the gold?'
'I am sure you know the answer. No.'
'I have to go now.'
'Please stay for a few more minutes, let me look at you, I might not see you for another few weeks as you might decide to hide away from me.'
'Looking at me is not good for your heart, you seriously need to think about this situation you're in and you put me in.'
'Promise me you will meet me at least once a week?'
'No, I don't want to meet you again.'
'Please bhondu, don't say that.'

'It is not right for me to meet you.'
'Come on bhondu you know I like meeting you.'
'I will see what I can do.'

Shabana was taking the bangles off. Foriz asked her if he could take them off for her. She told him that she didn't want him to touch her. They walked to the bus stop, went into a 25 bus and chatted to each other until they reach the last stop. In their conversation she told him that he was crazy and he told her that it was because of her.

Later on Shabana called Lana and updated her about the presents. Lana told her that she should be very pleased that someone was crazy about her. She wanted to know how she could face her parents. Lana told her that she doesn't have to, all she needed to do was run away with him, get married and live with him. She didn't like that idea. Shabana was in a dilemma, on the one hand she had her parents and on the other hand a lover who was crazy about her and willing to do almost anything to win her.

The restaurant competition in Brick Lane was irritating Sabbir. He constantly had to think about new ways of advertising, and getting to the customers first. He produced a special offer leaflet. Employed a person to distribute the special leaflet outside the Aldgate station from 5.30 pm. He felt that if he got to the customers first then he will have good chance that the customer would come to his restaurant. More restaurants were opening by the months, at the same time more customers were flowing into Brick Lane. Every new restaurant tried to create contemporary interface. But the menu stayed very similar to each others. The only difference was some restaurants had their own special curries and designed the menu with a different format.

Sabbir and Azima went to the Heathrow airport to welcome Kawsar. The immigration officers asked Kawsar a few questions then let him enter. Kawsar looked smart with shirt, tie, suit and didn't look like a freshi which was a good news to Azima. She wanted him to look smart as relatives would come and visit him. His luggage was checked before he collected it – no questions were asked, no argument, very unlike Bangladesh airport. He came to Sabbir's home; other relatives came, visited him and gave him presents.

Azima already decided with her family, that's he wasn't going to work in a restaurant like the other sisters' husband. Kawsar spoke fairly good English but his accent was different. Azima took him to a local college and enrolled him to an English class to improve his English. His qualification had value but not the same value as in Bangladesh.

Azima was earning good money and she wanted to buy a house. Sabbir helped her out with the a deposit. She bought a house near Sabbir's house so it was easy for her to travel. She provided pocked money for Kawsar who continued to study a few evenings. Kawsar complained to her that he didn't like taking money from her, and he wanted to earn his own pocket money.

Chapter Twelve

2000

If one walked through Brick Lane in 2000 would have just seen Bangladeshi restaurants with different names and contemporary style. What a transformation it had had over the past thirty years. The Bangladeshi had put their stamp on Brick Lane with curry.

Kawsar spoke to Sabbir for a part time job in his restaurant. Without any hesitation Sabbir offered a part time job to Kawsar so he could earn some pocked money and get some work experience in London. Azima didn't want her husband to work in a restaurant. People would say what was the point of getting married to an educated man, if he was working in a restaurant. Sabbir told her not to worry, once he became good at English then he would get a good job, he would improve his English if he worked as a waiter. At the same time he would feel good as he would be earning some money rather then relying on her. Kawsar also needed to pay tax to show that he was able to support himself when he needed to reapply for a visa in three years time. She agreed to let him work, mainly due to tax payment and visa purposes. Azima took him out to Gallion's Reach shopping centre in Becton to buy him the restaurant's uniform. She gave him a tour of the shopping center too.

Sabbir's restaurant business was doing very well. He was making more and more profit. The businesses were booming in Brick Lane. Sabbir opened another restaurant with his relatives. The new restaurant cost them one hundred thousand pounds to complete. They made sure it had contemporary design and mouthwatering look. They used Sabbir's restaurant's menu with some changes, such as, layout, colour and a few words as most of the items were the same.

Gozafor Miah managed to produce a cricket team with other restaurant workers. Cricket run through his blood circulation twenty four seven. He invited some of his friends who worked in the other restaurants, and asked them to bring more players. It was good news for Gozafor Miah that more restaurants had opened as he managed to find more players. Others played according to Gozafor Miah's rules. He didn't even know some of the rules himself. Real cricket ball was too hard, they used a tennis ball instead. Some of the players went to the park just to entertain Gozafor Miah and make him laugh. Gozafor Miah took betel nuts and paan to the park and offered them to others for taking parts. Eating paan through out the day is a habit of some Bengalis.

One lunch time a Bengali girl by the name of Sultana came to Sabbir's restaurant. She asked Sabbir if there was any vacancy. Sabbir was surprised as it was the first time a Bengali girl had came for a restaurant job. He asked her to sit down and offered her a drink. She didn't want a drink but out of politeness he prepared a soft drink for her. He wanted to find out more about her and the causes why she was looking for a restaurant job. Even though he didn't have a vacancy and he never employed a Bengali female, he asked her what kind of experience she had and what position she would like to work in. She told him that she had some cooking experience that she picked up from her mother and she spoke good English so she could work as a waiter and she was keen to learn. He asked her what part of Bangladesh and London she was from. She was a Sylheti and lived in Ilford, but left home due to many problems. She now lived on her own. Sabbir felt that there must have been some kind of serious problem at her home.

He had a few other ideas about how he may be able to benefit from her. Sabbir told her to stay seated while he went to speak to the boss in the kitchen.

He spoke to Gozafor Miah and told him about her. They discussed the risk, such, as if she was a thief or a business girl it would be embarrassing if local people found out. But they also spoke about the other benefit that they had in mind. And they concluded that they will give her a part-time job as a waitress and assess her suitability.

A few days later they received information that she was a drug addict. There were times she took breaks during work and they thought it was because she was taking drug while working. She needed money to feed her addiction. They felt that she had stolen some tips from the customers but didn't have any concrete evidence. Waiters were not allowed to keep the tips. It went to the restaurant. Sabbir felt that he had to make a decision whether to keep her or whether to see if she would agree to his plan or not. He didn't want to ask her directly as if anything happened the blame will come to him. He hired his cousin, Jamal to come to his restaurant as a visitor and told him about his plan for this girl. Jamal came to the restaurant a few times to make her notice him, and allow her to familiarize herself with him. Then he could talk to her freely. From time to time late night Jamal delivered Sabbir's restaurant's customers home where he never paid any tax on his earning. According to Sabbir Jamal knew how to scam the government like no one else.

A few days later as planed with Sabbir, Jamal came to the restaurant and asked Sultana to sit down with him in the restaurant table number one. All the other staff were told about the plan. Jamal said to her, 'I like to ask you one or two questions if you don't mind.'

'No problem you can ask me many questions as you like as long as the boss don't mind.'

'Boss won't mind he is my friend.'

'If you are illegal don't ask me to marry you.'

'No, I am not gonna ask you that.'

'Now I know why you have been around the restaurant a lot lately.'

'Sultana, I like you to earn a lot of money and I got this big plan for you.'

'Do you want me to be a prostitute?'

'No, ow no, I am not like that.'

'So what's the big plan than.'

'Before I say it, I just want to say, please don't scream just think about it.'

'Ok.'

'There are two options if you like; one is here in London and one in Bangladesh.'

'I got that.'

'Ok, you ready.'

'Yes.'

'It is five thousand pounds for here and ten thousand pounds if it's in Bangladesh.'

'Just tell me what it is?'

'All you need to do is, if you can that is, I have a cousin brother and he needs a passport.'

'You want me to get married to him.'

'I haven't finished yet.'

'Gone then.'

'All you have to do is just register for marriage and that's all you have to do. You don't have to live with him.'

'And you will give me five thousand pounds for that.'

'Yes, but you have to wait a few years for him to get a permanent visa.'

'What is the other option?'

'If you go to Bangladesh and get married to another cousin brother then you will get ten grand plus free ticket and stay, all you have to do is take some wedding picture with him and there will be a fake video for the immigration to see and once you're in England we will do all the paper work, but you will only be paid once he is here.'

'I see.'

'So think about it, you can earn a lot of easy money. Here is my number.'

'Ok, I will think about it.'

'Another thing if you have any friends who are willing to do this kind of job then let me know. I have lots of customers.'

'Ok.'

Spices of Brick Lane

'Thank you for listening Sultana and I hope to hear good news from you.'

Sultana took few days to decide what to do. She spoke to her friends and asked them for their advice. One problem was that she couldn't get married to a real husband until the dodgy marriage was over and that could take up to three to four years. She needed money to serve her drug addiction. She phoned Jamal to meet up. Sultana told Jamal that she was willing to get married here in London but she wanted ten grand for that. Also, she needed some advance payment. He told her that he cannot pay more then five grand. She told him that she also had a friend who was willing to go to Bangladesh but wanted fifteen grand. Jamal told her to give her friend his mobile number and he would negotiate if she was serious about it. After some negotiation and haggling they agreed on six grand. Jamal told her that she will get five hundred after their court marriage and the rest when the client gets the residency visa. Sabbir wasn't interested in making any money from this deal. All he was interested was to get a visa for his village cousin - Yahya. Yahya's father sold his land to send him to London. Yahyah had travelled through many countries and risked his life to get in to London.

The dodgy marriage took place and it was registered, and the paper work had started rolling. Only a few of the relatives were invited and were told about Yahyah's wedding as they didn't want people to know about the scam. They decided that if he got the visa then they would inform others.

Sultana's friend Shakira called Jamal and met up with him. She said that she was willing to go to Bangladesh but she needed fifteen grand for that journey. Jamal told her that was too much because everything was free and she would get ten grand tax free, the government won't touch a penny. They agreed on twelve grand. Jamal and Sabbir spoke to Sahim in Sylhet and informed him to find out which close relative was willing to pay close to twenty grand to get to London.

A few days later Sahim called and told Sabbir that he had found many relatives who were ready with their money on the table. She was offered to Belal, the closest relative who was willing to pay the asking price.

Shakira went to Bangladesh with Jamal to get married to Bilal. Sabbir and Jamal prepared most of the dodgy documents, such as payslips showing good income and a house with enough space to bring her husband. When outsiders saw Shakira in Jamal's house they thought it was his new wife and his family was hiding her. In Jamal's house they couldn't believe how a girl could do something like this for money. They didn't seem to understand people could have so many problems and problems made them do unbelievable things. If they had a TV they would have been able to see how people blow themselves up in Palestine. It was a wedding in a house which they decorated cheaply and invited fake people from the village and told them to come for free meal. They filmed it and took pictures for the immigration purposes. A man was hired who dressed like an Imam, read some Arabic sentences for the video camera, and they said 'Kobul' to each other. Obviously Bilal wasn't allowed to sleep with her. The English translation of the Bengali marriage certification was produced. In her marriage certificate fake parents' names were given.

Shakira went to the Bangladesh embassy in Dhaka for Bilal's visa. She took all the relevant documents with her. The immigration officers asked them a few questions which they answer. After a few hours of interviewing Bilal was given the visa. They returned to London. She was paid most of her money and the rest to be paid once he had a permanent stay visa. Bilal's father paid the money by selling his land. There have been thousands of bogus marriages in England. People from all over the world were paying British woman money for bogus marriages. Once it was reported a lady had married seven times in different registration offices and charged two thousand pounds each.

Sabbir's family bought another house in Ilford, Essex. A large four-bed roomed house with two reception rooms, two toilets and a large garden. They wanted to invest the money in London rather then Bangladesh like they used to do before. Their intention was that if Upton Park got too congested then they would move there. They rented out the house through an agent. The rent didn't cover the mortgage. Sabbir had to pay a little bit extra to cover the mortgage. Sabbir hoped if the house price goes up then they could make some profit from the house in the future.

Sokina's cousin's who was seriously ill with cancer called from the village for financial help, who didn't have enough money to go to Sylhet town for treatment. Sokina told her cousin that she will try her best to collect much as she can and send it to her as soon as possible. In the evening Sokina made calls to her sisters, daughters and other relatives and informed them of the news and collected three hundred pounds. Sokina asked Sabbir to send the money back home to her cousin. She became the money collector for the poor relatives. She liked doing charity work and it kept her busy.

Lana and Joynul went to a local cinema for personal entertainment and enjoyment. Joynul allowed her to choose what movie to watch. They bought the tickets and some pop-corns and went into the cinema hall. While they watched the movie they also watched each other physically. There was a third uninvited guest who watched them without their consent. As they came of the cinema hall the third person was waiting for them outside with his mates pretending that he hadn't notice them before and said, 'Hello Lana.' 'Hello, I got to go now, bye,' she replied and vanished with Joynul. She was shocked to see him. He was Lana's cousin – Liakot. Lana knew that she was in trouble. Liakot had tried to go out with her since she was thirteen, but she had refused him. Lana asked Joynul what to do as she knew Liakot would grass her up. The only solution he had was that she should tell her parents that she was in love with him and that they would get married once they finished university. She knew that would get her into more trouble and she may end up with an unrecognizable face.

Lana had no choice but return to home not sure of what was going to happen to her. She tried to act normal. She observed that her parents behaved same as before, they didn't say anything to her. She assumed that Liakot hadn't grassed her up. Lana called Shabana to tell her what had happened, and wanted advice. The door bell rang. Her old man opened the door. Lana heard, 'Ass-salaamu aaleykum uncle,' a male voice said. She stopped the talking with Shabana. Lana realised Liakot had arrived, and she had started to panic. She came down to the ground floor to hear what he was talking about. Her father and Liakot sat in the living room chatting about family matters and Bangladesh. She came in and gave her salaam and asked Liakot how many sugars he liked for his tea, 'One spoon please.' Lana made the teas and delivered it with biscuits. She left the door a bit open so she could hear them talk. Lana waited outside pretending to tidy the shoe shelf. Liakot asked his uncle to pray for him as he was about to open a new restaurant in Brick Lane with his friends. The old man told Liakot to wait as he went out to do one of the daily prayers.

Lana took the advantage of the situation, and went in to the room to speak to Liakot. She asked him if he was going to tell on her or not. He told her that he didn't want to grass her up but his going to think about it. Lana insisted that he gives her the answer so she knows where she stood. Liakot told her that if she goes out with him then he won't grass her up. She felt like calling him a bastard but she restrained herself. Lana told him that she liked her boy friend and wanted to marry him. Liakot told her that he had liked her for many many years and wanted to marry her too. She wanted to be polite to him and told him that she didn't have the opportunity to get to know him to like him. They knew the old man was going to return soon and swapped their mobile numbers, they decided to talk later.

Lana went in to her room, cried and called Joynul. She told him what happened and how Liakot was trying to back-mail her. He told her to meet Liakot and then he would beat the shit out of him. She didn't think that was a wise idea. Lana called Shabana but she didn't have any answers to her problems. Shabana told her that she had advised her not to go public places with him. Lana panicked even more, not certain what would happen next. She ended up having sleep less nights of many night mares.

Next day Lana called Liakot as she wanted to end the mess. They met up in the library near her house on the Romford Road. She told him categorically that she liked Joynul and wanted to get married to him. But he refused to listen or understand her situation. Liakot wanted her to dump her boyfriend and go out with him, and get married to him. Lana told him, if he loved her then he would want happiness for her and leave her alone. She never liked him because he worked in a restaurant and she always wanted an educated husband. At the end of their meeting nothing had changed. He told her that he will think about it. She told him, 'I hope you'll make the right decision.'

Liakot called Lana's father and told him what had happened with extra 'ingredients' to spice it up. When Lana came home, her father beat her up with a cooking pan. He wanted to know what she was doing with the boys on Mile End Road. She told him that she was with her girl friends but the boys were trying to talk to them. The old man said that this was the reason he didn't want her to go to university because he had a feeling she would mix with boys. He said to her, 'Number one you shouldn't have gone to cinema', 'number two you shouldn't have spoken to any boys and number three you should have worn your niqab. He also took her mobile to investigate if she had any boys' number. Liakot told him to check her mobile. Lana told her father that she was with Shabana and to Shabana about it. He told her that she couldn't go to university anymore. She had to stay home and help her mother with cooking and he would find a suitable boy for her and get her married as soon as possible. She ended up with bruises on her head and body, unable to move for a few days and unable to contact anyone. Her mother didn't show any remorse at all.

Joynul was worried as he couldn't get in touch with her. He knew that she was in trouble. He contacted Foriz and asked him for advice. He told him to contact the police and tell them that she's gone missing or her father probably killed her. On a serious note, Foriz told him that if he contacted the police then the father would know that boys were involved in it. They came up with plan B to get Shabana involved in it. Foriz contacted his love – Shabana and asked her to visit Lana, which Shabana did. Shabana contacted the police and told them what she had witnessed. The 'coppers' gave the old man a visit and arrested him. Lana didn't make any formal complaint. The police released her father.

The old man looked through the mobile's data storage file and found girls' names and numbers also Liakot's digits. He called the numbers, he had the feeling she may have had given her boy friend a girl's name in order to deceive him. From his investigation he concluded that there were no boy friends' numbers on her mobile. Lana knew that if Liakot grass her up her father would take her mobile. She had two sim cards. The old man wasn't sure who to believe. Lana begged her father to let her finish her university. She only had a few more months left to finish her exams. Her father decided to give her the last chance and told her that if he hears once more that she is near a boy then he would kill her. She promised him that she wouldn't go near anyone and if any boys spoke to her then she would let him know.

At the beginning of July Karim telephoned his wife in London and informed them that Sabbir grandfather wasn't well and he might pass away soon. The school holiday for the children was three weeks away. Sabbir thought that it would be best if the whole family went. Everyone would get to see his grandfather also make use of the summer holidays too. Sabbir contacted Badol Miah and he managed to get urgent flights for the family. Sabbir really wanted to see his grandfather for the last time.

Sabbir's grandfather was very happy to see them. Motlib hugged Sabbir and told him that soon he would leave this world, and Sabbir should pray for him. Some how the family worked out that Motlib had hit well over a century for his age. There was no record of his age. It wasn't necessary in the village as no one ever needed to produce one unless if they were going abroad, and if they did then they made one up. Sabbir went to the local bazaar and bought fresh fruit for his grandfather.

Two weeks after Sabbir's arrival his grandfather became really sick. The doctors were called. The doctors informed them that he had very weak heart and gave him an injection to boost his energy level. A few days went past but Motlib never recovered. Late one night he said that he was about to die and everyone should pray for him. Everyone from the house gathered around his bed and read Arabic suras from the holy Qur'an. Motlib read the four Kalimas and then he passed away from this ugly world. Most of the family members were crying. The mature family members told others not to cry, but to pray for him.

The next morning as soon as the sunlight came out everyone went out to the relatives' house and informed them of his death and told them what time his funeral would be. All the relatives came. He was buried with a white cloth wrapped around his body. No coffin allowed. He didn't take anything else with him, he couldn't if he wanted to, could he? He had to leave behind all the wealth he made. Imams were hired to read the Qur'an in his name. A week after his funeral, Sabbir's uncle bought four cattle which Sabbir had paid for to hold his grandfather's charity prayer to poor people. It is a religious act that Bengali people carry out when a person dies that they give food to poor people. The poor people from the surrounding villages were invited. They came and ate and took food with them for their next dinner. A few days later Sabbir ordered a headstone for his grandfather's grave. He knew it was important to mark Motlib's grave so his children and grandchildren would know his grandfather's grave.

Sabbir investigated and found out that Abdul Hannan had come for holiday during the previous year. Once again he failed to meet the man whom he remembered for so long. He decided to be patient and believed the time would come when he would meet him and pay him back.

Foriz and Shabana continued to chat on the email and met when ever she allowed him to. It was Foriz's final year and he had a few months left on his contract. He wanted to know whether Shabana liked him enough. They met in the Moorgate canteen as usual. Foriz wanted to get it off his chest and get on with his life. He could no longer wait to know whether Shabana was going to be his wife or not. Foriz told her that he wanted to tell her something every important and wanted an important answer. 'You have told me so many important things,' she said.

'Yes I have but this is the most important thing I am going to tell you.'

She had a good feeling what it could be but she wanted to hear it from the horse's mouth.

'Go on then tell me what is it so important?'

He composed himself, looked at her eyes and said, 'I truly love you a lot Shabana and I would like you to be my wife,' he kept his eyes fixed on her face. She hid her face with her hands for a good few seconds. Shabana's heart beat faster – she took some deep breaths. She was embarrassed to hear it even though she knew he loved her.

'Tell me, will you be my wife?'

She hid her face again and said, 'I don't have an answer, I need to go home now; I don't have anything to say.'

'Please don't go, I will be upset, just wait a few minutes, I had to get it off my chest, now the choice is yours.'

Shabana removed her hands from her face. She took a sip at the coffee, looked at his eyes and said, 'I am not sure what I should say now, I have told you before I wasn't available for love, I am not allowed to talk to anyone and like anyone and I don't have a say to whom I get married. It's my parents' decision.'

'Just tell me if you like me or not. If you do then I can propose to your parents.'

'I don't like this conversation we are having, this is something I wanted to avoid, and this is why I never wanted to meet any boys.'

'I understand what you're saying, I didn't know I was going to like you but I did, you know you can like me, I am Bengali, Muslim and good looking.'

She smiled as she heard the latter part of his sentence.

'I don't think you're good looking enough to change my mind,' she said with a smile.'

'Maybe not, but I do want you to be part of my life.'

'I know what you're saying but I am not in charge of my decisions. This decision belongs to my parents.'

'This is your life, I am sure you have a say.'

'I wish, I don't want to hurt my parents, I told them I won't hurt them if they let me go to university, they didn't want me to come to university, I promised them I wouldn't' do anything to hurt them.'

'Ok Shabana, can I propose for you?'

'No, you can't do that.'

'Let me propose to your parents for you, I promise I will look after you.'

'Will you let your wife work?'

She tried to change the topic. In her mind she was confused how the situation could be solved.

'No, I won't let my wife work if she is beautiful like you.'

'Why not?'

'Because I will look at her twenty four seven.'

'How would you love your wife?'

'I will make sure I don't hurt her, and give her lots of children.'

'Giving children is not loving, that's giving pain.'

'I heard woman enjoy giving birth.'

'I wouldn't know.'

'Anyway let me tell you the ways I will love you.'

'I am listening, you carry on.'

'Once I am married to you; I will never hurt you, I will love you from top to the bottom.'

'You Idiot!'

'I will look at your gorgeous face 24/7.'

'That's good I can sleep without any problems.'

'I will wash your saris for you.'

'That's even better.'

'I will wash your bra for you.'

'Stop it now.' She gave a little smile.

'Sorry, I will make love to you non-stop.'

'How?'

'I will take you out to restaurants and buy you nice saris and gold.'

'Really.'

'I will give her a lot of children.'

She smiled once again.

'How many children do you want?'

'One every year.'

'You are disgusting, you will kill your wife.'

'I am sure if a man had a wife like you, he won't be able to keep away from her.'

'You have to think about how difficult it is to bring up kids.'

'I know, I think our children will be gorgeous. What do you think?'

'What made you say that?'

'Look at it both of us are good looking. So our children will be good looking.'

'You are such a joker, tell me will you let your wife work?'

'I told you before if my wife is beautiful like you I won't let her work because I don't want another man to look at her.'

'Don't propose to my parents for me, you evil man.'

Hearing that Foriz gave a big smile. Shabana decided to drop a hint that she doesn't mind getting involved with him.

'I see, you do like me, so if I let you work then I can propose to your parents for you.'

'No, I didn't say that.'

'But you meant that. Just admit it that you fancy me.'

'No.'

'I don't care if you become my wife or not, but just tell me if you don't mind if I am your husband.'

'I won't answer that question, but if you promise me that if you propose for me, you have to let me work, you cannot say that you know me from university or you have met me any where at the university.'

'Ok, I promise, I will only let you work until you are pregnant.'

'Shut up you, get lost, you are so dirty.'

'So you do like me Shabana Begum?'

'I didn't say that and I won't tell you.'

'Why don't you just for once admit it that you like me?'

'Look, I will eventually be married to a man and I wouldn't mind if my husband looked as stupid like you.'

She covered her face with her hands when she said that.

'Nice to hear that you like me. I am so happy now.'

'Shut up, I never said that.'

'Say it then.'

Shabana had melted while she sat in front of him. Foriz felt he had managed to crack her with his sweet psychological talks.

'No, listen, if you propose for me and if my parents say yes then I will tell you.'

'So you want to be my wife?'

'No, what ever, stop asking me the same question.'

'I am very happy now that you are going to be my wife. Can I give you a hug?'

'No you can't. but you may if I become your wife.' She said with a raised tone.

'I see.'

'You better propose now as you know my parents get so many proposals.'

'What is the point of proposing now, you are still at university.'

'Yes I know, but they might say yes to someone else. If you do it now then if they say yes to you then we might get married later when I finish university.'

'You clever girl, you should have told me a long time ago that you wanted to be my wife.'

'You are the one who is desperate to get married, I am not.'

'Are you sure?'

'I am very sure.'

'I think you also want to get married to me since you saw my handsome face.'

'Haa haa ha, Get lost and don't push your luck.'

'Shabana just tell me once that you love me.'

'Do I have to?'

'Yes please darling.'

'Close your eyes first.'

Foriz closed his eyes.

'I like you Foriz.'

'Say, I love you Foriz!'

'No, you say I love you Shabana one million times.'

'Look who's talking.'

'If we are married I won't let you touch me for a year because I want to work.'

'Get lost, I will make you pregnant on the first night.'

'Stop it now, you suppose to be nice to me or I won't give you my address.'

'I can find your address easily. Plus its called making love, not dirty.'

'How are you going to find my address?'

'I know so many people who live in Manor Park, if I tell them your father's name, I am sure they would direct me to the right house, or perhaps I can ask people where the most beautiful Bengali girl lives.'

'What ever - you think too much!'

'What if your parents say no to me.'

'No means no, mate.'

'No,' he said with a raised voice.

'Yes.'

'Aren't you going to do anything if they say no?'

'I can't do anything.'

'Of course you can.'

'I can't, I have no say.'

'Of course you do.'

'I wish.'

'I don't believe you.'

'We are going round in circles.'

'I know.'

Shabana looked at her watch and it was getting late. She made a move. Foriz went with her in the bus and dropped her off to the nearest bus stop to her home in Romford Road. She waved good bye to him; he blew a kiss in her direction. She grabbed it and put it into her heart.

Chapter Thirteen

2000 Continued

Foriz informed his big sister about Shabana and asked her to propose for his marriage. Foriz's sister spoke to her parents and explained the situation to them. His father Rokib and his sister decided to go to Shabana's house with some Indian sweets from Green Street. Shabana didn't tell her parents that Foriz's family would be visiting otherwise they would think she was linked in the puzzle, but she told her young sister - Sabina. They kept the living room neat and tidy. Foriz's sister knocked on the door. Shabana's sister opened the door. The visitor said that they were there to see Shabana's parents and they were invited to go into the house. Shabana's father, Shujon, asked them if they were a new family arrived to their Avenue. Foriz's father said that he was there to talk about Shabana's marriage. Shabana's father wanted to know how they knew that he had a daughter. Foriz's sister said that they met his daughters in a sari shop in Green Street, and spoke to them as they liked them. He was content with the answer but found it a bit fishy. Sabina served teas and biscuits to the guest.

Foriz's parents told Shabana's parents that they would like to propose for their daughter Shabana. Both the old man asked each other questions and found out about their village details. Shabana's mother told them that there were hundred of proposals for Shabana and they hadn't looked at any yet. At the end of the discussion Foriz's father left his telephone number with Shabana's father to let him know if he would consider the proposal.

A few days later Shabana's father called Foriz's father and told him that they wouldn't consider the proposal as they will be going to Bangladesh to get her married. Foriz's father tried to convince him but he said it wasn't possible.

Foriz spoke to Shabana on the phone but she couldn't do anything. She told him that it was her parents' call and she didn't have a say in it.

Foriz found the rejection unbearable. He was hurt like if someone dear had died. Her parents' decision froze his brain cells. He believed that he did everything in his ability to win her heart but couldn't believe his 'takdir' (fate). It took a few days to sink into his brain that Shabana wasn't going to be his wife. He spoke to himself and tried to explain that in life one cannot have what one wants and one has to go through the unexpected results as one can't control another's decisions. Foriz told himself that he must stop thinking about her and get on with his own life otherwise he would lose his degree on top of her – double loss. After a few days, he managed to slowly come to terms with the loss of her and continued to concentrate on his studies.

July 2000

It was the end of July. Lana and Joynul finished their exams. She eloped to be with Joynul. Lana made the decision as she felt that it was best if she ran away from home. She knew her parents would never accept Joynul. Joynul managed to hijack a local Imam and had a few of his friends to attend his Islamic wedding. Lana called her mother that she wouldn't be coming home again and she was getting married to Joynul. Her mother started to cry. She told her not to cry and she should tell her father that she did it because of him. They had to get Islamically married in order to live together as Muslims. The Imam read the relevant Arabic text and asked them to accept each other by saying, 'Kobul,' which they did. From a local estate agent, Joynul hired a one bed room flat to further experiment his love with Lana.

Panna came to Sabbir's house after working for three years in a restaurant. He asked Sabbir to do him a big favour. 'What kind of favour do you want?' Sabbir asked. Panna said that his passport had expired and wanted Sabbir to call the police and grass him up. Sabbir told him that he could buy a ticket and go to Bangladesh. Panna wanted the police to catch him so he could return to Bangladesh free of charge. Sabbir asked him to give him time to think and find the best way to grass him up. He called Badol Miah, discussed the situation and found a solution. Next day Sabbir told Panna to go to Badol Miah's estate agent pretending to be looking for work. Sabbir called the police and grassed him up. The police officers came, took him away and then they deported him back to Bangladesh. A few days later Panna called Sabbir and thanked him for the favour.

Foriz worked part time during the weekend in Musa's restaurant, his neighbour. He had been working in Musa's restaurant for number of years to support his pocket. Musa had a beautiful Bangladeshi wife, Mishna, whom Foriz admired. When Foriz went to work, he first went to Musa's house and then went to work with Musa. Musa's restaurant was in Kent, and the business was doing well. Foriz couldn't understand why Musa was having an affair with a white lady when he had such a beautiful and decent wife. He met Mishna many times in his house but never 'grassed' on Musa as it wasn't his business. From time to time Mishna came to Foriz's house and they exchanged salaams.

As usual one Friday Foriz left home to go to work. As he arrived at Musa's house there was a bad news. Musa's son, Motiur had broken his hand, by falling from his bike. Musa told Foriz to go to work by himself, while he took his son to the local hospital for emergency check-up and medication. But Foriz had another idea. He told Musa to go to work as it was Friday. One of the busiest days, while Foriz took Motiur to the hospital. It was a better idea as Musa would be a better person to manage the restaurant. Musa agreed to that as he also wanted to meet his girl friend in the restaurant.

Foriz took Motiur and Mishna to the emergency section of the Newham General hospital. It was the first time Foriz had the opportunity to speak to Mishna for more than a few words. Foriz and Mishna exchanged general conversation while in the car. Foriz didn't know much about Mishna's life, apart from the fact she was a decent wife, who arrived from Bangladesh. She was a polite woman who looked after her family very well in terms of cooking food and being nice to her in-laws. Foriz's mother told him that she was a nice lady who spoke with respect, perhaps she tried to influence him to go to Bangladesh and get a wife from there. She could tell a Bengali woman's psychological motives!

They had to wait for a long time to see a doctor. The queue was quite long. This provided an opportunity for them to get to know each other. Foriz had great respect for her as she was a married woman and he usually called her a bhabi. He continued to speak to her with respect and chose words with great care. Soon he realized that she wasn't what he thought from her responses. She had started to show a great interest in him and wanted to know more and more about him.

'So do you have a girl friend Foriz?'

Foriz wasn't sure what to say and instantly tried to come up with his best answer.

'Why do you want to know?'

'Well, I heard that boys in London have girl friends and it's easy to find one.'

'I wish I had one. You see bhabi I am not good looking enough that a girl would go out with me.'

Motiur didn't seem to be in much pain. He continued to play with the toys provided by the hospital with his unbroken hand. Every word Mishna spoke Foriz started to learn more and he wanted to extract more from her as he thoughtfully started to think about more effective questioning.

'Don't be shy you can tell me if you have a girl friend, I am your bhabi after all, you know what people say, 'You can talk to your bhabi about anything.'

'Well bhabi, if I had one I would have told you, but if it makes you happy then I can say that I have a girl friend even though I don't have one.'

'That's fine, I thought someone good-looking and smart like you would have one.'

'Now you know being smart and good-looking doesn't guarantee a girl friend. Girls are very choosy these days and I find it difficult to chat up girls.'

As their conversation continued, Mishna's smile expanded to sexiness in Foriz's eyes. Foriz didn't mind waiting for the doctor. He had started to enjoy the kind of sensual conversation.

'Bhabi tell me did you have a boyfriend in Bangladesh?'

'You silly boy, you know how it's like in Bangladesh. I went a girl's school and left school at the age of fifteen and got married and here I am in your country where I don't know anything, Can you teach me how to speak English?'

'Bhabi, I think you are very friendly and a nice person, I am sure your husband can teach you how to speak English'.

'Thanks, I also think you are a friendly and nice boy; you know it is strange that before we never had the chance to talk to each other even though we lived so close to each other. Every time we met at each other places what did we say, 'Salaam and how are you - that's all.' Both agreed.

'Well, bhabi this is our opportunity to be friends, get to know each other, probably our only chance to talk.'

'Make sure when you come to our house you talk to me, come early when you go to work then I can make a tea for you and talk to you. When I visit your home, you know you can talk to me and joke with me, I like talking to people, I feel so lonely at home.'

'Do you know something; we are talking to each other like we know each other for ages.'

Both agreed and nodded their head. A doctor came and called to see Motiur. Foriz translated as the doctor spoke because Mishna didn't speak English. The doctor carried out an ex-ray on Motiur's hand to find out if he had broken his hand. He had. The doctor said that they needed to keep him in hospital and operate on his hand on the next day. Through mobile communication Foriz up-dated Musa regarding the situation. At about 9:30 he was informed that Motiur needed to stay at the hospital over night for an operation. Musa told Foriz to wait in the hospital until they are not allowed and then go home with his wife. Musa believed that he could trust Foriz and his wife that they wouldn't get up to any dodgy business. This was even a greater opportunity for Foriz to spend more time with Mishna.

Motiur was taken to a children's ward where he was going to spend the night. Mishna comforted him by saying 'Everything will be alright, you won't feel any pain tomorrow they will give you more medicine.' Motiur slept within half an hour. Foriz said to Mishna, 'We should go home now as he has slept. There is no point of staying here any more.'

'It's only ten o'clock; I thought we could stay here until late.'

'Yes we can, but your son has gone to sleep. There is no point of waiting here any longer.'

'But if you don't mind, I like to wait here and see my son. If you give me company it would be nice but if you insist then I will go home now.'

'Don't worry, I can stay here as long as you like as I have been enjoying talking to you and I don't feel like going to work so late. Anyway, what are you going to pay me for tonight?'

'I would like to pay you in a way that would make you very happy.'

Foriz didn't understand what she meant, but had a feeling something saucy was going on in her head.

'I take it you are thinking about giving me a lot of money as your husband is a rich man.'

'No, that's nothing.'

'What is it then?'

'You have a guess.'

'You're going to make me really nice coffee when we get home.'

'No.'

Foriz had started to take time to think about what he should say. He thought about other things that she could give him, a kiss on his lips, a hug and finally maybe more then a kiss, but there were no way he could have said that.

'I give up.'

'You give up so easily.'

'So tell me, what are the things that you could give me that would make me very happy?'

Mishna requested for time, 'Let me think,' she thought about a few things, such as, give him a nice kiss and obviously the most enjoyable thing he would like would be to sleep with her. But she couldn't say 'I like to give myself to you, would you like that? She thought in her mind that he had done a lot for her. He had come to the hospital instead of her husband, basically doing her husband's job.

'You ready.'

'Yes I am ready.'

'I can give you my cousin's phone number and I can put a few words in for you so hopefully you would get a date. She is a beautiful girl. I am sure you would like her and want to marry her once you see her.'

'Is that it?'

'Ain't you happy?'

'Well, something is better then nothing. Is she beautiful like you?

'If you think I am beautiful then she is extremely beautiful. If you see her you won't blink, you will be thirsty for her very quickly.'

She said that to arouse his feeling and get his desire ignited.

'I think you are very beautiful, you must give me her phone number, I can't wait to talk to her.'

'I will talk to her first and try to convince her then I will let you know what she says. Anyway, so you think I am beautiful? My husband doesn't think I am beautiful.'

'Yes, I do think you are a beautiful woman; I don't mind having a wife as beautiful as you.'

He said that to arouse her feeling and see how she reacted.

'O well it's sad I am a married woman, if I were a single girl then I wouldn't have minded having you.'

She was getting him more sexually excited.

'What does your cousin do?'

'She goes to college, listen I need to go to toilet; can you show me the way?'

'Come with me, I'll tell you something it's not difficult to find a toilet. You have to look for this picture of a female on the door, which means it's the women's toilet.'

It was about eleven o'clock, she came out of the toilet with a different appearance. She took her hijab off. Foriz asked her if she still wanted to stay in the hospital or go home. She replied, 'Ain't you enjoying your time with me. If not then we can go home.'

'I am enjoying myself very much as I am getting to know my bhabi.'

'I hope you didn't go through my bag'?

'I did, I wanted to see how much money you have.'

'I don't believe you.'

'If you don't believe me then ask me some questions about your bag's contents and see if I can answer them.'

'Tell me what is in my bag?'

One answer he thought that he could have said was tampex but waited as he felt it wasn't appropriate time to say that.

'A lipstick'

'Correct'

'Some money'

'Correct'

'Husband's and child's photo'

'Half correct'

'Why half correct'

'I do have my child's photo not my husband's'

'Don't you love your husband?'

'Why do you want to know that?'

She replied in an un-convincing voice which made him think there was something wrong with the relationship and he may have the opportunity to exploit that gap. They realized that every other parent had gone from the hospital and it wasn't an appropriate place to talk. Mishna said to Foriz, 'We should go to your car and talk.' They walked to the car, Foriz felt that she had half melted and he needed to do very little work to taste her. He asked her another question 'Bhabi, if I get five things right that is in your bag, what would you give me?'

'You can have what ever I can afford, does that mean if I ask for a grand you would give it to me.'

'If I have it then I would give it.'

'Are you sure you would give me what I want?'

'Yes I am sure.'

'Ok, so far I have got two and half correct answers.'

Spices of Brick Lane

They sat at the back of the car stirring at each other's face. 'Come on then, are you going to have another guess or give up,' said Mishna.

'Sorry, I think you have your house keys.'

'Correct, you are getting close now, what, if you don't get five correct answers, would you give me what I want?'

'Yes madam, you can have what you want.'

By now he wasn't sure whether to try and get five correct answers or not. Mishna realised she had a good deal and she was going to experiment something new.

'Come on then tell me what I got in my bag or give up, time is running out.'

'I am not going to give up, I know I can get it, but I need time.'

'We don't have enough time, I have to be home soon, I can't stay here whole night with you, hurry up little boy.'

'Give me a few seconds,'

He thought about what would she choose if she was given the chance and what he would choose. If he won he wouldn't be able to say, 'Can you get naked I like to taste you,' he was more likely to get a big slap on his face. Foriz felt it would be better to lose and give her the chance to see what she does.

'I think you have some kind of receipt in your bag'

'No, I don't, just give up.'

'Even though I don't like losing just for you I give up'

By now Mishna's sari had dropped from the top part of her body, only her Indian bra could be seen. Foriz could notice the difference between now and before.

'So I can have what I want.'

'Yes madam, you can have but don't forget I am not a rich man, I am your husband's servant.'

'First thing get your wallet out and take all the money out.'

'That's easy. You don't need money.'

'It's going to get tough soon.'

'Why do you need money, your husband is a rich man?'

'Shush! Do what I tell you, I am in control now, take your jacket off?'

'I am not going to take it off. Are you feeling cold that you need my jacket?'

'You have to take it off, you lost, remember! Close your eyes for thirty seconds and don't open them until I say so.'

She instructed him to come close to her, she jumped on his laps. She grabbed him and then told him to open his eyes.

'I am your present for today's hard work, do you like it?' she said. He nodded yes and they kissed each other continuously for a long period of time where he was able to feel her oranges with his chest and hands. Both of them moaned and groaned. He moaned that he couldn't believe that he was enjoying such a beautiful woman and she moaned that she couldn't believe that she was enjoying such a young and good looking boy.

'Thank you for the present bhabi; you made me a very satisfied customer.'

'I thank you for satisfying me too.'

Foriz wanted more of the same. He asked her to close her eyes for a minute. She was ready for more or what ever was on offer. Foriz grabbed her slowly and started to kiss her on the neck, chick, chin and then moving onto her lips. She got aroused and was asking for more and more. She moaned, 'You are allowed to do what ever you want.' 'I know darling, but I need more time to get to the other enjoyable places,' he replied.

'When are we going to meet again? You have to meet me more often.'

'I love to meet you again and again, but how could we do that as it's very difficult for you to get out of your house.'

'Give me your mobile number and I will see if I can come-up with a plan. By the way, I usually go shopping to the supermarket by myself every Wednesday.'

'I am sure I will see you soon and never know maybe next week.'

He dropped her off and she arrived home as if nothing had happened with her hijab back on. Her husband arrived home late about one o'clock. She up-dated him about their son without mentioning the time she spent with Foriz.

September 2000

Foriz decided to do a master in IT and continued to stay at London Guildhall University. It cost him three grand as he was a home student. He took a loan out to solve his financial problems. He just wanted to be-friend Shabana for another year. He thought maybe Shabana would change her mind. Maybe her parents would change their minds. Foriz couldn't keep away from her even though he knew that he had almost a zero percent chance of having her.

Foriz came to conclusion that finding a suitable girl wasn't in his Takdir and he wasn't going to love any girls who ever came his way. He would just enjoy them. When he started his masters there were some foreign students. He liked a girl that he wanted to play with. She was a Chinese girl. Soon he was put into a group where the girl was part of his group. This was a very good news to him. They were introduced and all the group members chatted and got to know each other. They exchanged email addresses and telephone numbers so everyone could be contacted when necessary. The group had to investigate different parts of a project life cycle. The Chinese girl found it difficult to do her task as she was new to the British education system. Foriz volunteered to help her out, there were strings attached to that but no one else knew. There is nothing free in this world! Foriz told her to meet him in the afternoon so he could help her.

They met and discussed the project first; then they had coffee which he offered and paid for. He learnt that she was single and lived by herself which was great news. They met a few times to do their project. He decided to make a move on her as he couldn't resist her looks. He asked her if she knew how to play pool. She said that she never played pool before. He offered to teach her which she agreed to take part in. Foriz took her down to the basement of the Moorgate canteen, where there were a few pool tables. It was a late evening and it was quiet. He inserted a fifty pence coin in the pool tables' slot and the balls came out. He explained the basic rules to her but he knew she would find it difficult to play. He showed her how to hold the cue and take shots. As she was a novice it was difficult for her to play and this was where he took advantage of her. Foriz started to demonstrate physically how to play the game, he held her left hand's fingers and made a v shape, where the cue rested and told her that if she kept a v shape then the cue wouldn't move.

Later on, he showed her how to bend down and take a shot. In order to demonstrate he bent down with her while his body touched hers. Soon he had the feeling that she was on the same wave length as him. He moved in with his winning shot. Foriz told Li to stand up. Then he pulled her onto the pool table and hugged her, at the same time she hugged him too. The chemical mixed well, they kissed. Li helped him to forget some of the pain he had from Shabana and he also wanted to show Shabana that he could get on with his life after all. Another beautiful girl in his portfolio which he wanted to keep and show off with. From time to time Foriz had lessons in Moorgate. He went into the canteen with his Chinese girl friend to make Shabana notice. He saw Shabana a few times in the canteen and they said hello to each other but never had a long conversation.

One evening Shabana called Foriz and asked him how he was and then asked him what was he doing with the Chinese girl. He asked her why was she bothered if he was going out with a Chinese girl. Shabana told him that she wasn't bothered but as a friend she felt that he shouldn't go out with a girl as it was sinful. Obviously she didn't know much about his past. Foriz told her that going out with the Chinese girl helped him forget her. Shabana told him that if he was going out with the girl to make her jealous then he was a loser.

Foriz graduated with a 2:1 honors degree, the first person to do so in his family. This was a special moment for him and his family. Graduation pictures were taken, framed and kept displayed in their living room for visitors to see the achievement of Foriz which showed the family in good light. Pictures were also sent to Bangladesh for the close family members to see. Shabana also texted him and congratulated him for his achievement.

Sabbir's uncle Kolim applied for 'indefinite stay.' He had been living in England for more then fourteen years as an illegal person with his wife and child. In his application he needed to show a permanent address. He asked Sabbir if he could use their address, he had problem using his brothers' address. His brother had kicked him out as there was no space in the house. Sabbir had to change his name on a utility bill to Kolim's name and register him on the voting list to fool the immigration officers. Sabbir had to help him other wise his mother would be upset. He asked his mother if he was running a charity for all the relatives and if he was going to get any money for helping Kolim. But he knew that he wouldn't get anything, maybe a box of sweet Pakistani mango, which he hates because it's Pakistani.

Mishna called Foriz on his mobile. He was pleased to hear from her. He felt that he was going to get interesting satisfaction from her. He felt that he needed this ready made solution in order to get rid of Shabana from his mind. Mishna was out of her house to shop in the local supermarket. Foriz met her in the car park and she went into the back of his car. They talked in the car for some time. Then they enjoyed each other like boy friends and girl friends. Foriz kissed her non-stop for long period of time and played with her water melons. While he played with her, he also thought about Shabana. Mishna only had a maximum of two hours to do the shopping otherwise her mother in-law would get suspicious. He felt what he was doing was wrong but took advantage of the free offer. Foriz felt that he was hard done by Shabana's parents and it helped him get over some of the pain.

Someone knocked on Sabbir's door. A man and his wife came. Sabbir opened the door, gave his salaam to them and invited them into the house. Sokina came to meet them as she was likely to know who they were and she recognized them. They lived in the same village in Sylhet but the children hardly met before. The man came to invite them to their son's wedding.

Sabbir went to the wedding because it was important to know the people from the village. He took a sari as the present. The man had invited all the people from the village. Sabbir met many of his village people and chatted about what they were doing, he boasted about how many restaurants and houses he had. About five, six hundred people turned up. It is a tradition that Sylheti people invited all their relatives and village people. A wedding provides the opportunity to meet other relatives.

The man wanted to show off to the others. He had hired DJ to play music. Some elderly man complained why the hell he had music. There were two professional video cameramen recording and many hand held video cameras were taking shots. It seem like if it was a wedding of a famous person. There were people saying, what a stupid idiot wasting money for no reason when he could have donated the money to the thousands of poor people in Bangladesh.

As Sima was at home all the time she had nothing better to do than sewing and thinking about her parents back home. She told Sabbir that she wanted to sponsor her sister, Uma to come to London. It wasn't a problem to Sabbir. He organised all the dodgy documents for Sima to sponsor her sister. It took three months for Uma to get a visa. She told the immigration officers in Bangladesh that she was going for a holiday to see London and her sister's family. Uma looked beautiful, she was the kind of girl that most Bengali men go back to Bangladesh to marry. Uma had a three months visa to stay in England.

Sima had other ideas. She told all her relatives to find a husband for her sister so she could stay in England, atypical Bengali idea. A few proposals came and they selected a groom. The groom was informed of her status and the groom was willing to marry her. Sabbir had to get involved and negotiated everything for Uma. As there was no one else to help financially, Sabbir paid for all the expenses for Uma's wedding. She got married, which cost Sima and Sabbir a lot of money.

There were many Bengali girls who came on a holiday visa, got married and stayed in London. A lot of people do that to help their relatives come to London. Sylhetis are well known for taking advantage of opportunities. One can bet there are many applications in the immigration office now to be considered for holiday visas.

Mishna called Foriz again to meet her. They met at the usual car park. She felt very lonely at home, needed some happiness which she wasn't getting from her husband. Meeting Foriz provided her with some comfort. She felt that she had a friend and she was getting some kind of revenge for her husband's affair. Mishna told Foriz to take the car to a quiet place where people won't see them. Once he parked the car, she gave herself to him. He enjoyed this with great satisfaction. Getting physical with Mishna helped him to keep Shabana out of his mind. Once they were tired of enjoying each other physically, Mishna hugged him and cried. 'Why are you crying?' he asked.

'I am trapped in this house. I have no one to help me.'

'Don't cry darling. You got me.'

She slowly stopped crying, he cleaned her tears with a tissue.

'I am sure there must be a way out.'

'Tell me how; I want some happiness and a life.'

'Do you have any relatives that can help you?'

'I don't have any close relatives that can help me; I come from a very poor family.'

'I am not sure what to advice you.'

'As soon as I get my permanent visa I want to leave this bastard. Look what he has done to me, look at the cut on my ear. He slapped me so hard because I didn't get his breakfast ready on time.'

'In the restaurant he behaves very well with people.'

'Because they are men, I am a woman this is why he beats me up and swears at me if I make a little mistake.'

'Like you said, once you get your visa just let me know if you want, I can get you in touch with the council and they will give you your own house. The Government will give you money to survive.'

'What am I going to do with my own house and money, if I don't have a family and people around me don't like me?'

'At least you can keep away from the bastard.'

'I know, but I need happiness, which no one can give, except Allah.'

'How about if you go back to Bangladesh to your parents.'

'My parents will curse me if I do that.'

'Why?'

'It is very difficult for a poor family to get their daughter married, I was lucky that I had a white face and he married me. If I go back to my parents it would be extremely difficult for them to get me married as no one will marry a married woman.'

It was getting late for Mishna. Foriz had to drop her off. She had to be home on time or her mother in-law would ask her questions about where she had been.

Kawsar had applied for a few new jobs. But he didn't get any interviews. He continued to work part time in Sabbir's restaurant and study in the evenings. During the day Sabbir managed to get Kawsar a job in Badol Miah's travel agent so he could get some experience. Kawsar thought that it was an opportunity for him to work in an office and get some experience of speaking to English customers. When he started work he realised all the customers were Sylheti. Badol Miah did a bit of everything in his travel agency. He sold plane tickets, let houses, a visa renewal, transferred money to Bangladesh and provided employment service to restaurants. The money wasn't very good as he was paid on commission.

Mishna called Foriz once again on his mobile as he wasn't allowed to call her incase her mother in-law picked up the phone. Her mother in-law went to her sisters' house. She had the opportunity to meet him for longer. They met; he kissed her freely and passionately. She asked him jokingly to show her around London. He told her he loved to hold her hand and show her London town but there wasn't enough time. Then he remembered and asked her;

'You supposed to give me your cousin's phone number, what happened?'

'You have got a good memory, I know, but ain't you happy I gave myself to you?'

'I am very happy. I just wanted to know if you really had a cousin.'

'No, I didn't have a cousin, I made that up to arouse you.'

'You clever kut-ti.'
'You clever kut-tha.'

Both of them laughed.

'I actually believed you.'
'You silly boy. That was my trick to get you ignited.'
'Tell me more about your husband, what else does he do?'
'He doesn't love me, I think he has another wife or girl friend outside. He doesn't do it with me all the time, only sometimes.'
'If he does it all the time, he won't have enough energy left to work.'
'Shut up. How do you know? Who have you been doing it with?'
'I assumed but I am hoping you might give the opportunity to learn from your experience.'
'You are becoming a dirty clever boy.'
'I am learning it from you.'

They smiled at each other. He felt that was a yes from her.

'Does my husband have a girl friend in the restaurant?'
He felt there wasn't any point of lying to her as she was giving him free love. He said softly.
'Yes, he does have an English girl friend in the restaurant and most of the lunch time he spends with her, not in the restaurant.'
'I knew it.'
'How did you know?'
'Because he must have been getting it from someone else.'
'I see, what else?'
'I have seen sperm marks on his underwear.'
'You must have been doing some investigation.'
'I had to.'
'I am sure it is good for you that you get the chance to rest.'
'I don't need a rest, I need satisfaction.'
'I am here to give you satisfaction.'
'Looks like you have to satisfy my needs.'
'I love to help.'

'And how do you intend to do that?'
'In the car.'
'You must be kidding, people will watch.'
'Don't worry I will put some newspaper on the windows, no one will be able to see.'
'Go on then, hurry up, I don't have too long to stay.'
'You take your sari off and I put the newspaper up on the windows.'
'Ok, you hurry up.'

Foriz put up the newspaper around the inside of the car with sellotape. Then they got down to business and he gave her what she wasn't getting from her husband. Both enjoyed each other's meat freely. He thanked her for the special gift and she thanked him for the revenge she had been able take on her husband.

Chapter Fourteen

2001

Many Indian restaurant owners lobbied the local ministers regarding shortage of restaurant workers. They proposed if the government provides visas for employees to come from Bangladesh then that could solve the problems. Many restaurant owners complained that their businesses were loosing money because they weren't able to find appropriate skilled workers. Some argued that if they don't bring new staff then many restaurants would have to be closed down. The ministers were probably not sure about the hidden agenda of some of the owners like Sabbir. In a meeting a minister argued that there were ten thousand young Bangladeshi out of work. They should train them and employ them. But some restaurant owners argued that these people didn't have the right skills and weren't looking for restaurant work. Perhaps they were all addicted to drugs. It may be possible that they were happy with the unemployment benefit they received and did dodgy jobs on the side like mini cab driving.

Yasin asked his father if he could buy the latest lap top computer. His father told him that he could buy it, if it was going to help him with his studies. It is a common respect that decent children ask their parents for permission before they buy anything that might upset their parents. Financially it wasn't a problem for Yasin to buy one as he had enough money from his part time work. But his father gave him a grand to buy the lap top. He also bought a new mobile. This time he didn't tell his father in case he might say no. Once he had the mobile, he told his father that he liked the mobile and bought it. Sabbir allowed Yasin to have the mobile but told him not to spend too much time on it.

11 September, 2001

On the eleventh September everyone watched on TV what happened to America's twin towers. When the staff met in the restaurant they only talked about one thing - The Twin Tower crash. Most human being were shocked to see the human life lost in such a way but in some part of the world like Palestine people celebrated the event probably because they had been losing humans everyday because of America's financial support to Israel. Everyone in the restaurant couldn't believe that America could be hit like that. Not America – a super power! A country with super power couldn't prevent something like that. Gozafor Miah said to Goni, 'How can this terrible act be justified by the terrorist. Killing innocent civilian must be an act of animals.' They also couldn't believe that Bin Laden had such power as that. Maybe they didn't know Bin Laden. They wanted to know more about Bin Laden. Bin Laden became super famous. His name was on everyone's lips. The restaurant was very quiet, only a few customers came in. Gozafor Miah was concerned about one of his relatives who worked in a restaurant in the Twin Tower building. A few days later news came through that Gozafor Miah had lost a relative who worked in a restaurant. Perhaps the man had travelled too far from Sylhet. He ended up losing everything. Gozafor Miah wanted to kill Bin Laden but he didn't realise the most powerful country on the earth was finding it difficult to get close to him.

Sima had started sewing Indian dresses at home. The other work that she used to do had dried up. She had good sewing experience, she made Indian dresses for the children and relatives. It wasn't long before everyone knew she had the skills and she was busy counting extra dosh. Sabbir told her not to work at home. He had enough money for the family and for her parents. She wanted to be busy and she enjoyed making dresses. She continued to work as it also helped her to keep her mind away from the village.

In the restaurant's kitchen Gozafor Miah and Goni discussed the attack of Bush and Blair in Afghanistan. They agreed that the main reason for the attack was that Bush and Blair didn't like Muslims and they wanted to kill Muslims to show how strong they were. They couldn't understand why the killing of thousands of Afghani could be justified just because they wanted to kill one man – Bin Laden. The killing of innocent civilians is an act of animals. And none of the Arab leaders were able to do anything. They couldn't believe the kind of Muslims the Arabs were because they didn't help their own people. All they had to do was to say to Tony and Bush that if they attacked Afghanistan then they wouldn't supply any oil. Maybe they thought if they said that then USA would attack them too or take over their own country. This is how the world works, whether in the East or West, one person makes a mistake but so many innocent people pay in blood. The big question was whether Bin Laden, Bush or Blair could justify the killing of innocent human beings anywhere in the world. Could they bring back the people they killed through their vanity? Who were the real Terrorists? Would these three be ever brought to justice for killing innocent people. Was there anyone in the world who could charge this big three B's for their day-light murders and criminal activities.

Peter came to the restaurant for a take away. He asked Yasin, 'So shouldn't you be on the plane to Afghan to help your Muslims brothers and sisters.' Yasin poured a half pint bear for Peter and said, 'I have sent my fundamentalist friends, but I will supply the money'. Yasin didn't get too worried about the war, he was too busy thinking about his girl friends. Sabbir came in late to the restaurant and gave his 'hello' and 'how are you' to Peter. 'Ain't you going to fight for your Muslim brothers,' asked Peter.

'If I was in Afghan then I would have fought.'

'This is what happens when someone touches the super power. They get bombs left right and centre.'

'To me the three of them are the real terrorists.'

'The world is watching but no one can stop them bombing.'

'When the rest of the world is impetus they can't do anything.'

'It is a warning to the world if they touched America, then they would get done. They could go anywhere and bomb where-ever they wanted.'

'I am sure others will come up with other strategies like suicide bombers to kill the Americans.'

'I won't be surprised.'

Shabana texted Foriz to arrange a meeting. Foriz asked her why she wanted to meet. She told him that she wanted to return the gold bracelet and the necklace that he had given her. He told her that there was no need to return it, she should keep it. She insisted that she couldn't keep those kind of presents from a friend. But he insisted that she should keep them as it was just presents that he gave her. Foriz told her that he didn't mind meeting her but he wouldn't take the gold back. They met in the university's canteen once again.

'What would you like to drink Shabana?'

'For the first time will you let me buy a drink for you?'

'Ok, no problem.' He said with a genuine smile.

'What would you like to drink then?'

'I let you choose what ever you want me to drink.'

She went to the counter and bought a lucozade for him and a bottle of water for herself.

'I bought you a lucozade, you need energy to keep up with all the exam stress.'

'Thank you Shabana.'

'Foriz, I am sorry about everything because of me you and your family had to go through so much of trouble.'

'Don't worry Shabana it's not your fault. It's my Takdir, because at the beginning you told me about your parents. I am very sorry I have put you and your family through so much hassle. Will you forgive me for the trouble I gave you and your family?'

'Don't be silly, of course I forgive you, I told you to propose.'

'I am very happy that I have tried my best, I am very happy with my Takdir because Allah has given me so much. I live in a country where there is no war and I can walk safely, and I think this has happened for a good reason.'

'I really wanted to give the gold back to you.'

'No, I want you to keep it because I really liked you and I want you to be happy and remember me when you wear it.'

'Thanks bhondu.'

'Have you got the gold with you?'

She nodded her head up and down with a wide a smile.

'Can you wear it for me please?'

She took the gold out from her bag and wore the chain and bangles as he watched her.

'You look so beautiful, I never seen a beautiful girl like you in my life.'

'I hope you get a wife more beautiful than me and someone who will love you a lot.'

'Thanks.'

'I wanted to suggest something to you, if you don't mind.'

'What is it?'

'I think it would be easy for you to get over this situation if we don't talk to each other for sometimes.'

'Ok, no problem, but I am sure you can always call me if you need any help, I am old enough to get over it.'

'Good.'

'If I ask you a question will you tell me the truth?'

'Do I have to?'

'If you do I will be happy.'

'For you I would.'

'My question is, did you really like me?'

She smiled and paused for a few seconds then covered her face with her hands and nodded her head up and down.

'Tell me with your lips please?'

'My answer is, I did.'

'I have to write a book on this story, do you mind if I use your name?'

'I don't mind but you have to give me fifty percent if you use my name.'

'Shabana, I am going to say something mean, I hope you won't mind.'

'How mean?'

'If I tell you then you will know.'

'Go-on then.'

'If you get divorced from your husband then do give me a call, I will marry you.'

She laughed.

'You are a crazy man. Don't you want me to be happy? When I get married, how will you marry me? You may have a wife.'

'I do, but it is a possibility that you might get divorced, I like to keep my option open. I don't mind having two wives.'

'I wouldn't share my husband with anyone. Anyway it was really nice knowing you and I am sure we will continue to be good mates and I am sure we can keep in touch through Lana.'

'Yep, that's the way it is, good mates, hey if you get married here do invite me, I love to come to your wedding just to say a final good bye.'

'I will see, lets go home now and I like to you to take me home today please.'

'Ok my dear Shabana, I wish I could take you to my home.'

'I am sure the lady that will go to your home will be a very beautiful one.'

They talked and walked to the bus stop. They caught a 25 bus. They talked more in the bus. As usual he dropped her off near her house. She waved good bye to him then she went home. Foriz boarded another bus and headed home thinking about her furiously.

―――

Gozafor Miah came to the restaurant for his afternoon shift. He first read the Bengali newspaper for the main headline before he did any work. He read the headline and called out, 'Bastards.' When the other kitchen staff arrived he told them congratulations to Bangladesh we have become the number one corrupted country in the world. Goni had learnt a lot from Gozafor Miah and learnt to talk like him in order to get his support. 'You're right, how the hell are we going to go forward when the government is so corrupt,' said Goni. 'Why don't these bastards do their job honestly?' 'Because they are bastards.'

'You're correct, how can a bastard work honestly.'

Sabbir's car was stopped as he drove to work on the Mile End Road. He was asked to pull over by the police. One police officer asked him to get out of the car. Sabbir was calm as he had nothing to hide. He got out of the car. Sabbir remembered Charles DeMenzes and reminded himself to be extra calm in case he did something suspicious then he might get shot. Another officer spoke on the walkie talkie to gave Sabbir's number to the central database. He was asked to open his boot, which he did. They checked it and found some spices that he had bought for his restaurant. The officers smelled it but it wasn't the kind of drug they were looking for. The other officer asked him what his name was and whose car it was. After investigating for a few minutes they let him go. They probably tried their best to link him to some kind of terrorist group but failed to find any DNA otherwise he could have been behind the bars without charges for a few weeks.

Foriz completed his MSc and went to his graduation ceremony at the Caribbean centre in Moorgate. He knew Shabana would be there, she had completed her LLB. While he was getting the robe for the Masters graduation, he saw Shabana was also getting ready for her graduation. He didn't want to ignore her. He decided to wait for her to look at him and then he said, 'Hello and how are you?' She replied but she didn't look comfortable, her sisters were with her. Shabana told her sisters that he was a classmate. Foriz knew it wasn't a good time to have a conversation with her.

While Foriz was waiting to go into the ceremony hall, he saw an old man and gave his salaam to him. The man looked like a Muslim, who had long white beard. The man asked Foriz if he was Bengali, and they started to have a general conversation out of nowhere. Soon Foriz found out that he was there for his daughter's graduation and he lived in Manor Park. Foriz had a very good idea that he must be Shabana's father. He was right, a bit later Shabana arrived to pick him up to go into the ceremony hall. He felt like introducing himself to the old man, 'My name is Foriz; I am the person who proposed for your gorgeous daughter.' Then he realised that it wasn't needed and wouldn't make any difference. What had happened had happened. Foriz thought that this man had no idea that how crazy Foriz was about Shabana and he had rejected him.

After the ceremony Foriz queued to get his graduation pictures taken with his sisters. He noticed Shabana was in the queue too. She looked awesome with the graduation gown. He told his big sister to take a look at Shabana, which she did. On the way home he felt he needed to propose for her again. Foriz was still a friend of Shabana but didn't speak to her too often. In the evening through texting they congratulated each other. She told him that she was sorry that she couldn't talk to him earlier. He called her up later on to listen to her voice and congratulate her again. Shabana told him that her parents were taking her to Bangladesh within two weeks. Foriz asked her if she could meet him for the last time before she went to Bangladesh. She agreed to meet up the next day.

Shabana's father Shujon and mother Ragana had an argument regarding whose relative Shabana should get married to. Shujon wanted her to get married to his sister's son. Ragana wanted her to get married to her brother's son. Her father said that he was the head of the house and he made the final decision but her mother refused to agree with him. Ragana said that she was the one who went through all the pain to give birth and the one who nurtured Shabana. She had the right to decide who Shabana should get married to. But his argument was that he was the father and because of his sperm she was born so he was in charge of the decision. Ragana said that her bother's son was better looking then his sister's son. Shujon said that his sister's son was more educated then the other one. Ragana said that education meant nothing because when he arrived here he would be cooking for white people. They were not getting any further with their decision. Sabina, Shabana's young sister decided to interject and told them 'Shouldn't you be asking Shabana to decide who she would like to get married to.' 'We don't have to ask her, we know what is best for her,' said Ragana. 'Well, then your mother will tell her to choose her brother's son,' replied Shujon. They went around the same circle over and over again.

Shabana and Foriz met in East Ham in a pizza restaurant for the last time. Foriz arrived ten minutes before her and ordered a pizza and drinks. They sat back of the restaurant where people couldn't see through the windows.

'So Shabana, how are you?'

'I am surviving, how about you?'

The drinks arrived to the table. Foriz drank some drink from his glass and asked Shabana to drink too.

'I am breathing without a life.'

'I am in a similar situation.'

'What you mean?'

'You know what's going to happen when I get to Bangladesh.'

'I don't, tell me?'

The pizza arrived to the table. Foriz put two slices of pizza on her plate.

'My parents were arguing about who I should get married to. My father wants me to get married to his sister's son and my mother wants me to get married to her brother's son.'

'Why don't you say that you don't want any of them but you want some one else?'

'I wish I could say that.'

Foriz asked Shabana to eat the pizza. She told him that she didn't feel like eating.

'Shabana we live in England and I am sure you have a choice.'

'Yes I know about choice but I can't hurt my mother, she has done so much for me, I probably didn't tell you when I was born my mother was unconscious for some time and my father wasn't sure if she was going to live.'

'I understand your situation and your feelings for your parents.'

'I am worried too, how am I going to get married to a man I never met before?'

'Tell me what shall I do, I am finding it difficult to erase you from my memory.'

'If I can survive then I am sure you can survive, you are a man.'

'Can I propose to your parents again Shabana?'

'What's the point, you know they are stubborn and they will reject you and you'll be more upset.'

'You never know they might change their mind.'

'I won't stop you from proposing, the choice is yours.'

'Thanks, I will ask my parents to visit your parents with in next few days.'

'No problems, if that makes you happy.'

The waitress took the plates away and cleaned the table.

'When my parents visit your house can you tell your father that you would like to be my wife.'

'I can't, I don't want them to know that I have spoken to a boy, if they find out that I did then they will be so cross with me. They won't forgive me.'

'Anyway what ever happens I will always remember you and love you and keep you in my heart.'

'I will always have respect for you and remember you for the love you gave me.'

'Shall I come with my parents?'

'Please don't, if you do my father will recognise you.'

'Ok, I won't.'

'I better go now.'

'Please don't, I want you to stay with me for ever.'

'I wish.'

'I love you so much Shabana.'

Shabana didn't respond. She looked at his eyes.

'Can you hear me, I love you so much Shabana.'

'I know, but try not to love me; it will get easier for you.'

'Will you give me a hug please?'

'You know I can't do that.' She said that with a soft tone.

'Can I hold your hands once?'

'Come on Foriz you know I can't do that, you should know that.'
'I know. I was just trying it.'
Shabana paused and after a few seconds she said;
'Listen Foriz, I will place my hands on the table and close my eyes and you can hold them. Is that ok?'
'Are you sure, if you don't want, I won't hold them.'
'Don't worry; I want you to hold my hands only once.'
Shabana closed her eyes. Foriz held both of her hands and kissed them and said, 'I love you Shabana more then the world.' She opened her eyes and said, 'Are you finished?' 'No I haven't finished, I won't let go off your hands.'
She looked at his eyes and had tears in her eyes. He let go off her hands. She took a tissue out of her bag. Foriz took the tissue from her hand and wiped her face.
'Foriz, you are the first man to touch my hands.'
'I like to be the first man to be your husband.'
'I hope, your hope will come true but I doubt it.'
'I have got this idea. It just came to my head.'
'What is it?'
'How about if I kidnap you.'
'And.'
'Keep you safe, away from your parents for twenty four hours.'
'Not a good idea.'
'Listen, they will realise it happened because they refused me, then they might change their mind.'
'I don't want them to go through any pain.'
'You love your parents so much but all they want is to help a relative to come to London and I find that unacceptable.'
'What can I do, I can't change their mind and I can't change my takdir.'
'Look Shabana, Lana did it, why can't you do it?'
'I am not Lana and I am not as beautiful as her!'
'I know who you are.'
'Can I go home now, please bondhu.'
'Yes bhondu, you can go now but don't forget I will be thinking about you non-stop, with every breath I take, every blink I make, every day I live. I love you'

'I love you too but I got to leave you.'

Foriz's parents visited Shabana's house again. Proposed for her once again, hopping that her parents' might change their mind. Shabana's father told them that they had arranged to take her to Bangladesh. His parents requested to her parents that if they could kindly accept their proposal, they would be very happy. If the changed their mind then Shujon should let them know and they would pay for the cancellation of the tickets. Once they left Shabana's house, Shujon told his wife that he didn't mind if his daughter married Foriz, but Ragana refused to consider.

'What's the point, they are not related to us and the marriage won't be any benefit to our family,' said Ragana.

'I know they are not related to us but the family sounds like a good family and the groom is educated, I am sure they will keep our daughter happy.'

'No, no chance, we will take her to Bangladesh as we have planned, I don't understand why the Satan comes in when we plan something.'

'I think father is correct we should consider this proposal as they really want her,' said Sabina. 'Who are you to talk, you are not mature enough to talk,' replied Ragana.

Shabana texted Foriz and told him that her mother refused the proposal again but her father didn't mind. Foriz was extremely upset and initially didn't have much to say, he felt gutted. He had the feeling like his life was empty without Shabana. Foriz felt that he did his best to achieve her but she wasn't in his Takdir. She wasn't meant to be his wife, life had to carry on, like people say, 'There are more fishes in the sea.'

One of the Sabbir's cousin, Abdul Harshim was working in a supermarket as a cashier after working his way up from a fast food chain. Harshim had some criminal friends and always spoke about making quick money. While he was working as a cashier he started to accept dodgy credit cards for purchase payment. He thought he could get away with it. He was caught. The police investigation started. When the family members heard that he was a criminal they thought that he would give the family a bad name. They sent him to Bangladesh. The police couldn't trace him. Typical Bengali plan. When problems arose send them to Bangladesh. He stayed in Bangladesh like a king in the village as everyone liked Londoners. After staying for a year he returned to London and assumed that the police won't chase him.

Gozafor Miah bought a Bengali newspaper, which he did most of the time to keep up to date with Bangladesh's news. He usually read it and then told others in the restaurant about the main stories. He read the main story; The Bangladeshi police department is reported to have compiled figures showing that four out of five officers have a criminal record. The figures published in a national newspaper, shows that in the past five years 85,000 of the country's 100,000 strong police force have been punished for their involvement in criminal activity. About 12,000 were sacked or forced to retire. The rest were given warnings or other disciplinary action and were allowed to stay in their jobs. A recent report by a watchdog organisation, Transparency International, described the Bangladeshi police as the most corrupt professional group in the country. Gozafor Miah asked the other staff, 'how the hell are we supposed to go forward when we have so much corruption in our country?'

Chapter Fifteen

2002

Many Indian restaurant owners continued to persuade the government that there was a need for more restaurant staff. They needed to bring staff from Bangladesh to cope with the demand. The government approved ten thousand employees that can be brought from Bangladesh for jobs. As soon as the news broke through almost all the Indian restaurant became short of staff. The news spread to Bangladesh like a wild fire. The restaurants in London that were not making any money had started to make money and were short staffed too.

Within a few days Sabbir's home telephone became unusually busy with calls from Bangladesh, twenty four seven. Some of the peasants never had the brain to realise that there was a time difference between the both countries. Sabbir's relatives asked him to sponsor them for restaurant work. Some of the relatives visited Sabbir's father in the village and spoke to him to speak to Sabbir for a sponsorship. Some relatives asked other relatives to mention to Sabbir to sponsor them. Even Sabbir's mother's relatives called her to ask her son to sponsor them. It wasn't long before one relative offered Sabbir fifteen thousand pounds for a sponsorship.

Sabbir's restaurant was fully staffed. He didn't need to bring anyone from Bangladesh. Sabbir couldn't stop the temptation of not making some easy money. He decided to apply for two employees, one kitchen staff and one waiter for each of the restaurants. Sabbir ordered his accountant to produce the business account to show that the restaurant was doing fine and had a good balance sheet. He didn't have to look for customers. The customers already had tracked him. All he had to decide whom to bring and how much to charge. In order to qualify they needed skills and qualification but in the village no one had ever worked in a restaurant or ever had a cooking qualification. There was zero percent chance for any one to meet the two basic criteria.

Sabbir found out from other restaurant owners that in Sylhet a restaurant provided fake qualification and skills for a few thousands takas. For the waiters position they needed to meet the criteria of speaking some English which was extremely difficult for any villager. Sabbir decided to charge his relatives ten thousand pounds each and the non-relatives fifteen thousands pounds each. And this was just to get to London. The potential employees paid the sum to Sabbir's uncle as a trusted person that both side can trust. When they arrived in London the money would be transferred into Sabbir account. From each of the other restaurants other partners' relatives wanted to come. That wasn't a problem as they were paying customers. It was a golden opportunity for so many people to bring their relatives and no-one wanted to let go off the opportunity. Sylhetis won't let go off any opportunities! If they do, then they are not Sylhetis!

Shabana's parents took her to Bangladesh as arranged. Her parents didn't consult her regarding what kind of husband she would like to get married to. Shabana's parents decided after many arguments that she should get married to her mother's brother's son. She didn't get to see the groom before the wedding. The wedding and the 'extras' were arranged by her father. She was married within ten days. For her dowry the groom's father gave a plot of land in her name in Sylhet town. Shabana accepted the marriage just to obey her parents,' and to make them happy. Even though she would have liked someone who was educated and from London. Inwardly she was very angry and sad that the social ideology didn't allow her to have a choice. She controlled her anger by justifying it through the ideology that it was written in her Takdir to get married to that man.

Shabana's young sister Sabina was with her. Her parents' promised her she won't get married but as they arrived in the village they changed their mind. Sabina told her parents that she won't get married to anyone as she was there for a holiday and to be part of Shabana's wedding. They told her that if she didn't then she wouldn't be coming back to London. She felt like killing her parents. Sabina told them that if they got her married then she would kill her husband and they should not blame her if she did so. Her wedding was arranged with a village man who paid her father twenty laks. Ten laks advance and ten laks once the groom got to London and became a permanent citizen.

Sabina was in a trap, no where to run. She wanted to run but she didn't know the way. The roads didn't have any names on them or directions. Sabina had to go with the family to do Shabana's wedding shopping. While they were at the shopping centre Sabina noticed two white men. She waved at them and invited them to come to her with her hands. As they came, she said hello. Her parents told her not to speak to the men. She asked them, 'Where you guys from?' 'England.' She felt so much better. Her parents persisted that she shouldn't talk to them. Sabina told the men, 'You guys have to help me, I am trapped, I need to get to England, please help me escape. My parents are forcing me to get married here.' The men became interested in the story line instantly. One man said, 'Its sounds like a Bollywood film, I can't see any camera and action,' 'This is real, not Bollywood,' she replied. The men were doing some kind of investigation in Bangladesh – no wonder. They told her that they could help her. Sabina told her parents, 'Good bye, I am going with the white men to London, catch me if you can.' Her parents tried to stop her but the men called the police and the British High Commission. Lots of people gathered around the shopping centre. Her parents and the relatives stopped her from leaving.

The police came and heard both sides of the argument. Then the police officer asked Sabina to say who she wanted to go with. And she did. The police told her parents they couldn't stop her from going to London. Her mother cried and told her not to go. Sabina told her, 'I won't listen to you, you are an evil bitch. You fucked up Shabana's life, I won't let you fuck up my life, go to hell.' The police took Sabina and handed her over to the British High Commission. In a special flight The British High Commission sent her back to England.

Sabbir's children watched many adverts of the Spiderman movie on television. They wanted to watch the movie in a cinema but due to Sabbir's ideology they were not allowed to go to a cinema. He believed that by going to cinema they would become too westernised. He didn't wanted to be too strict. He felt by being too strict he may lose the love of his children. Sabbir promised his children that as soon as Spiderman came out on DVD he would buy it for them. A few months later it was released on DVD. He bought it for them. He also wanted to watch it as he liked the advertisement clips he had seen. The whole family including Sima watched the movie. The children were very excited and loved the action. During the kissing screen, Sabbir forwarded it as it was embarrassing to watch kissing in front of the family. Sima couldn't understand how a man could jump like that. The children told her that' she won't understand because she was from the village. The children watched it over and over again. Every time Sabbir came to the living room the little kids were watching Spiderman and sometimes he had to watch it to keep the kids happy. While he watched it again, he came up with an idea of his own Spiderman like movie that he would have liked to make if he had the resources.

Sabbir thought about it and came out with the idea that the movie would be called 'Ligerman.' In his head he planned how the movie would evolve and who the character would be. His film would be based on two people who are married, go to honeymoon in China, namely Mr. and Mrs. Tiger. While they are in their apartment, some local gangster come in and tried to mug them, but Mr. Tiger tries to defend himself. A gangster shoots Mr. Tiger dead. The gang take Mrs. Tiger with them and dump her in a near by jungle where a lion first attacks her and scratches her. Her blood comes out but the lion for some reason doesn't kill her. She survives and returns to England with her husband's dead body. She would become pregnant with Mr. Tiger's vitamin and the lion's scratching will take effects like the Spider's bite. A son will be born to Mrs. Tiger and she will look at him and think that he looks a bit like a lion so she names him Liger-man. Takes name from lion and her husband; namely 'Li' from Lion and 'ger' from Tiger.

When the child grows up, he would have this un-usual look, bit of Lion, Englishness and Chinese in him with make up – he will have very good strength and natural ability of karate skills which leads him to take further training in karate. He will become a good fighter like Bruce Lee with dash of lion's attributes in him.

While at school other kids would take the piss out of him but he would try his best to keep away from trouble. When he has no choice, time to time he would get in bother and beat up the opposition. His reputation would go up. The best fighter in the school would challenge him. He would initially ignore it as he didn't want to get into trouble. The strongest boy, who would be tall and big, would call him a chicken for not fighting. After a few months of ignoring he would agree to fight outside the school so he doesn't get suspended. Most of the school pupils will come to watch. Everyone believing that Ligerman would get thrashed. No one would have seen his body naked or muscle apart from his best friends. At the beginning of the fight every time the big boy try to hit Ligerman, he would just move quickly, which the crowd enjoy and suddenly Ligerman would go for one punch and it would be all over. He would become the best fighter in the school. All the girls would come after him. The best looking girl would dump her boy friend as usual and become his. He would leave school with good GCSEs grades and go to college. He would have a few best friends, an Asian, A white and a black to make sure it would not be a racist movie. Also to sell it all over the world. Maybe have an Arabian girl in their to sell it in the Middle East. Perhaps he has to make two versions of the movie, one with nudity for the West and one without for the East; then no one would complain everyone satisfied.

At college Ligerman would try his best to get on with his studies, others would pick on him and his mates. He would beat them up. A few fighting scene to make it interesting. A student would try to rape a teacher. Ligerman would go and save her. The big boy from his school would attack him with his gangs but Ligerman would fight them like Bruce Lee with bit of Lion action to make it very interesting. He would regularly go to gym and get fit.

Ligerman would return to China for revenge. He would go to China with his friends and mother and stay in the same hotel that his parents went for honeymoon. Slowly they would hunt down the criminals that had killed his father. Ligerman's friends would also help him track down the gang members and provide other technical support. He would beat them up using natural strength and some movement of lion and then returns to England, that where it would end. And it's where Sabbir become a movie maker rather then a curry seller. Once Sabbir finished plotting his idea of this Ligerman movie he was quite happy and seriously thought about investigating whether he could make such a movie called Ligeman.

Priya telephoned her sister to let her know that her husband had received indefinite visa to stay in the UK. Kolim waited for more then three years for that decision. Sokina was very pleased for her sister's family. Sabbir couldn't believe how the fuck the government could have given that man a visa when in the eighteen years he lived in the UK he never paid a penny in tax. All his earning was tax free. Priya invited everyone to her rented flat to celebrate. Sabbir didn't want to go as he had seen them so many fucking times in his house he was glad that they had left.

Gozafor Miah read the Bengali newspaper that he had bought. From the newspaper he found; The Danish Government has publicly accused the Bangladeshi shipping minister of being corrupt. That was no surprise. It had withdrawn $45 million in aid from the Bangladeshi shipping sector and accused the minister of behaving dishonestly in his ministry's attempts to offer a tender for the repair of four ferries. Gozafor Miah commented front of the other staff 'How the hell are we going to go forward when the bastards ministers are so bloody corrupt, the stupid bastards are mugging our country.' This is why we are going backward,' replied Goni.

Many families approached Sabbir and Sima regarding their daughter's marriage. Most of the talks were from graduates and high cast families. Khadijah didn't want to get married. She wanted go to university and study Islam. Sabbir wanted to get her married as he was a bit skeptical about her going to university. But all the other family members wanted her to go to university and further her knowledge. Sabbir had to allow her to go to university without much of a fuss. Maybe he had learnt that he didn't live in Sylhet. He had to follow the Western waves.

―

Badol Miah telephoned Sabbir. First he asked Sabbir how he was and the family. Then he told Sabbir to look out for a suitable boy for his daughter, Shuma, who was aged twenty-two and recently completed her masters in economic. Sabbir asked what kind of boy they were looking for. He replied preferably a legal man with a degree at least and obviously from Sylhet and good family background. Most people didn't want to go outside their little world. It is their comfort zone and they wanted to stay in it. Sabbir told Badol Miah that he would lookout for a suitable boy.

―

The United Nations has accused Bangladesh's state-owned telecommunications company of corruption. The UN said that it had received bills for more than $16,000 for international telephone calls that were never made. Did they not know that they were in number one corrupt country in the world. Gozafor Miah wasn't surprised by what he read, 'Bastard,' he said aloud. He also celebrated with sarcastic enthusiasm that Bangladesh had topped the public sector corruption list for the second year running, a survey by the business funded lobby group Transparency International suggested.

―

December 2002

Yasin graduated in business studies with a honours degree. He made his father and the whole family very proud. Sabbir and the other children went to the graduation. Sima didn't bother, she didn't like travelling. They took pictures, framed them and displayed it in their living rooms wall. Yasin showed his certification to Sokina. She looked at it and jokingly said, 'So you worked three years for this piece of paper.' He told her that this paper was worth thousands of pounds. Yasin invited his friends to the restaurant to celebrate his degree. His friends were allowed to have a fee meal at his father's expense.

2003

Shabana told her husband politely that he should pray his daily prayers. He told her that he didn't have time. She didn't like it that her husband didn't pray at all. She told him, 'You have time to work and you don't have no time for Allah?'

'I will pray to Allah when I become an old man.'

'How can you say that?'

'When I am old, I won't be able to work so I will just stay in the mosque and pray to Allah all the time.'

'That's nonsense and I don't find it funny.'

'You don't worry about me, if I don't pray I will get the sin, not you, so leave me alone.'

'I should be worried, I am married to you, if you don't pray when our children grow up they won't pray too, they will say father doesn't pray, why should we pray?'

'I will send them to the mosque so they will learn to pray.'

'Do you know that if you don't pray I can refuse to sleep with you?'

He laughed sarcastically.

'Have you got another husband to sleep with, maybe you got someone at work?'

'Can you kindly stop talking rubbish.'

'I am not talking rubbish. If you have a boy friend I won't be able to tell.'

'That's it, I am not talking to you, I am going up stairs now.'

Day by day Shabana was getting more and more pissed off with Shundor's attitudes and behaviour. She wasn't getting the respect that she expected.

Yasin found a new job as a junior accountant. He continued to help his father in the evening in the restaurant. Sabbir never told his son not to work in the restaurant, but he always told Yasin to go home after a few hours. Sabbir wanted his son's interest to stay in the business so eventually Yasin can take over when he retired. Yasin enjoyed working in the restaurant, he met different types of people and liked mingling with the regular customers.

Sokina kept on receiving calls from Bangladesh. So many of Sabbir's relatives wanted to speak to him regarding restaurant's work permit visa. The relatives knew Sabbir had a few restaurants. Some of them were so stupid they didn't know the time difference as they called during late knights. Some of the relatives went to see Sabbir's father in the village to ask him to speak to his son for a work permit sponsorship. Work permit sponsorship was another opportunity for large waves of Sylheti men to come to London. Majority of the men who came didn't have the intention of returning back to Bangladesh unless they are caught by the immigration. They will stay in London as long as they can and if possible get married to a British subject.

Abdul Harshim was caught drug dealing in Whitechapel. He didn't realise the police had very tiny cameras fitted on the hot spot and caught him. He was supposed to attend a hearing in a court. But before that his family sent him to Bangladesh to avoid any sentences. He got married there to a young innocent girl. The girls' parents didn't ask any question. As soon as they heard that he was from London they just agreed to the marriage. He stayed in Bangladesh for long time and became a father.

Spices of Brick Lane

After lunch one of Mr. Ali's student had gone missing from his lesson. He asked the other students 'Where is Hamza? 'You don't want to know sir, his gone home to go to toilet,' One student replied. Sarcastically Mr. Ali replied 'Is there no toilet in the school?' 'There are toilets; but they are too crap, no one can use them; there is no toilet seat, no toilet roll and not even a lock on the doors; if you want to use one; you have to use one leg to keep the door shut,' replied one student. Mr. Ali couldn't believe that in this day and age in London the toilet condition could be that bad. At the next opportunity he visited the student's toilet and witnessed it himself. He thought, how could this be possible that a student had to go home because of the conditions of the poor toilets? The government was spending all the money killing innocent Iraqis, Afghanistanian and Palestinian. The government doesn't see the shortage of money in our door step. He felt like taking picture of the toilet and sending it to BBC news.

Five people arrived through the restaurant's working visa sponsorship scam. One didn't get his visa, he struggled to answer the immigration questions. Sabbir made an appeal against that decision. Actually there were no vacancies in Sabbir's restaurants. That didn't stop him and his partners making some extra cash. That was what he aimed to do and that's why he was here in London to do. His relatives stayed in his house for a few days. Then he found them work as far as possible so they didn't come to his home too often. Sabbir sent one to Isle of White, another to Scotland and others to different parts of the country. He told them the further they went the more money they would earn and the less chance there was of the immigration catching them, this was partly true. But this was not the end of it. Sabbir received calls from his relative's parent's back home that he needed to try and find wives for them so they could stay in London forever. Sabbir told them he would look out for brides but it was difficult to find any as they demanded too much dowry money.

Foriz was doing his Eid shopping in Green Street. He bumped into Shabana in a sari house. She was with a man; he assumed it was her husband. He looked at him and couldn't believe that she could marry a man like that. The man had no style; definitely a 'freshi' from Bangladesh. He told himself how could she marry a man like that; all she had to do was, run away from home. Foriz waited around to say hello to her but knew if he did then her husband will ask her millions of questions like, 'How do you know this man?' So he decided to catch her attention, which he did a bit later and nodded his head up and down to alert her, she replied with a smile. Then she came to talk to him. That surprised him. Shabana asked him how he was and what he had been up to. She introduced him to her husband and told him that Foriz was her university class mate. They shook hands but Shundor didn't look comfortable meeting Foriz.

When Shabana went home her husband asked her if Foriz was her boy friend. She told him no. Then he asked her if Foriz had liked her. She told him that there were so many boys that liked her but she told them to get lost. The man didn't know when to stop. He continued like a detective. He said that Foriz looked nice. Why had not she fancied him. She told him that she wasn't interested in boys. Shundor wondered how he could trust her. She was pissed off so she said, couldn't you tell when you slept with me if I had one. Shabana started to dislike her husband more and more. She felt there was far too big a gap between their ideologies.

An author released a book about Brick Lane which was good news. The problem was it caused an uproar in the Sylheti community. Some of the quotes from the book were published in the front pages of a few Bengali newspapers. Sabbir wanted to read the book and find out for himself what was written before jumping to any conclusion.

By reading the book he realised why the Sylheti community was upset. The comments were absolutely nonsense and one-sided. He felt that the author only wrote lies about the Sylheti people. She only wrote about the negative side of the Sylheti people. Nothing positive and that was diabolical. She should have been sued for making lying and stereo typical comments.

Sabbir and Miton arrived at work, after getting all the basic stuff ready. Sabbir asked Miton, what he thought about the comment made in the book.

'Well, I read the comments in a newspaper and I found it abysmal.'

'I don't understand why she had to lie about what she wrote and be rude to us Sylheti people. What have we done to her? We are from the same country.'

'You know what people say. When people become intelligent they also become stupid.'

'Stupid is not the word. She is s brainless bitch. iI we see her near Brick Lane, we will teach her a lesson.'

'You know what the other thing people say, when people are not happy with themselves or life they try to find weaknesses in others to make themselves happy. That is what she was trying to do. She is someone mentally ill, depressed and trying to find happiness by throwing insults at others.'

'I understand what you're saying. The main problem was that she wasn't nurtured properly, if she was then she wouldn't have made them lies up.'

'I think the reason she wrote that was, she wants to be famous and people would go and buy the book to find out what she had written so she can make some money.'

'If she was so desperate to be famous she could have become the best paid madam in Brick Lane.'

'I know what you're saying. She could have said some of the positive things Sylheti people have done over the past thirty years.'

'When people give one side of the story, you can say that only one side of their brain works.'

Simultaneously the kitchen staff were discussing the same issue as they read it in a Bengali newspaper.

Gozafor Miah spoke, Goni and the others listened to him as he had more to say and had been through many problems. 'These people don't know what we have gone through to establish ourselves in Brick Lane and England, since we arrived. We have taken so much abuse from the honkies, so many of our Sylheti brothers were seriously beaten up, a few brothers died in order to establish ourselves, and she insults us. Because of us Sylhetis, other Bangladeshi can come and live in this area without problems. Because of our numbers, we were the people who stood against the racist while people in the sixties and seventies and she calls us peasants, this woman doesn't know the basic history of Bengali in this area, how did she become a writer?'

Customers came into the restaurant so everyone had to stop the talking of the subject. It didn't look like an issue people were going to forget easily. Some people felt so upset that if they had found her they would have beaten her up. Next day Sabbir told Miton that he was thinking about inviting that woman to his restaurant and then insulting her. Miton told him that wasn't a good idea. And he didn't think she would come after what she had written.

'I am still so upset, how can she say so many stupid things about us when we have created an industry that is worth over 1.5 billion pounds.'

'Stupid people come up with stupid things.'

'If we were peasant then how could we have created such a big curry industry with probably close to ten thousand restaurants and takeaways?'

'Exactly, we have been probably more successful in terms of the number of businesses we own than any other foreigners who came at the same time as us.'

'She wrote that we are un-ambitious, if we were not ambitious then why did we Sylheti people open about ten thousand Indian restaurants.'

'Probably she doesn't know these facts'

'If we are illiterate then how come we are running thousands of restaurants?'

'Exactly, where is the evidence that we are peasants?'

'Ok, if we are close-minded, how come we are opening more and more businesses. Just look at Brick Lane. What we Sylheti created!'

'I know, I wish she would look at these facts and say sorry to us.'

'African were here before us. What industry did they create?'

'None, actually they are good at drug dealing and screwing white women.'

'What is the point of being educated if you don't have any money or if you can't earn enough money.'

'People who are educated they think they are the best even though they are not rich. It's a way of keeping themselves happy.'

'There are thousands of people in Bangladesh that are educated but there are no jobs for them.'

'We found an opportunity here and took advantage of it and are making good money.'

'Tell me how many educated people are making ten thousands pounds a week, that's how much roughly I make from my restaurants.'

'I don't know, maybe five percent of England's population.'

'Not even the PM earns what I earn a week, so what if I am an uneducated Sylheti man?'

'We are better off being uneducated and rich.'

'A doctor, a professor, an MP doesn't even earn much as we restaurant owners earn.'

'It doesn't really matter if you're educated or not in our circumstances.'

'We made Sylhet district the richest district in Bangladesh with the profits we made from our businesses and it's a fact.'

'Looks like she needs to do a lot more research about us.'

'The weaknesses she tried to find in us is nothing compared to the strengths we Sylhetis have.'

'We should send her the real facts.'

'Richard Branson left school without completing it, look at him, he is a multi millionaire, so what he doesn't have a degree, he has the brain.'

'So she has a degree, but she is still not happy. She is lying about people, insulting people without any provocation.'

'Main problem with the educational system is that they don't teach people to give fair views, only one sided or lies.'

'Exactly, like newspaper, you always get Muslims doing bad things, but you never get any thing about other religion because they are the racist against Islam.

Shabana and her husband sat down to eat dinner together. She had cooked all the food. 'Why is there not enough salt in this curry?' Shundor said.

'I might have forgot, there is the salt you can add it.'

'You are so stupid, you don't even check your curry to make sure that there is enough salt in it.'

'People make mistakes and it's only a bit of salt and you can add it if you want.'

'That's not the point, you should check to make sure it is perfect.'

'Well, in that case you should have asked me when you got married if I was a perfect cook or not.'

'If I knew you were so sloppy I wouldn't have got married to you.'

'And if I knew you are like this I would have told my parents to reject you.'

'I only married you because I needed to come to London.'

'I know.'

'Looks like I have to get another wife who can cook.'

'I know once you get your passport you will divorce me and go back to Bangladesh and get another wife.'

'No, I won't divorce you because aunty will get upset, so I will just keep you here and have another wife in Bangladesh.'

'If you do that I will divorce you.'

'I will see about that.'

Later on when Shundor went out of the house Shabana called her mother and told her all about it. Her mother told her, 'Men have light blood and they loose temper on little things and you should forgive him and carry on with your life.'

'If he talks to me like this now, how is he going to behave once he becomes legal?'

'People change, I am sure he will change and love you more once he realises.'

'When is he going to realize? I brought him to England and he doesn't respect me.'

'I will talk to him.'

Shabana's mother tried to calm her down. She would never allow Shabana to divorce her husband that would bring a bad name to their family.

Mr. Ali went to a trip with some of the students to the Thorpe Park. He looked forward to seeing the adventure as it was his first visit. They went by a coach. Mr. Ali enjoyed different rides and the atmosphere of the park with the colleague. He couldn't believe what happened at the end of the trip. Some of the students went into a shop and filled themselves with all sorts of goods, as they were there to loot everything. Quickly the shop keeper called the police. A few police officers came and checked all the students. All the stolen goods were taken from the students. It was a very embarrassing moment for Mr. Ali and his colleagues. The school was barred from taking students to the Thorpe Park again. The students' parents were invited to school and were informed of their actions. All the parents were gob-smacked that their children had done something like that. One parent said, 'Why did you not beat my son up, I give you permission to beat him up.' Another parent said, 'Where were the teachers when the children stole the goods? A teacher replied that they were allowed to go to shops by themselves; do you go with your child every time he or she goes to the shops? That shut up the imbecile parents.

Shabana's husband swore at her because she had put too much salt in a fish curry. While Shundor was eating, he said, 'How can you put so much salt in the fish curry, you stupid bitch, don't you look when you cook?'

'There is no need to swear at me, it was a mistake. I might have put the salt twice, anyway eat the other curries.'

'Did you not learn how to cook in your parents' house?' Maybe you were too busy talking to your boy friend.'

He threw the plate on the table and washed his hand.

'Don't give me a lecture, why don't you do the cooking sometimes and don't accuse me of things that you don't know about.' She said with a soft tone incase he got more angry.

'It's your job to do the cooking not mine.'

'It's not only my job, I also work outside and earn money and I have to cook too.'

Shundor left the kitchen. Shabana didn't like his swearing and attitude. She felt very upset because she married him and bought him to England, and this was how he treated her. He didn't have any respect for her. At the next opportunity she called her mother and told her about it. Her mother had no answer to why Shundor was behaving like that. Shabana told her that if he continued to behave like this then she would divorce him. Ragana told her 'You don't divorce for something so little as that, there are men who beat up their wife but they still don't get divorced, you have to make it work.' 'If he touches me I will get him killed.' Ragana told her that she would speak to Shundor's mother back home. Shabana remembered Foriz and thought that if she was married to him he definitely would have loved her so much more.

Sabbir's uncle Rahim called from Bangladesh and spoke to Sokina. He told her that he was sorry that he going to put them through a bit of bother as his underage son would be coming to London next day. Sokina asked him whether he had spoken to his brother about it. He said that he had spoken and his brother told him to speak to them in London but everything happened so quickly he didn't have chance to phone. Sokina told him that there was no space in the house as it was and it would be very difficult to fit an extra person in the house. Rahim told her that the carpet in London was very good and if they could provide some space on the carpet it would be very helpful. In the olden days ten to fifteen people used to live in one room on the carpet. Sokina told him that they would do their best to look after his son.

When Sabbir heard that his cousin, Shiru was coming to stay, he became very pissed off as there was no fucking space in the house. Also who was going to deal with all the problems and immigration business? The next day a person telephoned Sabbir and told him where to collect his cousin from. He didn't want to go and collect the boy. Sokina told him to do so other wise all the relatives would look down on them. Sabbir went to the given address and collected his thirteen year old cousin. Then he telephoned his uncle and to let him know so that he will pay the trafficker the money. Karim telephoned Sabbir and asked him to pay four thousands pounds for the child to the trafficker in London. He didn't want to pay, because his father told him he had to pay, but Sabbir told his father when the child grew up he had to pay him back.

Two weeks later Sabbir's uncle Sahim called and spoke to Sokina that he wanted to send his young child to London and if they would look after him too. She said 'As it is there are no rooms and one had arrived two weeks ago.' 'If I don't send my child, who will help me to survive financially later on and the opportunity doesn't come like this,' he said. Sokina told him that she will speak to Sabbir and let him know what to do. When Sabbir heard the news this time he became extremely angry and pissed off and told his mother, 'If uncle calls again then tell him to use his brain and find an extra room in the house; we are not running a refuge camp in London that they can send their child here; if he can't look after his own child then he shouldn't have given birth to the child. I am not the father, why should I look after his child?'

The following week Sabbir's cousin, Ariful arrived in London but Sabbir didn't know about it until the next day. Sahim called and told Sokina that his son was picked up by another relative from the Heathrow airport and Sabbir needed to pick him up. Sabbir refused to pick him up. He knew if he picked him up then Ariful would be staying with him. He told his mother that Ariful should stay with that relative as it was difficult to fit another person in the house. The news went to Bangladesh that Sabbir hadn't picked up Ariful yet. His uncle was very upset.

The telephone rang; Karim called, spoke to Sokina and Sabbir. He told Sabbir to pick up Ariful. Sabbir said that he won't pick up Ariful because there was no space in the house. Karim told him that he needed to help his brothers and Sabbir should make some space on the carpet. He also asked him to give four thousands pounds to the trafficker. Sabbir stood his ground, disobeyed his father's order and said

'I am sorry father but I am definitely not giving another four thousand pounds.' Later on Sabbir picked up his cousin as he had no choice. Sahim was preparing to sell some land to pay off the trafficker but Sabbir changed his mind and paid the trafficker.

This was a time when almost everyone in Sylhet were sending their young child to London, not thinking who will look after them. For them back home sending their children to London was like sending them to a money bank where they would go and pick up as much money as they wanted. The mentality of the people back home hadn't changed. They were sending children like they did thirty years ago. Who could blame them? The opportunity was too great to miss out on. One has to remember Sylhetis are probably the most opportunistic in the world.

Sabbir and his family had no real choice but were forced to look after the two illegal children. Not only that, he had to find way to make them legal in England. The family interviewed them about how they had arrived in London. Every relative who came also asked them the same questions. Shiru and Ariful told everyone how the trafficker trained them in Dhaka. They had to learn some English and their fake parents' name. With the fake parents they came to the UK. A few weeks later the parents returned to Bangladesh to bring more children. The traffickers were making million of pounds through bringing hundred of children every year. For each child they charged between seven to ten laks takas (seven to eight thousands pounds). Where was the British intelligence, couldn't they catch them? Actually they were too busy plotting which Muslim country to attack next.

Sabbir telephoned Jamal and other relatives and fished around to find out what they were doing with the illegal child they had. What process they were going through to make them legal. He found out that solicitors were charging up to a thousand pounds per child to apply for residency visa. Sabbir carried out further investigation to find out about a cheap solicitor. Through Badol Miah's recommendation the best deal he was offered for two children were fifteen hundred pounds. A problem was that for each child he needed a granter who would look after them. Sokina become the guardian for one child. Everyone asked Sabbir to be a guardian but he refused. At the end Jamal agreed to became guardian for the other child.

Sabbir arranged to meet the solicitor. The solicitor produced all the documents including a blue print of the story how they arrived. Sabbir couldn't believe the dodgy Bengali solicitor, and how they got away with the storyline. Once again Sabbir had to cough out another fifteen hundred pounds. Illegal children weren't allowed to go anywhere. They had no official documents. They had to stay home and watch television most of the time. When they were bothered they prayed. Sabbir gave them books to read. After a few months the immigration department replied, giving each of the children one year's permission card, which had their picture on it with the relevant information. The immigration officials were so stupid that they believed what the solicitor had written. One could argue how could they believe the story that was provided to them about the children arrival and situation. Then again there are loopholes in the system which the solicitors explored. Probably the government doesn't have enough money to investigate the child trafficking issues, but money is available to bomb humans in other parts of the world. With the immigration card, Shiru and Ariful were able to go to school which was free. Sabbir also had to send them to the local mosque to read the Qur'an, which cost him another ten pounds per week.

Sabbir's children complained to him that they didn't have enough space to study in their own home. He noticed and understood but couldn't do anything to create more space. There were times his children sat on the stairs to do their homework. Their house had been taken over by refugees. His children wanted to know why they had to look after everyone who came from the village. There were other problems, such as there being hardly any space to do the daily prayers.

One major problem was the usage of the toilet. When it was necessary for someone to go to the toilet they became really annoyed as most of the time it was busy as one after another were going to it like a public toilet. Mostly it was a problem in the morning when the children woke up to get ready to go to school all at the same time. Sabbir had no option but to build an extension at the back of the house to create more space. The extension cost him fifteen grand. At last, that provided a bit more room for everyone to get more oxygen.

Mr. Ali was doing his break duty. He came across a group of year eleven boys smoking. He told them to stop the smoking. And they did. One of the student asked Mr. Ali if he wanted to try some. Mr. Ali wasn't sure what he meant so he asked what he meant. The student asked him if he wanted to try some ganja. He couldn't believe that the boy had no respect for a teacher and openly talked about drugs. The boy continued to offer and asked Mr. Ali if he wanted to sell some to his colleague. It was an embarrassing situation for Mr. Ali. The student asked him how much he earned. Mr. Ali told him enough to keep his bank manager happy. The boy said, 'Sir, what you earn in a week I earn that in a day.' At the end of the break duty, Mr. Ali reported the boys to the deputy head teacher. The boys were checked, drugs were found and they were suspended from the school. Drugs were a major problem in the local area. It was so easily available and young children were taking it for fun and then getting addicted. Another issue the government doesn't have money to tackle. Why had Tower Hamlets became the drug capital of England. Then again did the government care about Tower Hamlets's Sylhetis. Probably to the government, they were just foreigners and no one cared whether they were successful or not.

Gozafor Miah asked Goni in the kitchen if they heard that a ship had sunk in the Meghna River in Bangladesh, killing up to four hundred people in what was believed to be the country's biggest shipping disaster. Most of them didn't hear it as they didn't have Bangla TV, except Sabbir. Goni chopped onion and said, 'We keep on getting ferries sunk but we never learn from our mistakes.' 'How can we learn from our mistakes, when people only think about money, not the safety of other people, they should never overload a ferry and they should never use a ferry when the weather condition is not good, but these greedy people will never understand they just want to make money what ever the condition is.'

CHAPTER SIXTEEN

2004

Sabbir had to reapply for further residency for the illegal cousins as their one year permit had expired. The solicitor obviously needed more money which Sabbir had to cough out. This time it cost him another eleven hundred pounds. The solicitor made the claim that these children don't have anywhere to go and they needed permission to stay in England. Where were they before they came here! You would expect solicitors to tell the truth, but they are the biggest crooks. They tell people how to lie so they can make money. What did these solicitors learn at university? Didn't they have a topic where they were taught about honesty. If they don't tell the truth then who will?

Sabbir's cousins spoke about how other children at their school spoke to them. Some of the children called them 'freshi,' illegal and kept on asking them for their real age. They found it difficult to avoid the other children as they were always approached by them. Sabbir told them to ignore them and go to the library and read books. It was very difficult for the kids in schools as they were bullied like that. When others called Shiru a 'freshi', he told them, 'Yes I am fresh from Bangladesh.' Other children knew they were illegal mainly because they had illegal relatives like that and they never spoke English. If anyone didn't speak English it meant they were illegal.

Peter sat at the table two and ate his meal with his wife, Sheila. If he ate in the restaurant then he always sat at table two because it was the closest table to the bar which provided the opportunity to talk to Sabbir and the bar staff. One thing led to another thing they ended up talking about animal rights. 'So why do you people like animals so much? asked Sabbir.

'Because we care about animals,' replied Sheila.

'Of course, you do. We also care about animals but we don't go that far,' said Sabbir.

'You people don't understand the feeling of having an animal as you lot don't like dogs.'

Peter didn't get bothered joining in the conversation. He was too busy drinking.

'We don't mix with animals because they are animals.'

'They are beautiful, I love my doggy.'

'We don't have space for human in our houses, how can we fit an animal too.'

'That's a valid point,' said Peter.

'Even if you lot had space you lot don't look after animals.' 'We are too busy looking after humans.'

'If you had lots of money and space would you look after a dog?'

'No, I would never have a dog in my house because if a dog touches me I have to change my clothes before I can pray. Don't ask me why.'

'Why are you people are so mean towards animals?'

'Not mean, it's just one of those things, but I think before one looks after an animal we need to see how we can help the humans all over the world that are dying because of no food. Once the humans have food we should look after the animals.'

'It's not our fault in the poor country the government keeps all the money for themselves and don't distribute it to their people.'

'I still think we should save human life rather then an animal's.'

'You give money to the poor country, I bet it won't reach them. The corrupt government will keep it.'

Suddenly through the post Sabbir received a notice to pay £80.00 fine for driving into the 'conjunction' area. He was quite sure that he didn't drive into that area. He refused to pay so they increased the fine to £120.00. He complained to them. They told him that they had his Mercedes number plate and he had to pay. He started to receive more fines through the letter box and couldn't believe why he was receiving them for no reason. He continued not to pay. A court order came and he had to attend the court. He hired a lawyer to look into his case. Sabbir went into court ready for battle.

In the court a lawyer asked him, why he hadn't paid the fines. He replied that he never drove into an area that was conjunctional so he refused to pay. They showed him some pictures of the Mercedes that they had caught on camera with the number plate that was registered in his name and asked him 'Is this your car?' Sabbir looked at the car and he was surprised to see his car in the picture. 'It looks like my car but it is definitely not my car,' he replied. 'What do you mean this is not your car?' the lawyer replied. 'Mr. Lawyer you have wasted your time and the judges time and most importantly my time by bringing me here. The car in the picture is not my car. My car is parked outside in the car park. If you like you can go and have a look, this car has two doors but my car has four doors, so please explain to me how this could be my car. I like to know how you are going to compensate me for wasting my time?' The lawyer took time out and went out to check his car. When they returned they discussed it with the judge and gave the 'not guilty' verdict, apologized to Sabbir and told him he didn't have to pay any of the fines. The lawyer said that they would investigate why there were two cars with same number plate. Sabbir said, 'Thank you' and left the court. A criminal had used Sabbir number plate to drive in the conjunctional area and probably got away with it.

Foriz was eating in a restaurant in Green Street. He noticed Shabana at another table with her husband. He just couldn't believe why he kept on bumping into her. Her husband went to the toilet. He called her by her name. She looked at him. He asked her how she was and they chatted for a few seconds until her husband was due back. Shabana told him that she worked in a solicitor's farm and her husband worked in a restaurant. She told him that if he needed a solicitor when he wanted to buy a house then he should give her a call. Foriz was surprised to hear that she wanted to communicate with him. She gave her business card to him. She was very friendly with him. He was confused by her behaviour and softness. Foriz felt that there might be something wrong with her relationship. He thought that soon he was going to find out.

Mr. Ali called a parent to complain about their son. He told the father that his son had called him 'Son of a pig.' The father told him 'I am sorry, tomorrow you will see how sorry my son is'. The next day the boy came to school with black eyes from his elder brother and said sorry to Mr. Ali. Some Bengali parents were so streaked that they don't like it if their child is rude to the teacher. On the other hand there were others didn't have interest in their child's education, they were too busy working in the restaurants. A recent report pointed out that Bengali children don't do well because their fathers don't give anytime to their children. How can they give time, they work seventy hours, six days a week.

In one of Sabbir's Bengali neighbour's houses a fight started. Every one heard shouting and screaming. Sabbir knew some of the brothers of the house. Being a neighbour Sabbir visited the house to help out and find out what was going on. He was surprised by what he saw. He realised his own life was in danger. Sabbir looked for away out but there wasn't one. He was in the thick of it.

Affilia had called the Brick Lane gang to come and kill her brothers. She had a meeting with her brothers regarding how much money she should get from her father's property. The father had passed away a few years ago. They couldn't sort out their differences. Wahid, one of the brothers had Affilia's husband under his control with his knife as Affilia called the gang. Wahid told her that if the gang arrived and tried to hurt him or his brother, he would kill her husband. That's when everyone had started to panic, shouted and screamed. Wahid's mother, uncle and other sisters were also in the house. Sabbir wasn't sure of the full story of what was going on. On the surface of it he saw that it was something ugly. Sabbir told Wahid no one would come into the house. He knew most of the Brick Lane boys, they would not hurt him. Quickly Sabbir made some calls to find out if there was any truth that the Brick Lane boys were coming over. He was told by his contact that it was true. Sabbir told them there should be no fight. The family was his neighbour and friends. They told him that wasn't a problem but they had to visit and then go. Sabbir told Wahid to release his sister's husband. No one could hurt his family. Everything was under Sabbir's control. He told them that he had spoken to one of the gang members. No one would touch them. He would be standing out-side the house. Soon some Brick Lane boys arrived in a van and Gunda Miah – one of the gang leaders, came out of the van spoke to Sabbir tended to be aggressive for a few minutes and then they left.

Later on Sabbir asked his mother if she knew anything about the fight. Sokina knew a lot from Affilia's mother. Affilia asked her brothers to re-mortgage the house and give eighty grand for a joined restaurant business. Money was given to Affilia's husband. He was in charge of the new restaurant to be bought. They opened the restaurant in their name but it was supposed to be a fifty - fifty partnership. The restaurant business was doing well. Affilia's husband didn't give any profits to Wahid. Wahid's family wanted the money back. They were paying an extra mortgage but weren't getting any benefits. They refused to pay. She said that she took the share from her father's property, and she wouldn't give it back. They arranged a family meeting with some of the relatives. During the meeting everything went wrong.

Mr. Ali stood near his door as soon as one of his students, Basith came through the door he sprayed an air fresher that he had on his hand. 'What the hell is that for sir,' said Basith. Mr. Ali told him that he stank and he needed it. Basith refused to agree that he stank. But Mr. Ali explained to him that every time he came into his classroom he stank of cigarette's smoke. If he continued to smoke like this he wasn't going to live very long, and when he tried to get a life insurance it would cost him much more then a non-smoker.

In the restaurant two female customers came in sat down on the table fifteen. First they order a bottle of red wine, some papadums which came with four types of chutney; mango, lime, onion and kebab. The customers ordered their starter, lit up their cigarettes and blazed away. Both ladies were in their thirties and looked stunning. It was late at night. The customers had finished their meal. Before they went out they kissed each other on the mouth. The waiters couldn't believe that people could be lesbians so openly. They didn't find it a major problem but felt that they didn't have to do it so openly. They hadn't seen a female kiss in Bangladesh so it was strange for them to get some new experience. Minto asked to the other waiters, 'Why would they want to be lesbian when they are so beautiful and can get men easily?' Perhaps he didn't know that they weren't interested in men and their equipment.

In May a T.V. program showed some of the Brick Lane's restaurants touting customers. They offered customers big discount to get them into their restaurant but once they ate they only gave a little discount. It was an embarrassing moment for the restaurant owners. Sabbir told his staff never to lie to any customers about any offers. One has to understand that there are about fifty restaurants and when there is a competition people will try to get to customers first. In most industries companies offer bribes to get contracts. There are many governments in the world that offer bribes for custom.

The Baishaki Mela came again. Thousands of people from all over the country came and enjoyed the occasion. Sabbir opened his stall outside his restaurant where he sold curries, rice and soft drinks. He also had his illegal cousins working at the stall so they got some experience, Sabbir just relaxed in the restaurant. From time to time he came out and checked how they were doing. Ariful and Shiru enjoyed meeting some of the passers by that they had not seen in Bangladesh or London. They came across foreigners who didn't speak much English like them.

After more then a year the other work permit employee managed to get his visa to come to London. It was worth the wait for Sabbir. He made a cool fifteen thousand pounds. One of the other employees who came a year ago was caught in an immigration raid in a restaurant, and was deported to Bangladesh. During the work permit visa season thousands of Sylheti flooded London. There were thousands on the waiting list too. If the work permit season was available for a few more years then all the Sylheti bachelors would have come to London.

Gozafor Miah was excited once more. Bangladesh defeated India by 15 run in a one day match at the Bangabandhu National Stadium in Dhaka. The man was crazy about cricket even though he probably didn't know all the rules and the rules of the game.

Sabbir's house was claustrophobic due to overcrowding and their belongings. He needed to make some space in the house so the oxygen could get through. At the same time Sabbir thought about making use of the illegal cousins' spare time. His garden was rather big. He decided to build a shed at the back of the garden. Sokina told him not to as she didn't want to lose any space for her coriander patch. Sabbir explained to his mother that more space was needed in the house and building a shed was the best solution. He bought all the necessary materials, had the others began digging the ground to build the basement. They needed to make it quite big as there were so many stuff needed to be removed from the house. He wanted to store the big cooking pots that they used on special occasions.

After working in the first day, the next day morning Shiru and Ariful complained that they had pain in their bodies. Sabbir gave them a day off as they had done quite a lot of digging and mixing of cement. Shiru was the clever one and Ariful was the big one. They had some ideas about building a house. Back home they had helped their father build cattle sheds. Shiru told Sabbir he was an expert in building houses. He had built a dog and chicken hut in Bangladesh where he mixed cement and nailed wood. 'How about you Ariful, what experience do you have?' He didn't make a comment but Shiru replied, 'He was too busy bunking off to his mother's parents' house to avoid school.' 'How can he go there by himself that's quite far?' 'The local rickshaw driver knew the house and dropped him off for free and later on charged his father.' 'Did you bunk school because the teacher beat you up?' 'No, he used to bunk because his nani (grand mother) used to give him lots of sweets and rice. This is why he is big and fat.' They laughed together.

They continued to work on the shed for two weeks to complete it. When the shed was ready, Shiru asked Sabbir if he could live in the shed as it was quite nice and there was not enough space in the house. Sabbir told him it was no problem and that it was a good idea but he needed to ask Sokina. To Shiru the shed was good enough to live in and much better then some of the houses in Bangladesh. He didn't think about how he would live during the winter. Sokina told him no. He became upset. 'How you going to live during the winter? You will die from cold.' They managed to remove a lot of items from the house into the shed.

Shabana and Shundor had a big argument. Shundor kept on sending all his earning back home and hardly spent any money on her. She complained that he shouldn't send all the money back home as they lived here and they needed to do things here rather then in Bangladesh. He didn't like it. He thought it was better to invest in Bangladesh. Shabana told him not to send money back home any more. He lost his temper. He asked her who the hell she was to tell him what to do.

She should listen to him all the time and obey his decisions; he was the decision maker in the family. Shabana argued with him that he hardly paid any bills. She had to pay all the bills and the house mortgage. He lost control of himself and held her by her throat and told her, 'Don't you ever argue with me and if you do I will kill you, you daughter of a bitch.'

'Let me go or you will pay heavily.'

'What you going to do.'

'I said let me go now or you had it.'

'Are you going to divorce me, if you do, no one else will marry you as you are a married woman and if you do divorce me then you will only get an ugly husband who would only marry you for your passport so don't think about it.'

'I won't come to you for ideas.'

He let her go. She ran upstairs, locked the door, dialed 999 for the police. On the phone Shabana showed her emotion with by crying. She told the operator her husband was threatening to kill her and they should come urgently.

Within a few minutes the police officers came, knocked on the door. Shundor never thought she would call the police. He was shocked to see the uniformed officers. A police officer asked him where his wife was. He understood the word wife and with his hand he directed them up the stairs. Two officers went upstairs and knocked on her door. She asked who they were. Then she opened the door. She had tears in her eyes. The officer asked her, 'Are you ok madam?'

'I have just about survived.'

'Did your husband beat you?'

'Yes.'

'Would you like us to arrest him?'

'Yes please, can you see the marks on my throat?'

'Yes we can see the red marks.'

'Would you like to go to the hospital for a check up?'

'Yes I would.'

'We would take you to the local hospital.'

'You also have to arrest him for another reason.'

'And what is that reason?'

'He is an illegal immigrant, his time has expired.'

'Thanks for the details.'

'Here is his expired passport, as you can see his visa has expired and I haven't made a new application yet, I am sure you can lock him up and send him back to Bangladesh.'

'Thanks for that too.'

The police officers took Shabana to the hospital. They arrested Shundor and took him to the police station. She didn't inform her family, she knew they wouldn't let him go to prison and definitely wouldn't let her charge him.

The main reason she went to the hospital was to have evidence to charge Shundor. From the hospital she called her brother and told him to pick her up. Shabana went to her parents' house and told her father and mother what had happened. Her father said that he didn't know what was the best solution now and if people heard it then they will laugh at their family. Her mother, Ragana became all emotional, cried and said that Shabana should drop the charges and get him out of the jail as he was her brother's son. 'How am I going to show my face to my brother?' said Ragana. 'You don't have to show your face to your brother, just cover it with a veil,' Shabana replied. For the first time Shabana told her mother on her face, there was no way she was going to drop the charges and her crying wasn't going to get her far this time. Shabana's brother supported her. He said that when Shundor got out he would beat him for touching his sister. 'Women become more patient when they are married but you have become more evil,' said Ragana. 'You were evil from day one, you had me married to your nephew because of your selfishness, you didn't want anything good for me. He had no respect for me, and the only thing he knew was money,' replied Shabana. Then Shabana told them that she had given Shundor's passport to the police just to put salt into the wounds. Her mother didn't like that too. 'Why did you do that?' she asked. 'Well, ask your nephew why did he hit me?' 'What's going to happen now. Is he going to be sent back home?' 'I hope so.' Ragana asked her husband to make Shabana understand that what she was doing was wrong and she should get him out. He said that he had spoken to her enough and it was her call now. She is mature and he won't force her to make any decision. 'What kind of father are you, you are encouraging your daughter to lose her husband. How would we get her married again? Don't you know it is extremely difficult to get a divorced girl married again,' said Ragana. 'I don't care if I do not get married again,' said Shabana and left the room. Her mother asked her father to do something. He told Ragana to do something as she had been making most of the decisions about their daughter's life. Ragana made a call to her sister and told her to come and explain to Shabana.

Ragana's sister came to the house. Shabana knew what they would talk about. Ragana and her sister went into Shabana's room to talk to her. She didn't want to be rude to them. The aunt spoke to Shabana, told her that it wasn't good to send her husband to jail, she should forgive him and get him out. She asked whether it wasn't good to beat up a wife. The aunt said that he probably lost his temper so she should forgive. 'If someone loses their temper and kills someone, a judge doesn't let them off, they pay for their mistakes and he needs to pay for hitting me and I don't care whether he lost his temper or not, there is no way I am going to get him out, I have given him many chances. He thinks I am his servant,' she said.

'Some men are stupid and they do stupid things that doesn't mean you should get rid of them, if you do then all the people who know us will laugh at us and especially your father and mother,' said the aunt. She knew being a solicitor, they were trying to play a psychological game and twist her decision. She stood her ground and said 'I don't care anymore.' 'You should care if you divorce him. Do you know how difficult it would be for us to find another husband.' 'I don't mind staying single rest of my life.'

Shabana contacted the police to find out what had happened to Shundor. The police told her that they would keep him locked up for the moment, and were investigating the case. She told them that if they released him then they must let her know and they should put a curfew on Shundor so he doesn't come near her house. Shabana filed for divorce. Ragana eventually learnt that she wasn't in control of Shabana any more and Shabana wasn't going to obey her anymore.

Chapter Seventeen

2005

It took four years and thirty-five Test matches but on Monday 10th January Bangladesh had finally celebrated the first victory in Test cricket. It put a smile on everyone's face in the restaurant even though they played a very weak Zimbabwean side. 'All we were concerned about was a win and we had our first win before India and New Zealand – that's the bottom line,' said Gozafor Miah with excitement.

Sima continued to make Indian dresses for the girls and the close relatives. It wasn't long before everyone knew she had the skills. She was busy making different types of dresses and earning money. Sima watched channel S, a Sylheti TV channel at a neighbour's house and she wanted it. Sabbir ordered the channel S on Sky which provided programmes in Bengali. Sima and Sokina enjoyed watching the news and Bengali programmes as they were able to understand them. Some of the programmes Sokina didn't understand as she didn't understand the Bengali language that is spoken in Dhaka. The Bengali channel helped Sima and Sokina to improve their knowledge of Bangladesh. They also improved their knowledge of Islam as there were programmes where an Imam explained different issues of Islam. There were times Sima telephoned the Imam and asked him questions. Before the Bengali channels Sokina hardly watched TV. She became a new fan of channel 'S.' Sima and Sokina needed a channel like that. It provided them with important news and issues about Sylhet and Bangladesh.

All of Sabbir's restaurants were doing very well. He was getting profit from all of the restaurants. Jamal wanted to buy a take away but didn't have enough money. He wanted Sabbir to take a fifty percent share and help him with the finance. Sabbir took a twenty five percent share and lent him the money without interest because Jamal had helped him out in many occasion, also when ever he needed something dodgy, Jamal always supplied it.

The great Bengali festival session came in the shape of Baishaki Mela. Sabbir had different ideas about it this time. He decided to open an extra stall for his illegal cousins – Ariful and Shiru. In his stall the kitchen staff sold the typical products made from his restaurant – curries and rices. Gozafor Miah had the opportunity to wear his Bangladesh's green cricket t-shirt, cap with Bengal tiger's logo printed. For Ariful and Shiru's stall Sabbir bought Bombay mix and all the relevant materials for them to mix it up. They mixed up Bombay mix with coriander, dash of lime, touch of salt and sold to the passers by. Shiru manage their stall and he made Ariful do most of the hard work. He collected the money and gave out change. They loved the new experience as they were busy non-stop serving customers.

At the end of the day Ariful and Shiru made four hundred pounds. Sabbir gave them three hundred pounds and kept hundred pounds for his expenses. They were delighted to earn so much money. They gave the money to their aunty Sokina to keep. Sokina told them that they should send the money back home to their parents as they will be happy to receive it. Ariful and Shiru agreed to send the money back home. They asked Sabbir to send it for them. Sabbir took the money to Badol Miah, who sent it without charging any commission. Shiru told the relatives how hard he worked and managed Ariful. He told them how he collected money with both hands and same time he mixed it up. Shiru said that he should have had more money then Ariful as he did more work then him. Ariful said that he did most of the work because he mixed all the ingredients most of the time. Shiru also said that next year he wants his own stall and make more money.

In Cardiff Bangladesh pulled off one of the biggest shock ever in cricket with a five-wicket victory over world champions Australia. Gozafor Miah and everyone else in the restaurant were ecstatic and smiling as if Bangladesh had own the cricket world cup. Sabir offered free drinks to his regular customers to celebrate the win. Gozafor Miah was so happy that he didn't know what he was cooking. Customers complained about some of the dishes, they didn't taste as usual. He told Peter next it was England's turn to get defeat. Peter told him in order to beat England, Bangladesh needed to practice for anther quarter of century.

Sabbir receives a telephone call from a cousin from the village. His cousin told him that everyone from the village had sent their child to London, he needed to send his child so he will have someone to help him out when his old. Sabbir told him that there were no space in his house and it was very difficult to make children human in London's society. There were many children have became gangsters as they didn't have any one to nature them. Then his cousin refused to listen to him, told him that he will sale his land and prepare the money but just needed Sabbir's help to look after his son for a few years. Sabbir stood his ground and told him no, if his son comes he won't open the door; he had enough of illegal children. People in the village don't understand anything about the life in London. They think it is some kind of heaven and they must be part of this even though it may involve life and death. Can you blame these people? They are always trying to build their living stability and thinking about the future.

Sokina received a telephone call from the village, a cousin of Karim called. The man told her that he wasn't fit enough to work anymore.

He fell from a tree while cutting its branches, now he needed money to build a house as his current house had a hole in the roof. She told Sabbir to give some money, which he did. Once again Sokina informed the relatives and collected money for him. She managed to collect four hundred pounds from everyone. Sabbir used Badol Miah to send the money to the uncle. Once the man received the money he telephoned to thank them for the charity. The poor people in the village did appreciate the help a lot. And the people in London liked helping the poor in the village as some of them thought that they were lucky to be in London and it was their duty to help the poor. Allah will be pleased with them and bring prosperity in to their life.

    Sabbir decided that he needed to promote himself and the family once again from the area he lived in. Due to the fact that he was earning thousands of pounds every week from his restaurant businesses. Sabbir asked his mother to view some of the houses. She refused. She didn't like travelling. She gave her views, which was that the house must have a big kitchen and at least two toilets. They viewed a few houses before making their mind up on a half a million pound mansion. He decided to buy a five bed room house in the area of Chigwell. He felt like a millionaire with that house.

    Sabbir invited all of his close relatives to his house to show off. All the relatives who knocked him down, now he could tell them that he lived in a half a million pound house. He was in a league of his own. Some of their relatives accused him of being stupid, buying a house in an area where there were hardly any Bengali people and a mosque. Sabbir replied that there were no mosques when Bengalis came to Brick Lane. It took Bengalis nearly twenty five years to have their first mosque. When there are enough Muslim we will open our own mosque here. Not bad for a man who made it from a mud hut to a million pound mansion by selling rice and spices.

Foriz called Shabana on her mobile. He had some kind of feeling for her even though he knew she was a married woman. He asked her how she was and general questions. She spoke with joy and gave him the impression that she was happy to receive the call from him. He told her that the main reason he called her was that he was buying a house and wanted her to do the paper work. She told him that it was not a problem that she could do that for him. He wanted to know roughly how much it would cost. She said that for him it would be free if he had dinner with her to discuss the property. He couldn't say no to an old lover, could he? It seemed like the pain in his heart had vanished over the years. They decided to meet after work in a restaurant in Green Street.

Foriz was punctual as always. He arrived in the restaurant twenty minutes early. He took a bunch of roses, hid them in the restaurant and sat waiting for her with mixed feeling. Shabana arrived five minutes early. She came into the restaurant, looked around, he put his right hand up in the air to signal where he was. She noticed him, came to his table and took the seat front of him.

'Hello Shabana.'
'Ass-salaamu-aaleykum.'
'Wa-aaleykum-ass-salaam.'

They ordered starters and main courses. Foriz and Shabana caught up with the missing five years actions in some details. She said that first she wanted to say sorry for what had happened five years ago. He told her that the past had passed and let look forward to the future. She agreed. Shabana asked him if he had any children.

'No, not yet.'
'Is your wife beautiful?'
'First you have to define beautiful, then I will tell you if she is beautiful.'
'Someone who looks beautiful, has a nice face and body structure and when you look at them, you like to be with them.'
'If this is how you describe beauty then she was a beautiful woman.'
'What do you mean she was?'
'She is no longer with me as she is very beautiful.'
'Sorry too hear that.'

'Don't be sorry, I am happy she isn't with me as I get to find someone new and carry on with my life.'

'So what was wrong with her?'

'Nothing wrong with her, she was too beautiful and too educated that was the problem.'

'What's wrong with begin educated and beautiful?'

'Nothing wrong, but the thing was that she was too career minded and it was a big problem for me and my family.'

'Did you not let her work?'

'I did but she didn't let me have any children and told me to wait five years, so I called it a day.'

'I am sure you can go to Bangladesh and bring a wife who would let you have kids from day one.'

'Maybe that's what I have to do, anyway tell me about your married life?'

'Not so good as yours.'

'What's wrong, I hope you're not divorced like me.'

'Yes I am.' She nodded her head too.

'I can't believe it. How can a man divorce someone like you.'

He raised his voice with a bit of disbelief.

'Why do you say that?'

'Well, I think you are a very decent girl.'

'My decency wasn't good enough for my husband, I divorced him at the end of last year.'

Foriz thought that could be the reason why she wanted to meet him.

'I didn't know you were such a dangerous woman.'

'I am not but he used to swear at me and beat me up, so I got rid of him.'

'When did you learn to stand up for yourself?'

'I learnt if from you.'

'Ha ha ha very funny.'

Shabana looked at her watch and said that she needed to be home and would talk next time. He told her 'That's fine, thanks for coming.' She wanted to pay the bill. He told her not to. 'We didn't have the chance to talk about the house details,' he said. She told him maybe we have to meet again for that. On the way out he gave her the roses, she took them with a big smile that nearly killed him once again. She waved her hand as she left.

He didn't understand how come she had become so nice over the five years. Foriz tried to analyse why she was acting so nice. He told himself, to calm down and let not think too much in advance. Foriz felt that she had definitely changed, and it must be her marriage life that had changed her. He thought maybe she wanted him that's why she wanted to meet him.

A new student arrived in Mr. Ali's class from Bangladesh as usual. Mr. Ali knew intuitively that the child wouldn't speak English. He was correct. Looking at the boy or young man he wanted to laugh, but he couldn't. Mr. Ali couldn't believe how this child could be in year nine. The child looked more like a sixteen or seventeen year old. He understood that's what it said on his paper but he didn't looked like a fourteen year old boy in a million years. The child had a proper shave. He couldn't hide his look with his age. It wasn't his fault. It was the solicitor's fault or the people who made the application for his residency visa. It is unbelievable to see the corruption going on in the child trafficking world. Then again Sylhetis are opportunists and they were taking advantage of the loophole in the system. It is similar to five hundred years ago when the British took advantage of the opportunities in India.

Shabana called Foriz on his mobile, told him that she was not feeling well. She had a problem with a client and wanted to meet him if he was free. Foriz was free for her twenty four hours but he didn't mention that. They arranged to meet in a restaurant in Green Street again. It was a suitable location. This time she was in the restaurant before him. He came in, looked around. She waved her right hand in the air to signal the beauty queen's position. They exchanged basic etiquette. Then he asked her what was wrong. She said that she had an argument with a customer, who kept on calling her. Maybe the customer was crazy about her, anyway she didn't want to talk about work.

'You look very nice today Foriz!'
'Isn't that used to be my dialogue.'
'Guess what?'
'What do you want me to guess?'
'Anything nice!'
'You are having a baby.'
'Shut up man, you have not changed much.'
'What now, you asked me to have a guess so I did.'
'One day Insha-Allah I will have children with a man who loves me.'
'Tell me what you wanted me to guess?'
'I am going to be officially divorced at the end of this week.'
'Good news for you, shall I look for an illegal husband for you?'
'No thanks, my mother already has a long list of illegal men.'
'Ain't you happy that I am divorced now.'

Shabana was trying to give him the hint that she was available. He knew what she was playing at but he wasn't going to give in easily.

'Why shall I be happy, I am not related to you.'
'Don't you want me to be happy?'
'I am not really sure.'
'You don't understand how much I was suffering with that man.'
'Good to see you happy now.'
'Thank you, that's what I wanted to hear from you.'
'I think an illegal man would be good for you, he will love you until he gets his passport and as soon as he gets his passport he will dump you.'

He was trying to wind her up and to see how she reacted.

'So you want me to be dumped again, you have no feeling for me.'
'I don't mean that. Anyway how could I have feelings for you. You have destroyed it a long time ago.'
'You do mean it. You don't care about my life. You want me to suffer for what I did to you five years ago.'

'I was joking man.'

'Now you think I am a man.'

'Ow shut up woman. If you nag like that no man will marry you.'

'No problem I can always go back to Desh.'

'Why not, another 'freshi' can come to London; you can charge about fifteen laks for the service.'

'Now you think I am a prostitute, I am going now; you haven't been nice to me.'

'I never said anything about being a prostitute.'

'Why did you say I can charge fifteen laks?'

'That's what some girl's parents do.'

'So how much would you pay if you find some one like me?'

He knew she was trying hard but refused to admit anything so easily.

'I don't go for second hand women.'

'Ow my God, I can't believe it, how could you say that to me.'

'What can't you believe?'

'So you think I am second hand.'

'You know you are.' He gave a little smile as he looked at her face.

'I better go, you don't have any respect for women, good job I never got married to you in the first place. I don't know how you would have treated me. Maybe you would have treated me like a slave.'

'Don't go yaar, you know I was joking.'

'Right, so you call that a joke by insulting me and all of the divorcees.'

'Don't you want to know how much I would pay for some one like you?'

'Go on then, blow it up, probably another insult.'

'I will give you two prices, one five years ago and one for now.'

They looked at each others' faces. She was half smiling.

'I am waiting, hurry up.'

'Five years ago I would have paid everything that I had, but now I wouldn't pay anything. But if you were the last woman on the earth then I have to pay what ever it takes as I do need one.'

'I am very upset with you Foriz, so in five years I lost all my values?'

'Yes you have. You lost the most important thing that you had.'

'I know where you are coming from but I wasn't expecting that from you. Good to know your opinion and how you look at woman.'

'I take it you will be on your way to Desh.'

'By the way I will not go to Desh again to get married. Once was enough; it's your turn to go now.'

'I have thought about it, that's what my mother wants. She thinks girls are more decent in Desh.'

She looked at the time and told Foriz that she had to go home. Foriz didn't want to stop her, he felt she had melted towards him. 'I will let you go if you come to cinema with me next time,' he said.

'What's the point of meeting you again, you don't have any respect for me. You think of me as second hand, and all you will do is insult me and hurt me.'

'I don't do that, I just joke with you. I like joking with you.'

'You do, your jokes hurt me a lot.'

'Sorry bhondu, I will try to make up soon.'

'Not good enough, you don't know how to joke.'

'Will you be coming then?'

'Say you are really sorry and you won't hurt my feeling again.'

'My dear Shabana, I am deeply sorry for what I said. Please forget and forgive me darling.'

'Ok, I will come but if you insult me I will never meet you again.'

'Why don't we meet during the weekend?'

'We could go to the cinema.'

'No problem, I will let you know the time.'

On the way out, she gave him a yellow rose that she had hidden under the chair. Foriz analysed her reactions. She wasn't like this before. She wanted to go to restaurants and cinema – this woman had changed – she had become a different Shabana.

―

On the 7th of July the bombing of the London underground killed fifty six humans. This was a shock to the local and national community. Four suicide bombers blew themselves up. The explosion had killed people from different countries and religious backgrounds. The Aldgate bombing was just a few hundred yards from where one of the largest Muslim communities had lived. This was deeply upsetting for the local Bangladeshi community as they had survived the early racism from the BNP and now they had Muslim kids blowing themselves for some kind of jihad. How this attack could be justified only the dead suicide bombers would be able to explain or could they? They killed in the name of Islam but Islam doesn't allow killing of innocent people. What direction were they coming from? None of the Muslim communities supported their mission and condemned it as an un-Islamic attack. Those young Muslims were brain-washed and their minds were twisted by some kind of guru who had his own selfish motives.

In the evening Peter arrived to the restaurant. He didn't look charming to the waiters. One could tell everyone was upset by what had happened next door to them – Aldgate East. Peter sat down, threw both his hands in the air and said, 'What's happening man?'

'I told you before; these people will get into England and America.'

'We don't want the suicide bombers here.'

'We definitely don't want them, do you know what's going to happen now, some of the Muslim people will get attacked from the racist people even though they are not involved.'

'I know what you're saying, why don't these people have any respect for their own life, why do they want to kill themselves.'

'Basically, what I think is that these are the people who are not very happy with their lives and want to do something to get noticed. You know some serial killers they kill people to get attention, and it's like that.'

'It's scary man; you don't know when and where the next bomb is going to explode.'

'I know, we are worried too. The BNP might attack Brick Lane in revenge. We have to watch out.'

'Why do these people want to die at so young an age?'

'I wish I can explain that, I think they could be brain washed to fight in the name of Allah. I am sure they were told by their master that if they kill British people then they would go to heaven, but far as I know as a Muslim we are not allowed to kill another human.'

'How can they go to heaven when they kill innocent people?'

'That's my point too. How can these killers go to heaven when they kill innocent people without any justification.'

'One bomber had a young family. Whose supposed to look after his family.'

'They would say Allah will look after his family.'

'Is their Allah going to work and earn money for their family?'

'I don't know mate.'

'It's the government whose going to pay for his family now, and we tax payers' money they will get for nothing.'

'I suppose so.'

'Do you know what?'

'No, I can't read your mind.'

'I think their families should be sent back home and the government should make a new law where if anyone blew themselves up then the whole family would be sent home. It doesn't matter if they are British.'

'Why not?'

The next day news came out that a young Bengali girl had died in the explosion. Gozafor Miah exploded with anger and said, 'I like to get hold of these bastards and kill them myself. If they want to get Blair then they should go to Blair's house and blow themselves there, not here killing innocent people. What did the Bengali girl do to these bastards? Nothing.'

A week later, Jean Charles de Menezes was shot seven times in the head after being mistaken for a bomb suspect. The police lied about the whole issue. They killed an innocent Brazilian thinking he was a suicide bomber. In the restaurant Gozafor Miah and Goni discussed why it wasn't safe for them to use the underground anymore. Gozafor Miah told others that, 'The police will shoot you if you look like a Muslim.' Goni told others that if they were on the street they must not run, act suspicious or they would get shoot. The kitchen porter said that he wouldn't use the underground until he feels safe. But the question was when was he going to feel safe? When would he know that there won't be a suicide bomber on the underground anymore?

The killing of Jean Charles de Menezes made the Muslim community confused. They weren't sure how to go into the street, not knowing how the police would responds to them. How were they going to walk on the street not knowing what made a person suspicious?

It became difficult for Muslims to go to public places as everyone else kept on looking at them as if they were some kind of terrorists. Many female Muslim were attacked by the racist and their hijabs were torn off and some were spat on. The Muslims in London didn't tell Bin Laden to blow up the Twin Towers. Why the hell were they attacking the Muslims here? Racist people don't seem to understand it could be worse if the Bin Laden supporters started a war in London. We would be very un-safe as suicide bombers would be blowing themselves up everywhere in the capital like they were doing in Iraq, Israel and Palestine. We definitely didn't want that in UK.

Sima had been nagging Sabbir to go back home once again. Sabbir decided to take his family to Bangladesh for a holiday. This was the only place his wife wanted to go to. One of the main reasons he went to Bangladesh all the time with his family was that he wanted the children to learn about their roots and family background. Sabbir bought a small camcorder and recorded images of the close relatives that had came to their house before they left. The relatives back home could see the images now rather then pictures. Pictures started to go out of fashion as the new technology took over. Their flight was with the Bangladesh airline, Biman. The reason they booked it through Biman was that it allowed them to take a larger amount of luggage and went direct to Sylhet. Once they were in the aircraft, Sabbir couldn't believe the condition of the Biman airline. The service they received was diabolical. The toilet doors were broken, the flash didn't work. He couldn't understand how they could be allowed to fly an aero plane that was in such poor condition. Don't the health and safety inspector check the Bangladeshi airline. Maybe the Bangladeshi official had paid off the health and safety inspectors. He decided to report them once he got back from his holiday. The poor qualities of service made Sabbir decide never to use Biman again and tell everyone else not to use it again.

Shabana and Foriz met in the Beckton cinema. She told her mother that she was meeting a female friend. Ragana wasn't bothered about Shabana anymore. She was a married woman. While they were choosing what film to watch, Shabana looked for a film that was romantic, so she could see if Foriz got any romantic ideas about her. On the other hand Foriz was just looking forward to getting into the cinema hall and experimenting with her. Foriz let her choose the movie.

He paid for the tickets, she paid for the popcorns. They went inside, he asked her where she wanted to sit. She said that she wanted to sit at the back. Her reason was that she didn't want anyone else to see her. They sat and watched the movie while eating the pop corns. When Foriz picked up the popcorns from the carton, he made sure her hands weren't in there but when she picked up the popcorns there were a few times she touched his hand, and he took that as she wanted to get physical. Foriz left his hand inside the carton intentionally and waited for her to put her hand in it. When she did, he held her fingers and waited for her to react. She didn't. This was a sign she was eager to respond to him. He realised that he had her in some control. He can experiment a few things now. After a few minutes or so, she asked him what he was doing with her fingers, as they do not talk. He said, they do talk, they told him a lot about her. She asked him, 'What did they say?' 'Turn around and I will tell you.' She turned around, he wiped his hand on his trousers to get rid of the sticky popcorns. Foriz said to her 'Do you really want to know what your fingers told me?' She nodded her head up and down. He asked her to give him her hands, which she did. He held her hands, told her to come close, which she did. He moved his head towards hers. She didn't move. He kissed her and she kissed him back. Then he said to her, 'This is what your fingers told me.' 'Not bad, you did tell me in one of your emails that you studied girls, I am impressed.' He kissed her again, he almost ate her tongue. She told him that if he kissed her like that she wouldn't have a tongue left.

They held each others hands through out the movie. From time to time he kissed her which she willingly returned. While kissing, he *muttered* that he loved her. She whispered, 'I love you too.' Maybe they couldn't control the love they had for each other. When they finished the movie, they went into his car and sat at the back and hugged each other and developed their love further. Foriz told her that he was so happy to have her and this time she shouldn't betray him. She told him this time she was in charge and she would make up for the five years he missed her. They finished the evening in a restaurant sealing their love. It looked like love was from the both sides.

Sabbir found out that Abdul Hanna was in the village. He didn't want to miss this opportunity to meet him face to face. He managed to get his troops together and told them once again he needed to catch a big fish. There would be a big party if they could catch it. Most of his mates were ready to listen to him. Sabbir went to the local bazaar everyday to grab him because he knew Abdul Hannan would go there to visit his mates. Sabbir only told Munna Bhai to look for his target and let him know. Within few days they noticed Abdul Hannan in the bazaar. Sabbir was ready with the troops and weapons to attack but Allah saved him. It was raining heavily. They had to give it a miss for the moment. It would have been difficult to move about.

Sabbir remembered that the last time he was in Bangladesh. He had opened a bank account at a local bank. He went to the bank to find out how much money he had and if he could make the account active again. The manager told him to get a report from the police station that he had lost his account details. He went to the local police station. All the officers were non-Sylheti but that didn't bother him. All he wanted was a report. The police officer asked Sabbir if he agreed to an officer filling the form-in for him and earning ten taka.

Sabbir said, 'No problem.' For him ten taka was like ten pence. Once the officer had completed the form, Sabbir gave him twenty taka. The officer refused to take it. The office said, 'You are giving me twenty taka for that. I have written such an important document and you only gave me twenty taka.' Sabbir told the officer that he had only asked for ten taka to fill in the form and it should be free anyway. The officer got pissed when Sabbir said it should have been free. The officer raised his voice and said, 'My father had to pay for my education and that wasn't free. You think I should write it for free.' Sabbir cousin was with him, he asked Sabbir if he should call Munna Bhai, but Sabbir told him not to. He wanted to see how far the officer would go. 'How much do you want me to give you for the form,' Sabbir asked. 'Five hundred taka.' Sabbir laughed sarcastically. 'If you laugh like that I will lock you up.' Sabbir decided to introduce himself. 'How about if I lock you up in the cell.' 'Who the hell are you to lock me up; you don't know that I am the main officer of the police station.' 'Well you won't be the officer any longer hopefully after today, Insha-Allah.' The officer pushed Sabbir and said, 'What are you going to do, get me killed?' Sabbir didn't react to the push. He said, 'Let me tell you a few things. I like to buy you some sweets when you finish work and then I will tell you how rough your life is going to be.'

'So you are threatening me in my own police station?'

'I have not finished yet; let me tell you few more things, do you know Munna Bhai?'

'Yes I do know him.'

'Well, I have created his power with my money and he is my cousin.'

The police officer went down on his knees and held Sabbir's feet and said 'I am so sorry, why didn't you tell me before. Please forgive me big brother, if you're Munna Bhai's brother then you are my big brother too.'

'Get off my feet and next time, don't harass people like that because everyone is different. You could have lost your life.' Then he left the police station. Munna Bhai a well know village gangster reputed to have beaten up a few people severely. The police know about him but don't have any evidence against him as the witnesses are scared to give evidence.

Chapter Eighteen

2005 Continued

It didn't take long to track down his number one enemy. Munna Bhai noticed Abdul Hannan with his mates in the local bazaar in a restaurant. He had the weapons ready, hidden in his friend's tea bar. The weather was hot like their minds. Sabbir decided to break the ice and told them the big fish was – Abdul Hannan. And he didn't want him dead, he just wanted him badly hurt, disabled but alive. Sabbir told them that he wanted Abdul Hannan's hands and legs broken. He shouldn't be able to walk again. It was about eight o'clock. Sabbir sent two people at the back of the restaurant in case the target runs. He told all the members to put their masks on. He didn't put one on. Sabbir wanted people to recognise who he was. They went into the restaurant and told Abdul Hannan's friends to move which they did very quickly. Sabbir told the restaurant owner that he will pay for the damages and gave him five thousands taka in his hand. They had surrounded Abdul Hannan. One person had a rope around Abdul Hannan's neck, two held his hands, four held his legs so he didn't move. Abdul Hannan shouted, 'What have I done, why you lot doing this to me.' Sabbir appeared and said, 'Do you recognise me? He twisted his head left then right.

'Of course I do.'

'No, you don't, you son of pig.'

Two men stood near the door and locked it so no one could come in. Sabbir told the guys to soften him up. They hit him with big torch lights; punched him; kicked him; Sabbir punched him on the face as well. He then took out the hammer he had. Abdul Hannan was screaming like hell. News went around the bazaar and everyone was waiting outside the restaurant. Sabbir smashed Abdul Hannan's kneecaps and told the boys to break his hands and legs, which they did knowing that they would also get financial satisfaction from Sabbir. Abdul Hannan's relatives tried to break into the restaurant. They smashed the glass but when they saw the boys with swords they backed off. The job was done. Sabbir went out of the restaurant. All the boys surrounded him with the swords. No one could touch him.

Abdul Hannan's relatives took him to the local hospital. The doctors bandaged him. Sabbir went home with the boys and took five eight seater vans with him. He told his father and uncle briefly what had happened. His father wanted to know why he had beaten up Abdul Hannan. He told his father that there was no time to explain. Then he told his father and uncles not to tell the women or they would panic. He had to get rid of them from the house for few nights. Sabbir sent his wife and mother to his father in-law's house in case Abdul Hannan's people attacked at night time or burnt the house. He also told his aunties and step mother to leave home with the young children for safety. Karim told Sabbir to go but he refused. All the boys stayed in Sabbir's house for the night.

Some of the men from the village came to see Karim and wanted to know what had happened. Why had his son beaten up Abdul Hannan? He told them that he didn't know the real reason. The people from Karim's caste also came to support Karim's family and wanted to know if he needed any back up for the night. Sabbir told the young guys to stay for the night. Some of them were already working for him. Sabbir told the people from his caste that the reason he had beat up Abdul Hannan was that when he was young Abdul Hannan had beaten him up. So he took revenge thirty five years later. They wanted to know more. He told them that it wasn't a good time and soon they would find out more.

About eleven o'clock Abdul Hannan's brothers and some elderly village men came to Karim's house. They were asked to sit down in the guest room. Karim and his brothers came to meet them. Sabbir waited outside the room to hear what they were talking about. Abdul Hannan's big brother - Abdul Monnan, said that Karim's son had beaten his brother so badly that he may not be able to walk again and may not be able to eat with his hands. Sabbir felt very good hearing that bad news to his ears. Abdul Monnan was in tears as he spoke. Karim told them that he didn't know why his son had beaten Abdul Hannan and he would find out soon. Abdul Monnan told Karim that he wanted justice for his brother's pain. The guests were offered teas, biscuits and betel nut with paan. Karim told them what ever happened he couldn't make Abdul Hannan same as before but he would pay for his son's mistake if it was his fault. Monnan said that people told him to report it to the police but he didn't. One of the guests said, 'We should hold a public justice meeting with five laks on the table, who ever loses the case, loses the money.' 'Five laks that's too much,' said Rahim. 'Your nephew has broken someones hands and legs, he needs to pay.' 'We will find out why he did it first then we will hold a public justice meeting.' 'We must hold a meeting because the people in the village want to know why your son has beaten up someone so severely.' Sabbir sent Munna Bhai into the meeting with some information. 'I like to say a few words if you don't mind uncle.'

'What is it?' Replied Karim.

'If they can afford it we like to have a public justice meeting with thirty five laks each, winner takes all.'

Every one was shocked to hear that and raised their eye brows.

'What are you talking about, are you out of your mind,' said Rahim.

'Well, brother Sabbir said that there is no way he is going to lose the case. He was first provoked by Abdul Hannan.'

'We can't afford thirty five laks,' said Abdul Monnan.

'If you can't afford thirty five laks then we won't have a meeting,' replied Munna Bhai.

After much of discussion they came to conclusion that they would hold a meeting in two weeks with five laks on the table. The deposit would be given to the village's chairman in advance. All the village elderly and educated people would make the judgments about who was innocent. Karim gave five thousands taka to Monnan for his brother's treatment and told him that he didn't want to see any one touch his son or any member of his family. If anyone touched his son or any member of his family, there will be no public meeting. Monnan promised he wouldn't attack Sabbir or any member of Karim's family.

Earlier Sabbir called his cousins and told them to come to his home with any weapons they had. One by one most of his cousins arrived. He briefly told them what had happened. Sabbir told everyone to stay ready for the night as Monnan may attack.

Karim and his brothers told Sabbir to leave the house and go to his father in law's house for the knight, but he refused. Sabbir told his father and uncles to keep their mobiles on. If they heard of any attack they should call him. He told his father that all of the back up would be in the guest room for the night and they wouldn't sleep. Teas and biscuits were supplied by Tazul.

Sabbir was pretty sure there would be an attack as there were a few enemies in the village. Moskond's relatives visited Monnan. They asked him what action he was going to take. He told them that Karim had paid him five thousands taka and he would attend the public meeting. Moskond's young brother – Toskond told him that this was the best chance to get revenge while his blood was 'hot' and everything was fresh in his mind. People would understand why he attacked. Monnan told them that he had promised Karim not to attack anyone. They told him to forget about promise. Sabbir had almost killed his brother. He must take revenge and they would help him attack Karim's family on the night.

Sabbir asked eight guys to hide on top of trees in the four corners of the house. Two persons were in each tree so they were not scared. Before they climbed the tree, they burnt some leaves near the tree to get rid of any snakes. If they noticed anyone then they should call Sabbir. They put the lights off in the guest room. Sabbir put two people top of the cattle's house in case Monnan tried to burn that. They felt the attack most likely to happen between 2 a.m. to 5 a.m. Sabbir had bought thirty big torch lights to use them as weapons, and gave everyone, one each. He also gave them a big light that could be seen from far and they should turn it on if they needed help. Sabbir told them that if they turned that big light on that meant they needed urgent help. He also told them to flash the light on the enemies face so they would know who the individual enemies were, if the enemy attack them and if there are too many of them then they should do a runner as he didn't want to see any one hurt.'

The village was dead quiet. Everyone was supposed to be asleep. At about 3 a.m. two men entered Karim's house's boundary through an alley way which was noticed by two of Sabbir's men from a tree. One man was Abdul Hannan's brother and the other was Moskond's young brother. Men from the tree called Sabbir and informed him. Sabbir told everyone to get ready with the big swords. They called others on the other trees and told them to block all the entrances. Sabbir and others also called their friends to come from surrounding villages with weapons.

They waited for the enemies to attack. The two enemies went to the cattle's shed and put petrol around the house and burnt it. The two guys who were in the cattle's shed, screamed, 'FIRE, FIRE, FIRE.' Everyone went out and attacked the enemies. They tried to run away but were out numbered. From every angle Sabbir's back up attacked them. Sabbir had sent one person to the mosque to make an announcement that there was a fire in Rahim's cattle's shed. A physical fight had started - punching, kicking, and wrestling! Sabbir's back up had the advantage; they used the torch lights to hit the two men. At all times Sabbir had four people around him. He instructed his back up to break the enemies' hands and legs. Munna Bhai called the police. Once they had the men roped up, they went to put off the fire. People from the village came to help. People were given buckets to get water from the pond and put out the fire. When the village people saw the two men lying on the floor they couldn't believe how severely they had been beaten up. They were crying. No one was seriously hurt from Sabbir's side. News went around the village and everyone started to come to Karim's house. More of Monnan's and Moskond's relatives came to beat up Karim's family with long bamboos and swords. When they saw all the people were standing up with their weapons they retreated. And they said that they would take revenge soon. Karim saw Monnan's brother on the floor and said to him, 'I told your brother not to attack my family and son, why didn't your brother listen.' Karim also asked Moskond's brother, 'Why did you come here, my son did nothing to you.' They didn't have any reply. Police officers came. Sabbir gave them five thousands taka for turning up. They arrested the disabled men and took them away.

About two hundred people gathered around the court yard of Karim's house. The village elderly men said to Karim that his son had turned the village upside down. He had made the village people very upset, worried and unsettled. Karim told the villagers that everything happened for a reason.

The next day morning the sun rose. Abdul Monnan came to Karim's house and knelt down at Karim's feet and cried. 'Uncle it wasn't my fault I tried my best to stop him but when I slept he came to your home and burnt your cattle house,' Monnan said.

'Get up from my feet now, I don't want to see your face. You promised me you won't attack.'

'I know, he didn't tell me he was going to do that.'

'How come Toskond was with your brother?'

'That bustor (bastard) came to my house yesterday and told me to attack you but I refused. He spoke to my brother and then he left.'

'Are you telling me the truth?'

'On my mother's life I am telling you the truth.'

'Do you know why Toskond wanted you to attack my family?'

'He said, they think you had Moskond disabled.'

'I didn't get Moskond beaten up. Do you know if they have any evidence against me?'

'I don't know.'

'See what happened, now you almost lost anther brother.'

'It's all Toskond's fault. He encouraged my brother to come.'

'I will see what happens. Wait here.'

Karim went into his room and took five thousand taka out and then gave it to Monnan for his brother's medication and told him not to blame his son for any incidence.

A few days later news came through to Karim's family that there was a shooting in the village. A man was killed during a dispute over land with his neighbour. Everyone went to see the dead man. He was only thirty years old. The victim's family didn't say who had killed the man. They were too scared to mention the suspect's name. They said they heard a shoot, came out and found him reading 'Kalimas' with his last breath. In the evening Sabbir went to the local bazaar and heard that Moskond had ordered his brother to kill him. This news irritated Sabbir. Nothing happened to the killer as they paid off the police. There was nothing surprising about paying off the police. It was common in Bangladesh that most officers could be bought – it's like they put their trust in their pocket.

The public meeting was held in the local MP's guest room. All the trustworthy elderly men from the village were invited. Men from Karim's and Monnan's family came. Women weren't allowed into the meeting. Before the meeting Karim told Sabbir that if he paid off Monnan then people in the village would be happy and wouldn't go against them. Sabbir told his father that he shouldn't pay a penny to Monnan and there wasn't any way he was going to lose the case. All the important people sat around the big table. On one side of the table, Karim's family sat. Opposite side Monnan's family sat, Abdul Hannan was on the wheelchair. On another side the village judges sat. On the other side some of the guest sat. In front of the guest an empty chair was left for the witness to sit. Most of the village men turned up. Some of the men stood around the room and the others waited outside the room. Sabbir stayed calm. Munna Bhai was next to him.

The MP said that the judges had some questions that they would ask and from the answers they would decided who was innocent and who was guilty. The innocent party would take the ten laks. If possible they would give the verdict on the day; if not they would decide when to give the verdict. Both parties agreed to the rules.

The first question went to Sabbir, 'Can you politely tell us why you have beaten Abdul Hannan so severely? Asked the MP.

'Yes I can tell you,' he paused and drank a bit of water and composed himself then continued.

'Is everyone ready to listen?'

'Yes we are.' Some of the people replied. Everyone was very focused.

'I will tell you why I did it but first, I like to, slowly get you in the mood and try to get you in the mind of Abdul Hannan's victim and Abdul Hannan's if possible. In order for me to do that I will ask you some questions and from the answers we will be able to understand much as possible. The pain the victim went through. My first question, I would like a few people to answer it. If someone kidnaps your twelve year old son, what would you do?'

'I don't think your question is related to the question we have asked you,' said the MP.

'I said, I need to get you in the right frame of mind before I tell you why I did it. Can a few people answer my question please.'

Most people weren't sure what to say or not sure if they should have a go first. Sabbir decided to get them started otherwise they would be having a meeting for a few days.

'I tell you what I will do, if I find out who kidnapped my son then in the name of Allah I will get that person killed,' said Sabbir.

'I will make sure the person pays for the pain he gave my son,' said the MP.

'I will kill the person myself,' said a guest.

'Fine, thank you very much for your answers. Now we know most people would take severe action. My next question is, what kind of pain do you think the twelve year old child would go through.'

'I think the child would be very upset and probably cry,' said an elderly judge.

'The child would go though trauma that will severely effect the child emotionally,' said an educated guest.

'Can you please kindly write down the two answers and the key words, 'cry', 'upset' and 'trauma.' My next question is, do you think a twelve year old child whose been kidnapped and released within a few minutes would go home and tell his parents what had happened?'

'That's difficult to say as every child his different. Some children might and some children might not,' said the MP.

'You have given a good answer. Let me expand, a child would tell his parents' if he thinks it is not embarrassing and a child won't tell his parents if he thinks it is embarrassing, what do you think?'

'That is a good possibility,' replied the MP. Everyone else were listening poetically.

'In 1968 in the days of East Pakistan in our village, one dark night, there was a boy who was kidnapped or on the way to be kidnapped from just outside where our mosque was. Does any one know that or heard it?'

Spices of Brick Lane

Everyone was surprised, looked at each other and shook their head meaning, no we can't believe it.

'It is a long time ago, nearly fourty years ago and I don't expect anyone to remember unless you were involved in it. Can you please ask Abdul Hannan if he can remember 1968, the dark night or the exciting night for him that shook a child's life?'

The judges and everyone looked at Abdul Hannan for an answer but he shook his head left and right.

'A twelve year old child had asked me to give justice to him for what had happened. I do know why the child has chosen me and I promised the child that if Allah allows me then Insha-Allah one day I would give justice to him. This child told me that in 1968, Abdul Hannan had attempted to kidnap him but with the help of Allah the child managed to escape from him.'

Everyone was shocked to hear that accusation. Their listening gear went up to the maximum limit, their eyes were wide open for more shocking discovery.

'Can you please ask Abdul Hannan if he can remember attempting to kidnap anyone in 1968?'

'I didn't kidnap anyone in my life,' the suspect replied.

'Who is the child, if we ask the child to name the kidnapper then we will know if it was him,' said the elderly judge.

'I have said the child told me that it was Abdul Hannan who attempted to kidnap him.'

'Are you saying because he attempted to kidnap a child nearly fourty years ago you have broken his hands and legs?' said the MP.

'I have to agree with you, that is correct.'

'How are we going to prove that it was him?'

'Well, we can give him a Qur'an to touch and say that it wasn't him.'

'I can't remember what happened forty years ago, how can I touch the Qur'an,' angrily Abdul Hannan replied.

'Can you please make note of the answer he gave, now he said he can't remember and before he said he didn't do it.'

'Were there anyone else there?' the MP asked.

'There were one other person with the boy and then a few more people were involved in the matter and some of the people are present in this room now. I believe I can get them to recall the incident.'

'Can you call the witness so everything will be in black and white?' said the MP.

'I would like him to admit it before I call the witness and I want to protect the child's identity.'

'Are you going to admit to the kidnapping charges Abdul Hannan,' asked the elderly judge.

'How many times does my brother need to tell you that he didn't do it,' replied Abdul Monnan with an aggressive high tone.

'I think you should talk with a low tone because I have saved your brother from getting killed.'

'You beat my brother up and you say that you have saved my brother from getting killed. What are you talking about?'

'The boy wanted to kill your brother and I had explained to the boy that he is Muslim and being a Muslim he should not get your brother killed.'

'Who is this boy, I want to know?'

'Do you think you can face that boy?'

'Yes I can face him!'

'Soon you will meet him.'

'You have to bring the witnesses otherwise we won't be able to find the truth?' said the MP.

'Abdul Monnan is a witness.' Everyone laughed.

'What are you talking about now,' said Abdul Monnan.

'I am going to make him a witness as I have no choice.'

'Go on prove it.'

'Can you remember in 1968 if anyone went to your home and complained about your brother's behaviour?'

Abdul Monnan held up both of his hands in the open air, looked around the room and said, 'How can I remember that. That's forty years ago?'

Everyone looked at Sabbir for a counter attack.

'That is understandable; it's very difficult to remember. Does anyone think the boy he kidnapped can remember that it had happened forty years ago? But Abdul Monnan should be able to remember if anyone ever complained to him about his brother's behaviour because the boy told me his uncle went to Abdul Monnan and spoke to him.'

'I can't remember if anyone ever complained about my brother forty years ago. He was involved in many fights when he was young, most kids get involved in fights when they are young,' replied Abdul Monnan.

'I am sure if it had happened then the child would be able to remember as it probably made a big impact on that child's life,' said the elderly judge.

'Thank you. Of course it made a very big impact on the boy's life because he couldn't forget the incident. It kept on coming back to him continuously since it happened.'

'We do understand that the boy went through a lot of pain and anxiety. Can you please prove to us whether it was him or not,' said the MP.

'Insha-Allah my next witness will prove it. Now, I like to ask you if I had asked all of you for justice for the boy and had proven in front of you what punishment would you have given to him?'

'We would have made him say 'sorry and promise' not to do it again,' said the elderly judge.

Sabbir waited for others to respond.

'It is difficult for me to say as we don't have a full picture of what had happened and there are 'ifs' and 'buts',' said the MP.

'Thank you. I am sure you wouldn't have passed on a sentence for his hands and legs to be broken for kidnapping a child, would you?'

Everyone looked at the judges.

'I don't think we have ever passed on any sentence to anyone as far as breaking hands and legs,' said the MP.

'Thank you very much. The reasons for you not passing on the proper sentence is because the village people don't want to create more enemies and the suspect may also take revenge on the victim that if the victim is weaker in strength,' Am I correct?

'That is a possibility,' said the MP.

'This is one of the reason I had to take the action I took as I felt that if I had asked the respected village people for justice then you would have used the so called village psychology to let him off through just a sorry and that wasn't good enough for the child.'

'You still haven't convinced us that Abdul Hannan did it,' said the elderly judge.

'Slowly, I will convince you but I also need to bring other important issues init too. Before I ask my next guest, I would like everyone to drink a bit of water to relax.'

Sabbir drank a bit of water to proceed to next witness.

'My next witness is dear respected Haji Abdul Kadir Jelani.'

He is one of the judges who made the notes. Everyone looked at him and he was surprised to be mentioned in the puzzle.

'I would like you to try and remember 1968 but not mention any names; one night in 1968, out of no-where two people visited your house about half an hour after magrib prayers?'

'No, I can't remember anything specific as that, but if you could remind me anything specific about the knight, I might be able to remember.'

'Insha-Allah I will try, once again if you do remember who the people were please don't mention the names at the moment. That day your son Abdul Sattar Jelani caught the biggest fish from the bill (big fishing pond) and at night time your wife was cutting the fish and you were helping your wife when two the people arrived at your home.'

'I do remember the day and I also remember the big fish but I can't remember who the visitors were.'

'Good to know someone remembered something. I think my next question will help you remember the people who visited you.'

Everyone was focused on the next question.

'You gave the head of the big fish to the young boy and told him to give it to his grandfather because his grandfather likes fish heads.'

Haji Abdul Kadir Jelani shook his head up and down slowly and said, 'I do remember who the child was.'

Sabbir slapped the table and said, 'Fantastic, we have someone who remembered 1968. I need more people to remember. The incident happened about half an hour before they visited you.'

All guests clapped their hands.

'My next witness was there with the child when it happened. Before I call him, I like to ask this question to everyone. Have I paid anyone at this meeting any money to give false information?'

The judges looked around the room to see if any one owned up. No one did.

'The reason for that question was that I don't want anyone to say I have paid someone to give false information. Now we are hundred percent sure that I have not paid anyone, I would like to invite Gulam Zia Hoque, eldest son of Gulam Zulfikar Hoque.'

He was standing amongst the witnesses; he came forward and sat on the witness chair.

'Dear brother Gulam once again I like you not to mention the child's name if you know who I am talking about. Firstly, I would like you to tell everyone whether I have approached you about today before or if I have discussed anything about today over the last forth years.'

'I like to say that brother Sabbir didn't speak to me before or discussed today's case with me before.'

'Now you know that I haven't tampered with this witness and I have not paid any bribes. My first question to Gulam, can you summarize how many families you have worked for since you were a little boy?'

Gulam slowly said all the families' names he had worked for including Motlib's.

'My respected elders, can you please note that he mentioned that he worked for my grandfather's family. Gulam can you remember roughly what years you worked in our house?'

'When I was a very young boy, probably as soon as I started to walk till I was about fifteen years old.'

'Ok, if you were about ten to fifteen year old then now you must be about fifty years old, am I correct?'

'Yes something like that, I don't have any record of my age.'

'Basically when the incident happened in 1968 you were working in our house. When people do big things they like to talk about it to their friends or the people they work with. I am assuming Abdul Hannan worked in the paddy fields. Do you know anything about a boy getting kidnapped in 1968 or did Abdul Hannan or anyone else ever tell you anything about how they tried to kidnap a boy while you looked after the cattle?'

'If it was 1968 then I can remember the day very well when the kidnapping happened.' He had tears in his eyes as he said that.

Everyone had a smile on their faces and they clapped their hands for an extended period.

'Thank you very much. Relax, drink some water. Its looks like we are getting there. When you say you do remember, do you mean someone told you about it or were you involved in it?'

'I was with the boy that nearly got kidnapped!'

Sabbir stood up and slapped the table a few times with his fist. Everyone had bigger smile on their face.

'My dear respected judges I think we should still offer Abdul Hannan the chance to admit that he did kidnap or tried to kidnap a boy of twelve before I ask my next question to Gulam.'

The judges looked at Abdul Hannan. The MP asked him if he wanted to admit to the charges. He didn't admit to it.

'Thank you for remembering the incident Gulam. Do you remember the person who tried to kidnap the boy?

'Yes I do remember.'

'Everyone got ready for the next answer. Who was it that tried to kidnap the boy?'

'Yes it is true it was Abdul Hannan.'

Everyone looked at Abdul Hannan with dirty looks.

'Did Abdul Hannan tell others in the cattle field that he almost kidnapped that boy?'

'He did tell others how the child just managed to escape from his hands, and he laughed and joked about it.'

What else did he say?

'He heard how the boy screamed like a girl, when he tried to kidnap him. I felt like stubbing him but I was just a kid.'

'My respected judges, please make note of that he told others and laughed and joked about kidnapping a child. Basically a child's life was a joke to him.'

'I would like to say thanks to Gulam from deep down my heart and kindly ask Gulam not to mention the child's name to anyone at the moment unless I ask you to. Yes I like to admit the boy had hired me to beat up Abdul Hannan for attempted kidnapping. My respected elders and judges you have heard the witnesses and I urge you to make the right decision about who is innocent and who is guilty.'

'Just because my brother touched a child you disabled him, that is unbelievable,' said Abdul Monnan.

'Do I need to answer that question? I think we have heard enough evidence of what your brother did,' replied Sabbir.

'So basically the reason for what you did to Abdul Hannan is that he attempted to kidnap a twelve year old boy in 1968,' the MP asked.

'Yes that is hundred percent correct,' I did it for the trauma he caused that child.

'That's insane for attempted kidnap breaking someone's limbs for ever. He needs to pay for my brother's family's cost for rest of the Abdul Hannan's life,' said Abdul Monnan.

Sabbir laughed sarcastically and said "Your brother is lucky he didn't die. If the boy had a knife then, then your brother would have been probably dead".

'We want to know who the child was and what kind of physical pain he had gone through. Did the child end up with broken hands and legs?' asked Abdul Monnan.

Sabbir looked at the judges and said, 'Do I have to answer that question?'

'If you want to,' said the MP.

'It doesn't matter who the child was. At the end of the day if the child was a rich or poor man's child the justice should be the same. The pain Abdul Hannan gave the child was very heavy that's why it has reflected on Abdul Hannan's body now for everyone to see. If the child hadn't gone through any pain he wouldn't have hired me to do such a nasty job. I am a business man, I have no interest in fighting. All I think about is how to make money.'

'You were just looking for a little excuse to beat my brother up so you could show the village people that you are a tough man,' said Abdul Monnan.

Sabbir refused to answer Abdul Monnan's accusation and sat quietly. The judges spoke to each other and shared their notes. Everyone else took a drinking break.

'We need to know more about the attempted kidnap, what exactly happened?' said the elderly judge.

Sabbir looked at some notes he had then he said, 'That night, after magrib the child and Gulam Zia Hoque went to the corner shop. On their way back, near the mosque, someone suddenly came from behind and grabbed hold of that child and tried to run away with him towards the forest, next to the mosque. The child tried to scream but he held the child's mouth with a cloth. He took the child about hundred yard away, the child scuffled and somehow with the help of Allah he managed to get away from Abdul Hannan's grip. The child saw the man's face as he did a runner. Gulam stood there screaming and couldn't help as he was just a child too.'

'Which direction was he going with that child?' asked the MP.

'He was going toward the west, just another hundred yards from the jungle. I am sure now you know what his intention was.'

'What kind of injuries did the child get?' asked the elderly man.

'We have discussed some of the injuries before. But I would like you to imagine that you were a twelve year old child and someone suddenly comes from the behind and tries to take you away, how would you feel for the rest of your life? I know it is extremely difficult to imagine unless it happened to you. So don't try. Only a person who suffers can explain what suffering is.'

'It would be very helpful if we could see the child. It would help us with our judgment,' said the MP.

'I didn't want to tell you the child as it is embarrassing but I will tell you as I also want you to know the power of that child who grew up to take revenge nearly forty years later. May I kindly request Abdul Hannan to name the child please?'

Sabbir said the latter with a wide smile.

Everyone looked at Abdul Hannan for a response. He didn't say anything.

'Come on man, say it, you can do it, I want everyone to know you had the guts to kidnap a child. You were so brave but Allah was there to stop you.'

Abdul Hannan refused to speak.

'The child is in this room and I want Abdul Hannan to mention that child's name. it would be very nice if he could mention the child's name as the child grew up to be so brave that he managed to take revenge for an awful act.'

Once again everyone waited for Abdul Hannan to respond. He didn't.

Sabbir stood up, slapped the table with his right hand and shouted, 'Come on you bastard say it now who that child was you tried to kidnap, come on, come on man, what happened to your guts now?'

Karim asked Sabbir to sit down. Sabbir sat down and drank some water.

'Looks like you have to tell us who the child was,' said the MP.

'Yes, looks like it.'

Sabbir stood up again and said, 'Oi you look at my face.'

Abdul Hannan refused to look at Sabbir's face.

'I am talking to you, look at my face.'

Abdul Hannan refused to look at Sabbir face again.

'You son of a dog look at my face?' Sabbir said in a loud tone.

'You son of a dog stop swearing at my brother,' said Abdul Monnan.

'You son of a pig don't swear at me or I will do the same to you, alright. You don't fucking know who I am.'

'No swearing please,' said the elderly judge.

'Sorry.'

Sabbir sat down. Everyone took another mini break.

Sabbir stood up again and said, 'Everyone look at me, I will tell you who the child was. Are you listening Abdul Hannan. The child is standing right here front of you now.'

'Son of an infidel, son of a dog, son of a bitch,' said Karim, Rahim, Sahim and went out of their chairs to attack Abdul Hanna. They intended to beat him up. The judges and middle men stopped them.

'Why did you not kill that bastard,' said Karim.

'Why didn't you tell me I would have killed him,' said Sahim.

'Did you touch my son, you son of pig?' Karim said to his son.

'I can shoot him dead now, if you want brother,' said Munna Bhai having his gun out.

'No, don't shoot him'

'I don't want him dead. I want him to suffer for the rest of his life.'

'Please everyone sit down,' said the elderly judge.

'There is no chance of them getting a penny of that money, I want that money back that I gave you for medication,' said Karim.

'People shouted, 'You did a good job Sabbir, well done.'

The judges said that they needed more time to make the final decision. They told everyone to wait and they went to another room and discussed their options. Meanwhile Sahim asked his brother Karim if they should attack Abdul Hannan's family at end of the meeting. Karim told his brother he had enough beating from Sabbir and not to attack again. Twenty minutes later the judges arrived with their verdict.

'After hearing all the evidence we have concluded that Abdul Hannan and Sabbir are guilty,' said the elderly judge.

'I don't agree with that decision my respected elders. How can I be guilty? I have suffered nearly forty years with the pain and trauma and you think I am a guilty man?' said Sabbir.

'How can you say he is not guilty. Look at what he has done to my brother?' said Abdul Monnan.

Karim told Sabbir there wasn't any point of arguing and Abdul Hannan got what he deserved. Sabbir told his father he needed to say a bit more.

'We have heard all the evidence and we felt what Abdul Hannan did was wrong also what Sabbir did was wrong. Two wrongs don't make a right,' said the elderly judge.

Sabbir stood up to talk as he felt that will force the issue further.

'I agree what I did was wrong but who made me do it? He forced me to do it. If he hadn't attempted to kidnap me I wouldn't have disabled him after thirty seven years. A tree doesn't fall with out wind. When the tree falls is it the tree's fault or the wind's. He made me disable him.'

'My brother didn't say to you to break his hands and legs,'

'Of course he told me, his actions made me do it. He is the one who provoked me without any reason what-so-ever. And he is getting away with it. How can that be correct?'

'We understand what you are saying but you have taken action and this is why you are guilty too,' said the MP.

'Now I have to say, you people made me take that action because your sloppy sentence for criminals made me do it. You people don't take actions. You forgive people for big crimes once they say sorry. Do you remember, that man stole the other man's cattle and sold it and all you did was make him pay for the cattle. You people didn't punish him.'

'We are not the real court hear. We try to do a friendly justice for people so we can continue to live in the same village without further problems,' said the elderly judge.

'I understand but there are times we shouldn't do short cut justice for people who suffer unquantifiable amount of trauma. We must work together and made them pay then we would have a much better society and people will be happy with the system,' said Sabbir.

'If people want they can always pay the police and make their complaint and try to get justice, but I am sure you know people don't like to complain to the police and create enemies,' said the MP.

'I like to thank everyone for attending, I hope I didn't injure anyone's feelings except them bastards,' said Sabbir.

The judges gave back both sides their money.

Chapter Nineteen

2005 Continued

Sabbir recorded images of the close relatives in the village house and the surrounding areas to bring back to London. Most relatives had something to say to their loved ones in London. His uncles and aunties spoke on video to their 'illegal' children and told them to study and listen to Sabbir's advice all the time. He even recorded one of the cattle employee, Tazul, who sent a message to Shiru to send money as he needed to buy a new cattle for farming. By looking at the camcorder, Tazul said 'The white people are so clever that they can produce intelligent things.' He asked Sabbir politely if he could touch the camcorder. Sabbir showed him how to look at it and take images. Tazul was only twelve years old, and lived in the same village as his parents were so poor that he had to start work from the moment he started to walk to support his family. His main job was to look after the cattle. He stayed in one of Sabbir's uncle's house where he received free food and accommodation. His father collected his five hundred taka salary at the end of each month, sometimes in advance. He never had the chance to go to school. In the evening when Rahim's and Sahim's children studied with the private tutor he sat on the side and listened to the children learn. The teacher gave him a piece of paper and taught him how to read the Bengali alphabet and the basic Maths. He wasn't able to count more then a few numbers as he hardly saw any of his pay and never had any pocket money. Sabbir went to his neighbour's house. He asked the grandmother to talk to the camera and send any messages to her relatives. She refused and said, 'I might be old but I am not stupid, how can I talk to that thing and they can see it in Landon.' Sabbir showed her some of the previous recordings. Then she believed him. Her messages to her grand children were that they should visit her and pray for her as she was going to die soon.

Foriz and Shabana continued to communicate and met each other every week. They met in cinema and at the restaurant and enjoyed each others' company. On another day Foriz sent her a text message telling her that he had to go to Bangladesh to get married. His parents don't trust the girls in London, he was going soon. She became extremely upset. She called him on his mobile. She was crying and wanted some answers from him.

'If you're going to Desh, then why did you have an affair with me and kiss me?'

'It was your fault that you allowed me to kiss you.'

'It was your fault because you started it first by giving me the roses.'

'You started it first by giving me your mobile number.'

'If I knew you're going to be like this, then I would never have let you kiss me. The reason I allowed you to kiss me was that I thought you really loved me and wanted to be with me.'

'I can be with you but not for long term. I need a wife and how can I marry you. You were married once, there are so many unmarried girls available.'

'So you kissed me without any feeling for me? I know the reason why you kissed me! You took the revenge for what I did to you five years ago.'

'I thought you wanted me to kiss you as I felt you were lonely so I tried to make you happy with the kisses, I bet you enjoyed it.'

'You are so evil.'

'Thank you.'

'How could you do this to me?'

'How did you kill me five years ago?'

'I did give you the chance.'

'That wasn't good enough.'

'If you didn't love me, you shouldn't have kissed me.'

'I kissed you because you are so fucking beautiful and I couldn't resist you.'

'I really thought you were a decent man.'

'I thought the same about you.'

'I will never forgive you.'

'How can I forgive you?'

'You never really loved me. If you had, you would accept me as I am.'

'I loved a complete woman, but now you are in complete.'

'I hope you get a horrible wife when you go to Desh.'

'I hope you get an ugly illegal husband.'

They continued to argue for an hour and repeated the same things over and over again. She was so pissed off, she hung up. He tried to call her back but she didn't answer for the next few days, he also texted her but she didn't reply either.

Mr. Ali was invigilating in a mock exam in the school hall. A tall student refused to listen and stop the talking. He told the child to leave the hall, but the student refused. Later on, the head of department Mr. Reed came in. Mr. Ali complained that the child had refused to listen to instructions. The head of department tried to remove the child but he refused once again but Mr. Reed took his exam paper and threatened to call the senior management team. The child went berserk and started to swear at Mr. Ali. 'You don't know who you are fucking around with. I beat the fuck out of you. After school, I am going to killed you, you better watch out, you son of a pig.' Mr. Ali ignored his abuse like an intelligent person would. He felt very hurt and thought that if this child was in Bangladesh then he would have sent him into a coma. He was very lucky that the British law protected him somehow.

At the end of the exam, Mr. Ali wrote a referral to the head of department, head of year and the head teacher. The next day morning Mr. Ali visited the head teacher with his referral and explained the situation. The child was internally excluded for five days and was allowed to take the exam in a room by himself. This child had previously sworn at Mr. Ali. He wanted to make sure that something happened to him.

Mr. Ali called the local police to report that he was verbally insulted and threatened by a student. The police responded very quickly. Two officers arrived and took a statement from Mr. Ali. The head-teacher wasn't very happy that according to him that was something minor and that Mr. Ali had called the police. To Mr. Ali it was something very serious. He told the police officers that he wanted the boy to be prosecuted for swearing and for his threatening behaviour. The police officers told him that there was no law that says you can prosecute someone for swearing. They told Mr. Ali that on the street people call them pigs and so many other things but they can't do anything. Mr. Ali told the police that he wasn't happy with the law and wanted to know what would happen if the boy attacked him on the street? They told him that if the boy attacked him or continued to harass him, then they could charge him. How can there be no law when someone swears at someone else without a valid reason or provocation. It's like a person attacks another person as if they are disabled, an attacker knows the other person will not react because of their job safety. What a fucked up law!

The senior management team called the child's father and asked him to come in. They also invited Mr. Ali to join the interview. During the interview they spoke about what had happened and at the beginning the child's father was very apologetic but later on he had started to get aggressive toward Mr. Ali as he wasn't very happy that Mr. Ali reported the matter to the police. In the interview Mr. Ali said 'Did you know if your son had called someone 'Son of a pig' in Bangladesh he would have mostly likely been shot dead.' The child's father didn't like that. He became extremely angry. The man only spoke a bit of English like most of the parents did; a typical un-educated Sylheti man tried to protect his stupid bastard son. What is the government doing to stop students from swearing at teachers? Why isn't there a fucking law which protects teachers? If a teacher swears at a student then he or she can lose their job.

Peter sat on the take away table drinking his free half pint beer. Lee didn't come, he had to pick up his children as his wife had to go out. Sabbir wasn't in yet. Peter had to talk to the other waiters for his company. 'Do you like working here?' Peter asked one of the waiter. 'Not too bad, it's okay, I have to work somewhere, and it's good to work in a place for long time if things go well.'

'It's very different now, when they started here first it was very difficult for Sabbir to survive.'

'We heard they had to fight a lot.'

'Yea, I was involved in a few of the fight.'

'Whose side were you in?'

'Whose side do you think?'

'Why did the people pick on us, I don't understand?' 'It's everywhere in the world, isn't it, when young people see others taking over, they don't like it. They attack the foreigners.'

'Tell us about a fight that you were involved in?'

'I was involved in a few fights, once I was here with my wife, about six guys were not paying their bill and they were about to start a fight. Sabbir bravely locked the door and called the kitchen staff.'

The waiters listened to Peter and nodded their heads with interest.

'The kitchen staff came with knives and the fight was about to start, I had to put my nose in it.'

'What did you do?'

'I knew it was going to be a big fight and people would get severely injured. I stood up and said, 'Hold it everyone.'

'Seriously!'

'Yes, the white guys thought I was going to take their side, I said to the white guys that they should pay up and leave the restaurant quietly or I have to get involved.'

'What did they say?'

'They said that why I was taking the Pakis side. I said that I wasn't taking anyone's side. I was here to have my food quietly. My wife asked me to sit down. They said that I should listen to my wife like a little child or I would get hurt. I picked up the wine bottle from my table and told Sabbir and other to move and let me take them all.'

'You must have been a strong man then.'

'No, I was just pissed off with them idiots, so I had the bottle in my hand, I pulled it up in the air and I said, 'Come on then I want to kill you all', Sabbir and others were behind me ready to attack.'

'One of them wisely said, we let you off this time and pay but we will be back.'

'You did a good job.'

'I told them if they come back I would be back with my mates and find them where ever they were and kill them.'

'Did they pay up?'

'They paid and left, but when they went out, they through a brick at the window, since then we became best mates.' 'Now we know why you get so many free drinks and special VIP treatment.'

'There you go I am the man, don't you ever forget my discount.'

Shabana texted Foriz a week after the last time they spoke. She texted him to tell him that her mother had found a husband for her; the groom was an illegal man; she will be getting married to him. After receiving the text Foriz called her on her mobile to find out the truth. He had a feeling she was winding him up and he wanted to wind her up further. He loved winding her up. He pretended to be crying and he said;

'Shabana you can't do this to me, I thought you loved me!'

'Shut up you little child and get a life.'

'What does your illegal husband do?'

'Mind your own business, you don't need to know!'

'Come on Shabana don't be angry. Does he work in a restaurant?'

'Yes he does before you ask me he is a relative of my aunt.'

'How cruel you will never get a decent husband, it is always a restaurant worker, see Shabana you should have run away with me five years ago.'

'Get lost, you probably would have dumped me, I can't trust you.'

'Of course you can trust me.'

'No, I can't trust you. Look what you did to me; you touched me, kissed me and you're going to get married to another woman.'

'There is a difference between going and gone, I haven't gone yet.'

'Does that mean you won't go?' she said with great enthusiasm.
'No, I meant, I haven't gone yet.'
'Stop twisting and turning just tell me if you are going or not.'
'Why are you so interested in my life when you're getting married to what ever he is?'
'Do I have to tell you why I am so interested, can't you work it out with your stupid little brain.'
'Let me think.'
'How can you think, you don't have a brain?'
'I think once your new husband gets his passport he will dump you as he is only interested in your red passport.'
'Why do you only think the worst of me. I bet when your new wife comes to London she will dump you once she gets her passport as I don't think anyone will live with someone sad like you.'
'I though just a moment ago you were willing to live with me.'
'In your dreams, I rather be single then have a stupid husband like you.'
'But I rather have someone like you than be single at least someone to tease and play with.'
'To you women are for teasing and playing, you are a racist.'
'I am not racist and racism got nothing to do with this. I think you selected the wrong word as you can't think logically.'
'Shut up,' she shouted.

They continued to argue like little children and winded up each other. Foriz knew Shabana wanted to be his wife but he liked teasing her.

'Guess what?' he said.
'You admit you are a stupid fagla.'
'I think you sound really sexy when you are angry. I like to look at your face when you're angry.'
'You can look at my foot.'
'That's ok, but can I also look at the other beautiful things that you have above your foot?'
'What beautiful things are you talking about, you dirty man.'
'I am talking about your beautiful coconuts.'

'You pervert, get a life there is no chance of that.'
'Please Shabana.'
'Shut up you foga.'
'If you want my beautiful things then why are you going to Desh for?'
'Because in Desh I will get a fresh one.'
'I am fresh, I had a shower this morning.'
'Can I taste?'
'You are so dirty; I never thought you could be like this.'
'What now, I was just telling you the truth.'
'You don't know how to talk to a girl, you just know how to hurt a girl, English men are better then you, they don't mind getting married to a married woman but most of you Bengali men don't like marrying a married women. You see, we Bengalis are more racist then the white people.'
'I am sorry Shabana, I don't mean to hurt you, I was joking with you, if you get upset like this then I won't joke with you anymore.'
'It is fine, I am getting to know the real you.'
'There you go. You're leaning something new.'
'I feel so happy that I didn't get married to you.'
'How is your work? He spoke softly and tried to change the subject.'
'Work is fine, I want to meet you.'
'Why do you want to meet me?'
'I want to return the gold you gave me five years ago, when you were crazy about me, when you used to send me millions of text messages, when you said you can't live without me, when you said you would do anything to have me, when you said looking at me is like looking at heaven.'
'I did, but you're not the same person anymore. You can keep it anyway.'
'No, I don't want to keep anything of yours anymore, I heard everything today.' She pretended to be very upset.
'I can meet you but promise me that you won't hit me with anything.'
She promised him and they agreed to meet.

Peter and Lee came to the restaurant for their regular drinks and take away. With respect Minto gave them their free half pints. Sabbir arrived with the restaurants' shopping and asked the kitchen staff to unload his car. 'How are you guys?' Sabbir asked them. Then he went close to the window to check if it had been cleaned by the waiters. Lee started to talk to a waiter about the problems he was having with his wife.

'I am fine man, busy as usual, how is business?' replied Peter.

'Yea, not too bad, surviving with all the problems.'

'Everyone has problems.'

'I know, listen Peter, I have given your mobile number to a cousin of mine, you need to give him a quote for his restaurant.'

'Shall I include your commission?'

'Up to you.'

'I am thinking about giving your number to the anti-terrorist expert.'

'Do you think I am a terrorist?'

'I didn't say that, they need advice on terrorist's mind set as you are a Muslim I am sure you can give some advice.'

'Ow yeah I can if they pay me, are you trying to say we Muslims are terrorist? I knew you are racist.'

'No, I am not racist. They are trying to understand suicide bombers in the UK and Europe.'

'That's easy; they don't have to spend millions to know that. I can tell them in a few minutes.'

'I know what you going to say.'

'You have a go. What am I going to say?'

'Because of the attack in Afghanistan, Iraq and the killing of Muslims all over the world.'

'You're not far off, but I would go into details, but I know they know the score.'

'I don't understand why would some one want to kill themselves in London when there are so many opportunities to have a good life.'

'Some people don't want good life, they want quick life.' 'What you mean quick life.'

'Well, they are brain washed to believe that if they fight against the people who are killing the Muslims, they will go to heaven, so they think it is a quick ticket to heaven. Why wait until the age of sixty or seventy to die and not be sure if you would go to heaven?'

'Is that what it says in the Qur'an?'

'I don't think so.'

'The Qur'an says one should not kill another, if you kill one, it's like killing the whole nation.'

'How did these people find a gap in the Qur'an?'

'They translated it into a way to suit them and to manipulate the less-able, misfit youngsters into it. Everyone wants attention. I think the drifters want attention so they try to do something to get it.'

'There must be a good reason for the suicide bombers, you know. In Palestine they are doing it everyday.'

'They have their own reason in Palestine. The land is like a mother to people.'

'I see.'

'If someone touches your mother, wouldn't you try to protect her?'

'I understand the point.'

'I think the Palestinians are brave people with a big heart.'

'I can't believe how a young child can have so much guts that he accepts he is going to die and goes out there to blow himself up, I can't get it through my brain.'

'You won't get it as you got too much beer in your head. Of course it is difficult for us to understand because we live in a different world to them. No one is bombing us. No one is taking our land, no one is killing our families, but if we were in Palestine then it wouldn't have been so difficult to understand their mindset.'

'I am getting brain washed by you. Can I have my take away before I convert to being a terrorist?'

Foriz and Shabana met in a pizza restaurant in East Ham. He sat in the corner of the restaurant facing the door. She came in on time and looked very upset. Both of them dressed to impress.

She said hello and sat in front of him. He smiled at her and asked her, 'What's wrong with you and why are you so upset?'

'Shut up, I am not in the mood to smile and laugh,' she spoke quickly.

'I have ordered an orange juice for you, what would you like to eat?'

'Order what ever you like.'

'You like spicy pizza, don't you?'

'What ever, I am not in the mood.'

They spoke in Bengali as they didn't want the waitress to know what they were talking about. Foriz ordered a spicy vegetarian pizza.

'By the way why are we meeting today?'

'I wanted to tell you that you are not a human.'

'What am I then?'

'Do you really want to know?'

'Yes please.'

'You are an animal. You have no feelings.'

'If I am an animal, what are you doing with me?'

'I am trying to educate you so you become a human and learn how to behave like one.'

'I thought I treated you very well.'

'No, you never treated me well, you talk rubbish, and all you think about is getting girls in bed. Sorry, you did have respect for me five years ago.'

'I never took you to bed or tried.'

'I never gave you the chance. If I had you would have.'

'No, no, I don't agree with that. I have never tried to get you to bed.'

'I don't believe you, I think you are a pervert. At the cinema you tried to get into my bra, do you remember, I had to stop you.'

'Look whose talking, I was only trying to find out how big your melons were, and anyway you're not that innocent too.'

Both of them looked at each others' face and smiled but she gave him a dirty look. The pizza arrived. Foriz put two slices on her plate and took the same for himself. He said to Shabana, 'Come on lets get some salads.' She went with him to get some salad. Foriz let her pick the salads and he stood behind her. While she picked the salads he pinched her bum. She knew it was him. She wanted to shout at him but due to the circumstances she didn't, she just turned around and gave him a dirty look as if she could have slapped him. He smiled back at her. They came back to their table. He sliced his pizza into small chunks and said, 'My nose tells me I have beautiful food in front of me, yum yum.' She waited to catch his eyes and gave him another mean look.

'Stop giving me dirty looks, I am trying to enjoy my pizza.'

'You eat like a Goru! And why did you touch me?'

'You eat like a princess! And when did I touch you?'

'Stop lying, stop giving me compliments, I won't fall into your trap.'

'You have already fallen in my trap.'

'Am I really, in your dreams, this is the last time you will see my beautiful face.'

'I am not so sure; I think you will meet me more because I have not finished with you. There are other things I want to enjoy with you.'

'I know you have not finished with me, but I won't let you get that far, I am not like other girls, I won't let you get there.'

'What are you talking about now?'

'You know what I am talking about. You have a dirty mind and I know where you want to get to.'

'I wasn't thinking about that yet but if you offer, I won't say no to that.'

'I will never offer, I am not that low.'

'Anyway, I really wasn't thinking about that, believe me.'

'Good boy.'

'I want to tell you something that will make you very happy.'

'I don't believe that you are going to talk some sense from now on.'

They finished eating. She picked up her orange juice to sip. She looked at him and said, 'Why are you looking at me for? Have you not seen a beautiful girl before?

'Shut up Shabana, I think we cussed each other enough today. Let's talk some serious business now.'

'When did you learn to talk seriously?'

'Sometimes I do talk seriously.'

'Ok, what is it that you want to get off from your chest.'

'Are you ready?'

'Yes I am ready.'
'Shabana I want to do it with you.'

Shabana kicked him on the leg. She looked at his face for a few good seconds, twisted her face and lips with anger.'

'You are a foga, I feel like throwing this glass of drink on you.'
'Why did you kick me for!'
'I am going to kick you again, if you don't stop the nonsense.'
'Come down, I am sure you would enjoy it.'
'You are going too far, you better stop it now or I will leave now.'
'Sorry, I was intentionally winding you up this time.'
'I know you are, why are you doing that. Grow up and act like a mature man.'
'Ok, I am serious now; I got something to show you.'
'Show me then, I haven't got whole day.'
'You have to come to my car.'
'I am not going in your car. I don't trust you, show it to me here.'
'I can't show it here.'
'Ok, in my car and we sit at the front not at the back.'
'No, we sit at the back because I need space.'
'No, I don't trust you.'
'Why not?'
'I can't trust you because you might try it on me.'
'Trust me, I won't do anything like that.'
'If you try anything against my will then I will sue you.'
'Ok.'

Foriz paid the bill. Shabana wanted to pay too. He told her that she could pay next time. They got up to go. 'Can I hold your hand Shabana,' he said softly. She looked at his eyes and gave a pause. He gave her a sexy blink then he said quietly, 'Please sweet Shabana, you won't regret it this time.' 'Ok.' He held her hand firmly as if it's something very important that he won't let go off. They went out of the restaurant. On the way to the car she said that she didn't mind going into his car. They went into his car, sat at the back. Foriz asked her to close her eyes. 'I won't close my eyes in case you kiss me.'

'I won't kiss you now, I have already tasted your lips before and they taste fantastic.'

'Shut up you. Ok. I'll close my eyes, you hurry up.'

He took the gift out of his pocket and told her to open her eyes.
'Foriz, What is it?'
'Open it?'
'Who is it for?
'Who else.'
'What you mean who else.' She had a feeling it's hers.
'It's for you my dear Shabana.'
'Why would you buy me a present?'
'I have my reasons.'
'I can't take presents from you.'
'Why not?'
'I have my reasons too.'
'Cut out the childish staff and open it.'
She opened the gift and it looked like the gift she chose for him to take to a wedding.
'It looks nice; I remember I chose a ring like that for you to take to a wedding.'
'Yes it's the same ring you chose, I asked you to choose it because I wanted you to like it but I gave you the wrong reason to choose it for.'
'So you bought it for me.' She gave a smile.
'Yes I did.'
'Why did you buy it for me when you don't even like me?'
She smiled again.
'Did I ever say I don't like you?'
'So what is the point of this ring?' She smiled as she spoke.
'Point is I want you to be happy and want to see you smiling.'
'If you bought it for me then why did to say you were going to Desh?'
'I am not, you told me your mum found someone for you.'
'So you lied to me, I lied to you too, my mum didn't find anyone for me.'
'Yes I did lie to you.'
'Why did you lie to me?'
'I wanted to know if you loved me and why did you lie to me?'
'So, do I love you? I also wanted to know if you loved me.'
'I think you do.'

'So what's next?'
'I think I deserve a big kiss and hug.'
'No, I don't think so.'
'Come on bhondu, let me give you a nice kiss on your lips.'
'No, just because you gave me a present, I won't give you a kiss, you need to learn your lesson.'
'Alright, let me hold your hands.'
'No, if you buy me a diamond ring then I will let you kiss me.'
'Get lost.'
'Do you love me Foriz?' She said with a serious face.
'I am not sure.'
'Tell me you love me.'
'You tell me if you love me.'
'First you tell me that you love me.'
'No, it's your turn.'
'Boys always go first.'
'I told you so many times before when I was at university, so I think you should say it now to make up.'
She hid her face with her hands and said, 'Ok, I love you Foriz.'
'Say it once more.'
'No, you say it.'
'Come on say it once more.'
'You close your eyes then I won't hide my face. He closed his eyes and she said, 'I love you Foriz.' And I want to be your wife forever. Then she hid her face and asked him, 'Did you like that?'
'Yes I did, please don't hide your face anymore look at me.' 'No I can't.'
'Yes you can, if you don't look at me how you gonna be my wife.'
'Shabana I love you and I want you to be my wife.'
'Really.'
'Yes.'
'So you gonna take me to your home.'
'Yes, Insha-Allah I will.'
'Let me give you a kiss and hug.'
'Come on then.'
They hugged each other for long period of time. They didn't want to let go off each other.

'Do you want a kiss?'
'If you let me.'
'I will close my eyes and you kiss me, ok.'
'No, please keep your eyes open, I won't you to see that it's me whose making love to you.'

They kissed each other affectionately and passionately. Then they moaned, 'I love you truly Shabana.' 'I love you too Foriz.' They stopped kissing after a long time. 'I need to take you home.' 'Take me to your home quickly then you can enjoy all the other things that you want.'

'Can't I enjoy them now?'

Shabana put her finger on his lips and said, 'You know it is not right, I will give you everything as soon as we are married, if we do anything now both of us will get sin.' 'Sorry, I was kidding.'

I better go home now as I have spent a very long time with you.
'Come here bitch and give me your lips again.'
'If you carry on kissing me like this, you will eat them.'
'They are mine now, ain't they?'
'Not yet, first you have to marry me to make them yours.'
'I will do that as soon as possible.'
'Lets go home now.'
'Ok I will speak to you on the phone.'

Foriz took her to her car and said good bye. Later on they texted each other through out the evening and deep into the night.

Outside Mr. Ali's room a female supply teacher was trapped by a few boys. The boys won't let her go unless she gave her mobile number to them. She gave a number but they dialled it and it was incorrect so they refused to let her go. Mr. Ali heard the noise and poked his nose to find out what was going on. He recognised the boys and told them to get the hell out of there, so they went. Then he safely took the sexy supply teacher to the staff room. He gave the 'desperado' boys' names to a deputy head. The head-teacher excluded the boys from school for a few weeks.

Peter came to the restaurant all smiling, dancing and singing like a little kid, 'We won the ashes, we won the ashes.'

'By the time you finish singing you'll probably lose it,' said Sabbir.

'We have done it man.'

'Congratulations Peter.'

They shook hands. Peter went to the kitchen and shook Gozafor Miah's hands too.

'Give me something really nice today, I am in the mood to celebrate.'

'I give you special curry every day.'

'Today I feel like having Tandoori mix grill with chopped green chilies.'

'You got it.'

'What do you want for your wife?'

'As usual, chicken tikka masala.'

'I think England were lucky to win it.'

'Lucky, what you talking about, we demolished Australia.'

'No, you didn't, they had a top bowler missing.'

'Shut it man, injuries are part of the game.'

Peter went on and on about the test match like Gozafor Miah does when ever Bangladesh won something.

―

Foriz told his sister to tell his parents of his intention to marry Shabana. They were opposed to it. They told his sister to tell him that he shouldn't get married to a married woman. There were so many single gorgeous women out there that they could find. He told them that he didn't want to lose her again. To him it didn't matter whether she was a single, married or unmarried. He loved her for her personality and beauty, not her marriage status.

CHAPTER TWENTY

2006

Foriz's sister proposed for Shabana for the third time. Rokib didn't go to the proposal as they had enough of her parents. Shabana told her mother that the guests would be visiting them. Raga had invited a few of her relatives to do the 'wedding talking.' This time her family accepted Foriz's proposal. They didn't demand any money for a dowry as they knew that he was a legal British man.

Shabana's father didn't have much to say. He was behind bars for 'honours' killing. Shabana's young sister Rabina had a Somalian boy friend. Her father found out about it. He sent his sons to beat up the boy. They beat up the boy so much that the boy died from the injuries. Shabana's father and her brothers were locked up for many years. From time to time Shabana took her mother to visit her father and brothers in prison. There are many Bengali men that don't like it when they find out that their daughter has a boyfriend. They find it difficult to accept that if their daughter chooses someone it would bring a bad name to the family rather then looking at their daughter's fault. If possible some people would try to kill the boy whose involved. It is a major problem in the Bangladeshi society that parents' find it absolutely unacceptable when their daughter dates someone. Sometimes some people accept it if their son dates a girl from another race and marries her. When it comes to their daughters their blood pressure jumps through to their skull!

Shabana paid for her wedding expense as there was no one else to help out. Her mother realised that it was wrong of her not to accept the proposal from Foriz at the first time.

During the wedding not many people turned up as it was Foriz's second wedding. Foriz's family did not tell the relatives that the bride was a divorcee, other wise they would have laughed. They probably would have said "Couldn't you find a clean one that you had to get a second hand one." It was a low key wedding. A lot of Shabana's relatives didn't come because she had divorced her previous husband. In the wedding hall some of the relatives were saying that Foriz had divorced his wife to get married to Shabana. They must wait and see the bride to check out how beautiful she was. Foriz invited Sabbir as he was the son of his father's best friend. Sabbir came to the wedding with his family and congratulated Foriz. In Foriz's home everyone was sceptical about Shabana and wasn't sure how to approach her. When she arrived and they looked at her, how beautiful she was they couldn't believe that how a man could have divorced her. They accepted her and liked her looks very much.

On the first night Shabana sat on the bed wearing the red wedding sari. Foriz came into the room and locked the door and sat front of her. He pulled over her sari from her head to see her awesome face. She gave him a heavenly smile that almost satisfied him. Foriz put an Indian song on, so no-one else could hear them talk from the other rooms. She quickly gave him a hug and said, 'Thank you very much for marrying me. Now you can have everything you wished for. I am all yours.'

'Tonight all I want to do is look at your beautiful face and admire Allah for creating someone so beautiful for me.'

'You have seen me so many times. I am the same person.' 'No, I have seen you with different eyes. Now I am looking at you as my wife, my gift.'

He looked at her face for a long time. She smiled at him and touched his face with her hands.

'Have you finished looking at me?'

'No I haven't, the more I look at you, the more I want to look at you.'

'Come on darling, don't you want me to take this heavy sari off or do you want me to sleep with it?'

'Shabana would you kindly come on the floor and stand up, I like to see you with the sari on.'

'No problem my sweet darling.'

She stood up on the floor. He looked at her from the top to the bottom. She hid her face with her hands then moved them. Foriz went close to her, hugged her then kissed her and then told her, 'I love you so much Shabana that I can't explain, I am so happy with Allah that I have you at last.'

'Now, you have me, make sure you love me today and for rest of my life.'

'Insha-Allah.'

'Shall I take the sari off or are you going to take it off for me?'

'Am I allowed to take it off?'

'Of course you are, I am all yours now. You don't have to ask me for permission all the time to do anything.'

He laughed sweetly.

'Ok, you take it off and I will just watch your beautiful body slowly.'

'Fine, be like that. If I take it off, it might take me half an hour as there are so many pins stuck on it, so I think you should help.'

'Ok, I will help, how much are you going to pay me?'

'You have me what more do you want.'

Foriz slowing took her sari off and kissed her as her body became visible to him. Shabana asked him if he was happy to see her in front of him. He told her it was the best day of his life. Foriz picked her up and laid her on his plate. Shabana told him again, 'I am all yours, I want you to enjoy me now.' Foriz slowly made love to her, kissed her on the eyes, neck, back and then he was ready. He drove through into her narrow but most secret garage, reversed for further satisfaction. Simultaneously he enjoyed her tangerines. Then he parked himself once he had run out of gas. While he drove, she made awesome noises that gave him even more satisfaction.

'Did you enjoy that ride darling?'

'I loved it. It was the most satisfying ride I ever had, Thank you very much.'

'I also thank you for the enjoyment you gave me.'

Sokina's young sister Sheena came to London for a holiday. She was sponsored by Sabbir. Sheena tried to get visa for the whole family but the immigration only gave her the visa. Her reason was to see her ill mother. 'Thanks to Allah,' said Sabbir as her whole family weren't given the visas. Sabbir was sure, if she was allowed to bring her children then she would have dumped one or two for the relatives to look after. When she came, she bought present for Sabbir's wife and the children and stayed at all the relatives' house. While she visited the relatives she told them to find a suitable husband for her daughter, who was only fourteen years old. Sheena showed her daughter's pictures to everyone so they could look for a British subject. Sabbir had to cough out five hundred pounds as a gift to her. He didn't want to give her any money. She was rich. There were so many poor people in the village who needed the money more then she did but Sokina told him everyone else had given her money. If he didn't, it would look silly and others will think his family was tight. After a month she returned to Bangladesh having arranged her daughter's marriage to a British subject; not bad she killed two birds with one stone. She decided that she would make a passport for her daughter aged eighteen so there wouldn't be a problem getting a visa to get to England once married.

Sabbir sat in his living room relaxing on his day off, a telephone call came, his wife picked it up. An English lady was on the phone. She passed it to Sabbir. He picked up the phone, 'Hello, who is it?' The caller said that she was calling from a bank and she had good news for him.
'What is the good news?'
'Before I give you the news I need to do some security checks.'
'How do I know that you are calling from a bank?'
'You have a bank card from us.'
'That's right.'
'Can you tell me, what's the first line of your address and post code?'
He gave the details.
'As you are a valued customer we can give you up to £7,500 loans at a special rate of 7.9%.'

'No, No, that is a too expensive, I had a loan last year at 5.9% from another bank.'

Their conversation ended shortly. He thought, do they think I'm stupid that I don't shop around for the best rate. They should have known he was a curry seller; one step ahead of their game. Some of these banks pissed him off calling him when ever they liked and came up with offers that he wouldn't consider.

February 2006

The Government voted with a majority that smoking should be banned in all public places. Peter and Lee arrived in the restaurant for their usual drinks and take-aways. Sabbir attacked Peter as he fetched a half pint of lager.

'Tell me Peter, why is your government 1400 years behind us.'

'What the fuck are you talking about now? To you everything is 1400 years ago,' said Peter.

'Yeh, what the fuck you said,' said Lee as he went to the loo to make some space for the lager.

'I am talking about the smoking ban.'

'I bet you gonna say now that it was written in the Qur'an that smoking isn't allowed.'

'Not exactly, but you're not far off.'

'Without reading the Qur'an I seem to know a lot, tell me what does it say about smoking?'

'In the Qur'an it says that one should not consume any substance that is harmful to our bodies, obviously smoking is harmful to one's body's so it isn't allowed.'

'I take it most of you Muslims can't even read your own Qur'an because if you lot knew how to read it then you lot wouldn't have been smoking.'

'We Bengali know how to read it but don't understand the meaning of it.'

'Why the fuck so many of you Muslims smoke then?' 'Especially you Bengali smoke a lot.'

'I wish I could answer that questions, I think people don't take it seriously. They probably think it's a minor issue but it's not.'

'Forty years ago they used to advertise smoking was good for you. It helped you relax.'

'Of course it does, it helps you to go to your death-bed early.'

'I have cut down a lot; I used to take forty once upon a time.'

'I never liked smoking anyway.'

'You never smoked because you are a tight git who wanted to save all the money.'

People don't realise that smoking causes so many deaths, roughly a hundred and fourteen thousand people die from smoking related diseases in UK every year.

'What is wrong with the world?' Sabbir asked Peter.

'Say that in full sentence please?'

'I mean the other day an author was sentenced for three years for denying the holocaust in Austria.'

'The Jews are a bit like you Muslims. You can't say much to them.'

'If you do, you will be prosecuted.'

'The Jews are running this country now, what ever they say happens.'

'How did the Jews become so powerful man?'

'I think when the Jews were getting killed by Hitler they got together and promised to work as a family and become educated in our country and rule it.'

'If that's the case they have done very well.'

'They have achieved a lot over the century.'

'There are some good Jews out there.'

'I wasn't expecting that from you.'

'My father told me in the fifties and sixties the Jews gave them work in their factories.'

'That's not because they were nice. They needed people to work for them so they could make money.'

'I know but still they employed Muslim people.'

'They thought of you lot as cheap labour that's why they employed Asians.'

'I am sure like the Jews we will be successful and maybe one day we will have a Bengali Prime Minister.'

Everyone laughed sarcastically.

'You carry on selling curry that's what you're good at, don't worry about becoming a Prime Minister.'

The telephone rung, Sabbir answered the call, Peter and Lee drank their second Lager.

'What is this world coming to man?' Peter said to Sabbir. 'What you mean?'

'Did you read the Metro today?'

'No, what's in it?'

'You cunts, don't you spend any money on a newspaper!'

'You have to save every penny man, you know every fucking thing is going up everyday, anyway tell me what happened.'

'I forgot, yea this cunt got £80.00 fine for swearing in a public place.'

'What the fuck are you talking about.'

'Yea, I am not joking, read the newspaper.'

'Tell me bit more.'

'Am I your news reader or what? You tight git, go and buy a newspaper and find out yourself.'

'This geezer was talking to his mate on the mobile and swearing and the coppers heard him swear so they caught him and fined him.'

'If the police hear you talk I am sure they will fine you a few hundred pounds very time you open your mouth.'

'I am sure if they check your restaurant they can find many illegal workers and fine you a few thousand pounds, how about that?'

Both of them laughed.

'That's enough.'

'How about this man whose got fined £50.00 for putting junk mail in a bin outside his house.'

'I thought bins are for people to put rubbish in.'

'Yes, but public bins are for public usage.'

'I can see what the government is trying to do with the public order act but I think this is going too far, there are so many important major issues they need to deal with before they deal with this kind of issues.'

'Why don't the government give fines to the people who smoke or drink alcohol on the street. How about giving fines to those advertisement company who display almost naked ladies on their posters. Isn't that rude and offensive? Perhaps the government likes looking at naked women.'

'I am sure the government likes looking at beautiful ladies displayed on the bill board when driving around the country.'

'I think the European governments are womenphobic.'

'You lot are womenphobic, you lot control your women and lock them up.'

'No, we don't.'

'You do, you lot lock them up like if they were some kind of object.'

'Why don't the government give fines to those women dress half naked?'

'The government likes looking at naked women.'

'I think the government is loosing the plot.'

'I think the government will soon be like the Taliban government.'

'What you mean?'

'Well, you Muslims have rules like, you can't do this, you can't do that, you shouldn't say this; you shouldn't say that. There are too many rules you Muslims have.'

'I got this feeling soon the government gonna have this law book full of rules that pupils have to study from primary school.'

'No comments.'

While Mr. Ali was teaching, suddenly the female teacher from next door came into his classroom and told him to close the door. A boy was after her. Quickly Mr. Ali went to close the door. He asked her what had happened. She said that a boy had threatened her with a knife in her classroom and she had run out. He looked through the window. There was no one outside. Mr. Ali took her to the head teacher's office and asked the senior management team to look for the boy. They found him. He smelt of alcohol. The police took him away. Then he was excluded from the school. This is what the government needs to do. Stop the abuse of the teachers. Not kill people in another country just to show off to the world. We have problem on our door-step and the government isn't solving them. What kind of government is that, interested in pretending to be solving another nation's problem by killing innocent people and getting own people killed in the process.

London's mayor had been suspended from office for four weeks for comparing a Jewish journalist to a concentration camp guard.

'You can't say nothing to the Jew's nowadays,' said Sabbir to Peter.

'If you say anything they suspend you or take you to court.'

'Are they trying to be super human?'

'You can't have a Jewish joke anymore.'

'I bet soon it will be illegal to say to someone, 'You are tight like the Jews.'

'And if you do say it then you would probably be prosecuted.'

'I know man, the way the law is changing you probably have to write down first what you want to say then check it with all the public order acts and then say it.'

'On the other hand you have a government that's killing thousand of people but no one can persecute them.'

'When are we going to stop this double standard?'

'It is proven like black and white that Tony misleadingly went to war. Shouldn't he be charged or prosecuted?'

'I bet the government will soon publish a book on what you can and can't say to a Jew and if you want to talk to a Jew, then you have to check to make sure you are within the law.'

Their discussion came to an end as customers arrived to the restaurant. They changed their subject. As usual Peter gulped a few pints of lager, which made him feel good, collected his take away and left semi-drunk.

Foriz took Shabana to the Newham General Hospital for scheduled check ups. Shabana could have gone by herself but he went with her to comfort her and to see scan image of their unborn child. Shabana asked Foriz if he wanted to know if the baby was boy or girl. He said that he will wait until the baby is born. He will be very happy whether it's boy or girl. It didn't matter to him.

Peter and Lee came to the restaurant to wind up Sabbir, drink and take away their curries. Sabbir asked Peter, 'So what do you think about Tony Blair when he suggested that his decision to go to war in Iraq would ultimately be judged by God?'

'I thought they don't do god.'

'I don't believe in no god,' said Lee.

'He is definitely doing God now, perhaps there is no way out.'

Most of the time Lee wasn't interested in their conversation as he was mostly busy drinking or talking to his wife, arguing about if she had slept with another man.

'He can say what ever he likes to convince people that he is innocent, but end of the day who is going to touch him?'

'At the moment no one can touch him, his got his father Bush with him.'

'How come he couldn't leave Saddam Hussain alone and leave it to God to judge him, is there a contradiction here?' 'If you believe what these politicians says then you must be a fool, I don't think anyone believes these politicians nowadays!'

Peter was correct about believing the politician. Just look at Tony Blair and Bush's propaganda war against the Iraqi people. They might attack Iran next, perhaps they are planning behind the back door what story to tell the world before they attack them. Maybe the blue print is ready, soon it will come out.

As the kitchen staff arrived to work in the restaurant, every one wanted to talk about Bangla bhai who had been caught in Bangladesh. The man was charged for planning five hundred bombs in sixty four districts.

The capture of Siddiqul Islam, one the most wanted Islamic militant in Bangladesh was an excellent news for the public. His arrest came just four days after the arrest of his mastermind guru Abdur Rahman. Islam, known as Bangla Bhai which meant Brother of Bengal, came to fame in 2004 as the leader of Jagrata Muslim Janata Bangladesh, the group blamed for a number of killings in Bangladesh. Perhaps he should have been named Dushman Bangla Bhai which meant enemy brother of Bengal for his killing. Gozafor Miah and his colleagues couldn't understand why the men whom looked so religious committed such crimes. Probably another one of Bin Laden's mate. What is wrong with this world, when ever people can't get what they want they start killing.

Priya's passport arrived with a three year visa after the original application. Their long wait was over. Can you believe it that in a country like England took three years for them to decide whether to give someone a visa or not. Why do they take so long? Then again the government is so stupid. Instead of sending these people back they give them permission to stay. Priya and Kolim invited the relatives around their rented house for dinner to celebrate the good news. Kolim thanked Sabbir for the dodgy documents he had given them.

Foriz received a leaflet through his door from the Respect Party. He read it. There was a meeting to be held at the East Ham Town Hall. It was close to his home. He went to the meeting to find out what it was all about. There were many speakers, namely the main candidate of Respect Party for the Newham's mayor's elections and council seats. He waited for George Galloway's speech. Mr. Galloway told the audience, 'If you vote for New Labour on the fourth of May then you will have blood of the Iraqis and Palestinians' on your hand.' Foriz previously had voted for New Labour but in this election he decided to vote for Respect. He also told his beautiful wife to vote for the Respect Party.

April 2006

In Fatullah, Bangladesh scored 427 runs in their first innings against the best cricket nation of the world. In the restaurant Gozafor Miah was excited as he couldn't believe that his country was capable of scoring like that. Through-out the night he spoke about cricket. A few days later Australia managed to beat Bangladesh marginally. Gozafor Miah took moral satisfaction out of the defeat as Bangladesh came close and pushed Australia into the fifth day.

'What happened to the best Prime Minister of the world? Sabbir asked Peter.

'You are talking about Italy's Berlusconi?'

'Who else!'

'Obviously he wasn't the best.'

'What's going to happen now, if he doesn't concede defeat?'

'They're probably going to do a recount, or he must concede defeat.'

'Big talk didn't get him very far.'

'Perhaps he shouldn't have stopped screwing his wife. Maybe women decided not to vote for him.'

'I am sure the beautiful secretaries they have in Italy voted for him. Do you remember when he said that people should invest in Italy because they have beautiful secretaries?'

'I can't, but I am not surprised.'

'That man used to come up with so many stupid comments.'

'No comments, this is why he lost.'

The telephone rang. Sabbir answered the call and took a 'collection order.'

'When are you Muslims going to learn and not execute people in public places?'

'What you talking about now?'

'I read a Somalian boy of sixteen executed his father's killer in a public execution order by the Islamic court.'

'I am sure the man did something wrong.'

'Yes, the man killed the boy's father. That doesn't mean the man should be stabbed in the head and throat in a public place.'

'It's the law, an eye for eye.'

'So you agree that people should be executed like that?'

'I didn't say that, but I don't know the full story.'

'Come on man what ever happened you can't kill someone like an animal.'

'Yes, but that man first killed someone that could have been very ugly, who knows?'

'I am sure they could have executed him by using a lethal injection or some other ways.'

'But what is the point of giving a killer easy death when he didn't have mercy when he killed.'

'I don't think we will get very far. We better stop.'

'Of course we will never come to the same conclusion. How can we? East and West are never the same. You can't compare fish and ships with rice and spice.'

Gozafor Miah had smile back on his face after the disappointment of losing to Australia as Bangladesh would host the 2011 Cricket World Cup with India, Pakistan and Sri Lanka. He discussed with Goni how the world would watch Bangladesh and it will hopefully give them the opportunity to improve their game. 'Uncle you going to watch Bangladesh get beaten in the world cup.' Yasin asked Gozafor Miah.

'Nephew, it's not all about winning, but for us Bangladeshi it is all about learning now, once we become good then we can challenge the world, like India,'

'How about football uncle, do you expect to see Bangladesh in the football World Cup.'

'We are not too bad in Asia, but it will take us probably another fifty years before we can get to the football world cup.'

'I am sure some of the Bangladeshi in England can play for Bangladesh.'

'No, I don't think so because the Bengalis here, as soon as possible they get a British passport.'

'I am sure in England soon we will get Bengalis playing in the premiership.'

'Problems are the Bengalis are too busy selling curry and don't concentrate on sports.'

'There was a Bengali player who played in West Ham United's reserve team but couldn't break into the main team.'

'There you go, all we need to do is practise and keep focus and we will be alright.'

'Uncle, make me a nice king prawn biryani.'

'No problem, do you want it spicy?'

'Yes please.'

May 2006

'I take it your Respect Party didn't win in Tower Hamlets,' said Peter.

'I knew you were going to say that,' replied Sabbir.

'Looks like it's going to take time to get rid of New Labour from Tower Hamlets.'

'Yes most definitely. It least Respect improved a lot, from one to eleven that's more then one thousand percent up.'

'I am sure if all the Bengalis voted for Respect then they probably could have won.'

'I know but quite a lot of Bengalis are brain washed to vote for Labour. These are mostly people who think that if they don't vote for Labour then they won't get unemployment benefits.'

'Are you serious?'

'I am being serious. There are so many Bengalis that think like that.'

'Maybe in the next round they might over take.'

'Maybe, I don't understand. How can a Muslim vote for New Labour anymore?'

'Why not?'

'Well, you know Tony is killing thousands of Muslims in Iraq and has killed thousand of Muslims in Afghanistan so for a Muslims to vote for New Labour basically according to my understanding, they are saying to Tony what you did wasn't a problem. We will still support you.'

'Who did you vote for before Respect?'

'I did vote for Labour and my father voted for them too, but I have promised, for as long as I live, I won't vote for them again.'

'Respect will never become the government though.'

'I know but it is a way of protesting against the war and a message to Tony.'

'Is my take away ready?'

'Let me check.'

Sabbir went into the kitchen to check.

'Few more minutes.'

'Give me another half pint.'

'No problems.'

Sabbir poured half a pint of lager.

'Anyway who did you vote for?'

'That's top secret, actually I voted for BNP.'

'You didn't.'

'I did.'

'I don't believe you.'

'Why not.'

'How can you vote for them, they are racist?'

'They are not; they stand up for the British white people.'

'They don't like non-whites.'

'They have their reasons. How can they like non-whites as you lot came over here and take everything from us, our houses, claim benefits the next day you arrive here and top of that take over our businesses.'

'Shut up man, we work hard for every penny.'

'I have not finished yet, top of all that you lot take our women too.'

'We don't, it's the African take your woman.'

'I actually voted for the conservative.'

'What's the reason then?'

'The leader looks smart and something for change.'

'I heard this Bengali man in Bow voted for BNP because he thought it was the Bangladesh National Party.'

'You are kidding me.'

'That's what I heard.'

The Baishaki Mela came again. It was an opportunity for the local and national people to visit Brick Lane and the surrounding area. This was also an extra opportunity for Sabbir to make more money. On the day Sabbir and his staff started work early as they prepared curries and rice for the stall outside his restaurants.

Sabbir had to get a stall for his illegal cousin Shiru as he insisted that he could manage it. He wanted them to learn about business so it would help them later. Sabbir liked Shiru's proactiveness and wanted to give him the chance. Shiru had planned for this Mela for many weeks and had made a list of things he wanted to sell. He hired another illegal cousin who came from the same village.

Sabbir also gave a stall to another cousin 'brother' - Ariful, but he didn't have the confidence that he could run the stall. Shiru had many contacts; he hired another illegal cousin to work with Ariful. They sold Bombay mix with added spice and soft drinks to the passers by.

A week before the Mela, Sabbir took his cousins to a wholesale warehouse and bought two large boxes of Bombay mix and a large quantity of soft drinks. They kept the stock in the restaurant so it was easy to get on the day. On the day he told them to buy other ingredients, such as, fresh coriander, salt, lime, chilies. This time Sabbir told them to keep a record of how much money they spent on the goods so they could work out how much profit they made.

People from all over the country came as usual and enjoyed the music, food, art and everything that was on offer. It was beautiful to watch people from different backgrounds mingling together without any problems and enjoying the day.

Sabbir's curry stall was busy from the word go. His cousins were also busy making money. On the soft drinks which cost them twenty pence to buy they sold it for a pound. On the day Shiru made five hundred pounds and Ariful made four hundred and fifty pounds. Sabbir told them to work out how much they spent on buying the goods. He gave him the money that he gave them and keep the rest for them self. Shiru's and Ariful's expenses were just over hundred pounds each. They paid their helper twenty pounds each and that was Shiru's deal with them. Ariful made about three hundred pounds profit. Shiru made nearly three hundred and fifty pounds profit.

When they were at home the cousins gave the money, back to Sabbir and asked him to send it back home to their parents. Sabbir was please as they were thinking about their parents. He told them to keep twenty pounds for their pocket money and take the money to Badol Miah who would send it for them.

When Ariful's and Shiru's parents found out that their sons had sent the money they were very proud and happy. They couldn't believe it, that in one day their sons were able to earn approximately thirty five to fourty thousand taka. This would last them for three to four months. In the next few weeks Ariful and Shiru bosted to the relatives how they made money on the day and they wished there was a Baishaki Mela every week.

Peter and Lee came in for drinks and take away and to relax as usual. After the general conversation – hello and how are you, Sabbir asked Peter what the latest news was.

'Go and buy a newspaper you tight Jew.'

'Why shall I buy one when I have you to supply me all the latest news with added spices.'

'Today I read Baa Baa Black Sheep to be changed to rainbow sheep.'

'I don't understand how that can be racist.'

'When a black person calls another black person black it is not racist, why is that?'

'There is a newspaper called, 'black newspaper' why it that not been banned, I don't understand the politics of this country.'

'I personally like the colour black. I think black is probably the best colour, because if you look at it percentage you would see almost everyone has a pair of black shoes or a pair of black trousers.'

'If black is not a good colour why do people wear it?'

End of December 2006

Peter came to the restaurant for the end of year drinking session. A new manager was in charge.

'You must be very unhappy that Saddam Hussein got executed today,' Peter said to Yasin.

'I don't care about Saddam Hussein, I am not related to him.'

'Come on Junior Sabbir, be honest.'

'Honestly I think he deserved to be executed as I believe if he was innocent then God would have saved him.'

'You talk different from your father, when is your father coming back from Arabia?'

'He should be back next week.'

'Are you ready to take over the business?'

'Well, my father can't carry on for ever and I don't mind managing it but I have other business plans on side too.'

'Why is it you Bengalis always think about business?'

'Because we are gifted.'

Peter laughed and said 'there is only one talent you Bengalis have and that is to sell curry.'

'No comment.'

Shabana was in pain. Foriz took Shabana to the Newham General Hospital, to give birth. They went to the labour ward. A male midwife wanted to check Shabana's condition. Foriz told the male midwife, 'Excuse me; I don't want a male to check my wife.'

'Why not?'

'I don't want a male to look at my wife.'

'I have helped many women to give birth.'

'You may have done that but I don't want a male midwife.'

'Well, we don't have a female midwife at the moment.'

'I was told that there will be female midwife.'

'They are busy with other clients.'

'If that's the case then I will have to go home and my wife will give birth at home.'

The midwife went to speak to his manager, told them to wait. Foriz asked Shabana, 'What should we do if they can't find a female midwife?' 'There isn't away I can allow another man to look at my things' 'This is why I love you so much Shabana.' After a few minutes another female midwife came and spoke to them, told them that she was supposed to finish her shift now but she would stay to check Shabana's condition. Foriz and Shabana couldn't understand how people could allow a male to look at their naked bodies and help them deliver their babies.

Don't people have any shame. Yes, one could understand if there was a situation if things went wrong and no female doctors were available then a male doctor could deal with a situation. Foriz said to Shabana, 'White women don't mind if a male midwife looks at them because they are doing a job.' 'That's why they are white and we are not.'

The midwife checked Shabana physically with her hands and told them to stay in the hospital. Slowly Shabana's pain increased. She was taken to the delivery room. Foriz told her that he didn't want to come into the room. He felt scared to watch her give birth. She told him that she needed him in there to support her. Foriz had no choice as he held her hand and watched her go through the pain. He managed to see how much pain a woman went through in order to give birth. He realised that he shouldn't hurt her ever again. Also he should be more nice to his mother. His mother must have gone through so much pain to give birth to him. It was an extremely useful lesson for him. She pushed hard and gave birth to their little baby. Within a few seconds the midwife told them it was a girl. Foriz was very happy to be a father. As soon as he had the chance he called his mother and gave her the news. She called all the relatives to let them know. Shabana was in the hospital for a few more hours before the midwife discharged her. In order to bring the baby home Foriz had to buy a car seat for the baby as it was illegal to transport a baby in the car without it. As they arrived home with the baby Foriz's family were extremely happy. Foriz told Shabana; 'I told you, if I get married to you then we will have beautiful children.' In return Shabana gave him an amazing smile.

Sabbir went to hajj to wash all his sins and complete one of the important pillars of Islam which a Muslim should undertake as its compulsory on them. Sabbir felt that he had done enough deals and monkey businesses and now it was time to see the house of Allah and ask Allah for forgiveness for all the sins he had committed. He calculated his time had come to call it a day. Sabbir felt that he made his life a successful one by managing to get from a mud hut to a millionaire's mansion.

GLOSSARY

Words	Meaning
Allah	The God.
Allah hafiz	Good bye in the name of Allah.
Appa	Big sister.
Bazaar	Shopping centre.
Bazaari	Shoppers.
Bustor	Bastard.
Bhabi	Sister In-law.
Bhai	Brother.
Bhondu	Friend.
Chadar	Blanket worn around the body.
Deshi	Belonging to ones homeland.
Dhada	Grandfather.
Fagla	Crazy.
Foga	Stupid.
Goru	Cow.
Hijab	Clothes that covers the face.
Imam	Islamic teacher.
Kalima	Declaration to Allah.
Kobul	Saying yes to a marriage's condition.
kut-thi	Bitch.
Londoni	Belonging to London.
Lungi	Sarong.

Mela	Street party.
Madrasa	Islamic school.
Magrib	Sun set prayers.
Naga	Extremely hot chilli.
Nani	Paternal grandmother.
Niqab	Face cover. Only the eyes can be seen.
Shatkora	A bitter lemony fruit of Sylhet.
Sari	Bangladeshi women's common cloth that they wrap around their body.
Taka	Bangladeshi currency.
Takdir	Fate.
Takbir	Having an attempt at something.
Yaar	Friend.

Acknowledgements:

My thanks and respect goes to Sarah Lamont and Zubida Christian for helping me with the drafting and also for giving me all the useful information regarding the structure and grammar of the novel.

I would like to thank Foysol Ali, Asma Begum, Aysha Begum, Abzar Choudhury and Tilok Das for their support and advice and also everyone else who encouraged and supported me through-out this book. Also, I like thank anyone who helped me with this project.

ABOUT THE AUTHOR

The author was born in a village in Sylhet, Bangladesh in 1975. He came to England at the age of 13 and he only had 3 years schooling in England, also he failed all of his GCSEs, however through self determination and ambition he ended up achieving BSc and MSc in IT. He Learnt the basic English language through selfstudy. The author having little knowledge of English language produced a novel based on his personal experience on the Bangladeshi culture here in East London and village life in Bangladesh. He previously worked as Junior accounts and in the Indian restaurant trade. Currently, he lives in East London working in the IT field that pays nearly 50K also has a business.

Lightning Source UK Ltd.
Milton Keynes UK
03 March 2010

150867UK00001B/6/P